AT THE COUNCILLOR'S;

OR,

A NAMELESS HISTORY.

BY

E. MARLITT.

TRANSLATED FROM THE GERMAN

BY MRS. A. L. WISTER,

TRANSLATOR OF "THE GREEN GATE," "THE SECOND WIFE," "ONLY A GIRL," "HULDA," "THE OLD MAM'SELLE'S SECRET," ETC.

PHILADELPHIA:
J. B. LIPPINCOTT & CO.
1876.

NOTE.

In Germany, the title of "Councillor" (*Rath*) can be purchased by those who achieve a certain eminence in their several walks of life, or it may be conferred as an honour by the Prince or King. The merchant who gives the name to this romance is thus "*Councillor of Commerce*," a compound word so unwieldy in English that the translator preferred to render "In the house of the Councillor of Commerce" by "At the Councillor's."

A. L. W.

AT THE COUNCILLOR'S.

CHAPTER I.

THE rays of a December sun shone dimly into a room in the large castle mill, calling forth feeble sparks of light from the strange objects lying on the broad stone window-sill, and then vanishing in a bank of snow-clouds that were rising slowly but steadily in the west. The objects sparkling so strangely on the window-sill were some portion of a surgeon's apparatus; those instruments the cold, steely glitter of which startles the eye and sends a shudder through the nerves of many a brave man. A huge bedstead, the head and foot-board clumsily painted with gaudy roses and carnations, and piled with feather-beds and patchwork quilts, stood directly in the broad light from the window, and upon this bed lay the castle miller. The skilful hand of the physician had just relieved him of a tumour in the throat that had several times threatened his life with suffocation. It had been a perilous undertaking, but the young man who now pulled down the window-shade and began to put up his instruments looked entirely satisfied,—the operation had succeeded.

The invalid, who shortly before, when only partly under the influence of chloroform, had pushed away the hand of the physician, abusing him in a hoarse voice as a robber and murderer, now lay quiet and exhausted among the pillows. He had been forbidden to talk,—surely an unnecessary prohibition, for it would have been difficult to find a face bearing so unmistakable an impress of dull taciturnity as did this square, clumsy countenance, which had but one beauty to boast of,—the thick, silvery hair that enclosed it as in a frame.

"Are you satisfied, Bruck?"* asked a gentleman, who now approached the physician from the foot of the bed, where he had been standing. His handsome features wore an expression of keen anxiety.

The doctor nodded. "All right so far; the patient's strong constitution will stand him in stead now," he said, quietly, glancing towards the old man. "At present all depends upon the nursing; I must leave. For some time he must not stir from his present position. There must be no hemorrhage from the wound——"

"I will see to that," the other interrupted him, eagerly; "I will stay as long as careful watching is needed. Will you not leave word at the villa that I shall not come back to tea?"

A slight flush mounted to the physician's cheek, and there was some embarrassment in the tone of his reply: "I cannot go round through the park. I must get to town as quickly as possible——"

"You have not seen Flora to-day, doctor——"

"I know that well enough. I——" He paused, compressed his lips, and took up his case of instruments. "I have some patients very ill," he went on, calmly: "the little Lenz girl will die before to-morrow morning. I cannot save the child, but the parents, who are utterly exhausted with nursing and anxiety, are counting the moments while I am away from them; the mother will eat only when I insist upon it."

He approached the bed, where the sick man raised his eyes to him with a look of perfect consciousness; there was even a glimmer of gratitude in them for the sudden and unspeakable relief he had experienced. He would have taken his

* Pronounced Brook.

benefactor's hand, but the latter imposed quiet with his own, as he reiterated the necessity for avoiding all motion whatever. "The councillor will remain here, Herr Sommer," he added, "and see that my injunctions are strictly obeyed."

This seemed to content the old man; he looked towards the councillor, who confirmed by a nod the physician's words, and then he closed his eyes as if to try to sleep. Doctor Bruck took his hat, gave his hand to the councillor, and left the room.

To an anxious wife seated by the bedside of the patient his departure would have been the signal for a weary sense of forlornness,—the opposite of the fresh courage with which his coming inspired the poor mother who took needful nourishment only at his request. But no such loving anxiety watched by this man's couch. The old housekeeper, who came into the room to put it in order after the doctor's visit, looked coldly indifferent; she flitted about like a bat, and seemed much more distressed by a few drops of water that marred the polish upon one of her tables than by the danger that had threatened her master's life.

"Pray let that be for the present, Susie," the councillor said, in his most courteous tone. "Your rubbing that table makes a noise very irritating to the nerves; Doctor Bruck prescribes absolute repose for Papa."

Susie hastily picked up housecloth and broom, and betook herself to her neat and shining kitchen, there to forget the stains upon the table. As perfect quiet as was possible in the mill reigned in the room she had left; up through the floor came the continuous, measured beat of machinery; the water tumbling over the weir outside sang its perpetual refrain, and now and then the doves fluttered against the window-pane, or cooed in the branches of the ancient chestnuts, through which the western light faintly illumined the room. These mingled noises did not exist as such for the sick man, however: they were as much part and parcel of his existence as the beating of his heart.

It was indeed a repulsive face which the elegant figure at the bedside watched, according to his promise, so carefully. Its coarseness, the hard lines of low vulgarity about the pendulous nether lip, had never so impressed and disgusted him as now, when sleep or exhaustion had robbed it of force and revealed all its original characteristics. Yes, the old man had begun life low enough in the scale, as a hard-worked mill-servant, but he was now the owner of untold wealth; trade had made a money-monarch of the invalid upon the clumsy old bedstead; and this fact, doubtless, had something to do with the familiar epithet of "Papa" bestowed upon him by the councillor, who was not bound to him by any tie of blood. The councillor had married the daughter of the deceased banker Mangold by his first wife. For his second, Mangold had wooed and won the daughter of the old miller. This was all the relationship that existed between the miller and his nurse.

The councillor arose and stepped softly to the window. He was a man of vivacious temperament, and sitting still in this way made him nervous; he could not bear the constant gazing upon that unsympathetic face, those coarse, sinewy fists, now buried in the down coverlet, which had once wielded the whip above the mill-horses. The chestnuts before the window had long since shed their last leaf; every opening left in the tracery of their boughs formed a rural landscape picture, each lovelier than the other, although for the moment the dark December sky dimmed the lustre that was reflected from the little lake, and veiled in misty gloom the hazy purple of the distant mountain-tops.

There, on the right, the river, after turning the wheels of the castle mill, made a sudden bend; a frame-work of boughs on that side enclosed a strip of its shining course, and a structure the purposes of which it was made to serve, a huge, square, unornamented stone building, with rows of windows enhancing its naked ugliness. This was the councillor's factory. He too was a rich man; he employed hundreds of weavers at clattering looms, and this property of his placed him in a kind of dependent position with regard to the castle miller. The mill, built hundreds of years before by a lord of the land, had been endowed with immense prerogatives, which, still in force, controlled a considerable stretch of the river, and were irritating enough to the dwellers upon its banks. Upon these prerogatives the burly master of the castle mill took his stand, and showed his teeth to any one who dared to lay a finger upon his rights. Once only a tenant of the mill, he had slowly but surely stretched forth the arms of his growing wealth, until not only the mill was his own, but also the baronial estate to which it had originally belonged. This he had accomplished shortly before the marriage of his only child to the respectable banker Mangold. The extensive forests and farm-land upon the estate were all that the miller cared for; the magnificent villa in the midst of its stately park had always been an eye-sore to him; nevertheless, he had kept the "costly toy" in perfect repair, for the pleasure of seeing his daughter rule as mistress where the former haughty lord had always disdained even to answer his salute. The councillor now rented the villa; there was every reason, therefore, that he should be upon the best terms with his landlord, and one who possessed such control of the river. And this was the case: the councillor was as a docile son to the surly old man.

Four o'clock struck from the factory tower, and the gas instantly lit up the counting-room windows. Twilight came on early indeed on this afternoon: the air was filled with that moisture that brings snow; the smoke from city chimneys hung low over the earth, while the slate roof of the factory and every stone door-step were glassy with intense damp; the doves, until now huddled together upon the bare chestnut-boughs, suddenly left them and flew to the warm, dry dovecote. The councillor looked back into the room with a shiver. By contrast it looked almost comfortable and cosy to the man to whose refined taste it was usually so repulsive, with its constant smell of cooking, its smoky ceiling, and the coarse prints here and there upon the walls; but Susie had just replenished the fire in the stove with pine wood, the old-fashioned sofa against the wall looked inviting with its huge soft cushions, and upon the bright panes of glass in the recess-door the last gleams of daylight were reflected. Ah, behind that door stood the iron safe: had he remembered to take out the key?

Just before the operation, the miller had made his will; as Doctor Bruck and the councillor entered the room, they met the lawyers and witnesses leaving it. Although outwardly composed, the patient must have gone through much agitation of mind: his hand had evidently been uncertain, for in putting away his papers he had left one of them lying upon the table. Noticing this omission, after the doctor's arrival he had requested the councillor to lock it up in the safe. A second door led from the recess where the safe was placed into an antechamber, and there were all sorts of people continually coming and going in the mill. The councillor had put away the paper, but left the door of the safe unlocked,—an inexcusable neglect,—and he hastily went to the little room. What would the old man, who guarded this precious place of deposit like a dragon, have said at seeing his money thus exposed! No one could possibly have entered the room, the councillor consoled himself by thinking; the slightest noise could not have escaped him; but he would make sure that everything was in order.

He opened the iron folding-doors as noiselessly as possible; there were the money-bags untouched, and before the packets of valuable papers were ranged columns of glittering gold pieces. He glanced rapidly over the paper, which in his former natural haste and agitation he had put carelessly into one of the neatly-arranged pigeon-holes: it was an inventory of the miller's entire possessions. What enormous sums those rows of figures represented! He carefully put it where it belonged, and in doing so he accidentally overthrew one of the columns of gold pieces: a number of napoleons fell noisily upon the floor. What an ugly sound they made! He had touched money belonging to another! A mixture of terror and uncalled-for shame sent the colour to his cheeks; he stooped in haste to pick up the money. As he did so, a heavy body fell upon him from behind, and hard, coarse fingers clutched his throat.

"You scoundrel, I am not dead yet!" the miller hissed in his ear, in a strange, muffled tone. There was a momentary struggle; all the councillor's strength and vigor were necessary to shake off the old man, who clung to him like a panther, grasping his throat so tightly that a shower of sparks seemed to flash before his eyes; he seized with both hands the mass that weighed him down, gave one strong thrust and push, and he was on his feet and free, while the miller staggered against the wall.

"Are you mad, Papa?" he gasped, breathlessly. "What vile suspicions!——" He paused in horror: the bandage beneath the old man's whitening face suddenly became crimson, and the dreadful colour crept rapidly downward over his white night-dress. This was the hemorrhage that was to have been so carefully guarded against.

The councillor's teeth chattered as in a fever-fit. Was this misfortune his fault? "No, no," he said to himself instantly, as he put his arm around the invalid to support him to his bed; but the old man thrust him away angrily, and pointed to the scattered gold; each piece had to be carefully picked up and arranged in place; in care for his money he either forgot or ignored the danger that threatened him. Not until the councillor had locked the safe and put the key into his hand did he totter back into his bedroom, there to fall helpless upon the bed; and when at last, summoned by the councillor's repeated cries for help, two mill-servants and Susie rushed into the room, there lay the castle miller on his back, his glazing eyes, from which all consciousness seemed to have departed, staring downward at the crimson dye which the welling life-stream was so rapidly spreading on every side.

A servant was dispatched to town to summon Doctor Bruck, while the housekeeper hurriedly brought water and linen. They were of no avail. The councillor anxiously applied cloth after cloth to the wound,—the stream would not be stayed. There was no doubt of it, an artery had burst. How had it happened? Was the old man's mental and physical excitement alone to blame, or—his heart seemed to stop beating at the thought—had he in defending himself struck and mortally aggravated the wound in the throat? How can there be any exact memory of the moment of defence against a furious assault? Who could tell whether, with murderous fingers clutching his throat, and his overcharged brain kindling thousands of fires in the air, he had seized shoulder or throat of his assailant? Why imagine so ghastly a possibility? Was not the spring out of bed, the excess of rage, quite enough to bring on the disaster which the physician had predicted would be the result of any sudden movement? No, no, his conscience was clear; he had nothing to reproach himself with, whatever might have been the cause of this terrible event. He had gone to the safe solely in the old man's interest; there had not been in his mind even a fleeting desire to possess any of that wealth; this he was sure of. How could he help the low suspicions of the miserable old corn-dealer, who saw a possible robber in every man, no matter what his position and culture? Anxiety and horror gave place to indignation in the councillor's mind. This came of his amiability, the innate courtesy for which his friends declared he was distinguished; it had often induced him to take upon himself responsibilities which had involved him disagreeably. Had he but stayed at home,—in his comfortable library, at the whist-table, or smoking a cigar in peace! His evil genius had prompted him to play the part of self-sacrificing nurse, and here he was in this terrible situation, shuddering with horror and disgust, his hands moistened with the blood of the wretch who would have strangled him.

The minutes were surely weighted with lead! The miller now seemed aware of the peril he had brought upon himself; he did not stir, but his eyes turned anxiously towards the door whenever footsteps were heard without; his hopes for rescue lay in the physician. The councillor, dismayed, marked the change in his countenance. That ashen hue was the sure forerunner of death.

Susie brought in the lamp; she had been repeatedly to the door to look for Doctor Bruck, and she now stood at the side of the bed, shaking her head in mute horror at the sight that the faint lamp-light revealed. A few moments more, and the miller's eyes closed. The key, until then clutched convulsively in his hand, fell upon the counterpane. Involuntarily the councillor extended his hand to put it away, but as he touched the bit of iron the thought suddenly struck him, like an unexpected blow, of the aspect this unfortunate accident might wear in the eyes of the world. He knew only too well what slander could do with its poisonous breath,—how it could glide through his halls and apartments, received by men as well as by women with malicious satisfaction, ambiguous smiles, and finger-pointings. If a single person should say, with a shrug, "Aha, what was Councillor Römer looking for in the miller's safe?" it would be enough. Such words would not be spoken by one voice only. Like all fortunate men, he numbered many among his acquaintances who envied and disliked him; he knew that it would be everywhere told in town to-morrow how the operation had been quite successful, but that the irritation produced in the patient by seeing the man self-installed as nurse secretly visiting his safe had brought on a fatal hemorrhage. And there would be a stain upon the name of Römer, the envied favorite of fortune, which no legal investigation could remove, for there could be no friendly witnesses. Would not his previous honourable career be sufficient testimony in his favour? He laughed bitterly to himself as he wiped the drops of cold perspiration from his brow. No one knew better than he how ready the world is to stigmatize as mere sham any uprightness of character as soon as appearances are against it. He leaned over the unconscious man, whose temples Susie was bathing with spirits, and suddenly regarded him in a different light: should he never recover sufficient strength to tell of what had occurred, it would be buried with him: there were no other lips to speak of it.

At last the watch-dog barked outside; hasty steps crossed the court-yard and ascended the stairs. Doctor Bruck paused for a moment, as if petrified, at the door of the room, then silently laid his hat upon the table, and approached the bed. The solemn moment that ensued seemed to throb with expectation of the verdict about to be pronounced.

"If he would only come to himself again, Herr Doctor," the housekeeper said, at last, in an anxious whisper.

"He will hardly do that," Doctor Bruck replied, looking up from his investigation. All colour had fled from his face. "Be quiet," he sternly ordered, as Susie was about to break out into loud lamentations, "and tell me why the patient left his bed!" He took the lamp from the table and pointed to the floor beside the bed: the planks were sprinkled with blood.

"That comes from the cloths we have been using," the councillor explained, in a decided tone, although he had grown very pale; while the housekeeper affirmed by all that was holy that the castle miller was lying just as the doctor had left him when she entered the room.

Doctor Bruck shook his head. "This hemorrhage never came on without cause; it must have been produced by some violent agitation."

"None that I know of; I assure you, none!" said the councillor, meeting the physician's keen glance with tolerable firmness. "What do you mean by looking at me thus? I cannot see why I should conceal from you that the patient had sprung from his bed in an excess of fever, if such had been the case." He would keep to the path he had chosen, although the last words seemed to stick in his throat. To save mere appearances he sacrificed his honour, he lied with a brazen brow; but then he had not been in fault with regard to what had occurred; his life had fairly been in peril. There was not a single consideration that could make an explanation of the real facts of the case necessary.

The physician turned silently away and busied himself with his patient. Once or twice the miller opened his eyes, but they gazed unmeaningly into space, and the effort to speak died away in a rattle in his throat.

A few hours afterwards, Councillor Römer left the castle mill. All was over. Across the doors of the recess broad strips of paper were already pasted. As soon as the miller breathed his last, the councillor advised the legal authorities of the fact, and, like a conscientious, prudent man, saw seals placed upon everything before he left the spot.

CHAPTER II.

He walked home through the park. The feeble glimmer of the mill-lights which accompanied him for a few steps of the way vanished behind him, and he went on alone in the black darkness. It was not the keen breeze sweeping by him, nor the few snow-flakes touching his cheek like some fluttering bird of night, but the memory of the last few hours, and his excited fancy, that made him shiver as if with bitter cold. That very afternoon he had left his well-furnished table, and along this path, where now the pebbles beneath his tread grated discordantly, he had walked, secure, as he thought, in the protection of his lucky star; and now, after so short a time, it would almost seem as if he, Councillor Römer, whose sensitive nerves would not allow him to witness the suffering even of a brute, had been partly guilty of the death of a fellow-creature. Surely the gods, impatient of a mortal lot without a thorn, had envied him, and had thus burdened his conscience that there might be some infusion of gall in the clear stream of his prosperity,—and all for nothing. He could be reproached with nothing but silence; and whom could his silence injure? No one,—no one in the wide world! Basta! no more of this. He turned into the broad linden avenue that led directly to the villa. A brilliant stream of light was issuing from the windows and glass doors of the lower suite of rooms. A life of luxury and enjoyment reached out white, rounded arms to him from those rooms, beckoning him away from the dark night and all his anxiety. He breathed more freely, threw off the evil influence of the last hours, and let it vanish with the sound of the mill-stream that was dying away in the distance.

There, around the Frau President Urach's tea-table and card-tables a numerous evening company was assembled. The large, low panes of glass, and the bronze tracery of the balustrade of the balcony outside, permitted an excellent view from without of the interior. The bright pictures on the walls, the heavy portières of violet velvet, the chandeliers of gilded bronze with their gas-lights shining through pearly glass shades, stood out in relief against the surrounding blackness of the winter night like a scene upon some fairy stage. A sudden gust of wind swept down the avenue, tossing snow-flakes and dry linden-leaves madly against the balcony, but the hurly-burly had no effect upon the dignified repose reigning within: there was not even a motion of the airy lace curtains; the fire alone flickering upon the marble hearth might blaze more brightly for an instant when breathed upon by the blast down the chimney.

The man outside looked in with a sensation of trembling delight upon the group assembled there. Not that he saw there fair and dark curls, slender women and girls to enchant his eye. No; the fairy heralds of spring painted on the ceiling extended their rosy flower-filled palms above matronly caps, gray hair, and bald heads; but then the names of their owners!—officers of high rank, pensioned maids of honour, and members of the ministry sat at the card-tables, or, leaning back in the velvet lounging-chairs, chatted by the warm fireside. The arrogant old councillor of medicine, Von Bär, was there too. As he dealt the cards, sparks of light flashed from the jewels upon his hands,—all gifts from royal personages. And these people were in his house, Councillor Römer's house; the ruby wine sparkling in the goblets was from his cellar, and the fresh, fragrant strawberries which liveried footmen were handing about in crystal saucers had been bought with his money. Frau President Urach was his deceased wife's grandmother, and did the honours in the house of the widower, with unlimited command of his means.

The councillor walked around to the western side of the house. Here only two windows on the ground-floor were illuminated; a hanging lamp between the crimson curtains of one of them gleamed out into the darkness, bathing in rosy light the white limbs of a marble nymph by a fountain in the grove. Herr Römer shook his head as he entered; then, giving his overcoat to a servant, he opened the door of the red-curtained apartment. The room was all red,—hangings, furniture, even the carpet was of the same dark crimson hue. Beneath the hanging lamp stood a writing-table of peculiar Chinese form, with golden arabesques covering its fine black lacquer; it was made for use in the fullest sense of the word; open books, sheets of writing-paper, and newspapers were scattered over it, with a manuscript, across which a pencil was lying, beside a small silver salver holding a goblet half full of a strong, dark-red wine. It was a room where flowers would not have flourished nor birds have sung. In each of the four corners stood a black marble pedestal, each supporting a bust of the same material, which brought into harsh relief the features it portrayed; book-shelves lined the long wall, harmonizing in colour and decoration with the writing-table, and containing finely-bound modern books as well as parchment-covered folios, and piles of pamphlets. It almost seemed as if the deep uniform crimson of the hangings and carpet had been chosen as the only fitting frame for the severe style in which the room was furnished.

As the councillor entered, a lady who had evidently been walking to and fro stood still. One might have thought that she too had just come in covered with snow from the flurry without, so dazzlingly white did she look upon the crimson carpet. It would have been difficult to say whether the soft folds of her long cashmere robe were draped so loosely about her waist and hips for the sake of convenience, or whether this strange and becoming toilette were the result of careful study; certainly the figure that stood out upon the crimson background was noble in outline, and as purely white as an Iphigenia. The lady was very beautiful, although no longer freshly young. She had a fine Roman profile, and a delicate, supple frame, but her light hair was wanting in thickness; it was cut short, and, smoothed away from the brow, curled in soft, flimsy curls about the head and neck. She was Flora Mangold, a sister-in-law of Councillor Römer, the twin-sister of his deceased wife. Her arms were lightly folded across her bosom, and she greeted her brother-in-law with evident eagerness.

"Well, Flora, have you left the drawing-room?" he asked.

"Do you suppose I could stay beside grandmamma's tea-table, in the midst of stockings and swaddling-clothes for poor children, and all that old woman's gossip?" she replied, in a tone of irritation.

"But there are gentlemen there, too, Floss——"

"Greater gossips than the rest, in spite of their orders and epaulettes!"

He laughed. "You are out of humour, ma chère," he said, sinking into an arm-chair.

She threw back her head and pressed her folded hands to her breast. "Moritz," she said, breathing hard, as if after a momentary struggle with herself, "tell me the truth; did the castle miller die beneath Bruck's knife?"

He started. "What an idea! No misfortune can be so black but that you women——"

"I pray you make me an exception there, Moritz," she interrupted him, haughtily.

"Well, with all due respect for your talent and remarkable powers of mind, are you in fact any better than the rest?" He got up and paced the room in great annoyance; this new view of the matter was startling indeed. "Beneath Bruck's knife!" he repeated, in an agitated voice. "I tell you the operation was performed before two o'clock, and the man died scarcely two hours ago. Besides, I cannot imagine how you of all others can venture to give utterance to such a thought so curtly and coldly,—I might almost say, so pitilessly."

"I of all others," she said, with emphasis, as she pressed the carpet with her foot; "I of all others, because I cannot endure to keep anything hidden in the depths of my soul. I am too proud, too unbending, to share and conceal the knowledge of wrong done by another, let that other be whom he will. Do not think that I do not suffer! It cuts me to the heart like a knife. But you have used the word 'pitilessly'; you could not better have confirmed my suspicions. Pity for bungling in science is absurd, impossible; and you as well as I are perfectly aware that Bruck's reputation as a physician has already suffered from his entire failure in the case of Countess Wallendorf."

"Oh, of course nothing could induce that worthy lady to moderate her appetite for pâté de foie gras and champagne."

"That is what Bruck says; her relatives tell another story." She pressed her palms upon her temples, as if her head ached violently. "Do you know, Moritz, when the news of the miller's death arrived, I went out of the house and ran hither and thither like one insane? Old Sommer was well known to high and low: everybody was interested in the success of the operation. Even if, as you say, he did not die immediately beneath Bruck's knife, every one of medical knowledge will maintain, and justly, that the further struggle with death was due to his strong constitution. Can you, who have no medical knowledge, be better informed? Rather do not deny that you are impressed with the same conviction! You have no idea how pale you are with agitation."

At this moment a side-door opened, and Frau President

Urach appeared upon the threshold. In spite of her seventy years, she entered with an elastic step; in spite of her seventy years, she looked a wonderfully youthful grandmamma. She was not apparelled in the dress of old age; a fichu of white lace was crossed upon her breast and knotted behind at the waist. The overskirt of her pearl-gray silk gown was richly trimmed. Her gray hair, still streaked here and there with its original hue of shining gold, was puffed thickly above her brow, and above these puffs she wore a veil-like scarf of white tulle, the long ends of which concealed the throat and the neck just below the chin, where age so surely sets its seal.

She was not alone. At her side there entered a creature most strange in appearance, evidently stunted in growth, not ill proportioned in figure, but extremely small, and very thin. This insignificant body was crowned by the strongly-developed head of a young lady of perhaps twenty-four years of age. The three women now in the room had a strong family resemblance in their features; the close relationship between grandmother and grandchildren was evident, but the noble, regular profile of the youngest of the three was too long for perfect beauty, and the chin was too broad and decisively prominent. She had a sickly complexion, and her lips were bluish in hue. In her fair hair was twisted a flame-coloured velvet ribbon, and she was in very elegant full dress, save that by her side, where other ladies wear a châtelaine, she carried a small oval osier basket lined with little cushions of blue satin, among which sat a canary-bird.

"No, Henriette!" cried Flora, impatiently, as the little bird left his nest and flew about her head, "that I will not have. You must leave your menagerie outside."

"Pray now, Flora,—Jack has neither elephants' feet nor horns on his head; he cannot harm you," the little lady replied, indifferently. "Come, Jacky, come!" she called; and the bird, after flying around the ceiling, dutifully came and perched upon the forefinger she held out for him.

Flora turned away with a shrug. "I cannot understand you or your guests, grandmamma," she said, sharply. "How can you tolerate Henriette's childish nonsense? Before long she will set up her pigeon-cote and daws'-nests in your drawing-room."

"And why not, Flora?" laughed the little lady, showing a row of small, sharp teeth. "They all tolerate you, going about everywhere with a pen behind your ear, your pockets crammed with bookish stuff, and——"

"Henriette!" the Frau President sternly interrupted her. In her bearing there was great dignity, and as she graciously gave her hand in greeting to the councillor, an unmistakable air of condescension mingled with the kindliness of her manner.

"I have just heard of your return, my dear Moritz; must we wait any longer for you?" she asked, in a gentle voice that was still musical.

Ten minutes previously he had come home, resolved to don his evening dress immediately. Now he replied, with hesitation, "Dearest grandmamma, I must beg you to excuse me this evening. The event at the mill——"

"True, it is very sad; but how can it affect us? I really cannot see how to excuse you to my friends."

"They can hardly be so dull of comprehension, those worthy people, as not to understand that Kitty's grandpapa has died?" Henriette remarked, looking back over her shoulder from where she was standing in front of the book-shelves, apparently reading assiduously the titles of the books.

"Henriette, I pray you spare me your pert observations," the Frau President said. "You can, if you choose, tone down your flame-coloured head-dress, for Kitty is your step-sister;

but with regard to Moritz and myself, the connection is so slight that we need take no conventional notice of the death, deplore it as we may. And, for Bruck's sake, the less said about it the better."

"Good heavens, are you all determined to be so unjust to the doctor?" cried the councillor, in despair. "No blame—not the smallest—can be attached to him; he brought all his skill, all his scientific knowledge, to bear——"

"My dear Moritz, you should hear what my old friend Doctor von Bär has to say upon that point," the Frau President said, in interruption, lightly tapping him upon the shoulder and making a significant motion of her head towards Flora, who had gone to her writing-table.

"Oh, do not mind me, grandmamma! Do you think me so blind and deaf as not to know what Bär's opinion is?" the beautiful girl exclaimed, with bitterness. "Bruck has, besides, condemned himself: he has not ventured to come near me this evening."

Hitherto Henriette had been standing with her back towards the rest. Now she turned round; a burning blush suddenly coloured her sallow cheek and as quickly faded. Her eyes were wonderfully fine, revealing depths of passionate feeling. They glowed like stars as she turned them, with a mixture of shy terror and positive hatred, upon her sister's countenance.

"Your last accusation he will refute in person; he will shortly be here, Flora," said the councillor, evidently relieved. "He will tell you himself that he has been driven hard indeed, to-day. You know how many patients he has seriously ill in town,—among them the poor little Lenz girl, who cannot live until morning."

The lady laughed a low, bitter laugh. "Is she going to die? Really, Moritz? Well, Bär, too, came here to me before going to grandmamma; he spoke of the child, whom he saw yesterday, and thought not very ill; he feared, however, that Bruck was upon a false track. Bär is an authority——"

"Yes, an authority filled with envy," said Henriette, in a clear, ringing voice. She had hastily approached, and laid her hand upon her brother-in-law's arm. "Give up trying to convince Flora, Moritz. You must see that she is determined to find her lover guilty."

"Determined? 'Tis false! I would give half that I possess to regard Bruck as I did in the beginning of our engagement,—with the same proud trust and confidence," Flora exclaimed, passionately. "But since the death of the Countess Wallendorf I have been a silent prey to doubt and mistrust; now I doubt no more: I am convinced. I know nothing, it is true, of that feminine weakness that loves without ever asking, 'Is he whom I love worthy my devotion?' I am ambitious, wildly ambitious; I care not who knows it. Without that mainspring I too might saunter along the broad highway of the commonplace like the weak and indolent of my sex. God forbid such a fate for me! How an aspiring and intellectual woman can pass her life quietly and composedly, linked to an insignificant husband, has always been incomprehensible to me; I should writhe beneath the shame of such a position."

"Oh, indeed! would it so shame you? Well, well, I suppose it would require more courage than is needed to hold forth to a roomful of students upon æsthetics and what not," Henriette said, with a smile full of malice.

Flora cast a contemptuous glance at her sister. "Hiss, little viper, if you will. What can you know of my ideal?" she said, with a shrug. "But you are right in thinking I should be more at home in the lecture-room than by the side of a man who has stamped himself a bungler in his profession; I could not endure such chains."

"That is your affair, my child," the Frau President coolly

remarked, while the councillor looked up in dismay. "You must remember that no one forced you to fetter yourself thus."

"I know that perfectly well, grandmamma; I know, too, that you would greatly have preferred that I should become the wife of the Chamberlain von Stetten, physical and financial bankrupt though he be. I grant you, also, that I refuse to allow myself to be influenced or led by others, since I know best what best beseems me.

"There, too, you are your own mistress," her grandmother rejoined, with frigid dignity; "only remember one thing,—you will find in me a determined opponent to anything like a public scandal. You surely know me well enough to be aware that I would far rather endure great personal annoyance than give any occasion for gossip. I reside here with you, and take upon myself the duties of mistress of the house with pleasure, but I must in return exact an unconditional respect for my name and position; I will not have society whispering and tattling about our affairs."

The councillor turned hastily away. He went to a window, pulled aside the curtain, and gazed out into the night. The wind, which had gradually risen to a tempest, rattled at the window-frame, and in the red light cast upon the bare, tossing branches outside, by the lamp hanging in the other window, the crimsoned snow-flakes whirled madly hither and thither like the tormenting thoughts in his own brain. He had a short time before debated in his mind whether he should not explain matters fully, at least to Flora; now he knew that she was the last person to whom he could speak upon the subject, if he did not wish that the whisper and tattle of society should drive the Frau President from his house. No; he saw clearly that his ambitious sister-in-law would publish his confession far and wide, less from solicitude for her lover than from a desire to prove that her heart, or rather her head, could not have been mistaken in its choice.

Meanwhile, Henriette turned a face of anger and scorn towards her grandmother. "It is solely to avoid furnishing gossip for society, then, that you would have my sister bear herself blameless? She can easily satisfy you. You will instantly acquit her if she can cover her breach of faith with a silken mantle. But indeed you need not be so sensitive upon the subject of scandal, grandmamma: those living in the world as we do, soon find out that society regards many a sinner of rank and wealth much as it does an old piece of valuable porcelain,—the more patched the more precious."

"I must request you to pass the remainder of the evening in your own room, Henriette," the Frau President said, now seriously angry. "In your present mood, I cannot permit you to return to the drawing-room."

"As you please, grandmamma. Come, Jack, we will go with the greatest pleasure," she said, smiling, smoothing with her cheek the bird's plumage as it sat on her forefinger. "You hate those old court-ladies, too; and you regularly peck at the great medical authority, Herr von Bär, and nip his finger, you good little fellow, when he tries to coax you with sugar. Good-night, grandmamma; good-night, Moritz." She paused in her hasty departure, and turned back. "That strong-minded lady there," she said, with cutting emphasis, "will probably pursue the path which her dead father would have inexorably forbidden to her; while he lived there was no chance for her boasted exercise of her own will. He would never have allowed her to break her troth with an honourable man."

She left the room with her head proudly erect, but, even as she crossed the threshold, the tears which had been plainly audible in her voice as she spoke the last words gushed from her eyes.

"Thank God, she has gone!" cried Flora. "What an amount of self-control is required not to lose one's patience with her!"

"I never forget her invalid condition," the Frau President remarked, in a reproving tone.

"And she is right, in a certain sense, Flora," the councillor ventured to interpose.

"You may think as you choose upon that point, Moritz," the young lady rejoined, coldly; "but I must earnestly entreat you not to make my task more difficult by your interference. I am used, as I said just now, to judge for myself in what concerns me, and I shall do so in this case. And you may be perfectly easy,—you and grandmamma. I excessively dislike any sudden and harsh measure, and I have a noiseless ally,—time."

She took the goblet from the writing-table and moistened her pale lips with a few drops of its contents, while the Frau President, without further remonstrance, prepared to leave the room.

"Apropos, Moritz," she said, with her hand upon the knob of the door, "what is to be done with Kitty now?"

"We must leave it to the will to decide all that," he replied, drawing a long breath of relief. "I have no idea how the castle miller has arranged matters. Kitty is his natural heir, but it is doubtful whether he has left all his property to her; he always resented the fact that her birth cost his daughter her life. In any case she must come here for a while."

"Do not trouble yourself about that; she will not come; she is tied as securely to-day to the apron-string of her detestable old governess as she was during papa's lifetime," said Flora. "That is easy to see from her letters."

"Well, perhaps it is better that she should stay where she is," the Frau President remarked, with a shade of eagerness.

"To be candid, I have no great desire to shelter her beneath my wing and waste my time in schooling her; it is very tiresome. I never really liked her; not because she was the child of my daughter's successor,—that I have always declared,—but she was altogether too much at home in the mill, getting her clothes and hair covered with meal; and then she was a self-willed little thing."

"A genuine 'child of the people,' and yet—papa's darling," Flora added, with a bitter smile.

"Apparently, my dear, because she was his youngest child," said the Frau President, who never permitted a suspicion, either in herself or in others, that any one belonging to her could be slighted. "You were just as much his darling at one time. Well, Moritz, are you coming?"

He hastily complied. As they left the room, Flora rang for her maid. "I wish to retire to my dressing-room to write; take my writing-materials and these papers there for me," she ordered. "Of course I can see no one this evening."

The red glow was no longer seen outside the windows, but the brilliant light from the drawing-room gleamed over the tempest-swept avenue until long past midnight. The councillor was at one of the card-tables. Upon his entrance every one received him with a kindly greeting or a warm pressure of the hand, that fell like sunshine on his anxious, troubled heart. Here, among these faces, stamped with the pride of noble birth or official arrogance, his line of conduct seemed so perfectly justifiable that he could hardly understand the tormenting scruples that assailed him. Why expose one's self to hostile criticism when one is conscious of entire innocence even in thought? And then such a low affair altogether! All this delightful scandal which was now whispered about, these stories over which each noble guest was glad to throw "a silken mantle," concerned high-born errors; but what mercy could these people show to one among them, not legitimately of them, accused of a vulgar attempt to rob the castle miller's safe? He could, however, no longer console himself with the idea that his silence harmed no one: it threatened to sever two human souls united by a betrothal ring. Pshaw! Flora was an eccentric creature. The next time some special distinction was awarded to Bruck, which his great learning and ability made certain, matters would be all right again. And with a glass of delicious punch he drained down his last scruple.

CHAPTER III.

THE castle miller had in fact left his granddaughter, Katharina Mangold, his sole heiress, and confirmed as her guardian the man previously selected as such by her deceased father. This guardian was Councillor Römer, who, at the reading of the will, shook his head and pondered deeply upon the inconsistencies that exist in the human soul. The old man who had wellnigh throttled him under the influence of a mad suspicion that he was robbing him of his gold, had, scarcely an hour before, appointed him his executor, with almost limitless authority. He had provided that in case the operation about to be performed resulted in death, all his real estate, with the exception of the castle mill, should be sold. With regard to this exception, he declared that the mill had made him a wealthy man, and that his granddaughter, even although she came to be as "proud and haughty" as her step-sisters, had no need to be ashamed of bringing it to her future husband. The baronial estate to which it belonged was to be divided, and each portion—forest-land, farm-land, farm-buildings, meadows, and kitchen-gardens—sold singly to the highest bidder. As for the villa, with its surrounding park, it was to be sold likewise, and Councillor Römer was to be allowed to purchase it, if he wished to do so, at the rate of five thousand thalers less than its taxable value. These five thousand thalers were his, not only as some indemnification for his trouble as guardian, but in token of the "esteem" of the testator for a man who had never been haughty "like the rest of them at the villa," but more like a kind and even devoted relative. The will further provided that the whole property should be invested in government securities and other solid stock, the choice of which should be left entirely to the guardian, as a prudent and careful man of business.

The young heiress had lived for the past six years away from home. Her dying father had left her in charge to a Fräulein Lukas, who had been her governess always,—in fact, had supplied a mother's place to her. Herr Mangold saw plainly that his darling, who had held herself shyly aloof from the step-sisters so much her elders, must not be deprived of her governess's tender care, and had therefore provided that she should accompany Fräulein Lukas to Dresden, whither the latter removed shortly after her employer's death, and upon her marriage with a physician to whom she had long been betrothed. In the young girl's letters thence to her guardian she had never expressed a wish to revisit her home, nor had it ever occurred to her grandfather, the castle miller, to recall her. He had acquiesced willingly in her removal to Dresden, because the sight of her constantly renewed his grief for his daughter, the only being whom he had ever really loved. Now, after his death, the girl's guardian requested her to return, for some time at least, arranging at the same time to be her escort himself from Dresden as soon as the weather should become warmer, towards the end of April, since—this fact, however, he naturally suppressed—the Frau President Urach had protested against her being accompanied by the former governess. His ward had acceded to everything, and, upon his asking her further whether she had any personal wish with regard to the disposal of her property, had begged that when the castle mill was rented, the huge corner room and the recess with which it communicated might be reserved for her, and that everything in them might be left exactly as it had been during her grandfather's lifetime. This was done.

It was March, and a young girl was walking from town upon the highway, here and there bordered by neat cottages. She turned into the broad road leading to the castle mill. The traces of the last snow-storm had not entirely disappeared, the water had not dried in the broad ruts left by the wheels of the mill-wagons or in the deep footprints of the passers-by; but the young girl's little feet were encased in stout leather boots, and her black silk dress was so well caught up that there was no trace of mud upon its edge. She looked no elf or fairy as she walked on with a sure, elastic step. No; she was rather like some fair Alpine maid, with veins and sinews full of vigorous health, nourished by the pure breath of the mountain air and the sweet fresh milk of mountain-fed cows. A close black velvet jacket, trimmed with fur, showed the full, graceful outlines of bust and waist, and upon her brown hair sat, a little to one side, a cap of marten-skin. Her features were far from classically regular: the aquiline nose was too short for the width and shape of the brow, the mouth too large, the dimpled chin too strongly marked, the eyebrows not sufficiently delicate; but all these defects were more than atoned for by the pure oval of the whole face and the incomparable freshness and beauty of its colouring.

She turned into the open door of the court-yard of the castle mill, scattering before her a number of chickens assembled upon the wagon-road to pick up some scattered grains of wheat. They flew hither and thither with a loud cackling, and a couple of watch-dogs, roused from their lazy doze by the noise, barked furiously. How bright and golden the warm spring sunshine looked, flooding the walls of the grand old pile of masonry heaped up in ancient times beneath the eye of its noble builder! The day before yesterday the last thick icicle had fallen clattering from the open jaws of the lion's head at the end of the gutter on the roof, above which the air was now quivering with heat from the sun-baked slate. The sap was swelling in the big brown chestnut-buds, making them glisten as if powdered with diamond-dust; a couple of pots containing some languishing plants had been put outside of the window of one of the miller's rooms, to enjoy the first breath of spring; and upon the well-worn wooden steps leading from this very room was seated a dusty miller, eating a huge piece of bread-and-cheese.

"Moor! Watch! good dogs!" the young girl called across the yard in a coaxing voice. The dogs leaped about madly, whining as they tugged at their chains.

"What do you want?" asked the miller, rising clumsily.

She laughed gently. "I want nothing, Franz, except to say 'good-day' to Susie and yourself."

In an instant bread, cheese, and knife were thrown down on the ground. The man was not tall,—shorter than the young girl,—and he looked up speechless into the blooming face, which he had seen last belonging to a sickly child not tall enough to reach to his broad shoulders. She used to be called the "miller's mouse," and, swift and agile as any mouse, would follow him about the mill and granary for hours at a time; now she was mistress here, and he, the former foreman, her tenant. "Queer enough," he said, shaking his head in loutish wonder; "the eyes and the dimples in the cheeks are the same, but what a size she is!" And he measured her with shy, incredulous glances. "Aha, she gets it all from her Sommer grandmother; she was just such a white-and-red creature, and—— Be quiet, you rogues!" he interrupted himself, shaking his fist at the barking dogs. "The fellows really know you, madame."

"Better than you do; the 'size' has not led them astray," she replied, going over to the dogs and caressing them as they leaped up upon her. "You give me a wonderful title, Franz; I have not been promoted in Dresden, I assure you."

"But the Fräuleins over in the villa are always called so," he said, doggedly.

"Indeed!"

"And you are worth ten of them. So young and rich,—so immensely rich! There's the mill,—the finest far or near. Zounds! 'tis a prize indeed. Good gracious!—only a girl, hardly eighteen years old, and the owner of such a mill!"

She laughed. "Yes, it is mine; and a dreary life I shall lead you, old Franz. But where is Susie?"

"Keeping her room; 'tis in her right side again, poor old thing! Her own doctoring did no good, and Doctor Bruck is there now."

The girl gave him her hand and went into the house. The heavy oaken door swung to behind her with a jar that resounded from all four walls of the large hall. Beneath her feet the floor trembled and shook with the dull sound of the machinery that was heard through a low, open door in a stone-vaulted archway, and the odour of freshly-ground grain filled the air. The young girl breathed it in eagerly; a flood of memories overcame her; she grew pale with emotion, and stood still for a moment with folded hands. Yes, she had indeed loved to make herself "at home" in the mill, as the Frau President had said, and her father had often brushed the flour from her dress and braids and laughingly called her his "little white miller's mouse." The stern old man, her grandfather, whom she could best remember shouting down his orders, in a harsh, authoritative voice, from the first landing of the stairs, had never loved her; she had almost always fled from his cross looks either to Susie's bright kitchen or to Franz; and yet she now thought of him with deep regret, and wished he were just descending the stairs that had creaked beneath his heavy tread; perhaps she should no longer have feared his face, repulsive, as she now knew, with the insolence of wealth; perhaps he would have been gentler and kinder, now that she had grown like her grandmother.

She found the door of the corner room up-stairs locked, but along the narrow passage connecting the back building with the main part of the mill she heard Susie's wailing voice. Ah, yes, there was the poor old servant's sleeping-room,—a dark little chamber, with round, leaded panes of glass in the windows, through which were seen the gray thatched roof of a wood-shed, and the pavement, always damp, of the side-yard. She shook her head impatiently, and walked along the passage.

As she entered the sick-room, the close, heated atmosphere of which was filled with smoke, she saw in the dim light that penetrated the old green glass of the window a man standing with his back towards her. He was very tall, much taller than she, and broad-shouldered in proportion. He was apparently about to depart, for he had hat and cane in hand. Ah, this, then, was Doctor Bruck, of whom her brother-in-law Moritz had told her when he informed her of the betrothal of her beautiful sister Flora,—how, as a student, the young doctor had secretly loved the much-admired and fêted belle, but had not dared to aspire then to the hand that was at length his own; this, then, was he. She had almost forgotten the engagement, and had never during her journey thither remembered that she should see this new member of the family.

The opening door had swung noiselessly upon its hinges, but perhaps the girl's silk dress rustled, or the stream of fresh air that she brought with her, and that seemed laden with the breath of violets, startled the young physician; he turned hastily.

"Doctor Bruck? I am Kitty Mangold," she said, briefly introducing herself; and, passing him quickly, she held out both hands to Susie, who sat propped up with pillows in an arm-chair.

The old woman stared at her with bewildered eyes.

"I seem fallen from the skies, do I not, Susie dear? But just at the right time, I perceive," she said, stroking back the old woman's dishevelled gray locks beneath her night-cap. "How comes it that I find you here in this wretched little back room? The stove smokes, and does not give out heat enough to dry these damp old walls. Did they not tell you that you were to take possession of the corner room and sleep in the recess?"

"Yes, yes, the Herr Councillor told me all that; but it seemed such a crazy thing for me to be stuck up all alone in the best corner room, like a lady, or like your blessed grandmother herself."

The young girl suppressed a smile. "But, Susie, you always sat there in grandpapa's time, did you not? Your spinning-wheel stood by the window; I am sure I have often enough put it out of order for you; and your work-basket had its place on the table. Will you not allow a change of apartment, Herr Doctor?" she said, turning to the physician.

"I not only allow it, I have urgently advised it, but have been met by the patient's most determined opposition," he replied, with a shrug. His voice was gentle but sonorous, and just now tinged with the pitying tone one so readily adopts in the presence of suffering.

"Well, then, we will not lose a moment," said Kitty, as she laid her fur cap upon Susie's bed and drew off her gloves.

"Nothing in the world shall induce me to go there," the housekeeper protested. "Fräulein Kitty, *don't* ask it!" she entreated, peevishly. "That room is the very apple of my eye; I have been cleaning it and rubbing it up every day since the Herr Councillor told me you were coming. I had fresh curtains put up there only the day before yesterday."

"Very well; stay here, then. I meant to take tea every afternoon at the mill, as I used to do in my childhood. But, since you are so obstinate, I will not come at all, depend upon it. I shall only be four weeks here in M——, and then you can show your 'cleaned and rubbed-up' room to any one whom you choose."

The effect was instantaneous. The grave decision in the young girl's face and bearing showed that she was not dealing for the first time with a querulous and obstinate invalid.

With a deep sigh Susie drew out the key of the room from beneath her pillow and handed it to her young mistress, who was hastily pulling off her velvet jacket. "Of course the corner room is not heated," she said, taking up a basket of wood by the stove.

"No, 'tis impossible you should do that," said Doctor Bruck, with a glance at her rich dress. He laid hat and cane on the table.

"I should be very much ashamed if I could not," she replied, gravely, but with a blush, as she noticed his glance.

She went out, and in a few moments a fine fire was crackling in the stove of the corner room, where Doctor Bruck opened the windows, that the fresh warm breath of March might replace the odour of soap and water.

Kitty entered. "I beg you to observe, Herr Doctor," she said, "that I am still fit to be seen," displaying as she spoke, not without some scorn in the gesture, her small, rosy hands, their wrists encircled by snowy linen cuffs.

An expressive smile lit up his grave face; he said nothing,

however, but turned away to close again the southern window, through which a strong draught came so freshly that it fluttered the brown curls upon the girl's forehead. The curtain, too, blew into the room; Kitty seized it with a skilful hand and tried to replace each stiff fold as it was before.

"Poor dear Susie! if she only knew how I detest these curtains!" she said, half laughing, half provoked. "They must stay now whether I like them or not, for she must have coaxed them out of my guardian entirely for me. Figured muslin curtains before such arched windows in the finest mediæval room that can be imagined! I meant to arrange and furnish it just as it might have been three centuries ago, with round, leaded panes of glass, and broad, oaken, cushioned window-seats; and there, upon the huge door leading out upon the stairs, I meant to have large antique brass bolts and hinges. Grandpapa must have had the old ones taken off; the marks are still there to show where they were. And then, with old Susie sitting by the window at her spinning-wheel!—I had imagined it all so pretty and cosy,—and now I shall have to give up the whole thing."

"But I can't see—— Are you not mistress here?"

"Oh, I shall never be able to do anything in such a case; I know myself too well," she replied, almost dejectedly. "In such matters I am a terrible coward." The contrast between this frank confession and the young girl's commanding exterior was so great that there needed indeed a keen glance into her hazel eyes to convince one that she spoke only the simple truth. These eyes were not very large, but well shaped and clear; their calm gaze was in thorough harmony with her independent, self-assured bearing. How quietly and practically she arranged everything for the coming of the invalid! A bed was made up on the sofa; the castle miller's huge leather-cushioned arm-chair was drawn out of the window-niche and placed so as to shelter the patient from every draught. She brought a little table from the recess, and placed the well-scoured footstool before the high sofa, and all was done as regularly and easily as if she had never been away from the mill. She was so absorbed in the occupation of the moment that she seemed to have quite forgotten the presence of the man standing by the southern window. Only when she opened the table-drawer and took out a white cloth with a woven red border, to spread it upon the little table in front of the arm-chair, did she turn to him and say, "There is something delightful in this old bourgeois order; nothing is ever out of place. Here it all was before I was born, and in all these six years that I have been away nothing has been changed. I am at home at once." She pointed to the mirror above the table. "There, behind the frame, I see the corner of the almanac, where grandpapa kept his accounts, and over the top is still sticking the rod, with its faded ribbon, once my mother's terror."

"And yours too?"

"No; grandpapa never paid me, poor little thing, enough attention to care about my improvement." She spoke entirely without bitterness, rather with a kind of smiling resignation. She went on to remove every particle of dust that had accumulated during Susie's illness upon tables and chairs, and closed the other windows. "There must be some flowers upon these stone window-ledges; their fragrance will refresh my poor Susie. I shall beg brother Moritz for some hyacinths and pots of violets from his conservatory——"

"You will have to apply to Frau President Urach; she has absolute and sole control of the conservatory; it belongs to her apartments."

The young girl opened her eyes. "Is etiquette so strictly observed at the villa now? During papa's lifetime the conservatory was the common property of the family." She shrugged her shoulders. "True, my father's distinguished mother-in-law was, at that time, only an occasional guest at the villa." Her melodious voice sharpened slightly in tone as she spoke these last words, but she tossed her head as she finished, as if she could thus shake off a momentarily disagreeable sensation, and added, with a smile, "'Tis all the better that I came first to the mill to acclimatize myself."

He left the window and approached her. "But will they not be vexed over there that you did not immediately upon your arrival place yourself under the protection of the family?" he asked, seriously, as one who would like to hint a gentle word of advice without presuming.

"They have no right to be so," she hastily and eagerly replied, with a blush. "Those 'over there,' 'the family,' as you call them, are alike strangers to me; I cannot beforehand feel as if I belonged to them, not even to my sisters. We do not know one another; there has not been even the slight tie of an interchange of letters between us,—I have corresponded only with Moritz. While papa lived, Henriette resided with her grandmother; we saw each other but seldom, and then always in the presence of the Frau President. My sister, Moritz Römer's wife, lived in town, and died long ago. And Flora? She was very beautiful and charming,—a belle who was at the head of papa's household while I was a child. Flora must have been wonderfully gifted, one always felt so timid and awe-stricken in her presence. I never ventured to talk to her, or even to touch her beautiful hands, and to-day I feel it would be very presuming for me to adopt towards her the familiar tone customary between sisters."

She paused and looked to him for a rejoinder, but he was gazing away far over the distant prospect, and said no word by way of encouragement. Had he not served for the lovely girl as Jacob served for Rachel? Possibly he did not even like to think that love for a sister could find lodgment in the heart that was at last his own. In spite of the gentleness and courtesy which were his by virtue of his profession, he looked as if he could vindicate his rights with great decision and gravity.

"As matters stand, the villa is no longer my home; I can visit it only as a guest, upon the same footing with other guests," she began again, after a moment's pause. "Here in the mill I am on my native soil, the air of home about me, and the sensation of home in my heart; and Franz and Susie will as faithfully protect my minority as can be done at the villa, with all its strict etiquette." A rebellious smile hovered upon her lips. "Moreover, they will forgive this breach of decorum sooner than you think, Herr Doctor; nothing better could be expected of the 'miller's mouse.'"

The pet name her father had given her was certainly most inapplicable now; any name that suggested a timorous flitting and gliding hither and thither into holes and corners scarcely befitted this girl, so calmly presenting to the world the spotless shield of her fair brow, and with all the supple vigour of her healthy youth, bearing herself with a kind of calm dignity.

Gradually a comfortable warmth was diffused by the stove. Kitty took from her pocket a tiny flask, and, pouring a few drops of cologne upon the heated iron, the air was filled with a purifying fragrance. "Susie will feel very grand and fine when she comes in here now," she said, gaily, looking about her once more to see that all was as it should be. Everything was in order, except that the recess door was ajar, and through it could be seen the gay carnations upon the head of the bedstead near the window. For the first time the girl's eye fell upon the well-known, clumsily-painted flowers that had once been the delight of her childish soul; the bloom left her cheeks, even her red lips grew pale.

"Grandpapa died there?" she whispered, agitated.

Doctor Bruck shook his head and pointed towards the southern window of the room.

"Were you with him?" she asked, quickly, coming closer to his side.

"Yes."

"He died so suddenly, and Moritz gave me such an unsatisfactory account of his death, that I do not even know what caused it."

The doctor was standing so that only his profile was towards her; he wore a heavy moustache and beard, and yet she could see his lips close tightly, as if it were difficult for them to frame a reply. After a moment's pause, he slowly turned and looked her full in the face. "They will tell you that he died in consequence of my want of skill in surgery," he said, in a voice which emotion made almost husky.

The young girl started back in horror; the glance which had been fixed upon the lips of the speaker sought the ground.

"Solely and simply for your own satisfaction," he continued, with gentle gravity, "I should like to assure you that such an assertion is utterly untrue; but how can I expect that you should believe me? We have never met before to-day, and know nothing of each other."

She might have easily extricated herself from her present embarrassment with some superficial commonplace, but it never occurred to her to do so. He was right; how could she know if he were really blameless and public opinion in the wrong? True, his whole bearing was stamped with simple frankness and integrity. She could not but feel that it was not his nature to deign one word in self-justification in the face of unjust suspicion; nay, that even the assurance he had just given her was a condescension on his part. And yet she would not say what she could give no real reason for believing.

He evidently expected no answer, for he turned away, but

with so much dignity and proud composure that Kitty had a sudden sense of shame, and the blood rushed to her cheeks. "May I bring Susie in here now?" she asked, in an uncertain voice.

He assented, and she hastily left the room. In Susie's little bedroom she wiped away the tears that had gathered in her eyes, and learned from the old housekeeper the manner of her grandfather's death.

"It has done the doctor no end of harm in town," the old woman concluded. "He used to be thought the best there, and had more to do than he could get through with; now they all say he doesn't understand his business. That's the way of the world, Fräulein Kitty. And he was *not* to blame for the misfortune. Everything went well; I saw it with my own eyes. But the castle miller was to keep perfectly quiet. *He* keep quiet, indeed! I know better than any one how the smallest trifle would make him turn red as a turkey-cock. Why, if Franz only spoke too loud, or a wagon drove too quickly into the yard, he would fall into a rage. I have borne enough in his service, and not a penny did he leave me for my pains,"—she laughed, a short, angry laugh;—"if *you* had not cared for me I should be begging my bread now."

Kitty raised her forefinger gravely, to impose silence upon the peevish old woman.

"Just as you please; I will be quiet," she said, as she sat like a helpless child while her young mistress wrapped her up in shawls and coverlets. "I am only sorry that such a good gentleman as the doctor should be so abused, and the very bread taken out of his mouth; and it is too bad for his poor old aunt, for whom he works so hard. She gave him his education out of her scanty means,—the old Frau Dean. She lives with him: he was always her pride; and for her to live to see this——"

Kitty put a stop to this talk, which threatened to become very discursive, by carefully helping the old woman to rise from her arm-chair. She was too much estranged from her former home, her thoughts and hopes were too much concentrated in Dresden, to admit of much interest at present in the private affairs of Flora's lover. She certainly pitied the physician, whose failure to cure had so suddenly imperilled position, and even means of subsistence; but grief for her grandfather, who must have suffered much, far outweighed that compassion.

Supported upon the young girl's strong arm, old Susie hobbled along the passage. The door of the corner room was open, and at the foot of the stairs leading down to it stood Doctor Bruck, with arms extended, to receive and assist the sufferer. It was a characteristic group that met his eyes. Kitty had put around her neck the invalid's sound arm, holding the brown, bony hand firmly clasped in her own upon her left shoulder, while her right arm was around Susie's waist. The girl looked the embodiment of self-sacrificing compassion, as, bending over the crippled old creature, she laid her glowing young face upon the gray head, above the wrinkled brow.

In a few moments Susie was comfortably seated in the airy apartment. She anxiously examined the famous curtains, was much shocked at the bed upon the "beautiful sofa," and tried in vain to conceal her pleasure at being once more able to count every sack of grain that was brought to the mill or carried thence.

The girl looked at her watch. "It is time I should present myself at the villa, if I would not run the risk of intruding upon the Frau President's distinguished tea-table," she said, with a feigned shudder, taking her gloves from her pocket. "In an hour I will come back and make you some broth, Susie——"

"With those hands?"

"With these hands, of course. Do you suppose I sit with them in my lap in Dresden? Why, you knew my Lukas, Susie,—she is just what she used to be, always astir, not a moment lost. You ought to see her. Such another doctor's wife it would be hard to find." And she left the apartment to get jacket and cap from Susie's room.

CHAPTER IV.

The factory clock struck five as Kitty, accompanied by Doctor Bruck, came out into the court-yard. It had grown colder, and the antique sun-dial in the gable of the mill, which in the warm spring sunshine of the earlier afternoon had clearly marked the time, looked worn and indistinct again.

A clear peal from the bell at the gate summoned Franz from the mill, and his wife followed him, stretching her neck to see all she could of the newly-returned young mistress. Kitty begged them to pay every attention to the invalid during her absence, which they duly promised to do. Just then something rustled through the air, and a beautiful dove fell maimed upon the pavement of the yard.

"Drat 'em! will they never stop that rogues' work?" cried Franz, with an oath, as he sprang down the steps and picked up the bird. Its wing was broken. "Just see here, wife," he said to her; "it's none of ours,—I thought so. They're a God-forsaken pack of scoundrels over there. They shoot the poor lady's pet doves under her very nose. Ah, if I were the Herr Councillor!" And he shook his fist.

"Who is the poor lady, Franz? And who shoots her doves?" asked Kitty, in surprise.

"He means Henriette," said Doctor Bruck.

"And they shoot them from the factory," cried Franz, angrily.

"What! my brother's workmen?"

"Yes, yes, Fräulein, those men who eat his bread. 'Tis a sin and a shame! There's the mischief, doctor! You see now what rogues they are. You want to waste kindness on them; and a pretty business you'd make of it. What will you get for your kindness? Small thanks, and such work as this. No, no; down with them!—that's what I think,—or there'll be no living here."

"Are there strikes here too, then?" Kitty asked the doctor, whose face wore so grave and beautiful a smile that she could not help looking at him.

"No, that is not the matter here," he said, shaking his head. His calm voice was in striking contrast with Franz's angry gabble. "Several of the best workmen, having saved a little money, asked of Moritz that when the estate was divided he would allow them to buy a small piece of waste land near the factory,—of small value in itself. They wanted to build houses upon it to rent to the poorer workmen, who can hardly support their families in town, where rents are so high. The councillor encouraged their hopes, which he could do the more readily since the strip of land still belonged to his park——"

"Excuse me for interrupting you, Herr Doctor," Franz here interposed, "but that was the very reason why he could not let them have it. I never thought the Frau President would allow it. Who would have such neighbours if they could help it? The ladies over there were provoked, and right enough they were; they would not have the building lots sold; no, 'they would have it ornamentally planted,' and there was an end of the business. And now the factory-hands are furious, and play all sorts of tricks in revenge."

"A miserable revenge, indeed. Poor little thing!" said Kitty, taking the dove from Franz.

"The worst of it is that the worthlessness of single individuals is attributed to an entire class. No one can blame Frau Urach for not allowing such people near her," Doctor Bruck said, and his face darkened.

"I don't admit that. There are evil and revengeful people in all classes of life," the young girl rejoined, eagerly. "I see a great deal of the lower classes: my foster-father has many poor patients; and where good, nourishing food and other help is wanted in addition to his medicines, my dear Lukas comes to the rescue, and of course I accompany her. One meets with much coarse ingratitude, 'tis true, but there are also many true, noble natures to be found among those who are so poor, so distressingly needy——"

"Not so bad as you think, Fräulein; that kind of people will always deceive you," Franz interrupted her, with a contemptuous wave of his hand.

Kitty silently measured him from head to heel with a most expressive look. "Heyday, what a magnificent person Franz has come to be!" she said, with evident irony. "Whom are you speaking of? Are you not yourself one of them? What were you in the castle mill?—A labourer just like those in the factory; a labourer who was forced silently to endure many an injustice, as I can testify."

The miller's dusty cheeks grew crimson. He stood utterly confounded before the young girl, who had known so well how to remind him of the truth. "Eh, don't take it amiss, Fräulein; I meant no harm," he said, at last, in loutish embarrassment, extending his broad palm.

"I believe there really is no harm in you; but you have been lucky, and like to play the castle miller with money in his pockets," she said, after a moment, laying her little hand in his, although the frown of displeasure did not instantly vanish from her smooth brow. She took out her handkerchief, laid the dove in it, and tied it up by the four corners. "I will carry this little sufferer to Henriette," she said, holding the handkerchief carefully like a basket,—it looked like a scantily filled traveller's bundle.

The doctor opened a little side-door in the court-yard wall, leading directly to the park, and the young girl passed through it, but stood still, amazed, upon the other side. "I do not know myself here," she cried, looking around her with an air of bewilderment; and then turning to her companion: "it looks as if giant hands had shaken the park to pieces. What are those people doing?" She pointed towards an extensive ditch, where a large number of labourers heads were seen just above-ground.

"They are digging a pond; the Frau President likes to see swans mirrored in clear water."

"And what are they building there, towards the south?"

"A tropical conservatory."

She looked thoughtful. "Moritz must be very rich."

"So they say." It sounded cool and indifferent, to the extent almost of an intentional avoidance of hinting his own opinion upon the subject. He was a striking person, this Doctor Bruck, she could not but admit to herself, as he stood there in the red gleam of the late afternoon. There was something soldierly erect in his figure, while his handsome bearded face, embrowned by sun and air, expressed only a gentle gravity. There was not in his bearing a trace of the depression of mind that one might suppose consequent upon such a misfortune as had befallen him. "Let me show you the way," he said, as he saw her eyes wander irresolutely hither and thither over the unaccustomed surroundings. He offered her his arm, and she took it without hesitation. Strange,—just so her sister Flora, she thought, walked beside him; and the thought that a few minutes would confront her with this sister, intellectually so greatly her superior, fell upon her heart like lead.

She paused, and, after a deep-drawn sigh, said, with an embarrassed smile, "Oh, what a coward I am! I really believe I am frightened. Shall I see Flora as soon as I reach the villa?"

She saw the colour mount darkly to his cheek. "To the best of my belief, she is out driving," he answered, in an under-tone; adding immediately afterwards, as if to avoid further questioning, "You will find the household still in a certain state of agitation: the prince sent Moritz a patent of nobility a few days ago."

And he had just thought to tell her this! "For what?' she asked, amazed.

"Well, he really has done good service in the cause of national industry," he replied, quickly and eagerly, as if to bar any unfavourable judgment. "And Moritz is an exceedingly kind-hearted man; he does a great deal for the poor."

Kitty shook her head. "His good fortune makes me anxious."

"His good fortune?" he repeated, with emphasis. "That depends upon how he himself regards these turns of the wheel."

"Oh, be sure they are just what he delights in," she replied, decidedly. "I know from his letters that the getting and gaining of the goods of this world is his chief aim in life. His last communication to me was enthusiastic in tone, because my fortune had proved to be so much larger than had been expected."

He walked on silently for a moment, and then asked, with a side-glance at her, "And you,—does all this wealth find you coldly indifferent?"

Kitty leaned slightly forward, and looked him in the face with a pretty air of waywardness. "You doubtless expect a very grave 'yes' from my advanced age, but I can't bring myself to utter it. I find it excessively delightful to be rich."

He laughed softly to himself, and asked no further question. They walked on quickly, and soon reached the linden-avenue. It had not been altered; fresh gravel had lately been spread upon its entire length. "Ah, there I see a dear old-time friend!" the young girl cried, pointing to a decaying wooden bridge, the arches of which spanned the stream at some distance.

"It leads to the fields on the other side——"

"Yes, to the orchard and meadows. There is a pretty old house there,—once a dependency of the castle,—embowered in grape-vines, with a broad flight of stone steps before the door. Oh, it is deliciously home-like and peaceful there! Susie used to make the garden her bleaching-ground; it was blue with violets every spring; I used to find the earliest there always."

"You may do so still; the little place has been mine since this morning." And as he spoke he cast a satisfied glance towards it.

Kitty thanked him, and looked down thoughtfully as she walked along upon the fresh gravel. Was her beautiful sister to reign as mistress in that house? Flora, with her haughty carriage, her flowing robes! Flora Mangold, whose aspirations were so lofty that a palace could hardly content them, at home in the lonely house, with its huge green porcelain stove and its worn wooden floors! How she must have changed for his sake!

A distant noise of wheels startled her. She looked up, and found herself so close to the villa that she could distinguish the pattern of the lace curtains at its windows. All was quiet there, but along the drive that swept by the stately front of the mansion a barouche swiftly approached, drawn by a pair of magnificent horses and glittering in all the pride of fresh varnish and silver mountings. A lady held the reins with a firm hand; her figure, shown to advantage in a dark velvet costume, trimmed with fur, sat airily and gracefully upon the high cushion. White plumes floated back from her brow, and about her classic face and white throat clustered fair curls.

"Flora! Ah, how beautiful my sister is!" Kitty cried, with enthusiasm, extending her hand involuntarily towards the fair driver; but neither Flora nor the councillor, who sat by her side with folded arms, heard her exclamation. The barouche flew past around the opposite corner, and was heard to draw up before the principal entrance.

A pebble flew across Kitty's path,—the doctor's cane had playfully, as it were, tossed it away. Then first the girl observed that in her eagerness she was outstripping him, and she turned towards him. He was walking at his previous pace, but his bearing seemed to have become a trifle more erect, more proudly reserved. As she looked at him, his glance was hastily averted with what almost seemed embarrassment. She suppressed with difficulty an ironical smile, surmising that she had detected in him some such thought as, "Heavens, what a clumsy creature is here as compared with my graceful sylph!"

"Flora's courage in driving surprises me," she said, as they again walked side by side.

"Her companion's contempt of danger is much more astonishing. This was a 'trial-trip:' the councillor bought those young horses only yesterday." He was greatly irritated. She could hear it in his voice, and fell silent in dismay.

CHAPTER V.

NEITHER spoke further. They soon reached the house, entering by a side-door while the barouche was driving away from the front. A servant informed them that the ladies and the Herr Councillor were in the conservatory, in the Frau President's apartments.

Kitty had regained her self-possession. She handed her card to the footman with a "For the Herr Councillor."

"So formal?" asked Doctor Bruck, smiling, as the lackey moved noiselessly away and vanished.

"So formal," she assented, gravely. "The greater the distance preserved, the better. It would scarcely become me to present myself familiarly here. I am even afraid that my unannounced arrival may cause the 'Herr Councillor' some embarrassment."

She was not mistaken. The councillor came rushing from within, almost stumbling over the threshold in his eagerness, exclaiming, "Good heavens, Kitty!"

His surprise was ridiculous, for he evidently looked to see his ward's face two feet nearer the ground than he found it; and this well-grown, graceful figure advancing towards him said, with an inclination full of womanly pride,—

"Dear Moritz, do not be angry with me for not complying with your suggestions. Indeed, I am rather too big to give you the trouble of coming for me."

He stood astounded. "You are right, Kitty. The time is past when I could lead you by the hand," said he, slowly, as if lost in contemplation of her face, which was bathed in a rosy blush. "Well, you are heartily welcome!" Then, giving his hand to Bruck, he added, "Ah, you met in the hall. I must present you——"

"Don't trouble yourself, Moritz; I have attended to all that," the girl interrupted him. "The Herr Doctor was paying his visit to Susie when I reached the mill."

The councillor's face lengthened. "You went first to the mill then?" he asked, surprised. "But, my dear child, Grandmamma Urach was most amiably ready to receive you, and naturally expected that you would come directly to her, instead of which you have been first to your old flame Susie! Pray say nothing about it within," he added, in a hurried whisper.

"Do you seriously desire that I should not?" The firm, clear, girlish tone contrasted strangely with his timid whisper. "I cannot deny it if I should be questioned. I really do not understand concealment, Moritz——" She paused a moment, startled at the sudden flush that overspread his face, but concluded resolutely, "If I have done wrong, I will confess it: it cannot cost me my head."

"Oh, if you take my well-meant hint so tragically, there is nothing more to be said," he replied at once, with some irritation. "It will not cost you your head, to be sure, but it will imperil your position in my house. Just as you please, however. Judge for yourself what success will await your direct 'up-and-down' tongue in our refined circles."

His tone had already changed to playfulness; and, before anything further could be said to alter his amiable mood, he gallantly offered his arm, and conducted her to the former dining-hall, adjoining the conservatory, and opened the door.

Here was no longer the pleasant dining-room, with its comfortable old-fashioned leather-covered furniture. The wall that had once separated it from the conservatory had disappeared, and in its place slender pillars upheld the arched ceiling, which was painted with brilliant colours, after the Moorish style. Below, a grating of delicate gilt-bronze tracery ran from pillar to pillar, separating the mosaic floor of the Moorish room from the white sand and green sod of the conservatory. Behind this grating there was a wealth of greenery and bloom: tufts of May-flower and Parma violets grouped about the feet of dark laurels, and dragon-trees, with hosts of metallic-leaved decorative plants,—all this embowered, framed in, as it were, by the pillars, around which were twined clematis-vines, that wreathed with white and lilac flowers the slender shafts up to the graceful arches they supported.

Between the two centre pillars Flora was standing, still in her driving-dress, apparently on the point of leaving the room. The fountain in the conservatory showed its silver spray just above the plumes in her hat. One small gloved hand lifted the heavy brown velvet skirt, which the evening light tinged with faint gold, while the other, from which the glove had been withdrawn, rested lightly upon the pillar beside her, as delicate and fair as the white clematis flower that hung beside it.

As Kitty entered, she first opened her blue eyes wide with astonishment, then half dropped the lids in a keen, inquiring glance, while a sarcastic smile hovered upon her lips.

"Guess, Flora, who this is!" exclaimed the councillor.

"No need to puzzle long over that riddle; it is Kitty, who has made the journey alone," she replied, in her careless yet decided manner. "It would be impossible for any one who knew old Frau Sommer to doubt for a moment that this stout girl, with a face like a rosy-cheeked apple, is her grandchild; her eyes and hair, however, are strikingly like Clotilde's, Moritz."

She lightly disengaged herself from the hanging flowers, approached her sister, and, lifting the girl's chin, kissed her lips. Yes, this was the same incomparable Flora; but her long-continued sway over the hearts of men had robbed her actions of feminine tenderness. With the same negligence with which she tendered a kiss to her sister after a separation of six years, she greeted the doctor with a "Good-evening, Bruck," extending her hand to him, not as if he were her lover, but rather as though he were some fellow-student. He pressed slightly the hand thus given, and acquiesced in its instant withdrawal.

This outward reserve between the lovers seemed to be an understood affair. Flora turned gaily towards the conservatory, exclaiming, with a mocking smile, "Grandmamma, our heiress presents herself to the admiring gaze of yourself and your friends a month earlier than she was expected."

At Flora's first words the Frau President made her appearance from behind a group of camellias. Without being aware of it herself, perhaps, she had been watching the new-comer with that keen attention which most people are apt to bestow upon one whom men dub a favourite of fortune. Flora's half-malicious remark quickly altered this expression, however. The old lady knitted her brows disapprovingly, and a delicate flush tinged her pale face. "I do not remember having displayed any extraordinary interest in your sister's heiress-ship," she said, coldly, with a stern glance of reproof. "If I take great pleasure in Kitty's arrival, and welcome her most cordially, it is because she is my dear lost Mangold's daughter, and your sister."

She approached Kitty with outstretched hands, as if to embrace her, but the girl courtesied profoundly and formally, as if presented for the first time to her father's haughty mother-in-law. A keen observer would have seen in her conduct a shy recoil from all contact, but the Frau President apparently regarded it as simply indicative of profound respect. She withdrew her hands, and touched the girl's forehead with her lips. "Did you really come alone?" she asked, and her eyes turned towards the door, as if half fearing the entrance of some unwelcome companion to her guest.

"Quite alone. I wished for once to try my wings unaided, and my Frau Doctor willingly consented." As if unconsciously, she passed her slender fingers across her forehead where the Frau President's cold lips had rested for an instant.

"Ah, that I can easily believe; there I recognize old Lukas," Frau von Urach rejoined, with a gentle laugh of irony. "She, too, was always very independent. Your good father spoiled her a little, my child. She did as she chose; of course only what was right——"

"And sensible, and therefore papa was glad to intrust his wild young colt to her care," Kitty added, with all the frank gaiety natural to her. This freedom of manner, however, seemed to produce an unfavourable impression.

The Frau President slightly shrugged her shoulders. "Your father certainly had your welfare at heart, my dear Kitty, and I made it a rule never to object to any of his plans. But his nature was eminently refined; he thought much of a due sense of decorum. Might he not, perhaps, have slightly disapproved of his daughter's dropping down thus, sans gêne, unceremoniously in the midst of a household?"

"Likely enough," Kitty replied. "But papa would remember what blood runs in this daughter's veins,"—and there was a wayward gleam in her brown eyes. "'To wander when and where it would, ever beseemed the miller's blood,' Frau President."

The councillor cleared his throat and carefully smoothed his silky moustache, while the Frau President looked as dismayed as if an icy blast had suddenly affronted her delicate face, and Flora burst into a laugh. "O child of mortality, you are delightfully naïve!" she cried, clapping her hands. "Yes, yes,—'To wander is the miller's joy,'" she quoted. "Only let our youngest make her début with such words on her lips at Moritz's next grand soirée, grandmamma, and see how every one will stare!" She looked at the old lady with merry malice, but Frau von Urach had entirely regained her self-possession.

"I trust to your sister's inborn tact, my child," she said, as she extended her hand in welcome to the doctor, smiling as she did so a smile that just showed the tips of her teeth through her drawn lips and left one in doubt whether it were sweet or sour.

"Tact, tact,—of much use that will be," Flora repeated, shaking her head mockingly. "Her miller tendencies are just as much inborn. The worthy Lukas has failed to inoculate her with a trifle of worldly wisdom,—there's the rub. Indeed, I am really glad you are alone, Kitty; I am sure we shall like you far better than if you were pinned to the apron of your prosaic old governess."

Kitty had taken off her cap; the warm, odorous air had flushed her cheeks. Thus, her head crowned with thick golden-brown braids, she looked still taller.

"Prosaic? My Frau Doctor?" she cried, gaily. "No more poetical woman lives."

"Indeed? Raves about the moon, I suppose, copies sentimental verses, etc., or even composes them herself,—eh?"

The young girl's bright eyes were riveted for a moment upon the face of the mocking speaker. "No, she does not copy verses, but quantities of her husband's manuscript, because the printers of the medical periodicals declare that they cannot possibly decipher his hieroglyphics," she said, after a short pause. "She writes neither verses nor romances: she has not the time; and yet she is full of poetry. Ah, you smile just as you used to do, Flora, with those deep lines at the corners of your mouth; but I no longer want to run away from the sneer. There is a combative vein in me, and I maintain that there is real poetry in the way in which my dear

Lukas always knows how to grasp the truest and best side of life, in her knowledge of how to make home lovely and attractive, with beauty of various kinds peeping out from every corner, and in the talent she shows for making her husband, myself, and her chosen circle of friends content and happy."

As she finished, a shower of fresh violets came raining against her breast, whence they fell to the floor.

"Brava, Kitty!" cried Henriette. She was standing in the conservatory, close to the grating, her pale hands pressed to her panting bosom. "I should like to have my arms about your neck this minute, but—just look at me—would it not be ridiculous? You so thoroughly healthy, body and mind, and I——" Her voice failed her.

Kitty threw down the cap she had in her hand and flew to her. She tenderly embraced the poor, weak form, wisely suppressing the tears that were ready to flow at sight of her sister's emaciated face.

Flora bit her lip. "Our youngest" had not only gained dignity of appearance, but her clear eyes and outspoken tongue gave token also of a courageous independence of thought and of speech that might possibly be inconvenient at times. She was aware of a sudden foreboding that with the advent of this vigorous girl a shadow was to fall upon her path. She hastily took off her hat and passed her fingers through the curls that had been flattened against her temples. "Did you really bring that poetic traveller's-bundle all the way from Dresden?" she asked, drily, with a glance at the knotted handkerchief hanging upon Kitty's arm.

The girl untied it and held out the dove to Henriette. "This little patient belongs to you," she said. "The poor thing has been shot in the wing. It fell upon the pavement in the mill-yard."

This betrayed her visit to the mill, but Frau von Urach did

not appear to have heard her last words; she pointed indignantly to the wounded bird, and said to the councillor, in a tone of reproach, "That is the *fourth*, Moritz."

"And my pet besides, my little Silver-crest!" exclaimed Henriette, brushing away a tear of grief and vexation.

The councillor was quite pale with anger and dismay. "Dear grandmamma, I pray you do not blame me!" he cried, almost with violence. "I do my very best to trace these abominable outrages to their source, and to prevent them, but their perpetrators are concealed in the ranks of two hundred angry men,"—he shrugged his shoulders,—"and there is nothing to be done. Therefore I have repeatedly entreated Henriette to confine her doves until the excitement is over."

"Then it is we who are to submit? Better and better," said the old lady, satirically; and, as she spoke, she loosened and adjusted the cloud of lace about her face and throat, as if her agitation made her insufferably warm. "Can you not see, Moritz, that such compliance fairly challenges insolence? They will soon tire of permitted dove-shooting, and aim at some nobler game."

"Why dress the matter in such phrases, grandmamma? They themselves do not scruple to speak plainly," Flora remarked, carelessly. "My maid found another threatening letter on the window-sill when she opened the shutters this morning. She was forced to pick up the dirty scrap of paper with the tongs to let me read it, and it is now in her room, in case you wish it preserved, Moritz. Of course it contains nothing new,—the same old story! I should really like to know why these men honour me so especially with their hatred of a class."

Kitty could not help thinking that in this case the hatred was not so much of a class as of an individual. She could easily understand how this queenly figure, apparelled in rich garments, with scornful lines about her mouth and a masculine address, might well be held responsible by outsiders for all that emanated from the house.

"Their low attacks are all the more ridiculous, since I am particularly interested in the social question," Flora continued, with a short laugh, "and I have given to the world several telling articles in favour of the working-classes."

"Nothing can be effected nowadays by mere writing," Doctor Bruck said, from the window where he was standing. "The most gifted pens have written unweariedly upon the subject, and the waves of popular agitation rise higher and higher, and float all their theories from the paper."

Every eye turned towards him. "Ah! and what is to be done, then?" Flora asked, sharply.

"Meet the people and their demands face to face. What avails it to collect laboriously all the evidence 'for and against' from the mass of memorials and pamphlets that cumber your writing-table——"

"Oh, pray——" And her eyes lit up with sudden fire.

"And add your mite to the pile of dead published matter?" he went on, undeterred. "These people will scarcely read your articles, and if they should, what good would it do them? Words cannot build homesteads for them. The larger part of the solution of this problem belongs to the women of the families of our capitalists, to their mild influence in modifying masculine severity, their gentle mediation, their wisdom. But very few take the trouble to reflect upon the matter, or, what is more important than all else, to question their own hearts. They require at the hands of the men the means for providing for their needs, which at the present day are almost boundless, and never consider that the elements of a fearful conflict are gathering and growing at their very doors."

The Frau President slowly passed her slender hands down the satin folds of her gown, and, without heeding the last remark, said, complacently, "I like to give, but I am not used to put my alms directly into the hands of my beneficiaries myself, and thus it may easily occur that the number and value of my charities are not known. I am quite willing to have them ignored, even although I am thus made responsible, as it were, for the barbarities to which we are daily exposed."

"These barbarities are detestable. No one can condemn them more severely than I," Doctor Bruck rejoined, in a tone as cold as her own, "but——"

"Well, 'but'? You still maintain that we women of the capitalists' families have provoked them?"

"Yes, Frau President. You have deterred the capitalist from coming to the assistance of his people when their demand was not unreasonable, not one of those extravagant requirements that at present cast suspicion and discredit upon the cause of an entire party. They did not ask for charity, but simply to be allowed, with the help of their employer, to struggle upwards to a happier daily life."

The old lady tapped him lightly on the shoulder, and said, kindly, but in a curt, decisive tone, evidently intended to cut short all discussion, "You are an idealist, Herr Doctor."

"Only a philanthropist," he rejoined, with a faint smile, and took his hat to go.

Flora had turned her back to him, and walked to the other window. There never was a woman's face more fitted to express enmity than was that clear-cut profile, that mouth so closely shut over the teeth. Had not the man plainly said that she had laboriously sought to collect the ideas of others?—she, with her talents! To be sure, she had never soiled her dainty foot with the dust of her brother-in-law's factory; it was true that she knew nothing of the life of those people whom the clamour for reform had assembled beneath one banner, where they were grown to be a power that thrust itself like a wedge into social order, threatening to shatter it. And why need she know by sight and contact what she described? Nonsense! Of what use, then, were intellect and imagination? Until to-day the doctor had never uttered a syllable with regard to her literary efforts,—"from timid reverence," she had supposed,—and now he suddenly treated her work with such scant courtesy,—*he!* "I cannot conceive, grandmamma," she exclaimed, with flashing eyes, "how you can dignify him with the title of idealist. To my mind, Bruck handles the great subject prosaically enough. According to his plan, we must instantly strip ourselves of every elegance and comfort, and dress in sackcloth and ashes; never must we indulge in intellectual pursuits, but must concoct soup for the poor. To insist upon quiet and retirement in our own park is a deadly sin; of course we must encourage the hopeful school-children to romp and play directly underneath our windows, etc., etc.; and if we are not docile, he threatens us with a ghost at our doors." She laughed a short, hard laugh. "Our philanthropist overshoots the mark terribly with these sympathies of his. If the conflict that he foretells ever really comes to pass, the ghost will make as short work with him as with us."

"I have not much to lose," the doctor said, with a smile.

Flora hastily approached him. Her curls stirred lightly, and her heavy velvet skirt swept the marble floor.

"Oh, since this morning that is not true, Bruck," she said, ironically. "You are a real-estate owner, Moritz tells me. Seriously, have you fulfilled your yesterday's threat and purchased that wretched barracks on the other side of the river?"

"My threat?"

"What else can I call your presenting to me such a picture of the future? You have, as you spoke of doing yesterday, invested your savings in a spot that is to me the *ne plus ultra* of desolation, poverty, and repulsive ugliness. You certainly cannot have possessed yourself of this gem simply to feast your eyes upon its beauties, and therefore I ask you seriously, 'Who is to live there?'"

"You never need cross the threshold."

"I certainly never shall,—you may rely upon that. Rather——" The glance with which the doctor raised his hand to interrupt her was a riddle hard to read, but it had such power in it that it silenced those beautiful lips.

"I purchased the house for my aunt, only reserving one room in it for my use,—a corner where I can enjoy a leisure hour of study amid rural surroundings," he said, immediately, and far more placidly than could have been anticipated from the former expression of his face.

"Ah, I wish you joy of it! A special summer retreat! And in winter, Bruck?"

"In winter I must content myself with the green room, which you have assigned me in our future dwelling."

"To tell the truth, that house does not please me. There is such constant noise from the street about a corner house, it would greatly disturb me when I wanted to work."

"Well, then, I will simply pay off the house-agent, and look for another," he rejoined, with imperturbable equanimity.

Flora turned away with a shrug, so that Kitty could look directly into her face. It seemed as if she would have stamped upon the floor with vexation, while her head was thrown back and her eyes sought the ceiling, as if to say, "Gracious heaven, is there no way to reach him?"

At that moment the Frau President rang the bell so sharply that the sound echoed from the end of the long corridor. The old lady looked greatly aggrieved; explanations so devoid of all taste and tact as these should never take place in *her* presence. "You can scarcely have a high opinion of the hospitality and breeding of your brother's household, Kitty," she said to the young girl. "No one has taken off your travelling-jacket or offered you a chair; you are forced instead, whether you will or not, to listen to useless discussions, and left standing upon the cold marble, while warm rugs are at hand." She pointed, as she spoke, to two opposite corners of the room, furnished with luxurious chairs and lounges and laid with costly Smyrna rugs, and then she gave orders to the servant who entered to instruct the housekeeper with regard to apartments for the guest.

Thus the bystanders were relieved of the disagreeable sensation left in their minds by the sharp interchange of words between the lovers. The councillor hastened to relieve his ward of her jacket, and Henriette, her wasted cheeks flushed with a feverish colour, left the conservatory to attend to her dove.

"Will you not stay to tea, Herr Doctor?" Frau von Urach asked the physician, as he came to take leave of her. He excused himself on the plea of visits to patients,—a plea which Flora heard with a sarcastic smile. This, however, he did not appear to notice. He shook hands with her and with the councillor; to Kitty he made a chivalric and respectful inclination, not at all as if to a new young sister-in-law: she was still a stranger to him, and the others appeared to find this view of the matter entirely correct. Henriette left the room with him.

"My dear Flora, I must for the future strictly forbid the recurrence of such distasteful scenes as this which we have just been compelled to witness," the Frau President said, in a stern voice and with a deep frown, as soon as the door had closed upon the pair. "You have reserved to yourself entire freedom to attain your end in the manner that shall best please yourself; so far so good,—you have hitherto encountered not the slightest opposition on my part; but I protest earnestly as soon as you show an inclination to fight out the wretched affair in my presence. As I said before, that I strictly forbid! Must I repeat——"

"Dear grandmamma," the young lady interrupted her, in a tone of contemptuous banter, "do not repeat! I know it all." Commit murder or arson, if you will, in this house, only see that the Frau President Urach arises like a phœnix from the ashes. Forgive me, grandmamma; I will never do so again. The house is large enough; I need not carry out my designs directly in your sight. If my work were only not made so immensely difficult! I am afraid that some fine day I shall lose patience and——"

"Flora!" the councillor exclaimed, in a voice expressing both warning and entreaty.

"Yes, yes, Herr von Römer, I perfectly understand that I must pay due regard to your new honours. Heavens! how my poor shoulders are weighted down! And why should I do penance because hearts cling to me like burrs?"

She took her hat, and gathered up her train to go,—then paused as she passed Kitty.

"You see, my dear," she said, putting her forefinger beneath her sister's chin and turning her face up to her, "this all comes of a poor girl's giving way to sentiment for a moment and imagining herself in love. She suddenly finds herself in a trap, and admits sorrowfully that the trite old doctrine, 'See, ye who join in endless union, that heart with heart be in communion,' contains a terrible truth. Think of your sister, and take care of yourself, child."

She left the room, and Kitty looked after her in wide-eyed wonder. What a strange fiancée her beautiful sister was!

CHAPTER VI.

NEAR the western boundary of the park stood the remains of the former Castle Baumgarten. Of the entire structure, once surrounded by a fosse, only a single tower—of considerable dimensions, however,—was left, flanked on one side by the blackened ruin of an ancient wing of the building. Sixty years previously, the old pile had been torn down. Its possessor at that time, residing most of the year in foreign parts, had erected "Villa Baumgarten" on the opposite side of the estate, near the frequented road, in order that when in his own country he might "live among his kind," and the grandly-hewn blocks of granite from the old castle had been used in building the modern villa. The tower, with the ruin adjoining it, had been spared as an ornament to the park. It crowned an artificial mound covered with mossy turf. Its base was encircled by a wilderness of woodland shrubs and plants, hedge-roses and blackberry-vines crept in and out of the huge window-arches in the ruin and nestled among its fragments, while the wild hop clambered everywhere, covering the grim dark stones with a wealth of greenery.

This ruin, encircled by the water of the fosse, certainly answered the end for which it had first been preserved; but the succeeding generation, being of an eminently practical turn of mind, had drained the ditch, and planted vegetables in the damp, rich soil. The castle miller had declared upon purchasing the estate that this proceeding had been the only sensible thing done by its former possessors, and had appropriated this spot for his own special use. As a child, Kitty had taken great delight in the "little valley," as she called the former fosse. Of course, she then thought and knew nothing of how romance had been outraged in this transformation; she would while away hours wandering and plucking with Susie through the wilderness of bean-poles and young pea-vines, never dreaming that if the dam should suddenly give way the waters would overwhelm her with Susie and all the green luxuriance.

Now, on the fifth day after her arrival, she found herself for the first time in this retired part of the park, and paused bewildered. The hop-vines still wove a leafless net-work about the walls, and the turf on the mound showed as yet no green blade of grass, but the April sunshine lay broad and full upon the ruin-crowned hill, throwing it into picturesque relief against the background of dark firs that covered the mountain-range in the distance. There was no trace of fresh mortar on the walls to tell of modern repair, every stone was old, yet none were wanting; the high arched windows in the tower, formerly closed by decaying wooden shutters, gaped wide, and within the stone window-frames the sunny, tremulous air glittered as if some imprisoned sunbeam were weaving there a mysterious golden web. And fresh life was stirring about the ruined ancestral home of the Von Baumgartens; above the battlements of the tower white and coloured doves were wheeling in airy flight, and from the thicket beneath the ancient chestnuts which flanked it on the south, two roes came noiselessly and wandered about the hill. The "little valley" had vanished; and, as of old, a shining stream girdled the hill around, burying beneath its bubbling waters, as if no human hand had ever usurped its bed, all that had once bloomed and flourished there.

A bridge suspended by chains spanned the ditch, and, guarding its hither side, lay a huge bull-dog, his head on his forepaws, keeping a watchful eye upon the opposite bank of the stream.

"Here you have Moritz's Tusculum, Kitty," said Henriette, who was leaning upon her sister's arm. "Once a castle-keep, with its paraphernalia of instruments of torture and sighs of mortal agony; only four months ago an undisputed refuge for owls, bats, and my doves; and now drawing-room, bedroom, and even treasure-chamber, of the Herr Councillor von Römer. In truth, the place still looks ruinous enough, almost as if the next strong wind would overthrow the walls, but all is really strong and firm; and there, beneath those projecting stones, Moritz's servant has his room; the fellow is to be envied."

Flora had come with them. "No accounting for tastes!" she said, drily, with a shrug. "Really a striking and original idea for a plebeian brain, eh, Kitty?" She passed her sisters and crossed the bridge. A touch of her little foot thrust away the dog from her path, and she ascended the hill. The roes fled timidly from her rustling silken robes, the doves flew away from the lower window-sills, and the dog growled, and slowly followed the lordly lady for a few steps. Standing above, her slender hands upon the latch of the brazen-studded door of the tower, and dressed in heavy light-gray silk, gleaming like silver in the sunlight, with puffed sleeves and skirt caught up on one side, she was the living impersonation of the beautiful emperor's daughter of the Kyffhäuser.

Involuntarily Kitty looked from her to Henriette, clinging to her arm, and her heart ached. The frail figure, its emaciation showing plainly in the close-fitting gay-coloured dress, was actually balanced upon immensely high heels. Her breath came in short gasps; but her whole costume was gaudy, and had so coquettish an air that but for pity one could have laughed. Within the last few days she had had repeated attacks of asthma, almost to suffocation, and yet she *would* not be ill: the world should not know that she suffered. A single compassionate glance, any pitying remark, made her angry and bitter. She had been more ill than usual; for

Doctor Bruck, whose patient she was, and who could always give her relief, was away. A few hours after leaving the villa upon Kitty's arrival there, he had received a telegraphic dispatch from a friend calling him to L——g, to remain there for several days, he informed Flora in a short note. Any medical aid from Doctorr von Bär the sick girl persistently refused to accept. "Rather die!" she had whispered, when struggling with one of her attacks. Kitty had tended her sister with the greatest care, and now, putting her arm around her waist, she led her across the bridge towards the ruin.

How often as a child she had run up that hill and scrambled through the underbrush! How often she had peeped through the big key-hole of the door of the tower! The servants had said that in its cellars there was still stored powder from the Thirty Years' War, and that the walls were hung with "all sorts of horrid things." But she had never seen anything within but black darkness. A heavy, mouldy air had been wafted out upon her childish face with terrifying effect; and if an owl above happened to flap his wings, she would rush down the hill as if pursued by the furies, and cling with both hands to Susie's apron, quaking with fright. Now she stood inside, at the foot of a narrow, carpeted winding staircase, and admired the effect produced by the wealthy merchant's money. Without, a crumbling ruin; within, the home of knightly ease. The room her childish eye had never been able to pierce was a spacious vaulted hall, the massive arches of which supported the entire structure above. On the walls the "horrid things" were still hanging,—helmets and various weapons,—but they were tastefully arranged, and flashed back from their burnished surfaces the sunlight that streamed through the windows. To preserve the ruinous aspect from without, there was no division into panes of the glass in the windows; one unbroken sheet had been set into the stone frames, hence the strange glitter in them when seen from the outside. The place had been what was called in the olden time a fortress ward; in times of supreme danger, a place of refuge for the dwellers in the castle. As such, its upper story had been furnished after the most primitive fashion; now, its splendour far eclipsed that of the finest ancient banqueting-hall of the old castle, so long since swept from the face of the earth.

When the two sisters reached the first room of the upper story they found Flora gracefully reclining among the crimson cushions of a lounge, with a lighted cigarette between her fingers, looking on while the councillor brewed the afternoon coffee in the silver coffee-pot. He had invited his three sisters-in-law to take coffee with him this afternoon.

"Well, Kitty?" he called out to the young girl upon her entrance, directing her attention by a wave of his hand, as he spoke, to all that he had effected.

She paused upon the threshold, a black veil thrown loosely over her golden-brown braids, her eyes full of laughter, her young frame vigorous and supple as if sprung from the giant knights Von Baumgarten.

"Most romantic, Moritz! The illusion is perfect!" she answered, gaily. "That fellow down there," and she pointed through the nearest window to the gleaming girdle of water, "might terrify us with his martial air, did we not know that a councillor of commerce of the nineteenth century sits within his circle."

He contracted his fine eyebrows, and cast from beneath them a dubious glance at her face. She did not notice it. "It certainly was hardly fair to grow turnips and cabbages in the bed of the fosse," she continued. "I see that now, although the 'little valley' was a favoured spot in my remembrance. Still, it is a strange and interesting fact, that the merchant of to-day renews the barriers which even former knightly lords of the soil wearied of and at last destroyed as superfluous."

"Do not forget, my dear Kitty, that I myself now belong among these latter," he replied, in a tone of considerable pique. "It is sad to think that an ancient race should so adapt itself to the spirit of the age as ruthlessly to abolish old and honourable customs and institutions. It is a crying outrage upon us, their successors."

"Idiot! He is more Catholic than the Pope," Henriette muttered, angrily. She advanced farther into the room, while Kitty mechanically closed the door behind her without averting her half-startled, half-thoughtful gaze from her brother-in-law. As a child she had, in common with all who came in contact with him, been very fond of him. His father had been an honest, hard-working mechanic, and Moritz, left an orphan at an early age, of striking personal beauty and ingratiating address, had been received as an underling in the establishment of the wealthy banker Mangold, whose daughter he eventually married. Kitty knew how devoted he had been to her sister Clotilde until she died; she had always seen him submissive even to servility to her father, and he had been uniformly amiable and kind even towards those beneath him; and yet there was now hovering about those finely-chiselled lips a distinctly-stamped expression of arrogance. The rope-maker's son was contemptuously overthrowing the ladder by which he had climbed thus high, and was so dazzled by his good fortune that he fell naturally into the jargon of a genuine country squire.

Henriette had coiled herself up on a low cushioned seat, and, clasping her hands around her knees, said, sharply, "Dearest Moritz, I pray you do not take quite so much state upon yourself; you might provoke some old mistress of these walls to awaken and see her grand successor and lord of the castle making coffee, while the castle dame reclines comfortably, smoking cigarettes. Oh, how she would stare!"

Flora did not stir a hair's-breadth from her position: she

only took the cigarette slowly from between her lips, and asked, in a tone of assumed indifference, as she knocked off the ashes with her third finger, "Does it annoy you, my dear?"

"*Me?*" Henriette turned towards her with a hard laugh. "You know I am never annoyed by the freaks and follies of your genius, Flora; the world is wide: it is easy to avoid"——

"Hush! don't be so bitter, child. I asked from the purest sympathy for your poor chest."

The flitting crimson came and went upon the invalid's thin cheek, and tears glittered in her eyes, but she controlled herself. "Thanks; but expend your care first upon yourself, Flora. I know how your every fibre is longing to throw that smoky thing out of the window, for it discolours your white teeth like meerschaum, and sends a perpetual shiver of disgust through you, and yet you persist in the heroic self-subjugation. From a mania for the emancipation of woman? Pshaw! you have far too much taste, Flora, to have recourse to such distinctive signs of a blue-stocking, and you certainly would not sacrifice beauty to a rage for public glorification and applause——"

"See what a lofty opinion the dear creature entertains of me," Flora said to the councillor, shaking her head, and laughing ironically.

"You are practising smoking, and will probably continue to do so for three or four weeks longer," Henriette continued, undeterred, but with evident irritation, "because there are people who detest like the breath of the plague the odour of tobacco from a woman's mouth. You are trying to offend; this is your latest attempt to——"

Flora raised herself from her reclining posture. "And if it is, Fräulein Henriette?" she asked, with an air of lofty disdain. "Is it not my affair, solely, whether I choose to attract or repel?"

"Not at all. Your only duty in this case is to please," Henriette declared, with vehemence.

"Nonsense! There is no marriage ring here yet." And she pointed to the third finger of her left hand. "Thank God, no! And you of all others should be the last to lay a lance in rest in this cause. You are ill, poor child, and more than ever dependent upon your physician; but he prefers to take a pleasure-trip, and to remain weeks away perhaps, assigning no reason for his absence."

Here the councillor put in a word. "Assigning no reason, Flora, because he does not happen to have told you all the why and the wherefore of his absence!" he exclaimed, with irritation. "Bruck never speaks of his profession, or of anything connected with it, as you well know. He has doubtless been summoned to some patient——"

"To L——g, where distinguished professors from the university can be had? Ha! ha! a charming idea! Don't be ridiculous, Moritz! But this is a point upon which I positively decline to argue with you." She held out her hand for her coffee-cup, and slowly sipped the delicious beverage. Henriette sullenly declined the offered refreshment; she arose, and stepped to the glass door that led out upon the adjoining ruin. It was the remains of a colonnade which had once connected the tower with the castle, and two finely-vaulted arches, resting upon slender pillars, now formed a kind of balcony whence there was a magnificent view.

She tore open one of the glass folding-doors, and, pressing her clasped hands convulsively to her breast, greedily inhaled the fresh air. In vain; for a moment she seemed in danger of suffocation. Kitty and the councillor hastened to support the sufferer, and even Flora arose and reluctantly threw away her cigarette. "I suppose you will accuse these harmless wreaths of smoke of causing this attack," she said, fretfully, "but I know better. You ought to be in bed, Henriette, not out in this dry spring air, which is positive poison for your disease. I warned you, but you never heed advice, and would fain persuade us that you are glowing with health and strength. And you are just as obstinate with regard to your medical adviser——"

"Because I do not intrust my poor lungs to the first poisoner at hand," Henriette concluded her sentence in a weak but very decided tone.

"Oh, dear! you mean my poor old councillor of medicine," cried Flora, smiling, and shrugging her shoulders. "Go on, child, if it pleases you! I know nothing, it is true, about his medicines, but I can affirm that he has never yet been so clumsy as——nearly to cut a patient's throat."

The councillor turned a pale face towards her and involuntarily raised his hand, as if to stop the slanderous words upon her lips; he was speechless as he timidly glanced at Kitty.

"Heartless!" gasped Henriette.

"Not heartless, but bold enough to call things by their right names, even if the hard words make my own wounds bleed afresh. Where is the merit else of uncompromising truth? Think of that terrible evening, and ask yourself who was right! I knew that a fall from the heights of a mere superficial adventitious celebrity was sure to come. It has come, more disastrously and completely than even I feared, as you must admit if you would not dispute the unanimous verdict of the public. That I will not share this fall every one who knows me must be aware. I cannot smooth over and adjust matters as grandmamma so well understands how to do. I would not do so if I could. No part is more ridiculous than that of those simple-souled women who continue openly to adore where the world unites in pronouncing that there is nothing worthy of worship."

She opened the other folding-door and stepped out upon the balcony. She had spoken with passionate emphasis; the pale marble tint of her Roman profile, seen clearly cut against the blue sky of spring, glowed with a gloomy fire; her eyes were full of disdain, her nostrils quivered nervously,—she was the very personification of burning impatience.

"At least, it was his part to convince me.—How I would have defended him then, both with tongue and pen!" she continued, thrusting her slender fingers in among the rustling tracery of withered vines. "But he chose to reply to my first and only question upon the subject, by an icy look, haughty as a Spaniard——"

"Such a reply should have sufficed you——"

"Not so, my dear Moritz; it was a very convenient and easy answer, and I am sceptical with regard to speaking looks and gestures: I require more. But I show you that my will is good in the matter by repeating again what I said at first: 'Prove to me and to the world that he did his duty well, for you were present!'"

He retreated hastily from the threshold of the door and put his hand over his eyes: the sunlight shining full upon the balcony was insupportable to him. "You know well enough that I cannot do what you ask; I am no surgeon," he replied, in a stifled tone, that was lost in an almost inarticulate murmur.

"Not another word, Moritz," Henriette exclaimed. "Your every attempt to defend him gives some colour to this girl's cowardly indecision." Her large eyes, glowing with internal fever, were riveted with an expression of hatred upon her sister's beautiful face. "It would be best that your cruel designs should attain their end as soon as possible,—to speak plainly, that your evident estrangement should induce him voluntarily to break the bond between you. Your heart, cleaving as it does to mere externals, would be small loss to him; but he loves you, and would rather contract an unhappy marriage, knowing it to be such, than resign you. His whole conduct proves this——"

"Unfortunately," Flora said over her shoulder, by way of interjection.

"And therefore I will stand by him, and defeat your machinations if I can," Henriette concluded, in a louder voice, and with quivering lips.

The glance that Flora here bestowed upon her frail, agitated sister sparkled with cruel scorn, but, as she looked, a startling revelation seemed to dawn upon her; she suddenly put her right arm around Henriette's shoulders, and drew her towards her, as she whispered in her ear, with a sardonic smile, "Why not make him happy yourself, child? You will meet with no opposition from me,—be sure of that."

To such wanton malice can vanity prompt a petted, spoiled, and worshipped woman! Kitty stood near enough to understand the whisper, and, although she had hitherto held herself passively aloof, her eyes now fairly flashed with honest indignation.

Flora saw it. "Just look what a pair of eyes the girl can make! Can you not understand a joke, Kitty?" she asked, half startled, half amused. "I will not harm your petted nursling,—although it really would be well to put a final stop to Henriette's petty malice. These two people," she pointed to the councillor and Henriette, "imagine it their duty to form my morals, and you, our youngest, just out of school, your head filled with crochet, worsted-work, and a few French phrases, side with them against me. You little goose, do you really think yourself capable of passing judgment upon your sister Flora?" She laughed aloud, and pointed to a chestnut-tree, from the boughs of which a white dove was flying. The bird flew high in air, a dazzling point of light. "Look, child, a moment ago it nestled amid the branches among its fellows, now its outspread wings gleam like silver, and it hangs in the blue, lonely firmament a shining spectacle for mortal eyes to gaze upon. Perhaps you may one day understand what thirsting, aspiring soul it resembles. Apropos, Moritz," she suddenly interrupted herself, beckoning the councillor out upon the balcony, "the old barracks that Bruck has just purchased must lie behind that grove,—I see smoke curling above the trees——"

"Simply because there is a fire kindled upon the hearth," the councillor replied, smiling. "The dean's old widow arrived there yesterday."

"And is in that miserable old place just as it is?"

"Just as it is. Indeed, the castle miller was too careful a man to allow any of his property to go to ruin; there is not a nail wanting in the house, not a slate missing on the roof."

"Well, I wish the widow Godspeed. Her old-fashioned furniture and the late dean's portrait will suit those walls extremely well,—there will be room enough for her pickle-jars and bake-oven,—and the water for scouring runs past the very door." She affected a slight nervous shiver, and, as though involuntarily, lifted her richly-trimmed skirt, as if from a freshly-scoured floor. "We had better shut the doors," she said, hastily retreating into the room; "the wind blows the smoke over here. Pah!"—she waved her pocket-handkerchief in the air before her face,—"I really believe the worthy woman is baking her everlasting pancakes even before she has a chair in the house to sit down upon. She is never content unless she is cooking." And she closed the folding-doors.

In the mean time, Henriette had quietly left the room. She had started in terror at Flora's whisper, like some sleep-walker who, on awaking, finds himself on the brink of an abyss. She had not spoken since, and had now mounted to the uppermost story of the tower, where the doves and rooks had their nests. Kitty took up her parasol,—she knew that the invalid always desired solitude when she thus withdrew from the society of others; but this room within these thick walls, the oppressive splendour on every side, and her domineering, capricious sister rustling to and fro, had a most depressing effect upon the young girl. The air that Flora breathed always seemed full of inflammable matter. Therefore she determined to pay Susie a visit.

"Just as you please; go to the mill if you like," the councillor said, fretfully, after in vain endeavouring to detain her; "but look here first." He drew aside a heavy Gobelin curtain, and behind it, in a deep recess, stood a new iron safe. "That belongs to you, you lucky child; here is your 'Shake, shake, little tree, gold and silver over me.'" And he passed his hand almost caressingly over the cold iron. "Everything that your grandfather owned of real estate is in there, turned into paper. Those papers are working for you day and night; you may draw incredible sums of money from the world in this quiet corner. The castle miller knew how to grasp fortune at the flood,—his will is proof of that,—but even he could hardly dream how his wealth would increase metamorphosed thus."

"So that you are on the way to become the best match in the country, Kitty, and, like the man in the fairy-tale, can floor your dining-room at your marriage with silver dollars," Flora cried, from the lounge, where she was again reclining, with a book in her hand. "'Tis a pity! Don't be angry, child, but indeed I am afraid you have been drilled in too strait-laced a morality to know how to fling brilliantly abroad your golden shower."

"Wait and see," laughed the young girl. "In the mean time, I have no present right to take one dollar locked up there." She pointed to the safe. "With regard to the castle mill, Moritz, I should like to attain my majority, if only for a single day."

"Does it not suit you, 'lovely miller maid'?"

"My mill? As well as my vigorous youth, Moritz. But I

was in the mill-garden yesterday. It is so large that Franz is obliged to leave all that portion bordering on the high-road uncultivated, for want of time and labourers. He wishes to sell it to you,—it would divide very well into lots for villas, and would be a good investment, he says; but I think cottages ornées might just as well be built elsewhere, and I would rather let your people, who wish to build near the factory, have the land."

"Ah! make them a present of it, Kitty?"

"Such an idea never occurred to me. You need not smile so compassionately and contemptuously, Moritz. Such 'exaggerated sentimentality' would disgrace me, truly, in the Villa Baumgarten. And, indeed, the people do not ask a gift or an alms, as Doctor Bruck says——"

"Ah, 'as Doctor Bruck says'? Is he your oracle already?" cried Flora, sitting upright on the lounge and fixing her eyes with a strange, changeful expression upon her young sister's face.

Kitty's colour deepened for a moment, but she returned the gaze with cool gravity, and continued, without paying any heed to Flora's words: "I know, besides, how valuable is the fruit of one's own exertions. I prize what I earn myself more highly than the richest gift, and upon this ground the people should pay,—pay exactly what they offer for your land."

"You show a fine capacity for business, Kitty," laughed the councillor. "My barren strip of shore would be cheap enough at the price they offer; and that piece of fine arable land near the mill! . . . No, child; glad as I should be to please you, my conscience as your guardian cannot allow you to lay aside your minority for a single hour."

"Well, then, your enterprising 'hands' must content themselves for the present," she rejoined, neither surprised nor irritated. "I know that at the end of three years I shall think just as I do at present, and maybe then I shall even be rash enough to lend the people the money for their building, without interest."

She bade a smiling farewell, and left.

CHAPTER VII.

Slowly she descended the winding staircase, so narrow in the upper half of the tower that there would have been no room for anything more substantial by her side than the ghost of some ancestral dame. Poor ancestral dame! There was no place for her here now, even although the new-made nobleman above-stairs should desire that as an appendage to his greatness he should own a ghostly white lady to look after the fortunes of his house, could he but buy one by as heavy a drain upon his money-bags as his patent of nobility had already cost him! There upon the walls hung the armour of her knightly race,—the weapons with which the old giants had striven for honour and shame, for lands and blood. The heavier the dints upon the old breastplates, the more frequent the blood-stains upon them, the more precious would they have been held, the more caressing would have been the nightly touch of her ghostly fingers. Now they glittered without a stain upon the walls, and the weapons of the new inmate of the tower were his money-bags.

Yes, the strange foreign element that vibrated through all the social intercourse of the family at the villa, the money-fever, the spirit of speculation, had intruded here also in this mimicry of the old chivalric life. It infected the air, it glided up and down the stairs, and the mighty tankards on the sideboards in the hall were not more of a mockery in the soft hands whose only labour was to cut coupons than were the giant locks and bolts, but lately burnished afresh, upon the iron cellar-door that kept guard over the councillor's champagne, while money by thousands of thousands was locked up in the safe above, with its small decorated key-hole. The historic powder from the Thirty Years' War was still in the cellar,—tolerated there by the councillor, only, as Henriette averred, that the inquisitive visitor might have an opportunity of seeing the costly wines arranged beside it in well-ordered rows. It was this that made Kitty a stranger in the home of her childhood; this display, this estimate of effect, for which no outlay of money was too great; this feverish effort to proclaim to the world that the basis of everything here was of gold,—all this was in direct contradiction to the spirit of the old Mangold firm, which had never thus asserted its undeniable wealth and credit. Nor during her father's lifetime had money as power intruded upon his home; strict as he was in all his business relations in his counting-room, not one word with regard to them ever escaped him in the home circle. And now! even the Frau President speculated. She had thrown her small property of a few thousands into the huge lottery,—that is, invested it in stock,—and it was strange to see her face, usually so calm and impassive, work nervously, and flush with colour to the temples, when the subject of conversation was the money-market.

Kitty left the tower and crossed the bridge. She leaned for a moment over the railing and looked down into the water, as if she half expected to see in its depths her old friends the dwarf fruit-trees and strawberry-vines,—but she saw only her own head, with its crown of thick brown braids. This girl, oddly enough, was the heiress of the family; she was reminded daily that as such she was distinguished and flattered, and she was repeatedly taught that she never should arrange these same brown braids herself, that a lady's maid was indispensably necessary; but she opposed an energetic will to the Frau President's admonitions; nothing should induce her to resign her head to the hands of an artiste, to sit solemn as some heathen idol for hours in her dressing-gown. Oh, yes, it was delightful indeed to be rich, but her wealth should not make a slave of her, should not fetter her warm, active, shapely hands.

She left behind her the pretty grounds around the ruin, and walked along the unfrequented path through the meadows upon the banks of the stream. Chilled by the melted snow from the mountains, that swelled it to a torrent, the little river rolled along, clay-coloured in hue; but the minnows showed here and there like flecks of molten silver, the soft, downy buds were thick upon the osiers, and beneath their protecting net-work the blue flowers of the hepatica were spreading everywhere,—it was easy to make a spring nosegay.

With a bunch of them in her hand, she sauntered on as far as the ancient wooden bridge. There was Susie's old bleaching-ground, the meadow, planted with fruit-trees. The councillor had spoken truly; the low picket fence that enclosed the garden was in perfect repair, and everything about the house, from the old tiled roof to the latticed arbour for the grapevines, was in thorough order. And it was really a charming old house, the despised "barracks." It was situated in a very retired spot on the banks of the river, and the leafy grove behind it, on the other side of the fence, gave it the character of a woodland cottage. Its exterior was not imposing, to be sure; it had only one row of windows, directly above which arose the roof with its gilded weather-cock and massive chimneys, one of which was actually smoking,—an incredible sight. It was long indeed since a fire had been kindled on that hearth or a lamp lighted within those walls. During the lifetime of the castle miller it had been used as a store-house for grain; the shutters had always been closed, and the door of entrance locked, except during harvest. At that time, little Kitty used to slip into what was called the fruit-room, an apartment adjoining the kitchen, with whitewashed walls and a large green stove, and fill her apron with rosy-cheeked apples and mellow pears. To-day, the shutters were wide open, and the young girl saw for the first time in her life the glitter of the panes of glass in the large windows. It was now Doctor Bruck's home.

Scarcely knowing why, she crossed the bridge and passed around three sides of the house. Her heart beat slightly, for she really had no right to be seen here; but the soft turf smothered the sound of her footsteps, which indeed could never have been heard above the din of the rushing river and of the sparrows twittering upon the roof. Some of the windows were open; she could see, within, hanging baskets filled with green creeping plants and vines, and the bright glitter of burnished copper on the kitchen walls; the merry song of a bird, too, came through the window, mingling with the shrill chatter of the sparrows; but there was no sound of human life or occupation. She cautiously turned around the west corner to pass by the front of the house, and paused, startled.

In the large doorway that divided the front of the house into halves, and from which a broad flight of steps led down to the little lawn, stood a lady, slender, refined, almost virginal in appearance. A table standing beside her was piled with books and pictures, which she was engaged in dusting. She looked up in surprise at the shy intruder, and involuntarily dropped the picture in her hand,—it was Flora's photograph in an oval frame.

Impossible that this could be the dean's widow! After Flora's sneering description, Kitty had fancied her a little, bent, active housekeeper, her hands rough with hard work, grown gray amidst pots and pans, and liking nothing so much as baking pancakes; she could not reconcile the picture of her imagination with this lady, elderly to be sure, but with delicate, noble features, and gentle, earnest eyes, her still abundant fair hair covered with a kerchief of white lace.

Kitty grew more and more embarrassed, as, standing at the foot of the steps, she stammered out her excuses. "I used to play here as a child; I only came from Dresden a few days ago, and—— That is my sister," she added, hastily, pointing to the picture, and then breaking into a clear, merry laugh, and shaking her head at the extraordinary manner in which, in her confusion, she had introduced herself.

The lady laughed, too. She placed the picture upon the table, and, descending the steps, held out both hands to the young girl. "Then you are the doctor's youngest sister-in-law." A faint shadow crossed her face. "I did not know that there were visitors at Villa Baumgarten," she added, with the slightest tinge of irritation.

A shadow floated across Kitty's mind also at this moment. Was she, then, such a nonentity, such an entirely insignificant member of the Mangold family, that Doctor Bruck had not thought it worth while to mention having met her? She bit her lip, and silently followed the lady, who invited her into the house and opened a door in the large hall. Every movement of her slender figure was gentle and gracious.

"Here is my room,—my home for the rest of my life," she said, in a tone in which was plainly audible her satisfaction at having reached this harbour of refuge after years of weary wandering.

"Before my husband received the appointment of dean in the city, he had charge of a small country parish. Our means were not adequate, and all my economy in housekeeping was needed to maintain the dignity of his position; but it was the happiest time of my life. The dust and noise of the city were never good for my nerves; my longing for the quiet of woods and fields became almost morbid. I never spoke of it, but the doctor privately made the purchase of this place with his savings, and showed it to me as my own a few hours afterwards." Her voice was husky with emotion as she spoke the last words. With what pride did she call her nephew "the doctor"! and as she spoke she smiled pleasantly. "Is it not a charming place,—quite a castle?" she asked. "See these folding-doors, and the graceful decoration of the ceilings. Those leather hangings, with their tarnished gold, must once have been very splendid; and out in the garden there are the remains of clipped yews and old statues of stone. The place was originally the dower-house of one of the women of the Baumgarten family,—I learned that from an old chronicle. We have scrubbed and aired and warmed the rooms, but have altered nothing; we are not rich enough for that, and indeed there is no need of it."

Kitty was inspecting it all with silent satisfaction. The dark mahogany furniture suited the faded leather hangings admirably. Against the wall, not far from the large white glazed antique stove, stood a sofa covered with chintz, and above it hung the portrait of the late dean in his canonicals,—valuable, perhaps, as a likeness, but scarcely as a work of art. The plants at each of the high, broad windows decorated the room charmingly; there were various kinds of azaleas and palms, and magnificent india-rubber trees, just now tinged with gold by the sunshine that came broadly in through the net curtains. Gold-fish in a glass bowl, and a canary in a cage, —those favourites with lonely women,—were here also; and spring flowers, gay hyacinths, with here and there a white narcissus bending its fair head dreamily, were upon the window-sills, while the work-table was fairly embowered in laurel.

"They are of my own growing: almost from the seed," the old lady said, as she noticed the girl's admiring gaze. "Of course I put the finest in the doctor's room." She opened the door of the adjoining apartment and invited Kitty to enter.

"Of course!" There was a charm in her way of speaking these words, as if they sprang from a maternal devotion which must excuse any over-indulgence. "Of course" she had given him the pleasantest room in the house,—the corner room,—below the eastern windows of which the stream rippled past. On the other side of the water lay one of the finest parts of the park, and in the distance, behind the lindens, the blue tiles of the roof of the villa could be seen. Between these windows stood the writing-table, so that when the doctor raised his eyes from his work he could see the flag-staff of the villa pointing towards heaven,—towards heaven! Kitty suddenly felt her cheeks flush with shame as she thought how the tenderest care was watching over the man's comfort here, while there her faithless sister was employed day and night in devising some way to thrust him from his heaven. She had resigned all claim upon him with those frivolous words, "Make him happy yourself."

Did the warm-hearted, delicate-minded woman standing beside her dream, or perhaps instinctively feel, that the heaviest sorrow he could have to endure was hanging over her darling's future? She had received Kitty not as a new-comer, a stranger to the family relations, but as Bruck's youngest sister-in-law, who must of necessity be so well aware of everything connected with him that there was no need of any mention that she was his aunt. Surely she could not have known much of the inmates of Villa Baumgarten; and she confirmed Kitty's suspicion on this head by pointing to the wall over the writing-table, and saying, "All is not quite ready here; there I shall hang the photographs of his Flora, and of his mother, my dear sister."

Nothing else was wanting in the cosy room. The doctor, who was to return by the evening train, had no suspicion that his aunt had left the city. She had wished to spare him all the annoyance of moving; and the councillor had been so kind, she said, as to come to her assistance, by putting her in immediate possession of the house.

As she talked, the dean's widow went on putting a finishing touch here and there, gliding about with a step so noiseless that it could not have disturbed the doctor if he had been seated at his writing-table, deep in his new work, for the completion of which he had desired this retirement in the country.

She now opened a cupboard in the wall beside the book-shelves, and took thence a plate filled with delicate little cakes. These she offered to the young girl with a charming air of hospitality. "They are fresh; I made them to-day, busy as I was. The doctor always has a supply for his little patients, who often need a bribe. But I cannot offer you any wine, for the few bottles that we own I left in town, where they are required for the sick."

Kitty thought of the papers in her safe, "working day and night" to fill it with gold, of the well-furnished wine-cellar in the tower, and of her wayward, cigarette-smoking sister, buried amid the crimson cushions of the lounge. What a contrast it was to this simple content and self-denial! And how all this reminded her of her Dresden home! Her heart warmed to the dean's widow, and she told her of her dear foster-mother, of her wise and gentle ways of influencing those around her, and of her never-failing industry,—an industry to which she had trained her foster-child.

"But what does the Frau President say to such a system of education?" the aunt asked, with a smile, as her eyes dwelt with pleasure upon the blooming young creature.

"I do not know," Kitty replied, with a shrug and a saucy glance; "but I suppose my movements are too quick for her, my voice too loud, and I am too robust,—not sufficiently pale. Heaven knows, I am a trial indeed! Is that your sister's portrait?" she suddenly broke off to ask, pointing to an oil sketch of a very pretty woman, leaning in its frame against the wall.

The old lady assented. "I am sorry to have to leave it in so insecure a place," she said, "for the frame is old; but I suffer from vertigo, and dare not mount a step-ladder. A few weeks ago I was obliged to dismiss my servant,"—a faint flush tinged her withered cheek,—"and now I must wait until the charwoman comes to hang these last pictures, and the curtains to my bed."

At the first words of this explanation, Kitty had laid her parasol upon the writing-table and stuck her little bouquet of willow buds and hepatica into a pretty little milk-white vase that stood beside the inkstand. Then she pulled the table out into the room, and moved a chair up to the wall. "May I?" she asked, coaxingly, picking up the hammer and nails that were placed ready on the window-seat.

With a grateful smile the aunt brought her the portrait, and in a few moments it was hung upon the wall. Kitty shrank back involuntarily when the old lady then handed her Flora's photograph. Should she with her own hand place this picture where it would constantly meet the eyes of the betrayed lover? It was no longer his, it would in a few short days be reclaimed, with the ring which he still wore on his finger. How the thought pained her! The old lady passed her hand caressingly over the picture. "She is so lovely!" she said, tenderly. "I know her only slightly; she does not come often to see me; how could an old woman ask her to undertake so tiresome a task? but I am very fond of her, for she loves him, and will make him happy."

What an inconceivable absence of all misgiving! The girl's cheeks burned with a sense of her own imprudence. After all she had heard in the tower, she never should have set foot within these doors. She felt like a hypocrite for not snatching the picture from the old lady's hand and unmasking the serpent that was ready to dart at her heart. But she could say nothing. She hammered at the nail so vigorously that the wall shook, then she hung the photograph upon it, and pushed the writing-table into its former place. The seductive face of her sister looked down from the wall with the smile of a triumphant evil genius.

Kitty took up her parasol to leave the room as quickly as possible. As she crossed the threshold she saw through an open door the old lady's bed,—the step-ladder stood beside it. "I almost forgot that," she said, as if in excuse, as she entered the small apartment, and, taking the gay chintz curtains from where they lay ready, mounted the ladder. She stood so high in the dark recess beside the window that she could touch the projecting foot of one of the angels in the cornice, and began rapidly to slip the curtain-rings upon their brass rods, while the old lady, standing by the table in the middle of the adjoining sitting-room, mixed a glass of raspberry syrup for her kind assistant.

Suddenly Kitty saw a man of erect, stately carriage pass the window. She recognized him instantly, and started, but before she could determine whether it was best to stay where she was or to slip hastily down and away, he had come through the hall and entered his aunt's room. The old lady turned, and threw her arms around him with, "Ah, Leo, here you are already!" The raspberry syrup was entirely forgotten, as well as the kind assistant for whom it had been intended, and who was covered with confusion in her hiding-place behind the curtains, where she was now obliged to stay, if she would not break in upon the meeting of aunt and nephew.

She saw the doctor's handsome bearded face bend tenderly above the old lady's head as he drew her towards him and, taking her hand from his shoulder, kissed it reverentially. Then he glanced through the rooms.

"Well, Leo, what do you say to my coming out here without your knowledge?" his aunt said, noticing his glance.

"I cannot praise that proceeding. It was too much for you to undertake in so short a time, for you know how injurious all household confusion and worry are for you. Nevertheless, you look well and happy."

"I wish you did too, Leo," his aunt interrupted him; "you have lost the fine colour you used to have, and here"—she lightly passed her hand over his forehead—"there is something strange, something of pain and perplexity. Have you been annoyed during your absence?"

"No, aunt." The tone was frank and reassuring, but evidently intended to stop further question; the councillor had said that Bruck never spoke of his profession or of incidents connected with it. "How attractive this room is to me, in spite of its shabby walls!" he said, as, with hands clasped behind him, he surveyed her writing-table. "It breathes of the peace of mind of a self-forgetting feminine nature; that is why I like so to come to our quiet home, aunt, with its old-fashioned furniture and your orderly arrangements. I shall be here a great deal."

The old lady laughed. "Yes, yes, until a certain day in June," she said, archly; "you are to be married at Whitsuntide."

"The second day of Whitsuntide." The words sounded strangely cold and decided, as if nothing should postpone for a moment the appointed hour. Kitty felt something like a shudder of dread. She held her breath; it would never do to be seen now. Every minute she hoped that the doctor would go into his room and give her the opportunity of slipping down from her perch and leaving without meeting him. Her whole nature revolted at this involuntary part of listener that she was playing. But, instead of go'ng, he suddenly took up from the table a letter that had been slipped, apparently by chance, between two books.

His aunt made an involuntary gesture as if to prevent his reading it; her delicate face grew crimson. "Ah, heavens!" she exclaimed, "how forgetful my poor old head is growing! That letter came from town a few hours ago; it is from Lenz, the merchant, and I did not mean to let you have it to-day, but I forgot, and left it on my table. I think it contains your fee; and coming at such an unusual time, Leo,—I am afraid——"

The doctor opened the envelope, and hastily read the note. "Yes, he dismisses me," he said, calmly, tossing the letter and the paper money it contained down on the table again. "Does it worry you, aunt?"

"Me? Not for a moment, if I could be sure that you do not take the ingratitude of these foolish people too much to heart. I have firm faith in you, and in your skill, and in—your lucky star," the gentle voice replied, warmly and confidently. "The obstacles that chance and calumny place in your path do not mislead me,—you will succeed." She pointed towards the open door of the corner room. "Look at your little study; you can think and write there so comfortably, so secure from all interruption! Ah, I cannot help enjoying the thought of the time, short though it be, during which we can still be together and I can attend to your comfort——"

"Yes, aunt; but the retrenchments you have gradually been making lately in consequence of the unfortunate turn in my affairs must cease. I will not have you standing for hours upon the cold stone floor of a kitchen. You must send for our old cook to-day, if you can. There is no reason why you should not." He put his hand into his pocket, drew thence a heavy purse of gold, and poured out its contents upon the table.

The old lady clasped her hands in mute surprise at the golden stream rolling here and there upon her neat tablecloth.

"It is a single fee, aunt," he said, with audible satisfaction; "our hard times are past." And, as he spoke, he turned and went into the corner room.

It was easy to see that his aunt longed to know more; but she asked no questions as to the cure or the patient whence came so large a sum of money.

Kitty seized this favourable moment to get down from the ladder. How her heart beat, how her cheeks burned, at having overheard this familiar talk! The door of the room led directly into the hall: she could escape unseen; even the dean's widow might suppose she had left the bedroom long since, without hearing a word that had been said. She cast a stealthy glance through the door of the corner room, where aunt and nephew were standing by the writing-table. Just then she heard the doctor say, "Ah, here are the first spring flowers! Did you know how fond I am of these little blue blossoms?"

He was interrupted by an exclamation of surprise: "It was not I, Leo. Kitty, your young sister-in-law, put those flowers there. Indeed, I am absent-minded and forgetful!" The old lady hurried into the next room; but Kitty had already slipped out of the hall door into the open air.

Without, she sauntered calmly and leisurely past the windows. Through the first she could faintly descry the gay flowers upon the still unhung bed-curtain; then came two windows with pretty net curtains, belonging to the aunt's sitting-room. One of them was open, and from it came the fragrance of hyacinth and narcissus. Suddenly a man's hand, strong and shapely, placed among the flower-pots on the window-sill a milk-white glass filled with blue flowers: it was her spring bouquet, which the doctor had thus removed from his writing-table.

She paused, startled by the thought that in her heedlessness she had placed herself in a false position. Evidently he regarded the placing of the flowers on his writing-table as an officious act on the part of a thoughtless, forward young girl. With her eyes shining with ill-suppressed tears of indignation, she extended her hand to the window. The gesture attracted the doctor's attention; he looked up.

"Will you be so kind as to hand me out my flowers, Doctor Bruck? they belong to me; I laid them down for a moment and forgot them," she said, with difficulty preserving her self-possession.

For one moment he seemed to be startled by the sound of the voice so unexpectedly addressing him. Perhaps he was annoyed that Kitty had observed him; but, if so, he instantly suppressed the sensation, and said, kindly, "I will bring you the flowers." His deep, quiet voice disarmed her immediately: he had not meant to wound her.

A moment afterwards he came down the steps. His figure, with its broad shoulders and erect carriage, and the fine bearded face, belonged of right, it seemed, to a soldier, and should have been clad in uniform, were it only the green coat of a forester. He handed the glass to the young girl, with a courteous inclination.

She took out the flowers. "They are the first little determined things that were in a great hurry to get out into the sharp April air," she said, with a smile. "They need to be searched for, but, when found, are worth a whole hot-house full of plants." He certainly could not suppose now that she had so far presumed upon their future relationship as to ornament his writing-table.

His aunt appeared at the open window, and begged the young girl to repeat her visit frequently.

"Fräulein Kitty is going back to Dresden in a few weeks," the doctor answered instantly in Kitty's stead.

She was startled. Was he afraid lest she should enlighten the unsuspicious old lady as to his strange relations with his betrothed? The idea troubled her, but chiefly because of the sorrow which she saw he must lock up within his own breast. And she could not reassure him.

"I shall stay longer, Herr Doctor," she rejoined, gravely. "It may be that my stay in Moritz's house will be prolonged for months. You, as Henriette's physician, can best say how many may pass before I can leave my invalid sister without anxiety and return to my foster-parents."

"You propose to devote yourself to Henriette?"

"Of course," she replied. "It is a great pity that hitherto she has been left entirely to the care of strangers. The poor child passes nights of suffering entirely alone, rather than summon attendants whose sleepy, sullen faces irritate her diseased, sensitive nerves; and, besides, her pride rebels against any confession of dependence upon her inferiors. This must not be so any longer. I shall stay with her."

"You do not know the task you would undertake: Henriette is very ill,"—he passed his hands slowly over his forehead, so that his eyes were hidden for a moment,—"there will be many a long weary hour to live through."

"I know it," she said, softly. "But I have courage——"

"That I do not doubt," he interrupted her. "I have perfect faith in your patience as well as in your compassion; but no one can tell how long it may be before the invalid—— will need no further care. And therefore I cannot advise your undertaking the case so positively; you could not endure the physical strain."

"I?" Involuntarily she held out her arms and looked down at them with a proud smile. "Do not your fears seem groundless even to yourself, Herr Doctor, when you look at me?" she asked, gaily. "I am strong and well: in constitution like my grandmother Sommer, who was a peasant's—a woodcutter's—child, running barefoot in the fields and wielding the axe better than her brothers,—Susie has often told me."

He looked from her towards the open window, where his aunt, half hidden behind her flowers, was lost in admiration of the young girl; his face grew dark.

"The question is not one of the force and endurance of muscles," he said, obviously to end all discussion. "Such duties as you propose to fulfil act most disastrously upon the nervous system. However," he suddenly interrupted himself, "it is not my part to influence your resolutions. That is your guardian's affair. Moritz must decide, and will probably see that you return to your home in Dresden at the appointed time." These last words were spoken with a hard emphasis not at all in accordance with the doctor's usual gentle composure.

His aunt involuntarily withdrew a step from the window; Kitty stood still. "But why are you so decided, Herr Doctor? Why do you desire that Moritz should control me so strictly?" she asked, with great gentleness. "Am I desirous of doing anything wrong? Ought Moritz to use his authority to prevent me from fulfilling my sisterly duty? I think not. But there is a way out of the dilemma. Let Henriette go with me to Dresden. There my dear Frau Doctor will share with me the charge of her, and that will not harm my nerves." She smiled slightly.

"Well, I will try so to arrange it," he said, decidedly.

"Then I give you my word to be up and away as soon as possible," she rejoined, just as decidedly, with a meaning look, before which his glance fell as though he had been detected in some injustice.

His aunt suddenly leaned from the window and looked him wonderingly in the face,—he was so strangely silent. He stood plucking some withered vine-leaves from the trellis where they had lodged in falling from the vine, and did not open his lips.

"Do you so ardently desire to go?" the old lady asked the girl, kindly, but with some embarrassment.

Kitty drew her veil, which had fallen upon her neck, over her head again, and knotted it beneath her chin. Her face looked like a fresh peach-blossom amid the folds of lace. "Ought I to say 'no' for politeness' sake, madame?" she asked, smiling, in reply. "I think I have had the best of training, but nothing will eradicate certain prejudices and individualities from the hidden corners of my nature. I feel just the same repulsion for my sisters' grandmother to-day as when, years ago, my father used to command me to kiss her hand; hence I constantly come into collision with all kinds of irritating causes which do not exist for others, and which tormented and worried me as a child. And how chilly it has grown in my father's house!"—she shivered,—"there is too much marble beneath my feet; and Moritz has become so frightfully distinguished,"—two roguish dimples appeared in her cheeks,—"I am positively startled and mortified at the sight of my simple undecorated visiting-card. Yes, dear madame, I shall be very glad to return to Dresden, provided Henriette may accompany me; otherwise,"—she turned to the doctor, and the playfulness of her tone was changed to quiet resolution,—"otherwise, I shall do my best to conform myself to my present surroundings, and to remain, even although Moritz should attempt to force me to return to Dresden."

She bade a kindly farewell to the old lady, courtesied slightly to the doctor, and left the garden to go to the castle mill, although twilight was at hand.

CHAPTER VIII.

It had grown quite dark; seven had struck by the factory clock, and Kitty was still sitting in the bow-window in the large room at the castle mill. At Susie's entreaty, she had inspected the linen-closet, for the old housekeeper insisted that the miller's wife was not to be trusted, and that "no one could keep their hands off beautiful homespun linen." Then she had, as usual, prepared Susie's evening broth, and put her to bed; for, although much better, she was still very weak and helpless. But the girl had been sitting a long while in the recess of the window, her hands gravely folded on her lap, until the shadows of night wrapped her around. It was pleasanter here than at the councillor's, where there was no cosy talk in the twilight hour as in Dresden. No sooner had the sun set than the servants invariably drew the curtains, the gas was lighted, and its dazzling rays banished the shadows from every corner.

The muffled tick of the old clock against the wall sounded like a measured subterranean knocking, and through the thick green curtain before the glass of the closed door of the recess the night-lamp at Susie's bedside glowed like the eye of some gloomy gnome. What a breathless quiet reigned in the darkness! How intently, when a child, she had listened in such an hour for the rustle and tripping tread of the dusty brownies, while Susie told her how the cruel and superstitious lord who built the mill had buried a new-born babe in its foundations and had mixed the mortar for them with precious wine! All these recollections were but faintly present to her now: her eyes were fixed upon the southern window, whence a faint light was still visible in the sky,—upon the spot where the castle miller had breathed his last; and she was thinking of the way in which Dr. Bruck had told her of the verdict passed upon him by the public, and of his self-vindication, to which she now wondered more than ever that he had condescended. Why, even should the whole world insist upon it, she never could believe in a reckless disregard of prudence, an ignorant, unscientific over-estimate of himself, on the part of a man who was the personification of integrity and honour. And the hot blood stirred in her veins, and indignation possessed her, as she remembered the gross terms in which Flora this very afternoon had stigmatized Bruck's medical capacity. What a riddle Flora, admired and adored as she was, had become—once an object to the child Kitty of wondering awe and secret admiration!

Henriette, when alone with her young sister, was careful never to make the betrothed pair the subject of conversation; but from casual remarks of hers, Kitty had gathered that Flora must at first have shown a passionate affection for her lover.

Doctor Bruck, after serving as regimental surgeon during the Franco-Prussian War, and then remaining for some time in Berlin as assistant to a distinguished surgeon there, had returned to M——, principally in compliance with his aunt's entreaty. There the favourable reputation that had preceded him, and his fine person, had soon made him a popular physician as well as a great social favourite. It was therefore no condescension even on the part of the haughty Flora Mangold to yield him the coveted treasure of her hand. She had herself made decided advances to him in persisting in placing herself under the skilful young doctor's care for a painful sprained ankle; before the ankle had recovered they were betrothed, and the lady was much envied. This was, of course, why she wished to avoid any sudden breach of the engagement, and laid perfidious plans for inducing a gradual termination to it, founded upon mutual decline of affection.

Kitty started up; it was intolerable to her to think that if she remained she must be a witness of this distressing drama, —must see the unhappy man, in spite of his strong affection and efforts to the contrary, thrust forth from the paradise he had dreamed of. No; she sided with Moritz and Henriette. Flora could not and should not break her troth; the whole family must combine to prevent such wretched treachery. What folly so blinded her as thus to induce her to destroy her own happiness! Had she not seen him in his home with his loving foster-mother? Did she not know that the winds of heaven would never be allowed to visit her too roughly if she bestowed upon him the happiness he craved?

Kitty started and covered her face with her hands. It had grown so dark here, so black was the night, that it seemed a fitting time for sinful thoughts to creep into an unguarded soul. She ran across the room and threw wide the door upon the stairs; the large lamp was burning in the hall below, throwing slender rays upwards among the pillars of the gallery, even to her feet, while from the mill itself, the door of which opened at that moment, came the noise of loud voices. Light and sound instantly dissipated the alluring phantoms that were crowding into the young girl's mind. There was the huge whitewashed hall of the castle mill, and from its wall looked down in ghostly dimness out of the worm-eaten black frame the figure, in full armour, of its knightly builder. In former days the picture had terrified her; now it seemed to her an old friend, beckoning her back to reality from a treacherous dream in which she was playing a false part.

She descended the stairs, and left the mill. The night wind of spring refreshed her hot cheeks, and stars filled the clear sky with glittering arabesques. Kitty was ashamed of her idle dreaming; but had it not assailed her like a sudden vertigo which may suddenly attack even the healthiest and strongest of human kind?

From a distance she saw through the trees the glimmer of the lights at the villa; and as she entered the hall-door she was greeted by the sound of the piano. It was a magnificent instrument, but was being shamefully maltreated at present. This was one of the Frau President's reception evenings,—old and young came to take tea,—the elders went to the card-tables, and the young people amused themselves with music and conversation as best pleased them.

Kitty made a hasty toilette, and entered the drawing-room, —the large balconied apartment on the ground-floor. There were but few guests this evening; only one card-table was in demand, and the tea-table, usually surrounded by young ladies, looked lonely and deserted.

Henriette was seated at it, making the tea; again she had scarlet ribbons in her blonde hair, and a sleeveless jacket of the same brilliant colour over a light blue silk dress. Her small, pallid face looked ghostly in so theatric a costume, but her beautiful eyes shone with an almost unearthly fire. "Bruck has come!" she whispered, breathlessly, into Kitty's ear, pointing through the adjoining music-room, where the grand piano was being so punished, towards Flora's study. "Kitty, he really seems grown, so tall and majestic—— Good heavens! do not look 'so sober, steadfast, and demure'!" she hastily interrupted herself. She was strangely agitated. "They are all so cross to-day; Moritz has had a dispatch which has made him absent-minded, and grandmamma is dreadfully out of sorts because her rooms are so empty. But I am so happy,—so happy! Do you know, Kitty, that the day before yesterday, when I had that attack, I really imagined that Bruck would see me next as a corpse? That must not be. I *will not* die without him!"

It was the first time she had ever spoken to Kitty of dying; and it was well that the fingers scrambling hither and thither over the keys in the music-room seemed just now endowed with fresh energy, and that three elderly gentlemen, standing by the chimney-piece, raised their voices in the ardour of their discussion, for the invalid's last exclamation was loud and passionately uttered. Kitty gave her a warning glance, and the Frau President looked keenly and disapprovingly over her eye-glass towards the tea-table. Henriette instantly controlled herself. "Nonsense! how can any one object to my saying so?" she said, lightly shrugging her shoulders. "No one likes to die alone. One has a physician in order that his presence may inspire with hope even one's last breath."

Kitty understood now perfectly that the sick girl would never return with her to Dresden. She declined the cup of tea which Henriette filled for her with a trembling hand, and drew a small piece of embroidery from her pocket.

"Oh, let that miserable work alone!" said Henriette, impatiently. "Do you suppose I can sit here and watch you calmly stick in your needle and draw out that tiresome thread?" She arose and put her hand within her sister's arm. "Let us go into the music-room. Margaret Giese will shatter the instrument and our nerves at the same time if we do not put an end to this torment."

They went into the adjoining drawing-room, but the lady at the piano, lost in her own harmonies, remained undisturbed. The folding-doors leading into Flora's study were, as was usual when the reception was small, wide open, allowing a full view of the interior. Its subdued light made it seem almost gloomy in contrast with the other brilliantly lighted apartments, and the dark crimson of its hangings deepened to black in remote corners.

Flora was standing by the writing-table, her hands nervously clasped before her, while the councillor leaned back comfortably in an arm-chair, and Doctor Bruck stood looking through a new pamphlet. He was unusually pale; the light falling from the lamp above him brought out two dark wrinkles in his forehead and a deep shadow beneath his eyes, but his expressive head, nevertheless, looked very young in comparison with that of his future bride.

Henriette entered composedly; the lovers were not alone; but Kitty, whom she drew with her, paused upon the threshold, repelled by Flora's air, which was impatient, almost angry. She was evidently in an ill humour. She surveyed with a sarcastic glance her sister's dress, for Kitty had laid aside this evening, for the first time, her deep mourning, and wore light gray.

"Come in, Kitty," she exclaimed, without changing her attitude. "In stiff silk, I see, as usual, just like a paper angel, and enough to make the strongest of us nervous with the perpetual rustle. Tell me, for heaven's sake, why you always wear these frightfully heavy silks? Scarcely the thing, I should say, for your cooking cares in Dresden."

"Oh, 'tis a weakness of mine, Flora," Kitty answered, with a smile. "Childish enough, no doubt; but I like to hear an attendant rustle of silk,—it sounds majestic. In the midst of my 'cooking cares' I do not wear it, of course."

"Why, how proudly she admits the 'cooking cares'! You foolish child! I should like to see you in a linen apron among your pots and pans! Well, every one to his liking; I beg to be excused." Her large gray eyes slowly turned towards the doctor, who was just quietly closing his book.

Kitty felt Henriette's little hand clench as it lay within her arm. "Nonsense, Flora!" she said, in apparent amusement. "Five months ago you often paid a visit yourself to Christel's kitchen. Whether you were of any use there I cannot say; but the good intention, as well as your pretty muslin apron, became you admirably."

Flora bit her lip. "You make a good story of it, Henriette; you never were able to understand that jest or to take it for what it was,—a mere whim." She folded her arms, and, drooping her head as in thought, slowly walked towards the window. She looked very beautiful in her white cashmere dress, with its soft, sweeping train.

The councillor sprang from his arm-chair. "Come, Floss, will you not go into the drawing-room with me now?" he asked. "It is very empty, for a good reason,—the prince holds a diplomatic audience to-night," he added, by way of silencing his own discontent; "but we must do something to put a little life into it, or we shall have grandmamma out of sorts for a day or two."

"I excused myself to her for half an hour, Moritz," she said, impatiently. "I must finish the article I have on hand to-night. The manuscript would have been ready now if Bruck had not interrupted me."

The doctor approached her writing-table. "Is there such haste? And why?" he asked, not without a touch of merriment in his face and voice.

"Why, my friend? Because I wish to keep my word," she replied, tartly. "Ah, that amuses you! It is, to be sure, only a woman's work, and you cannot, of course, comprehend how there can be any hurry about such a trifle."

"These are assuredly not my views with regard to women's work in general."

"In general!" she repeated, with a hard laugh. "Oh, yes, the general world-wide idea,—cooking—sewing—knitting!" She counted them off upon her fingers.

"You did not let me finish, Flora," he said, quietly. "I had reference to mental as well as to physical labour. I am much interested in the woman question, and desire nothing more, in common with all thoughtful men, than that woman should be an intelligent assistant and co-worker with man in the department of the intellect."

"Assistant? How very kind! We want no such kindness, my friend; we want more: we would be the equal of man,—equal in our privileges as in all else."

He shrugged his shoulders and smiled. The mingled expression of merry scorn and indulgent gentleness became his fine face wonderfully well. "This is indeed the extreme of these claims. It has been abandoned long since by the most intelligent, and will be warmly opposed by all friends of reform in church and state so long as woman shows herself liable to such excesses as we have witnessed in the 'praying bands' of some of the American cities, and in their unscrupulous adherence here in Europe to the dark host of monkish confessors. To do otherwise would be to place the murderous knife in a small and inconsiderate hand."

Flora grew very pale, but said not a word in reply. She took up a new steel pen with apparent indifference and fitted it into a holder. Then she drew a casket towards her, and, with a hand that trembled slightly, took from it a small object.

Henriette withdrew her hand from her sister's arm and made one step forward, while the councillor left the room hurriedly, as if to fulfil some suddenly-remembered duty. Kitty was troubled. She saw the trembling taper fingers take up a penknife and cut off the tip of the cigar which had just been selected from the box.

"Such a knife as this, not for us to use in this way," Flora said, with forced gaiety, over her shoulder to the doctor, who had paced the room once or twice while speaking. "Strangely enough, however, the feminine brain, although weighing four ounces less than that of the lord of creation, shares with it this peculiarity: it thinks more vividly and works more easily while smoking." She lighted the cigar and put it between her lips, smiling nervously.

The performer upon the piano in the next room had finished her fantasia, and now appeared upon the threshold. "What,

Flora! smoking? Why, you never could endure the smell of a cigar!" she cried, laughingly, clapping her hands.

"Fräulein Mangold is jesting," Doctor Bruck said, with perfect composure, as he walked to the writing-table, "and will be quite satisfied with trying it once only. Another attempt might cost her too dear."

"Do you forbid it, Bruck?" she asked, coldly, a baleful fire glowing in her eyes. She had taken the cigar from her mouth for a moment, and held it delicately between her fingers.

It was what the doctor had evidently expected. Without haste, with imperturbable equanimity, he took the cigar from her hand, and threw it into the fire. "Forbid it as your lover?" he asked, with a shrug. "My rights, as yet, do not extend so far. I might entreat you, but I dislike repetition and useless words; and you know perfectly how I detest a cigar in a woman's mouth. In this instance I forbid it simply as your physician. Your lungs are not strong enough."

Flora stood for an instant confounded by this cool assurance; and his last words evidently impressed her, but she controlled herself. "A terrible diagnosis indeed, Bruck," she said, with a scornful smile. "And the Councillor von Bär, who has attended me from my infancy, never said a word of it. Tales to frighten children! Besides, I have no reason for so loving my life that I should deny myself an enjoyment to preserve it. On the contrary, I shall continue to smoke; in my intellectual vocation I need it, and this vocation is my delight, my moral support,—in it I live and breathe——"

"Until a certain inevitable crisis arrives to reveal to you your true vocation," the doctor interrupted her. His voice sounded hard as steel.

A burning blush crimsoned her cheek. She opened her lips for an angry reply, but her glance fell upon Fräulein von Giese, the piano-player, the sarcastic maid of honour, who was still standing in the door-way, her head and shoulders bent forward, as if eager to catch every word of this interesting dispute, that from it and from the embarrassed faces of the bystanders she might extract material for a charming dish of court scandal. This was certainly to be avoided. Flora turned away with a graceful pout. "Nonsense, Bruck!" she exclaimed. "How prosaic! You have just returned from a pleasure-trip, and have been amusing yourself——"

She stopped. Bruck laid his hand on hers with a firm pressure. "Will you have the kindness to leave my vocation out of the question, Flora?" he asked, emphasizing his words strongly.

"I was speaking of pleasure," she said, pertly, withdrawing her hand from his.

The Frau President's face, with its expression of cold dignity, was never a welcome sight to Kitty, and when unexpectedly seen, inspired her usually with a kind of shy terror; but now it was a positive relief when the old lady suddenly entered the room. She came in with unusual haste, and evidently in ill humour. "I shall have to order my card-tables to be placed here in future, if I would not have my friends neglected," she said, in an irritated tone. "How came you to leave the tea-table so early, Henriette? I shall be obliged to place my maid there. And, Flora, I cannot understand your withdrawing to your study when we have guests. If your publisher is really so impatient that you must work in the evenings, pray close your door, if you would avoid the appearance of ostentation and a desire to be thought a blue-stocking!" She must have been much vexed, to speak thus in the presence of the maid of honour.

Flora placed her manuscript before her, and dipped her pen in the ink. "Decide upon that as you please, grandmamma," she said, coldly. "I cannot prevent people from coming to me here, and I should have sacrificed myself long ago, and been seated at one of your green-covered tables, if I had not been interrupted."

Henriette stepped past her grandmother, and privately signalled to Kitty to follow her. "These exciting scenes kill me," she whispered, as they entered the empty music-room.

"Be tranquil. Flora's struggles are vain; he will yet bring her to his feet," Kitty rejoined, in a strange, agitated tone. "But I cannot understand him. Were I such a man——" Her eyes flashed, and she held herself proudly erect.

"Do you know what it is to love, Kitty? Judge not! You, with your cool glance and blooming cheeks, have no conception of the mad intoxication which can take possession of a human soul." She paused, and drew a long and labouring breath. "You do not know how enchanting and seductive Flora can be if she chooses. You know her only in her present mood,—cowardly, egotistical, pitiless. Once see her display affection, and you will understand how a man must prefer death to surrendering his right to her."

CHAPTER IX.

SHE went into the drawing-room to resume her neglected duties at the tea-table; but Kitty remained standing by the piano, turning over some music. Henriette's last words had moved her deeply. Could a despised love be so absorbing that for its sake a man would gladly die? Could it have such power over a man like Doctor Bruck?

He was just leaving Flora's room; the Frau President at the same moment rustled through the music-room,—two elderly ladies had just arrived, and she was hastening to receive them. The study-door remained open; the unfinished article was surely in process of completion, for nothing stirred there, even after Fräulein von Giese seated herself at the piano again and ran her fingers over the keys.

Kitty glanced towards the doctor, who had entered the drawing-room. He went to the tea-table to talk with Henriette, but one of the newly-arrived ladies detained him in conversation. His air was courteous and composed, but Kitty had seen his eyes flash and his cheek crimson at Flora's malicious words, and even now the colour in his face was deeper than usual,—he was by no means so calm and cheerful as he seemed. His beautiful adversary in the study was scarcely more composed; after about five minutes she pushed back her chair, with audible impatience, and came into the music-room.

"Well, Flora, have you finished already?" the maid of honour asked, as she went on striking thirds in quick succession on the keys.

"Nonsense! do you suppose an effective conclusion runs off your pen's point as quickly as that? I am not in the humour, and I will not write unless I am. The calling of authoress is too sacred."

Fräulein von Giese's eyes had a malicious twinkle in them,—their expression was never quite honest. "I am very curious to know what the critics will say of your great work upon 'Woman;' you have talked so much of it, Flora. Has the publisher accepted it?"

Flora had noted the glance. "Ah, how you dear creatures would rejoice if it were a failure! But that pleasure must be denied you, as I am assured by—well, by my little finger." She laughed a low, self-satisfied laugh, shook the light curls from her brow, and prepared to enter the drawing-room with the regal air she knew so well how to adopt.

"My dear, you stand there with those notes in your hand as if you, too, wished to besiege our ears," she said to Kitty, in passing, with a meaning glance towards the diligent performer at the piano. "Do you sing?" Kitty shook her head. "It would be an inheritance from the Sommers; our family have no voices for singing."

"Yes, Flora, Kitty plays on the piano," the councillor replied from the doorway, where he was standing with several gentlemen. "I know that from the bills I have received from Dresden. A great deal of money, Kitty,—I meant to tell you that you employ very dear teachers."

The young girl laughed. "The best, Moritz. We are practical people in Dresden. The best is the cheapest."

"Well, I have no objection. Have you really any talent?" he asked, dubiously. "A gift for music is not a Mangold characteristic."

"I have a great love for it, at all events," she replied, simply, "and a delight in composing melodies."

Flora, who was just upon the threshold of the drawing-room, turned in surprise. "Nonsense, Kitty!" she said, hastily. "Compose melodies! You look like it, with those red cheeks and your prosaic training. Quite natural that a polka or a waltz should sometimes flit through the brain of any one who is fond of dancing——"

"And I am passionately fond of dancing, Flora," Kitty interrupted her, frankly.

"I thought so. Scarcely compatible, though, with profound originality in creation. You have probably taken lessons in composition?"

"For the last three years."

Flora clasped her hands and came back into the music-room. "Your Lukas"—she always called the former governess thus by her maiden name—"must be insane, to throw money away in that fashion."

It was very quiet in the adjoining drawing-room. The three old gentlemen by the fire, and the lady who had been speaking with the doctor, had just seated themselves at a card-table; Doctor Bruck was talking in a low tone to Henriette; and Fräulein von Giese paused for a moment to listen; every one in the drawing-room could hear this tolerably loud conversation.

Henriette sprang up and came into the music-room. "You can play, Kitty," she said, surprised, "and have never touched the keys since you came?"

"The piano is so near to Flora's study, I could not presume to interrupt her work by my playing," the young girl answered, naturally and simply. "I have longed—I do not deny that my fingers have fairly burned to try this instrument, for it is magnificent, and my cottage piano in Dresden is not worth much. It was not new when we bought it, five years ago. My Frau Doctor wished to ask for a new one long ago, but I opposed it. I did not wish you to estimate my musical powers by such a demand. But after my glimpse of a certain safe to-day, I am wonderfully bold: I want just such an instrument as this."

"It costs a thousand thalers!—a thousand thalers for a girl's whim. It requires consideration, Kitty."

"Who in this house plays upon your instrument?" she now asked, in a hard tone, with flashing eyes. She was evidently deeply wounded. "To whose quiet enjoyment does it minister? It is here only for your guests. Must money never be spent except to make a show?"

The councillor approached her and took her hand; he had never before seen the girlish face so informed with energy and self-assertion. "Do not agitate yourself, my dear child," he said, gently. "Have I ever been a hard or grudging guardian to you? Go play us something to prove that music is really dear to your heart,—I ask nothing more,—and you shall have any instrument you desire."

"I do not like to play, after what has passed," she said, frankly, as she withdrew her hand from his. "I do not wish to buy my piano by playing for it; and who can tell what can convince you that my music is dear to my heart? But I will get my notes, for I detest being urged to play."

"Why get any notes? Play one of your own compositions," said Flora, only half suppressing a sneer.

"I do not know even those by heart," Kitty answered, as she left the room.

She returned in a few moments with a sheet of music. As she seated herself upon the piano-stool, which Fräulein von Giese readily vacated for her, Flora took up the notes she had placed on the music-desk, and asked, pointing to the title-page, "Who is the composer?"

"Why, did you not ask me to play something of my own?"

"Certainly; but you have made a mistake: this is printed music——"

"True: it is printed."

"Heavens! how did that happen?" Flora asked, hastily, surprised out of her usual self-possession.

"How does it happen, Floss, that *your* productions are printed?" Kitty asked, in jest, as she placed her beautiful slender hands upon the keys. "I will tell you how I was so honoured," she added, soothingly. Flora had evidently taken her reply very much amiss, for she had drawn herself up with an offended air. "My teachers had this fantasia printed privately, to give me a pleasant surprise upon my birthday."

"Ah, indeed! that I can understand," Flora said, putting the notes back upon the desk.

Henriette, who had meanwhile been standing behind Kitty, pointed over her shoulder to the title-page. "Do not let her impose upon you, Flora!" she exclaimed, with a laugh. "Look there!—Schott & Sons,—that firm would hardly lend itself to a birthday jest. Kitty, tell the truth," she begged, with beaming eyes. "Your compositions are popular,—there is a sale for them?"

The young girl assented with a blush. "But it is true,

also, that I knew nothing of my first appearance in public. I found my first printed opus upon my table with my birthday presents," she said, as she began to play.

It was a very simple melody that now fell upon the listeners' ears; but after the first few notes the players at the card-tables dropped their cards, so liquid and pure were the tones that filled the air, so touchingly were they rendered. The young composer sat there, her eyes earnestly riveted upon the notes, so calm and quiet that one could see the jet cross upon her breast rise and fall with each breath. Here was no brilliant execution, no crash of chords,—one hardly asked what style of performance it was,—there was no thought of the performance, any more than of the shape of a singer's mouth when an enchanting song is issuing from it; and when the melody ceased with a few low notes, breathed as it were from the instrument, there was a moment of breathless silence, as if all feared that any noise might scare the fleeting spirit of music. Then the drawing-room awoke to life. The gentlemen cried, "Brava!" "Charmante!" "Superbe!" and the ladies lamented that Herr Mangold was not alive to hear it. They were astonished and touched, and—took up their cards again.

"You must give me that charming fantasia, Fräulein Mangold: I will play it to the princess," said the maid of honour, with an air of patronage.

"And you shall have the finest 'concert grand' that can be found, Kitty!" the councillor added, with enthusiasm.

But Henriette caressingly laid her pale cheek against her sister's, and whispered, with tears in her eyes, "You gifted darling!"

At the first notes, Flora had retreated as if frightened away from the piano. She paced slowly to and fro in the red room, at each entrancing turn of the melody casting a half-scared glance at the performer, and, when the last tones died away, the restless white figure was no longer to be seen: it had probably withdrawn to the recess of a window.

"Ah, Flora seems to take it amiss that she is no longer the sole celebrity in the Mangold family," Fräulein von Giese whispered, maliciously, half to herself and half to the councillor.

The councillor smiled,—he always smiled when any one from the court addressed him,—but he forbore to reply.

"I am greatly provoked with your Frau Doctor for never telling us of your musical talent," he said to Kitty, who was just leaving the piano.

She laughed. "There is very little said about it at home," she replied, quietly. "The Frau Doctor is seldom profuse in words of praise; she knows how much I have to learn."

"Nonsense! That is Spartan training——"

"Or the most refined cunning in producing a grand final effect," interposed Flora, who now made her appearance. She looked flushed with fever. "You cannot mislead me, Kitty, with this modest self-depreciation, making so light of your talent that during the five days you have been here you have never betrayed your knowledge even of the notes of music. It is treating me—treating us all—deceitfully, unfairly." Her fine sonorous voice was thick with rising anger.

"That may well be your mode of judging, Flora," Henriette indignantly exclaimed. "You who are never weary of vaunting your literary efforts, and already base your pretensions in society upon a reputation yet to be acquired——"

"Henriette, your tea-table requires your attention," the Frau President called, in a sharp stern tone,—the talk in the music-room was growing too loud,—and Henriette sullenly returned to her charge.

"You are mistaken, Flora, if you think I undervalue my talent," Kitty said, gently, while her haughty sister bit her lip and followed Henriette's retreating figure with angry eyes.

"To do so would be untrue to myself, and most ungrateful, for it gives me hours of delicious enjoyment. Accident alone has prevented my speaking of my music since my arrival, for indeed it is the cause of my coming here a month earlier than was proposed. My teacher of composition was obliged to leave Dresden for a month, and because my waiting would have cost me two months of instruction, I hastily made up my mind to leave the city when he did so."

As Kitty finished speaking, Fräulein von Giese went into the drawing-room, evidently with great reluctance,—these explanations were so very entertaining; but her father, an aged and pensioned colonel, had arrived. The councillor followed her.

Flora again approached the piano, and took the sheet of music from the desk. Kitty saw her breast heave and her hand tremble with nervous agitation, and bitterly repented her thoughtless introduction of her little work.

"I suppose you have had all sorts of flattering things said to you about this?" Flora said, striking the title-page with the back of her hand, as she eagerly watched the lips opening in reply.

"By whom?" Kitty rejoined. "My teachers are quite as chary of praise as my Frau Doctor, and no one else knows of my authorship; you see, there is no composer's name there."

"But the thing finds a ready sale?"

Kitty was silent.

"Tell the truth. Has it passed through more than one edition?"

"Yes."

Flora threw the music upon the piano. "Fame comes in sleep to such a bread-and-butter miss as this, with her round red cheeks and phlegmatic nature, while others struggle laboriously up each round of the ladder; they almost die in the agonizing strife before they are even heard of." She folded her arms and paced to and fro.

"But what does it really matter?" she suddenly said, pausing as if relieved. "The most brilliant rocket vanishes and leaves not a trace in the air, while the fiery heart of Vesuvius throbs and glows,—the world knows of its burning core, and exults or trembles when the flames leap forth. Be it so. There are now two of the Mangold family to step forth into the arena. We shall see, Kitty, which of us will have the more brilliant career."

"Not I, you may rely upon it," Kitty replied, gaily, stroking back a rebellious curl from her brow. "I shall take good care not to enter the arena. Do not imagine that I do not care for results. It is an indescribable pleasure to know that one can sway and touch the souls of men, and I would not resign such knowledge for the wealth of the world. But to live for that and that alone? No; I see too much of the happiness of home, the delights of mutual sympathy in aim and labour. Of what use were fame to me if it left me lonely?"

"Aha! there we have the root of the matter, the quintessence of your whole homely training. You will attain the same end for which your Fräulein Lukas strove, and which she has attained,—you will marry." And a hard laugh accompanied the sneer.

The exquisite colour in the young girl's cheeks suddenly flushed her forehead to the roots of her hair, and even her snowy throat was crimsoned for an instant. "You sneer and laugh as if it had never occurred to you to do the same," she said indignantly, involuntarily lowering her voice; "and yet——"

Flora hastily extended her hand, as if to bar further utterance from the lovely lips. "Not another word, pray!" she exclaimed, authoritatively. Again she folded her arms and slowly inclined her head in assent. "Yes, my very wise young sister, I certainly was so weak and blind for a moment as to allow myself to be caught in a net; but, thank God! my head is free again, and is clear and strong enough to win back my liberty."

"And have you no conscience then, Flora?"

"A very sensitive conscience, my dear; it tells me that it would be most culpable frivolity to throw myself away. You remember your Bible well enough to know that we are each and all answerable for the employment of our talent. Look at me, and ask yourself if it is my rôle to play the Frau Doctor and devote my time to housekeeping. And for whom?" She nodded her head towards the drawing-room, where the conversation was just then rather lively: old Colonel von Giese's arrival had inspired the guests with some animation. Doctor Bruck, however, was sitting alone by the tea-table, looking over a newspaper,—he was apparently absorbed by it, and had hardly looked up upon Henriette's return to his side.

"Do you see any of the gentlemen talking with him?" Flora asked, in a suppressed tone. "He is ostracized, and with justice. He has deceived me and the world. His brilliant reputation was the merest tinsel."

She broke off, and retired to her room, obviously to avoid the talkative old colonel, who now entered the music-room with his daughter and the councillor to beg for an introduction to Kitty. At his request, the young girl seated herself again at the instrument and played. Strange! As she lifted her eyes from the notes, she found her brother-in-law watching her with an intense and indescribable expression, not at all like the brotherly air with which he gave her, as a child, a box of bonbons, or with which he had but yesterday brought her a bouquet from town. She willingly resigned her hand to him when he took it in conversation, and often permitted him to stroke her hair caressingly from her brow,—he did it much as her father had been used to do it; and now, when she had finished playing, and amid the enthusiastic applause that followed, he came hastily to her side and laid his hand upon her shoulder.

"Kitty, what a change is this!" he whispered, bending over her. "It is Clotilde, your sister, but infinitely more beautiful, more richly gifted!"

She put up her hand to remove his from her shoulder; but Moritz possessed himself of it, and held it as if in a life-long grasp. For the others it was only a pretty, innocent picture: the guardian was proudly caressing his ward,—the child entrusted to his care by his father-in-law. Henriette's pale face alone flushed crimson; she smiled oddly. Doctor Bruck, standing beside her, looked at his watch, then quietly gave Henriette his hand, and took advantage of the general commotion to withdraw unobserved.

CHAPTER X.

A WEEK had passed since the last reception-evening: "a terribly fatiguing week!" the Frau President sighed, in a tone of exhaustion, which did not, however, prevent her from immediately afterwards finding a great deal of fault with her modiste for not arranging with sufficient taste the toilette in which she was to appear on the eighth of these fatiguing evenings. The train was not long enough; the lace not broad enough; and the silk not so heavy as was desirable. There had been several large festivities in aristocratic circles, and, in addition, Flora had been requested to compose and recite verses at some tableaux vivants arranged at a small fête at court. "There was hardly time to breathe."

Henriette, in consequence of her invalid condition, could take no part in these exciting entertainments, and Kitty remained at home with her, although she was always included in the invitations to the family. They drank tea alone together in the music-room, and Kitty was unwearied in her efforts to dissipate Henriette's melancholy, by lively talk, and music. Keen as was the invalid's power of discrimination, impressed as she was by the superficiality and unreality of a life given up to society, she was, and always must be, a child of the world of fashion; she had grown up in the drawing-room of her aristocratic grandmother, and often, when the sound of rolling carriages bound for ball or opera was heard in the distance, she would smile bitterly, and liken herself to a broken-down war-horse, weak and lame, who nevertheless at the blast of the trumpet pricks his ears and longs for the strife.

Lovely as a fairy, Flora would glide through the music-room before her departure. There was almost always a frown upon her brow and a sneer upon her lip at sight of her grandmother's youthful toilette; she would lament the loss of precious time as, throwing a lace veil over her flower-wreathed curls and gathering up her train, she passed on to the carriage which was to bear the "victim to the sacrifice."

The councillor had been absent in Berlin, attending to business affairs, for six days. He wrote every day to the Frau President, and seemed "intoxicated with money-making," she remarked, with a significant smile. Four days after his departure, however, there arrived from him for his sisters-in-law three magnificent bouquets, at which the Frau President did not smile. The gallant brother-in-law had ordered camellias and violets for Flora and Henriette, whilst Kitty's bouquet was composed almost entirely of myrtle and orange-blossoms. This tender message from a distance might have escaped the Frau President's observation; she took the flowers from the box in which they were packed, and was about to send up to Henriette's room those destined for the two girls, when Flora, with a laugh, called her attention to the expressive arrangement of Kitty's flowers. The old lady's face lengthened as she looked. "But, grandmamma, did you really suppose that Moritz would purchase rank at such an immense price and then allow his race to die out?" Flora exclaimed, in her arrogant, frivolous manner. "You ought to have known that such a man as he—still young and rich and handsome—would not remain a widower all his life. And he will not woo Kitty in vain,—I am well assured of that."

After this a shadow haunted Villa Baumgarten. Kitty never suspected its presence; she sprinkled her flowers, all attached to wires as they were, with fresh water, to keep them as long as possible from fading, and never noticed their sentimental signification. Nevertheless, the gray, menacing phantom glided hither and thither through the Frau President's rooms; its presence dimmed the splendour of the costly satin furniture, the beauty of the bronzes, and the priceless porcelain; it occupied the Frau President's own favourite seat in the conservatory, and embittered her enjoyment of existence. The old lady was as anxious as to her future as if but half of her life lay behind her. The councillor should not marry again: so much at least he owed to her. She had made him what he was, by her aristocratic connections, her social influence; her incomparable taste had transformed his home into a palace, that impressed even the spoiled habitués of the court. Had she not sacrificed herself most decidedly in first consenting to take charge of his comparatively simple bourgeois household? And now, when everything was at last arranged precisely as she liked it,—when her efforts had been crowned with success,—a youthful Frau von Römer was to arise to take the lead in these splendid apartments, and those who asked to see the Frau President Urach would be shown up-stairs to some retired rooms appropriated to her use. Why, she would not have liked to see even Flora, her own daughter's child, in this position, much less the grandchild of the castle miller! The Frau President immediately manifested a deep interest in Kitty's Dresden home; she expressed great regret that so wonderful a musical talent should lie fallow for four long weeks, and even spoke of accompanying Kitty to Dresden in her own august person.

The young girl received this access of courtesy and interest in silence. She still hoped that Henriette might be induced by Doctor Bruck to visit Dresden. Hitherto he had made no attempt to do so, apparently for fear lest the invalid's irritability might be aroused in opposition; for just now she was irritable and excitable to the utmost. His visits were paid every morning at the same hour. The boudoirs of the two younger sisters were adjoining, and the door between them was almost always open. Kitty could hear his soothing tones, his gentle voice, and now and then a laugh so merry that the invalid could not but join in it. His ringing, musical laugh had a peculiar charm for Kitty: it seemed to come directly from a heart the youthful freshness of which was yet undimmed; it was a proof to her that he felt his future secure, that he was not in reality affected by the thousand trials which at present assailed him.

She herself seldom spoke with him. Sitting at her work-table in her room, she could see him walk to and fro at times; but, inseparable though the sisters usually were, Henriette always withdrew to her own room shortly before the time for his visit, and Kitty took care never to thwart her evident wish by taking part in the conversation either by word or by look.

She frequently saw the dean's widow, however, in the castle mill. The old lady paid Susie a daily visit, now that she lived so near, carrying her strengthening soups and jellies, and spending hours in cheering the poor old housekeeper, who was much depressed at being still unable to scrub or spin or even knit.

Those were happy twilight-hours in the old room at the mill. The widow would relate stories of her youth, when she had been the pastor's wife in her happy village home. She told of the sad, tearful time when she took her dear Leo, the doctor, then a boy only eight years old, from his home, where his parents had died within a few weeks of each other; and whatever else she talked of or dwelt upon, she was sure to return to the theme of which she never tired,—her delight in this nephew, who was, as she said, the very sunshine of her life.

Kitty used to accompany the old lady on her way home along the river-bank as far as the bridge across the stream. The little, wrinkled hand lay confidingly upon the girl's arm, and the two walked along as if they belonged to each other, and must together cross the bridge and enter the "Doctor's house" in its peaceful retirement among the trees in the twilight. The evenings were still cold, and from the dark forest the floating mists would moisten both hair and dress. The friendly roof and smoking chimney were very attractive. The lamp was usually shining brightly through the windows of the corner room, clearly illuminating the bridge. The old lady could not have missed her way even on a dark night. She would enter; the window-shutters would be closed; and there, in the cosy corner by the stove,—Kitty could see it all in her mind's eye,—where the faded green rug lay and the high-backed arm-chair stood, would be arranged the table for the pleasant evening meal, and his aunt would sit knitting until the doctor had finished his writing.

She had described it all often to Kitty as they walked along together, and she liked to pause for a moment upon the bridge and contemplate her pleasant home, pointing to her darling's head, with its dark curls, bending over his writing-table. He would suddenly spring up and open the window when the new watch-dog barked and rattled his chain at the sound of approaching footsteps. "Is that you, aunt?" the doctor would call from the window, and at his call Kitty would withdraw from the circle of light thrown by the lamp. With a hasty "good-night," she would run along the lonely avenue: she could not help feeling thrust out in the cold. And would not he at some future day, if he persisted in forcing Flora to be his, experience the same sensation when he went from the house here by the stream to his home in town and met but a cold greeting from his wife, or found her just arrayed for some evening entertainment?

On the seventh day after the councillor's departure, news arrived from Berlin that the factory was sold. The Frau President was so much pleased by the intelligence that she mounted the stairs in her dressing-gown and came into Henriette's room with the open letter in her hand. Flora happened to be already there.

The old lady seated herself in an arm-chair and imparted her news. "Thank Heaven, Moritz has done with it!" she said, in the best of humours. "He has made an excellent bargain; he himself is amazed at the price paid him." She folded her delicate hands upon the table before her and looked perfectly satisfied. "He can now break entirely with every connection with trade. There will be no more. I trust, of those dreadful 'business friends.' Only think how we have been forced to endure men at dinner whose proper place was in the servants' hall! Heavens! what moments of painful embarrassment I have had! Yes, yes; there has been much to be borne in silence."

Meanwhile, Kitty was standing at the window, whence she had a full view of the huge factory, with its still unfinished additions. The gravelled square in front of the building was swarming at present with people,—men, women, and children in a state of evident excitement,—gesticulating violently. The looms were deserted: there was not a workman occupied inside the factory.

The young girl pointed this out to her companions.

"I know it," the Frau President said, smiling, as she arose and came to the window. "The coachman told me awhile ago that they were in a very agitated state over there,—quite beside themselves,—because the factory has been sold to a joint-stock company, principally, they say, under the management of Jews. Yes, yes, they are now reaping what they have sown. Moritz would never have made such a sudden tabula rasa,—he clung to the factory in a manner to me perfectly incomprehensible,—but these last outrages have disgusted him: he does not want to have anything more to do with it."

"It looks very much as if our excellent Moritz were afraid," Flora remarked, with a contemptuous curl of her lip. "I, for my part, would not have parted with the factory at present for millions. Those scoundrels should first have been taught that they are beneath notice, that we laugh at their threats. I fairly burn with indignation at the thought that they may suppose their menacing letters to me have frightened us!"

"Make yourself easy, Flora. No one will suspect you. You have only to be seen to be recognized as an impersonation of daring and courage," Henriette said, with a sneer.

Her beautiful sister silently moved towards the door, ignoring the invalid's remarks with her usual cold smile, and her grandmother arose to go to dress for dinner.

"Bruck ordered you to take a short walk to-day, Henriette, did he not?" the old lady asked, as she was leaving the room.

"He wishes me to spend half an hour in the pine forest bordering the town, for the sake of the resinous air."

"I will go with you," said Flora. "I also need air, air to prevent me from suffocating beneath the burden of annoyances which fate imposes upon me."

She offered the Frau President her arm, and they left the room together.

Henriette stamped her foot angrily; she could have cried for vexation, but she could not prevent her beautiful sister from presenting herself in the afternoon in a white felt hat, fan in hand, ready to accompany her upon her woodland walk.

It was a glorious April day: the blue skies were cloudless, the glistening sunshine was bright on forest and fell, and the balmy air was fragrant with the odour of the first violets. The strip of forest which bordered, as it were, the dark mantle of pines was still light, light as if the dome of dark green had been removed from its shady aisles. The wealth of leaves that would shortly overpower each knotty bough and transform it to youth and beauty still lay compressed, a soft down, in millions of brown buds; the underbrush alone showed a pale, misty green, and from the damp moss the snow-drops hung upon long, slender stems. Kitty strayed aside, plucking these flowers, while Flora and Henriette walked on in the narrow path leading to the pines.

It was not quiet here to-day: it was the day upon which the poor of the town were allowed to gather fagots. There was the noise of the cracking of dry wood and of loud human voices, and in among the thickest bushes Kitty suddenly came upon a swarthy woman who was just tearing down a branch as thick as her arm that had been sawed from the parent stem. Irritated, perhaps, by being detected carrying off green instead of dead wood, perhaps by the sudden appearance of the commanding figure, the woman cast from beneath the purple kerchief she had tied over her head a savage glance at the intruder, and by the manner in which, standing erect, she trailed the bough to and fro upon the ground, seemed to challenge expostulation.

Kitty was not in the least afraid: she stooped to pluck a tuft of anemones from beneath a bush, when suddenly she heard a cry from the path,—a faint scream, followed by a tumult of voices in an under-tone.

The woman listened, tossed aside the bough, and dashed through the underbrush in the direction of the noise. Again the scream was heard: it was Henriette's thin, feeble voice. Kitty followed close upon the woman's heels; the thorns tore her dress, and the bushes which her forerunner parted with a strong arm flew back into her face, but she quickly emerged upon the path.

At first she saw only a knot of women and ragged lads gathered about the trunk of a pine-tree; but through the openings made here and there by the gesticulations of the throng Flora's white hat and blue feather could be seen behind the mass of bristly heads and dirty kerchiefs.

"Let the dwarf go, Fritz!" exclaimed a huge woman.

"But she screams like a fool!" said a boy's voice.

"What of that? not a soul can hear her little pipe." The woman had a broad snub-nose and small, wicked eyes, and towered like a giantess above all the rest.

Flora now spoke,—Kitty scarcely recognized her voice.

She was answered by a burst of contemptuous laughter.

"Get out of the way?" the tall woman repeated. "This wood belongs to the town, Fräulein; the poorest has just as good a right here as the richest. I should like to see any one drive me away!" She planted herself in the path more broadly than before. "Come, look, all of ye! Such as we don't often have a chance to see that face, except in a grand coach, with the horses tearing around the corners and trying to drive over poor people. You are a beauty, Fräulein: your worst enemy can't deny that. All real,—nothing laid on,—a skin like silk and velvet,—good enough to eat." She thrust her face close under the white hat.

The woman who had run before Kitty pushed herself into the circle. "Here comes another!" she cried, pointing back towards the young girl.

Those nearest her involuntarily turned to look, leaving an opening in their midst. There stood Flora, her lips and cheeks white as snow, evidently hardly able to stand, in vain attempting to retain her haughty carriage.

"We don't care for her!" a boy cried out, and the circle closed again more densely than before.

"Kitty!" Henriette's voice was heard in helpless terror from behind the living wall; but the cry was instantly smothered, evidently by a hand laid upon her mouth. In an instant three or four of the boys were thrust staggering aside, and even the gigantic woman yielded to Kitty's strong arm as she made her way to her sisters and placed herself in front of them. "What do you want?" she asked, in a loud, firm voice.

For one moment the assailants were dismayed; but only for one moment. This was but a girl, and of what avail could she be to help? They closed around her with loud bursts of laughter.

"Body and bones o' me! she asks her questions like a judge on the bench!" cried the giantess, putting her arms akimbo on her broad hips.

"Yes, and looks as proud as if she were come direct from the three kings of Cologne," added the woman with the purple kerchief on her head. "Hark ye! your grandmother belonged to my village; never when I knew her did she have shoe or stocking to her foot; and I remember very well, too, when your grandfather fed and drove old miller Klaus's horses——"

"Do you suppose I do not know it, or that I am ashamed of it?" Kitty interrupted her, calmly and coldly, although her stern face had grown very pale.

"What need?—you have his money,—heaps of money!" cried a third, pressing close to the young girl and snatching at the skirt of her dress, which she rubbed in her grimy fingers. "A fine gown this!—a holiday gown!—and worn, too, o' week-days, and in the woods, where the thorns might tear it to shreds! No matter for that,—there's money enough: they found basketfuls of it when the old man died. But no one asks where it came from. It's all the same to you, Fräulein, if the castle miller did buy away the grain from poor people who needed it, and lock it up in his granaries, and then declare he would not sell a shovelful of it until the price had risen to what he wanted,—no, not although the people squeaked like starving mice——"

"Lies!" exclaimed Kitty, exasperated.

"Lies, indeed? And is it a lie, too, that we are given up to usurers now, who will take our last potato from us? 'Tis shameful! My daughter shall drown herself sooner than work for those skinflints!"

"And my brother will shoot them dead if they show their faces here!" bragged a half-grown boy.

"Yes, like the dwarf's doves," said another, with a grimace, pointing to Henriette, who was clinging to Kitty, half wild with terror.

Suddenly the bark of a dog was heard near at hand. In an instant Flora stood erect, and all the haughty arrogance of her nature mirrored itself in her face. "What have I to do with the sale of the factory?" she asked, scornfully.

"Settle that with the councillor. He will know how to answer you. And now begone, all of you! You shall suffer for your insolence, rely upon it!"

She extended her hand with a lordly air; but the tall woman seized it as if it had been offered for a friendly grasp, shook it with well-feigned cordiality, and burst into a noisy laugh, in which the others joined uproariously. "Oh, Fräulein, have you grown so brave all of a sudden because"—and she pointed with her thumb over her shoulder—"a dog barked over there? That is Hans Sonnemann's terrier: I know his voice well. He will not stir from his master, who is stone-deaf. They are going to the tavern together, as they do every afternoon. Make yourself easy,—they'll not come near here. And you have nothing to do, my fine Fräulein, with the sale of the factory, eh? You'll find no one to believe that. They need only look at you to see which way the wind blows. You and the old madame rule the roast; the councillor must obey, and, now that he is rich enough, shake himself clear of all the common people who have earned him his money. No, we can't help it, but we can thank you for it, Fräulein."

She drew nearer, and her small, sharp eyes gleamed with a cat-like cruelty.

Flora, in horror, covered her face with her hands. "God of heaven, they will murder us!" she gasped, with white lips.

The whole rabble laughed.

"Not a bit of it, Fräulein," said the woman. "We're not such fools. Where would be the use of putting a rope here?" And she passed her hand beneath her chin, with a significant gesture. "But you shall have something to remember us by."

Suddenly, Flora, as in obedience to a momentary impulse, took from her pocket her porte-monnaie, opened it, and scattered its contents, gold and silver, upon the ground. Instantly the circle widened, and the foremost boys were about to scramble for the money. "Stop that!" yelled the giantess, pushing them back into a close crowd with her powerful arms. "There will be time enough for that afterwards. Afterwards, Fräulein." She turned slowly, and with an air of coarse irony, to the beautiful woman. "First, a token for you!"

"Take care how you touch us!" said Kitty. She perfectly retained her composure, while her two sisters were nearly fainting.

"Ah, you! What business is it of yours? Why should I take care? What signifies a couple of weeks in the cage?" She made a scornful gesture. "'Tis nothing; and the judge never gives more for—well, for a box on the ear, or a couple of scars on the face. And those you shall have, Fräulein, sure as I stand here!" And she turned to Flora and elevated her voice. "I will paint your snowy skin so that you will remember me as long as you live. You shall show as fine a striped face as any tiger in the menagerie!"

Quick as lightning she lifted her hands to bury her dirty nails in Flora's cheek; but Kitty was as quick. She seized the bony wrists, and with one vigorous thrust sent the huge woman backwards among the rabble, making a wide breach in their circle. An indescribable tumult ensued. The mob rushed upon the strong, steadfast girl, who stood full in front of her sisters, still deadly pale, but undaunted. Flora had sunk on the ground and thrown her arms around the trunk of the pine, pressing her menaced face against the bark. Her white hat had fallen off, and was trampled beneath the feet of the assailants.

"Help! help!" screamed Henriette, with one last superhuman effort, as the rush was made upon Kitty, whose black lace mantle was torn to shreds in an instant. Her hat was snatched from her head, and the loosened braids of hair fell down her back, when the boy who had again clapped his hand upon Henriette's mouth gave a howl of dismay. "Good

God! what ails her now?" he yelled, and dashed in among the crowd to escape.

A crimson stream was trickling from the invalid's lips, as, with failing glances, she clutched wildly at some support, while all recoiled in horror. Blood! In an instant the mob scattered in every direction. The bushes snapped and cracked on all sides, as when a herd of deer break through the underbrush, and then came a silence so profound that it seemed as if the rabble rout had sunk into the earth. Even if here and there a boy's head emerged from the bushes to peep greedily at the money scattered about, it did so without noise and with great caution.

Kitty threw her arms around her sister and sank with her upon the ground, leaning against the trunk of the pine and pillowing the invalid's head upon her breast. In this position the blood gradually ceased to flow.

"Go for help!" she said, without turning her tearful eyes from Henriette's death-like face, to Flora, who was gazing down upon the group, her hands clasped to her bosom in impatient terror.

"Are you mad?" she exclaimed, in a suppressed tone. "Would you have me run into the arms of those wretches? I will not stir from here alone. We must try to get Henriette away."

Kitty answered not a word: she saw how vain would be any appeal to such selfishness. With Flora's assistance she got upon her feet, Henriette lying like a child in her arms, perfectly unconscious, her head resting upon her sister's shoulder. Thus she actually glided over the ground, avoiding even the smallest stones that could jar and thus endanger her precious burden. Of course this precaution increased the difficulty of her task; but she could neither pause nor draw a long breath.

"Rest as long as you choose when we have reached the

open fields,—but not here, if you would not have me die of terror," Flora said, authoritatively. She walked close by Kitty's side, her head held high with her usual haughty air, nevertheless keenly scanning each bush on either side of the path, ready to take to flight at the first suspicious noise. Where was the courage to which Henriette had ironically alluded? Where the self-reliance, the masculine energy, she had herself so vaunted? In this terrible hour Kitty could not but reflect that where a woman ceases to think, to feel, and to struggle like a *woman*, her life is a farce, and a farce only.

CHAPTER XI.

At last they emerged upon the sunny open fields. Kitty leaned for a moment against the trunk of a huge oak-tree, while Flora walked on a few paces to be entirely free of the "horrible" forest. The danger was past: there were men ploughing within calling distance, the steeples of the city were in view, and directly in front lay the road leading to the gates of the park of Villa Baumgarten.

But Kitty's eyes were fixed upon an object which Flora did not see,—the low roof, with the tall chimneys and gilded weathercock, that lay so peacefully amid its surrounding fruit-trees. She could see distinctly the picket-fence of the garden,—it was much nearer at hand than the park gates,—and thither, after a brief rest, she silently directed her steps.

"Where are you going?" cried Flora, who was already on her way to the park.

"To Doctor Bruck's house," replied the young girl, walking quietly forward without pausing. "It is the nearest place where we can find a bed where Henriette can be laid, and all necessary assistance. Perhaps the doctor himself is at home."

Flora frowned and hesitated; but whether she fancied herself still followed by the revengeful woman with the long, bony fingers, or whether she, in the present state of her toilette and without a hat, feared to encounter pedestrians on the road to the park, she silently followed Kitty's lead.

Thus they crossed the fields. The task that Kitty had undertaken was laborious indeed. The unfrequented field was full of holes and very stony; at every false step she made, her blood fairly curdled with terror lest Henriette might have a recurrence of the last fearful attack. Then, too, the sun, hot as upon a day in August, beat down upon her unprotected head; now and then the world seemed to swim in a strange, lurid light around her, and she was in imminent danger of sinking down with exhaustion. But at such moments she riveted her gaze upon the doctor's house; it came nearer and nearer,—a lovely picture of rural peace and refreshing repose. She could now clearly see the order and care that reigned behind the picket-fence, and in the midst of her terror and fatigue she was aware of a sensation of pleasure. A man in shirt-sleeves was constructing an arbour, an arbour for the dean's widow: the old lady could not forget the vine-wreathed arbour in the parsonage garden of long ago. Again she would be able to enjoy a seat in the open air. How the simple pleasure would delight her!

She herself now descended the stone steps of the front door in her white cap and apron, bringing to the laborer some afternoon refreshment. She stayed for a moment, apparently talking to the man about his work; it did not occur to either of them to look abroad over the fields. Kitty was just considering whether she should not call to them for help, when the doctor himself came out of the house.

"Bruck!" Flora called across the field, with all the clear, silvery strength of her voice.

He paused, gazed for one moment at the advancing group, and then, tearing open the garden-gate, rushed towards them. "Good heavens! what has happened?" he cried, as he came up.

"I have been assaulted by a mob of savage Mænads," Flora answered, with a bitter smile, but with all her old scorn and proud indifference of manner. "The wretches meant mischief; my life was in danger, and this poor creature"—she pointed to Henriette—"has had a hemorrhage from terror and agitation."

He only glanced towards her—she was there, safe and uninjured—as he immediately took Henriette from Kitty's arms. "You have exerted a superhuman amount of strength," he said, scanning her face and figure anxiously. A nervous tremor possessed her frame, she bit her lip convulsively, and her cheeks glowed as if the heated blood would burst through the delicate skin. And beside her stood Flora, now cool and quiet, her cheeks flushed, to be sure, but only with the memory of what had occurred.

"You should not have allowed your sister to bear this burden alone," the doctor said to her as he carefully carried the still unconscious Henriette towards the house.

"How can you say so, Bruck!" she exclaimed, with an injured air. "Such a reproach from you is very unjust," she added, sharply. "I know my duty, and would have been only too glad to carry Henriette; but I felt it would be madness to attempt it with my delicate physical organization, while Kitty's is one of those sound, robust, Valkyria natures to whom such a task is a trifle."

He answered not a word, but called to his aunt, who was hastening towards him, to prepare a bed immediately. She hurried back into the house, and when her nephew ascended the steps to the hall, she was standing at the open door of a western room, into which, mutely and with an anxious face, she motioned him to enter.

It was her guest-chamber,—a tolerably large, sunny room, —the bare floor worn but white, the walls, once painted pink, much defaced, and a monster of a stove of black tiles. The gay chintz curtains before the two windows were perhaps the only luxury that the dean's widow had allowed herself in her new home. At the head of the bed stood an ancient screen covered with Chinese figures, and upon the walls there hung in black frames some illustrations, not very artistic, to be sure, of "Louise," a charming idyl by Vosz. The air of the chamber was deliciously fresh and filled with the fragrance of lavender.

The doctor's face was grave and anxious. It was long before his efforts were successful in restoring Henriette to partial consciousness. She recognized him at last, but she was too weak to lift her hand from the bed to extend it to him. He sent the man at work in the garden to Villa Baumgarten at once, to acquaint the Frau President with what had occurred, and she very soon made her appearance. Until her arrival, not a word was spoken in the sick-room. Flora stood at one window, gazing out over the fields, and Kitty sat at the other, her hands clasped in her lap, her eyes riveted upon the bed, while the dean's widow went and came noiselessly, fulfilling all her nephew's behests.

The Frau President seemed greatly shocked; she was startled afresh at the sight of Henriette's waxen face upon the pillow, and was prepared for the worst when she found that the sick girl did not open her eyes when she gently spoke to her. Henriette had closed them as her grandmother entered the room.

"Tell me, for Heaven's sake, what has happened!" the old lady cried, her soft and carefully-modulated voice sounding almost harsh in the intense quiet that had reigned in the room.

Then Flora came from the window and told the story. Indignantly, and with great distinctness, she portrayed the entire scene in the forest, of course never allowing it to appear that she had for a moment lost her courage or presence of mind, although she declared that in the midst of a throng of at least twenty furies even the strongest nature needed to summon up all its energy not to succumb to aversion and disgust.

Meanwhile, the Frau President paced the apartment in the greatest agitation, never heeding that her silken train rustled over the uneven floor in a way that might be torture to sensitive nerves. "What does the *philanthropist* say to all this?" she asked, at last, pausing to look at the doctor through her half-shut eyelids with intense irritation.

He answered not a word. His whole expression was that of calm strength as he stood holding Henriette's hand in his, seeming to have neither eyes nor thought for anything but the feeble spark of life which each moment threatened to extinguish.

The old lady again approached the bed, and leaned over the invalid.

"Herr Doctor," she said, after a momentary hesitation, "the case seems to me a very serious one. Shall we not call in my old experienced friend and physician, the councillor of medicine, Von Bär, in consultation? You must not take it amiss."

"Not in the least, Frau President," he said, laying the sick girl's hand, which just then moved convulsively, gently upon the bed. "It is my duty to do everything that can conduce to your satisfaction." He then quietly left the room to send for the required physician.

"Good heavens, what a mistake it was to bring Henriette here!" the Frau President exclaimed, in an under-tone, as soon as the door closed after him.

"Kitty is to blame for it," Flora rejoined, crossly. "It will be her fault if we are obliged to almost live in this tumble-down place for weeks to come——" And she glanced angrily towards the silent girl at the window.

"And what an oversight to place the poor child so that every time she opens her eyes she has a full view of that horrible stove! And these daubs on the walls!—'tis enough to frighten her!" As she spoke, the old lady turned away from her and examined the bed. "This seems to be tolerably comfortable,—the linen, at least, is white and fine; but I will send over Henriette's silken duvet, with a comfortable arm-chair for Doctor von Bär, and, above all, another toilette set. Stoneware!" she said, contemptuously, as she pushed aside the basin and pitcher upon the wash-stand to make room for the painted porcelain shortly to arrive. "Heavens, how wretchedly such people live! And they never feel it—— Do you wish for anything, my angel?" she interrupted herself, in a soft voice, as she hurried to the bedside.

Henriette had slowly lifted her head and looked about her for an instant; she had now sunk back again and closed her eyes, although her strength had sufficiently returned to enable her to push away her grandmother's hand as it attempted to stroke her own.

"Wayward as ever!" sighed the Frau President, as she sat down beside the bed.

The councillor of medicine was not long in making his appearance: he came in great consternation. He needed an explanation of what had occurred to account for the presence of his old friend in the house by the river. He was a handsome old man, excessively neat in his dress, and with an arrogant reserve of manner. He was family physician to the reigning prince, who had conferred upon him a patent of nobility in reward of his services, which had also obtained him quite a number of orders, diamond rings, and gold snuffboxes. His splendid equipage awaited him on the farther side of the bridge.

"Bad, very bad!" he said, with a critical air, going to the bedside. He looked at the patient for a minute, and then began an examination of her chest. He did it very carefully, but the sick girl moaned,—the repeated touch was evidently painful to her.

Doctor Bruck stood silently beside him with folded arms. He never moved; but, as Henriette moaned, his brows contracted: so thorough an examination at this advanced stage of the disease was entirely unnecessary. "Shall I give you my experience of the case, Doctor von Bär?" he asked quietly, but evidently with the intention of putting a stop to what gave the patient pain.

The old gentleman glanced towards him. No one could confront an enemy with a look of more bitter hatred than that which gleamed in the sunken eyes of the distinguished physician. "Permit me first to investigate matters myself, Herr Doctor!" he answered, coldly, and continued his examination. "Now I am at your service," he said, a few minutes later, retiring from the bedside, and following the doctor into his study.

As soon as he had gone, Henriette opened her eyes. Her cheeks wore the flush of fever, and, with what was almost violence, she demanded to see her own physician, Doctor Bruck.

The Frau President could scarcely repress her annoyance at such "utter waywardness," but she went, without a word, to fulfil the invalid's request. She did not, however, as she had feared she should, intrude upon a consultation: there had evidently been none; the councillor of medicine had paid no heed to the young physician's communications, but had seated himself at the study-table to write a prescription.

Doctor Bruck instantly left the room, and the Frau President stayed to hear her old friend's opinion. He was rather curt and out of humour, spoke of an entire misconception of the case, and lamented that the right man was applied to only in moments of the greatest danger. The grandmother should have overcome her grandchild's obstinacy long since, and consulted the old family physician who had treated her in her childhood. In such a case the consideration shown to Flora's lover was culpable. "First of all, we must see that the poor child is transferred as soon as possible, dear madame, to her own convenient and elegant bedroom," he added. "She will be better amid her accustomed surroundings; and then too I can be sure that my directions will be strictly followed, which could never be the case here."

He dipped his pen in the ink. Suddenly his eyes fell upon a beautiful little open box upon the table in the midst of the books and writing-materials; it had probably been received but a few hours previously, for the wrapping-paper still lay beside it.

Never had the Frau President seen the face of her "cherished friend" express such blank dismay as at this moment; the pen fell from his hand.

"Good heavens! that is the order of the royal household of D——!" he said, tapping the box with a respectful finger. "How comes it in this house, sent to this obscure address?"

"Strange!" the Frau President murmured, in a startled tone, her delicate white features flushed with a disagreeable surprise. She put up her eyeglass to examine the contents of the little box. "I do not know the order, or its value——"

"No wonder: it is very rarely bestowed," the councillor of medicine interrupted her.

"Or I might suppose its reception dated from his last campaign;" she completed her remark.

"No possibility of that!" he ejaculated, harshly,—he must

have been much agitated to adopt such a tone. "In the first place, the order is only bestowed as a reward for services rendered to the royal family; and then I should like to see the man who could possess such a decoration for more than a year without the world's knowing it. If I only knew why,—knew why!" He rubbed his forehead absently with a hand upon which three marks of princely favour glittered in sparkling diamonds; but of what value were they to him at this moment? They were all presents from his own royal family,—not distinctions awarded by a foreign court.

"This same order is the goal of the hopes of so many," he continued; "many a person of distinction has sighed for it in vain; and here it lies, as if carelessly thrown aside, on this miserable painted table!—thrown around the neck of a man, an ignoramus, disgraced by his repeated failures,—pardon me, dear madame, I cannot help saying so,—thrown around his neck, I repeat, and no one has an idea of the why or the wherefore!"

He had arisen, and was pacing to and fro in the room. The haughty old lady, who so seldom lost her self-possession, looked at him the while with a strange air of scrutiny. "I cannot believe," she observed, in an uncertain tone, "that the decoration has anything to do with his medical services. When was he ever at the D—— court?"

The councillor of medicine paused, and laughed aloud: but it was a forced laugh. "I must say, madame, such an idea never entered my head, simply because it is—impossible. The world must be turned upside down indeed before the quackery and ignorance of raw tyros can be crowned with honour, while genuine merit is trampled under-foot. No, no; that I cannot believe." He went to a window and drummed with his fingers on the glass. "But who knows what he may have undertaken to do? He vanished for eight days, and no one knew whither," he said, after a short silence, in an under-tone. "Hm! who knows anything of his outside relations? These schemers, who never speak of their profession, have good reasons for silence: there is much in their practice of medicine which no honorable man could countenance. Well, I say nothing. It has never been my way to lift the veil from the dark designs of others. We are all in His hands!" And he pointed upwards with such well-feigned reliance upon Heaven that only so intimate a friend as the Frau President could have failed to be deceived. He was always gentle and pious when he imagined himself slighted or defrauded of his rights.

He sat down at the table again, and wrote his prescription, but hurriedly, as if the proximity of the fatal box burned his fingers. "One thing I pray of your kindness, my dear friend," he said, as he finished: "try to get to the bottom of this affair. I should like to be au fait before Bruck begins to boast of his ambiguous distinction,—I should like to have some weapon at hand. No need to advise you to use the most refined diplomacy: there you are mistress and at home."

The old lady did not at once reply: she had watched him while he had been transcribing on paper the delicate, mysterious characters, and had admitted to herself that her old friend had suddenly grown strangely old. Not that wrinkles had invaded his still blooming cheeks,—his face was smooth and plump,—but at this moment, when he was entirely off his guard, there was in all the lines of his countenance an indefinable mixture of anxiety, depression, and peevish discontent; he looked like a man for whom some secret, disturbing thought ruins the day's enjoyment and the night's repose. Now first she remembered that he had of late occasionally thrown out delicate hints with regard to the caprice of princes. Heavens, what if she should lose this friend! Not that this thought had reference to his transfer from this earthly sphere,—she never, if she could help it, thought of death,—but he might be pensioned off. He could then stand her in no stead at court, and she dreaded to think of what this would cost her. Pshaw! why should she? The good old Von Bär was too fond of truffles and the like good but indigestible things; he loved strong wine and heavy beer; he was beginning to be hypochondriacal, to have whims and see phantoms; her refined sensibility was sure to warn her of the decline of any influence at court, and she had not as yet detected in that delicate weathercock the slightest disposition to veer.

"But, my dear friend, how do you know that this decoration belongs to the doctor?" she asked, with all the assurance of an experienced woman of the world. "I cannot believe that it does, because, with all the will in the world, I cannot see how it should. At all events, whatever is the state of the case, it will do him no good in our capital, where he is, as it were, dead. I will willingly investigate the affair, solely for your satisfaction——" She stopped; the door of the next room opened, and the dean's widow entered it to get something from her closet.

The councillor of medicine arose and gave the prescription to the Frau President. Then both passed through the room where the dean's widow was just closing the closet-door. Doctor von Bär would gladly have put an end to his anxiety by provoking an explanation by some facetious remark as he passed her; but the old lady made him an inclination so cool and dignified, so full of grave reserve, that he did not venture to address her.

In the invalid's apartment there was no better chance to satisfy his mind. The doctor had brought the glass globe of gold-fish from his aunt's room, and was busy arranging the apparatus of a little fountain attached to it; the maid was bringing fresh water to fill various deep plates on the tables and a bucket near the sick-bed,—all to moisten as much as possible the atmosphere of the room. Who could disturb a man thus given over to the performance of his duty by captious remarks with regard to outside affairs? And, besides, the councillor of medicine instantly felt relieved upon the subject. There must be some hidden and harmless explanation of the whole matter; for no man who had just been honoured by so rare a distinction could possibly conduct himself so quietly and unconsciously as the young physician.

Henriette was sitting propped up with pillows in bed; fever had set in. Removal to the villa was out of the question, however earnestly the Frau President might desire it. She was obliged to content herself with sending Henriette's maid to stay through the night, with everything that could make the sick-chamber "comfortable." Kitty's entreaty to be allowed to take charge of her sister during the night was set aside, not so much by the Frau President and Doctor von Bär as by Doctor Bruck, who was very decided in the matter. Tears rushed to the young girl's eyes as he refused to yield one jot of his opinion that the maid, acting under his directions, was all that was required. Accordingly, it was arranged that Flora and Kitty should remain until ten o'clock, and then give place to Nanni.

Flora maintained an impassive silence during this discussion. She was conscious, as was her grandmother, that she must not be outdone by Kitty in attention to her own sister in this illness, which, with the adventure in the wood, was likely to furnish talk for the capital the next day, and therefore she was satisfied to abide by the doctor's decision.

CHAPTER XII.

Soon after the departure of the Frau President and her friend, footmen and house-maids arrived from the villa, bringing all sorts of cushions, coverings, and furniture, which were noiselessly transferred to the sick-room. The simple but cosy apartment shortly wore the air of an auction-room: an embroidered screen before the shabby black stove, the gorgeous toilette set, shining apple-green satin arm-chairs,—how ridiculously unsuitable, as if blown hither by some unfavourable wind, they all looked within the faded, defaced walls!

Without a change of countenance, with all her own calm gentleness of manner, the dean's widow removed her despised belongings. Her eyes never once encountered those of the doctor, who stood, with folded arms, at a window, silently watching the alterations. Perhaps the old lady feared he might detect in her glance some trace of annoyance, and that must not be.

This invasion of accustomed elegance infused with fresh energy Flora's hitherto apathetic demeanour; she directed its arrangement,—put the green silk duvet upon Henriette's bed with her own hands, and sprinkled a whole bottle of cologne-water over the bare floor. Then she had a thick rug laid by the vacant window, and placed upon it an arm-chair, into which, as soon as the servants had left, she threw herself, crossing her little feet upon an embroidered footstool. It really looked as if she had fled to an oasis in the surrounding desert, she so gathered herself together, so coldly scrutinized everything outside of her carpeted corner. She had noticed, in the "ridiculously small" looking-glass enclosed in a brown frame, that her thin hair was disarranged. Therefore she had taken a little white lace fichu from her neck and tied it loosely over the dishevelled curls: the airy fabric crowned her charming head like a saintly halo. The dean's widow could not help gazing at her; she certainly was a wonderfully beautiful creature. For the first time she understood how, neither in his wild student days, nor upon the battle-field, had the doctor been able to forget this enchanting being, and her present strange conduct, her gloomy taciturnity, disappointing as it was, was but the natural effect of the terrible adventure of the day.

Meanwhile, the day drew to a close. The western skies were aflame, the wreaths of green trailing down from the hanging-baskets at the windows were tipped with gold, and the roses on the curtains looked like giant peonies, flooding the sick-room with fiery splendour.

Henriette lay back among her pillows, with closed eyes. She had protested against the drawing of the curtains "because the dull twilight would stifle" her, and she begged that every one would come in and go out of her room as usual and speak in ordinary tones,—she could not endure whispering and "tiptoe tread;" she was even afraid of it: it made her think that every one thought her dying. Her wish was granted. Without being noisy, all tried to preserve their usual manner of speaking and stepping.

When the doctor left the room for a few moments to get a book, the dean's widow entered, bearing a small waiter, and immediately a delicious fragrance of tea overcame even the strong odour of cologne water. The waiter was covered with a napkin of the finest damask, the cups were of old porcelain, and the antique silver spoons massive and thick, inherited through many generations. The red sunlight illumined and transfigured the elderly figure that, advancing in spotless purity of attire, offered some refreshment to the beautiful woman in the arm-chair by the window.

"Home-made waffles?" And Flora started up from her half-reclining posture. "Oh, yes! even in this corner I could smell them baking in the kitchen. How good they look!" She clasped her hands as if in naïve admiration. "Good heavens, one needs to be as entirely unfit for domestic cares as I am to be as utterly ignorant of how to produce such a little work of art! How much patience and how much time it must take!"

"Time flies so fast that I have learned to accomplish small tasks quickly," the old lady replied, with a smile, "so as to have many hours of leisure at my disposal. My household cares must not interfere with my intellectual pleasures. This last winter I completed the task I had undertaken of reading the Bible through from beginning to end——"

"For your spiritual welfare?" asked Flora.

"Not at all. I know by heart all those portions that can comfort and support me; but the fierce politico-religious controversy at present raging in the world should interest women greatly, and, although we may not enter the field, we ought to range ourselves intelligently beneath some banner, which we can do only by divesting our minds of prejudices and superstitions engendered by pulpit and school, and studying the sacred books themselves."

Flora looked at her in mute astonishment. Read through the whole Bible for such a reason! How intolerably dry and uninteresting! Her poetic nature could never have found patience for such a labour. Irritated by the discovery of such unexpected intellectual capacity in the woman whom she had described as given over to sweeping, baking, and darning stockings, she entirely forgot the part she herself hoped to play before the world,—that of an earnest and profound student. How had the dean's widow come to know anything about what was going on in the intellectual world? Now she knew who had so spoiled the doctor by filling his imagination with an ideal of a wife who should be housekeeper and intellectual companion at one and the same time.

Kitty had come forward and taken the waiter from the old lady. She marked the amazement painted on her sister's beautiful face, and, fearing lest she might give utterance to it in some thoughtless remark, hastened to offer her some tea.

Flora impatiently toyed with her handkerchief, and refused to take anything, upon the plea that she was "still too much agitated to taste a morsel," although a few minutes afterward the young girl saw her take a bonbonnière from her pocket and refresh herself with its contents; evidently she wished to avoid accepting any hospitality beneath this roof. Kitty perfectly understood that this visit to the old house—this glimpse of its simple bourgeois interior—had destroyed every vestige of self-control in Flora's mind; she could easily read in those large, gray-blue eyes, sparkling with impatience, that the moment was near at hand when the "yoke must be thrown off at all hazards." In her inmost soul the younger sister breathed a fervent prayer that the blow might not strike the unhappy man here by his own hearthstone. Fortunately, the dean's widow did not observe Flora's conduct. Never dreaming of the black, threatening cloud that overshadowed her peaceful life, she took her waiter from the room after Kitty had gratefully accepted a cup of tea.

The glowing sunset gradually paled. The crimson light faded in the sick-room until it illumined only the beautiful woman reclining by the window. Flora sat there like some evil angel around whom was playing demoniac fire.

The sick girl grew restless. She plucked at the green silk coverlet, evidently attempting to throw it off. "Take it away! the green is full of arsenic!" she whispered, with all the hurried vehemence of increasing fever.

Kitty instantly exchanged the silken coverlet for the cool,

white linen counterpane, which she laid smoothly over the emaciated body of the poor girl whom the mob in the wood had called "dwarf." In the glorious eyes there was now not a ray of consciousness: they rolled wildly hither and thither beneath the half-closed eyelids.

"That does me good," she said, stretching herself wearily. "And now do not let them come in again to smother me with that hot, poisonous silk. Grandmamma is false, as is all the society she gathers about her,—she and the old poisoner, the great authority. I will strike him if he ever dares to lay his hateful fingers on my breast!" she muttered, angrily, through her shut teeth. Suddenly she sat up in bed and seized Kitty's hand. "Mistrust him, Bruck!" she said, holding up her forefinger; "and grandmamma too! And she,—you know who I mean,—the one who smokes cigars, and drives the new horses furiously because you forbade it,—she is the falsest of all!"

"Oh, thank you!" Flora said, in an under-tone, with a malicious smile, as she nestled in among the cushions of her chair.

Kitty was indescribably distressed as her hand was thus firmly held. She never glanced towards the doctor, for whom the delirious girl mistook her, and who stood at the head of the bed, half hidden by the Chinese screen.

"Do you remember how it all used to be?" Henriette continued. "Do you remember how the footmen used to be sent after you through wind and storm with letters, four, five a day? Do you remember how she used to rush to meet you, half wild with longing, if you did not come at t' e appointed moment? And how she would throw her arms around you as if nothing should ever loosen their clasp?"

At this Flora started up, her silken robes rustling, and her face as crimson as if the lately-vanished western glow had left its stain on her white cheeks. "Give her morphia!" she cried. "This is madness, rather than the delirium of fever; she must sleep."

The doctor had just before given the sick girl a teaspoonful of medicine; he did not notice Flora's words, save by the slight, fleeting smile with which one receives some ignorant and foolish suggestion, never even changing his attitude; the flush called to his cheek by Henriette's last words instantly faded, leaving him as coldly calm and impassive as before.

Flora sank back angrily in her chair, then turned away her head and looked restlessly abroad over the darkening fields.

"Did you ever believe that all could be so changed, Bruck? That she could declare it had all been a mistake?" Henriette began again, clasping both her burning hands around Kitty's right. The young girl's heart seemed to stop beating; on those fever-stricken lips were hovering the words to which no one, not even Flora herself, had yet dared to give utterance. Hastily she leaned over her sick sister and instinctively laid her left hand upon her forehead, as if she could thus divert her thoughts into another channel.

"Oh, that is cool and kind!" Henriette said, with a sigh. "But do you remember how Flora used to thrust your hand away from my aching head? She was terribly jealous."

A half-suppressed laugh of contempt came from the window. Henriette did not hear it: she was deaf to the outside world.

"I cannot sleep, for distress at what must come!" she moaned, clasping Kitty's hand, locked in her own, passionately against her poor breast. "You will avoid us all and be a miserable man, never even uttering our names. Ah, Bruck, what can satisfy her boundless vanity, which she calls ambition! She wants to sever the bond between you, cost what it may."

Involuntarily, Kitty moved her hand as if to lay it upon the sick girl's lips. Henriette screamed. "Not on my mouth, like that terrible boy in the forest!" she gasped, turning away.

At this moment Flora stood by the bed and thrust aside her young sister; her face, her whole attitude, expressed a sudden determination. "Let her speak out!" she said, authoritatively.

"Yes, let me speak out!" Henriette repeated, in a voice hoarse from exhaustion, but in the tone of a child content at being indulged. "Who should tell you, Bruck, except myself,—myself? Who else should pray you to be upon your guard? Keep your eyes open! She will fly from you like the dove from the tree, white coquette that she is; she wishes to be free——"

"In all her delirium she tells one truth," Flora interrupted, resolutely advancing a step towards the doctor. "She is right: I cannot be to you what I promised. Let me be free, Bruck!" she added, imploringly, raising her clasped hands. For the first time Kitty heard how indescribably sweet her voice could be.

The decisive words were spoken for which she had planned and plotted for months. Kitty had supposed that their first utterance would annihilate the betrayed lover; but the lightning produced no visible effect; the man's unshaken composure was as inexplicable to Kitty as if one apparently struck by a murderous bullet should walk unharmed out of the smoke of the explosion. Grave and silent, he looked down at the imploring figure; but he was pale, pale as death. He withheld his hand which she tried to grasp. "This is not the place for such an explanation——"

"But it is the moment. Other lips have spoken what has hovered upon my own for months, refusing to be clothed in words——"

"Because it is a notorious breach of faith!"

She bit her lip. "Your definition is harsh and not correct;

the bond between us was not indissoluble, and I know that no other image has thrust yours from my heart. Do not smile so contemptuously, Bruck! By heaven, I love no other man!" she exclaimed, passionately. "But I will accept all reproach," she added, more calmly, "sooner than that we should both be miserable."

"Leave *my* happiness or misery out of the question. *You* cannot understand the meaning I attach to those words, but you must admit that they are not to be weighed in the balance when a man's honour and self-respect are at stake. And now let me entreat you, for your sick sister's sake, to be silent for the present." He turned away and walked to the nearest window.

She followed him. "Henriette does not hear," she said. The sick girl had fallen back exhausted among her pillows, and was whispering to herself incessantly, like a child telling itself some story; it was true that she did not hear. "You have said nothing decisive," Flora continued, in a tone of melancholy depression. "The final word must be spoken. Why postpone what one quick resolve will accomplish?" And as she spoke she turned and twisted the betrothal ring upon her hand.

Doctor Bruck looked down upon her over his shoulder. Kitty could not but be struck, as they stood thus, with his youthful air, which even his manly strength and vigour could not diminish. Beneath his moustache the lips showed a delicate, almost feminine outline, and there was something boyish in the moulding of the brow about the temples, in the graceful, easy carriage of the head, and in the quick, melting fire of the eyes. Now, however, his glance rested coldly upon the beautiful woman appealing to him.

"For what do you propose to exchange a life by my side?" he asked, so suddenly, so sharply, that she started involuntarily.

13*

"Do you need to ask, Bruck?" she exclaimed, stroking the curls from her forehead and taking a long breath, as if freed from an intolerable burden. "Can you not see how my whole soul is thirsting to embrace an author's profession? And could I ever succeed there as my gifts, my special endowments, so imperatively demand that I should, if I took upon myself the duties of a wife? Never! never!"

"Strange that this inextinguishable thirst should assail you for the first time within the last few months, after you——"

"After I have lived without this fame *twenty-nine* years," she completed his sentence with a burning blush. "Account for that as you please; call it a result of the feminine nature, which gropes and errs until it finds the right path——"

"Are you so sure that it is the right path?"

"As sure as that the needle seeks the pole."

He passed her without a word, took the medicine from the table, and approached the bed. It was time to administer it to the patient again, but she had fallen asleep, with Kitty's hand clasped firmly in both her own. He seemed to the young girl to be acting automatically, as if mental agitation were robbing him of control over his movements. He never looked at *her;* it might well humiliate him to have a witness present during this wretched scene; but had not she, too, suffered in remaining? She had several times attempted to withdraw her hand, that she might flee as far as her feet could carry her, but at her slightest movement Henriette would start in uncontrollable terror.

He attempted to feel the sleeping girl's pulse. Kitty tried to assist him by placing her left hand beneath Henriette's wrist; in doing so, her palm for a moment came in contact with his clasping fingers. He started, and changed colour so instantly that she withdrew her hand in terror. Why was it? Had what he had just passed through made him so nervous that any outward contact irritated him? She glanced aside at him. His breast heaved in a long sigh as he turned away to place the medicine again upon the table.

Meanwhile, Flora had paced the room to and fro in a state of indescribable agitation and impatience. Now she approached the doctor standing by the table. "It was unwise to confess my feelings so frankly," she said, with anger sparkling in her eyes. His silence and the quiet fulfilment of his medical duties in the midst of such a conflict had greatly irritated her. "You are one of those who despise a woman's mental power; you belong to the thousands of irreclaimable egotists who would deny permission to woman to stand upon her own feet——"

"Most certainly, if she *cannot* stand."

She clenched her small hand upon the table and gazed into his face for one moment, her lips compressed and white. "What do you mean by that, Bruck?" she asked, sharply.

He frowned slightly, and a faint crimson tinged his cheek and forehead; his was evidently one of those sensitive natures which an interchange of sharp words leading to recrimination stretches upon the rack. "I mean," he replied, with equal firmness, and with well-maintained coolness, "that for this 'standing upon her own feet'—to which woman certainly is entitled when by so doing she does not interfere with duties that have a prior claim—that for this 'standing upon her own feet' a firm, unbending will, an entire eradication of sensitive feminine vanity, and, above all, genuine talent, are indispensable."

"And you deny me the possession of these latter qualifications?"

"I have read your articles upon the 'Labour Question' and the 'Emancipation of Woman.'" His voice, usually so finely modulated, grew sharp and keen.

Flora started as if threatened with a blow. "How do you know that I am the author of the articles you have read?'

she asked, falteringly, but with her eyes intently fixed upon his face. "I write under false initials."

"But those initials were well known throughout your large circle of acquaintance long ago,—before the essays were published."

She looked confused and ashamed for a moment as she averted her eyes. "Well, you have read them," she then said. "And what must I think of your never alluding to these efforts of mine,—your never even mentioning your disapproval of them?"

"Could I have induced you to lay aside the pen?"

"No, no,—never!"

"That I knew, and therefore intended to say nothing until I should have the right to do so. Of course a sensible woman cleaves to her husband and does not isolate herself in special interests, even although in common with a keen sense of duty she possess great gifts, distinguished talent——"

"Which I of course do *not*," she interrupted him, bitterly.

"No, Flora; you have wit and intelligence, but no originality," he replied, gravely, shaking his head and resuming his usual calm manner of speaking.

For a few seconds she stood petrified by this simple sentence, evidently the result of entire conviction, and then, with a half-frantic mixture of affected merriment and unrepressed anger, she extended her arms. "Thank God, this puts an end to all hesitation, all uncertainty! I should have been a slave, a poor, down-trodden drudge, from whose soul the divine spark of poesy would have been torn—to light with it the kitchen fire."

She spoke too loudly. The sick girl, who had slumbered during the exchange of words in an even under-tone, opened her eyes wide and stared about her. The doctor hurried to the bedside; he gave her her medicine and gently laid his hand upon her forehead. Beneath his soothing touch the wild eyes closed again. Ah, could the poor sufferer have dreamed what a tempest she had invoked upon this man's head,—she who had hitherto done everything in her power to avert such a misfortune!

"I must seriously entreat you not to disturb your sister further," the doctor said, turning his head towards Flora as he bent over the bed, his hand still upon Henriette's forehead.

"I really have nothing more to say," Flora rejoined, with an unsuccessful attempt to smile, as she took her gloves from her pocket. "Everything is at an end between us, as, after your last offensive remarks, you must be perfectly aware. I am free——"

"Because I deny your possession of a talent to which you lay claim?" he asked, controlling his voice by an effort. And now his indignation mastered him; he suddenly stood erect and tall before her. Everything in his air and bearing that had bespoken youth and patient gentleness vanished: this was an angry, indignant man. "Let me ask you whom I wooed, the authoress, or Flora Mangold? As Flora Mangold, and only as such, you placed your hand in mine, knowing well that the woman who married me must be my wife, belonging to me alone, and no flickering will-o'-the-wisp of society. You knew this; you took pains to adapt yourself to my desire,—exaggerated pains, for I never should have required my wife to devote herself to cooking cares, as your zeal prompted you to do for a while. No; she was to be my intellectual inspiration, my pride, my sympathetic companion, the light of my household."

He paused for breath, never for an instant averting his indignant gaze from the beautiful woman, who looked mean and pitiable enough as she strove in vain to retain her usual arrogant demeanour and carriage.

"I have followed this change in you, step by step, from the first wayward frown upon your brow to the words that left your lips but a moment ago," he began again. "In the grasp of your own feminine infirmities,—arrogance, vanity, and caprice,—you are unutterably weak; and yet you would play the strong-minded woman, would espouse woman's cause, arrogating for your sex firmness of purpose, calmness of judgment, and strength of will that would usurp every manly prerogative! What I think of your conduct, what my inmost conviction is, whether I am to be happy or utterly wretched, is not the question at present. We have solemnly plighted our troth to each other for life—we are bound. Oh, it has been often enough said of you that you ensnare and play with men's hearts at first to make them a public scorn and mockery in the end! Mine you shall not thus place in the pillory, rely upon that! You are *not* free: I do not release you. Perjure yourself if you choose: I shall keep my word!"

"Shame upon you!" she cried, beside herself. "Would you drag me to the altar when I tell you that I have long ceased to love you? that at this moment, standing here, I can scarcely control my bitter hatred of you?"

At this terrible outbreak Kitty arose; she had succeeded in gradually withdrawing her hand from Henriette's clasp. She hurried from the room with averted eyes: she could not look in the face the man who had just received what must be his death-blow.

CHAPTER XIII.

TWILIGHT already reigned in the hall, which looked towards the north, but in the kitchen the last red gleam from the west played upon the walls and fell upon the red tiled floor.

The dean's widow stood there by the window, washing the tea-cups that had been used. The cook-maid whom she had been obliged to dismiss was to return on the morrow; she had been ill, and the chief household duties were therefore still performed by the old lady. She nodded kindly to Kitty and smiled: not the least suspicion of what was going on behind the opposite broad folding-door disturbed her gentle spirit. The young girl shivered, and hurried past her into the garden.

It had grown very cool. A strong breeze came blowing into her face and over her unprotected shoulders from the river. She ran towards it. Her temperament was sensitive, prone to emotion; the warm blood of youth circled in her veins; cheeks, eyes, her whole frame even to her tingling finger-tips, glowed, aflame with indignant agitation.

It had been terrible, that struggle between two human souls. And the guilty one, who alone was to blame for it, was her sister,—a faithless, frivolous woman, who could lightly bind the tie that should pledge her to a man for life, only to sever it at her wayward will, as if it were the merest summer gossamer floating on the air! This time, indeed, Flora had reckoned falsely: where she had expected to tread beneath her feet a heart subdued to submission by public condemnation and her own systematic ill treatment, she had encountered steel. But what would the firmness and energy with which he defied her avail him? He must succumb——

Kitty stepped upon the bridge, and, resting her hands on

the frail balustrade, looked down. The waters rushed beneath her feet, struggling against every stone that maintained its place in the bed of the stream, every root that projected from the shore, and in the struggle dashing up mimic showers of spray; but at a little distance the pale crescent moon was mirrored in its depths as though nothing could ever efface it. Was love thus steadfast in the human heart? Could the fiercest struggles beat around it in vain? Did it never fade, although its ideal were shattered? No; she had just seen that it did not.

Wondrous indeed must be this passion of love! Once already beneath that very roof it had hounded on a human soul through every stage of misery and despair. Many years before, as the dean's widow had related to Kitty on one of their homeward walks, the lovely young widow of a Baron von Baumgarten had lived in the house by the river. Her husband's heir and successor, the scion of a collateral branch, a handsome young cavalier, had daily come from his inherited castle to have one look at the lovely face shrouded in its widow's weeds. He might not enter the house, for she transgressed no bounds that custom had assigned to a young widow. But he would ride across the narrow bridge on his black steed and rein in the foaming fiery charger close to the wall of the house, that he might inhale the air she had breathed and kiss devotedly her small white hand. Those who saw him declared that when her period of mourning was past the beautiful widow would once more reign as mistress in Castle Baumgarten.

But once he was absent for some months at a foreign court, and it was rumoured that he would bring home with him a bride of noble birth. The fair young widow, when this rumour reached her ears, only smiled, and watched for him all the more constantly from her window. She never credited such treachery until the sound of trumpets and revelry from the castle announced the lord's return with his proud, stately bride, and that a gorgeous banquet had been arranged in honour of their arrival.

And the next day he rode across the wooden bridge with his wife, to present her to the fair dame in the house by the river. The gay tulips upon her brocade robe glittered in the distance, upon the fan in her hand a coronet gleamed in diamonds, and the greyhound that had formerly accompanied his master ran before her horse, not, as formerly, to hasten to the window whence a fair hand had fed him with sugar and bits of bread,—no, it ran along the river-bank to a spot where it barked and whined piteously. There upon the water lay a snow-white garment, tossed to and fro by the waves which could not float it down the stream, for the long, fair braids of its owner were entangled among the roots under the river-bank, and the pale, dead face was held fast, that the false love might gaze once more into the wide, glazed eyes.

The window whence she had looked so confidently to see him once more ride across the bridge was the same through which the doctor's study-lamp threw its nightly beam. There she must have stood in her bitter despair, watching the water hurrying past from the castle resounding with the marriage revelry, and she had been mastered by a fierce desire to plunge her fair body beneath the waves, that they might bear her far, far away from the scene of her past happiness. And now after long, long years the same struggle was going on in the same spot. No, not the same struggle! Was he not a man, strong of soul? Even should the unhappy woman, who had hidden all her misery in the grave by one swift plunge, arise from the water and stretch out her white arms to lure him in, he would not heed her. Kitty shuddered. Had not Henriette said that whoever had once seen Flora love could understand that a man would die sooner than resign her? And was there now any choice for him, since she had told him that she hated him?

Kitty ran hastily back into the garden, as if the drowned woman with the long, fair braids were actually arising by the dim shore to bar her way.

It was growing dark. The forest which had been the scene of the rude attack of the afternoon looked like a black pall over the low hills, and the ploughed meadow-land lay smooth and still, giving no token that millions of living germs were there thrusting forth tiny arms beneath the thin crust, ready to issue forth into the golden sunlight a waving field of grain. Upon the roof the weathercock creaked in the moaning evening wind, which was gradually increasing and would bring torrents of spring rain during the night. The boughs of the silver poplars by the fence tossed to and fro, and the loose branches in the half-finished arbour cracked beneath its strong breath. Those branches were still bare. When they were covered with leafy greenery, how would it be with everything that lay at present unsolved in the dark lap of destiny? Would the dean's widow ever sit there in the green retreat she so loved, peaceful and happy as in the little parsonage garden of long ago? Never, if her darling were unhappy or if she lost him.

Kitty timidly turned around the western end of the house. The softened light of a night-lamp gleamed from the windows of the sick-room: the struggle was not yet ended. The doctor stood by one of the windows, his back turned to the young girl, his right hand raised as if imposing silence. What had she just been saying,—that figure in the dim background, not tall enough to allow more of her to be seen than the defiant movement of the white lace fichu above the golden blonde curls on the forehead? Had she again impertinently alluded to his profession?

Kitty shivered with nervous agitation, and in her indignation she half resolved to interfere to recall the faithless woman to a sense of her duty. Should she not enter at once, place herself by his side, and confront her perjured sister with all the might of her maidenly scorn and anger? What an idea! What would he say to such interference on the part of a third person? Suppose he should look round at the intruder with cool surprise, or thrust her aside as he had lately done by the "determined" little blue flowers—shame and mortification would annihilate her.

She walked hurriedly on, shivering with cold. Robust girl as she was, clear in mind and sound in nerve, she was suddenly seized with a horror of the solitude about her, of the pale light of the golden crescent hung in the heavens, of the monotonous gurgling murmur of the rushing water. Through the kitchen window she saw the dean's widow seated by the shining kitchen lamp, engaged in some household occupation, —a peaceful contrast to the scene in the sick-room. Quiet and soothing as the picture was, in her present feverish state of mind and body she could not join the tranquil old lady, whose clear glance would soon have detected her agitation.

The house-door stood open, while the one leading into the kitchen was closed. Kitty slipped on tip-toe through the dark hall and entered the widow's sitting-room. Here she would try to become calmer, in this darkening, tranquil spot, full of the fragrance of flowers and a refreshing warmth. She seated herself in the arm-chair behind the work-table. The laurels arched above her, the violets and hyacinths on the window-sill sent forth a delicious odour, and the canary-bird, who was just adjusting himself in the gloom for repose, hopped from perch to perch, with an occasional shrill chirp: there was some life near her, if only in the breast of a timid little bird. But she did not grow calmer. Through these rooms the lovely forsaken woman had wandered in her widow's weeds, and the smiling cherubs still ornamenting the ceiling had looked down upon her outbreaks of anguish, her bitter despair. In vain did Kitty try to banish the phantom, and the thought that perhaps Bruck, too, might not survive the pain of separation. Had not Henriette said so? she had seen his intense affection in the early days of his betrothal; she must know how it would be.

The dean's widow entered with the lamp which she placed every evening upon the doctor's study-table. She closed the windows, pulled down the shades, saw that the fire in the stove burned clear, and then left the room, without having perceived the young girl in her retreat. Her gentle step died away as the door closed, but immediately afterward a manly tread was heard in the hall, and the doctor came into the room.

He paused for a moment upon the threshold, and drew a long breath, passing his hand across his brow; he was as unconscious as his aunt had been of the presence, behind the leafy screen at the window, of a human heart throbbing in mortal agitation. The girlish figure cowered, breathless, closer to the window. Was this a miserable, despairing, lonely man for evermore?

He hastily traversed this room and his own, and went to his study-table. Kitty noiselessly arose. Standing in the middle of the room, she could see him in his study where the light of the lamp clearly illumined his face, which still showed traces of the passion that had so lately mastered him. Cheek and brow were crimson, as if he had been walking far and fast beneath a noonday sun. He had indeed travelled a weary road, leading through ruined hopes and illusions destroyed! Had he reached the end, the dreary goal where the lovely Fata Morgana melted away and the terrible solitude of the future confronted him?

As he stood, he wrote a few lines upon a sheet of paper, which he then put into an envelope. He did it hastily, in evident agitation. He addressed it as hurriedly. Whose name did he write? Could he think of aught in this hour save the terrible crisis through which he was passing? The letter could be for no one but Flora. Was it a last farewell, or the crushing denunciation of a dying man?

And now he poured water into the milk-white glass into which she had so lately put her wild-flowers, and, opening a drawer in his table, took from it a tiny vial. From this, carefully holding it against the light, he dropped five clear drops into the glass of water.

The intense emotion which, gradually increasing, had hitherto seemed to paralyze the young girl as she stood thus watching the wretched man, now urged her to action. She suddenly stood by his side, and, placing one hand upon his shoulder, with the other seized the glass he was conveying to his lips, and slowly drew it away.

She could not utter a sound; but all the anguish, the compassionate pity, that filled her soul shone in the brown eyes raised to his in a mute entreaty more eloquent than words. She started back. Good heavens! what had she done? She almost sank on the floor beneath the gaze of astonished inquiry that she encountered. Stammering some inarticulate words, she covered her face with her hands and burst into tears.

He understood it all in a moment. Placing the fatal glass upon the table, he took both her hands in his and drew her towards him. "Kitty, my dear child," he said, in tremulous tones, looking into the tearful face which she tried to turn from him, as she shook her head. The girl, usually so self-possessed and strong, looked at this moment what she really was in years, in experience, and in unspotted purity; her sensibilities, warm and unhackneyed, had led her on to what now left her a prey to maidenly confusion.

She gently withdrew her hands, and hurriedly put her kerchief to her eyes. "Ah, I have deeply offended you, Doctor Bruck!" she said, still struggling with her tears. "You can never forget my folly. Good heaven! how could I suppose that——" She bit her lip to keep from a fresh outburst of weeping. "But do not judge me too harshly," she added, tremulously. "What I have endured to-day might well have confused a far stronger mind than mine."

He scarcely looked at her,—he only glanced at the tender, quivering mouth, as if he did not wish to show how he was moved by her self-accusation; but across his face there flitted the smile which she knew so well.

"You have not offended me," he said, soothingly; "and how could I dare to sit in judgment on your strength of mind? I do not know, I will not attempt to discover, nor even to dispute, the estimate you must have formed of my character, my mode of thought, my temperament, to lead you to such a conclusion. The error has given me a moment of life which I shall certainly never forget. And now calm yourself, or rather permit me to exercise my office of physician." He took up the glass and offered it to her. "I was not seeking in this glass the quiet that you feared——" He stopped, and there was a moment's pause. "I had been carried away, mastered by irritation, passion, and that, too, in a sick-room. I could not forgive myself, did I not know that I, in common with the rest of us, have nerves and blood that will not always yield the mastership to my will. A few drops of this"—he pointed to the tiny vial—"will soothe nervous agitation."

She took the glass from his hand and obediently drained its contents.

"And now let me entreat your forgiveness for the wretched hour you have so lately passed. I am responsible for that miserable scene, for I might have prevented it by a few words spoken at the right time." He smiled, so bitterly, so sarcastically, that it went to the young girl's soul. "Those few of my friends who, from pure goodness of heart, have not quite dropped me, accuse me of a crushing quantity of beggarly pride, because I am not fond of prating of myself. This 'beggarly pride' has been a kind of Cassandra-curse to me. The world takes silence for incapacity, for want of judgment, and so people see no necessity for imposing moral constraint upon themselves in their dealings with me. I see men professing to be talented and intellectual commit the clumsiest blunders, and I can predict with mathematical precision their conduct under certain circumstances—ah, it is too disgusting!" He lightly stamped his foot upon the floor, and shook himself, as if to be rid of some vile reptile.

He was far from self-possessed; the indignant blood was still in commotion, and the frivolous creature whose wanton hand had so made discord in this harmonious nature smiled down from the wall in white Iphigenia robes, her hands calmly folded, her expression thoughtfully spiritual, almost holy. Then she had prized and sought his affection, his approval; then she had been determined to be the realization of his ideal, the beneficent fairy of the home of the future illustrious professor. She never could have fulfilled this determination: that home would have been merely the soil in which her greed of admiration would have flourished. He might have had a brilliant salon, but no home; an ambitious woman of the world to do the honours of his house, but no true, loving wife, no "sympathetic companion." He was no longer blind, and yet he would not release her. Or was the link at length broken, now that Flora had flung so boldly in his teeth her hatred of him? Kitty did not know what had occurred after her departure; but, whatever it had been, there was no longer any reason for her remaining here in his study.

The doctor noticed the dark look she cast at the picture, and now saw that she was preparing to leave the room.

"Yes, go," he said. "Henriette's maid has come, and is already established for the night. The state of the invalid is now such as to allow you to return to the villa easy in mind, to assist the Frau President, according to her desire, at her tea-table this evening. I give you my word that you need feel no anxiety. I will faithfully watch over your sick sister," he repeated, as she tried to protest against being sent away. "But give me your hand once more!" He held out his own, and she quickly and willingly laid hers in it. "And now, whatever may be said of me to you to-day, do not let it influence you to misjudge me. In a day or two she"—he did not mention her name, but nodded, with a bitter smile, towards Flora's picture—"will be of an entirely different mind; it is this knowledge that makes me firm. I cannot lay myself open to the reproach of having taken advantage of a—favourable moment."

She looked up at him entirely mystified, and he nodded significantly with a strange air of resignation, as if to say, "Yes, thus matters stand," but neither of them spoke a word.

"Good-night, good-night," he said, immediately afterwards, and, with a light pressure, dropped her hand and turned to his writing-table, while she left the room. Involuntarily she looked round as she stood upon the threshold: he was, oddly enough, raising the empty glass to his lips, but, as he did so, it fell from his hand and was broken into a hundred fragments upon the floor.

In the sick-room she found Flora ready for departure, looking as if every fibre of her frame were thrilling with nervous excitement. "Where have you been, Kitty?" she said, crossly. "Grandmamma is waiting for us; it will be your fault if our tea is flavoured with reproaches."

Kitty did not reply. She threw over her shoulders the wrap which the maid had brought her, and went to the bedside. Henriette was sleeping quietly; the feverish colour was fading from her cheeks. The young girl gently breathed kiss after kiss upon the small transparent hand that lay relaxed upon the counterpane, and then followed her imperious sister.

In the hall a lamp was burning, and a footman from the villa stood waiting. The doctor came from his study at this moment, and the blush of shame returned to Kitty's cheek as she saw him hand to the man the note she had supposed to contain a last farewell to his false love, and which bore the address of a young physician in town.

Flora swept past him, as if unwilling to interrupt his instructions to the servant, and vanished in the darkness. But Kitty went into the kitchen to take leave of the widow. The old lady gravely shook her head when she found that Flora had actually left the house without even bidding her good-night, but she said nothing, and followed the doctor into the sick-room to see the invalid once more before retiring to her own apartment.

Flora waited just outside of the house until the servant's footsteps had died away on the other side of the bridge. The light from the open hall-door feebly illumined her angry face: it looked as if a curse were hovering upon the parted lips. With an air of unspeakable contempt her gaze rested upon the old house, marking the red tiled floor and bare walls of the hall, and the entire exterior of the dwelling, as if to make of the whole a complete picture in her mind.

"Oh, yes; greatly to my taste all this would have been,—'a cottage with the man of my choice!'" she said, with intense sarcasm, slowly nodding her head: "a husband without position or influence! a dreary old barn for a home in the midst of a lonely field! and an isolated existence for the means of which my own limited income must suffice! I have never known before what humiliation was. To-day, for the first time, in the midst of those sordid surroundings, I felt dragged down, as it were, from the pedestal where spotless descent, easy circumstances, and the possession of intellectual force have placed me. God grant that Henriette's illness may not terminate fatally! I could not bid her a last farewell, for this house shall never again see me within its walls. Never was woman more shamefully deluded than I have been; I could rage against myself for having been so blindly and unsuspectingly lured into such a snare."

She turned and hurried towards the bridge. The moonlight, gleaming like a thin silvery veil upon the water, shed its pale rays upon her; the wind, already rising, fluttered her dress and, tearing the shiny silken covering from her head, tossed up the light ringlets in snaky curls above her white brow.

"He does not release me, in spite of my prayers and struggles," she said, pausing in the middle of the bridge, to her sister, who had followed her, and now would have passed her without a word. "You were there; you heard what was said. He is acting without honour, without pity, like some usurer, who has failed to degrade his victim but yet insists upon the fulfilment of the bargain made between them. Let him content himself with the shadow of justice he boasts on his side. From this moment I am free!"

With the last words, she drew the betrothal ring from her finger and hurled it far into the rolling water.

"Flora, what have you done?" Kitty exclaimed, as she leaned over the railing of the bridge and stretched out her hand as if to catch the ring ere it fell. In vain: it had sunk beneath the stream. Would the waters bear it away, or would it fall and lie buried near the house where sorrow had come with the advent within its walls of faithful, loving human souls? The young girl half expected to see the pale, dead woman who had once found refuge beneath those waves arise from their glittering depths to bring back the rejected symbol of fidelity. With a shudder, she covered her eyes with her hand.

"You little fool, you look as if I had thrown myself in!" Flora said, with a cold smile. "A woman with less force of character and will might have done so perhaps. *I* simply cast from me the last link of a detested chain." She raised her hand, and seemed to caress the finger whence the ring had been drawn. "It was but a slender circlet of gold, simple as the man there"—she nodded towards the house—"would pretend to be with his affectation of Spartan manners, and yet it weighed upon me like iron. Let it lie buried and rust: I begin a new life."

Yes, she had thrown aside the burden,—thrown it aside "at all hazards," as she herself had said. The bugbear of a hated marriage vanished: the sun of fame would rise in its stead.

Flora hurried on as if the ground were burning beneath her feet, and Kitty silently followed her. In her young mind all was for the moment a wild tempest of confusion and uncertainty; the sound, healthy judgment she was wont to bring to bear upon men and things was obscured: she was tossing, rudderless, between right and wrong, truth and falsehood. Did not the beautiful creature beside her—the personification, as it were, of glaring wrong, arrogance, and cruel self-will—conduct herself with all the determination and complacent resolve of one to whom no other course lay open? Was not Flora trampling beneath her feet her plighted word, every consideration of truth and honour?

In the vestibule of the villa the servant informed the two sisters that the Frau President had visitors: two old friends had come to tea.

"So much the better," Flora said to Kitty. "I am really not in the mood to act Scheherazade for grandmamma to-night. Madame the general's wife always has her pocket full of gossip and news from town; so I can be spared."

She went in, as she said, to preside for half an hour at the tea-table, and then she retired to her room with her "surcharged heart." But Kitty excused herself on the plea of a headache. It seemed, indeed, as though what she had passed through were bringing illness to both head and heart.

CHAPTER XIV.

The next morning all were astir at Villa Baumgarten. Towards midnight a telegraphic despatch had announced the return of the councillor from Berlin, and an hour later he had arrived. He brought with him two business friends, commercial grandees, who were obliged to continue their journey in the afternoon, and for whom, to give them an opportunity of seeing several of their friends in the neighbouring capital, the councillor, before he slept, arranged a large breakfast for the next morning,—of course for gentlemen only. Cook and housekeeper had their hands full, and servants ran hither and thither noiselessly.

Kitty passed a sleepless night. The events of the previous day, and anxiety on Henriette's account, banished slumber from her eyelids. Sitting for hours at her window, she gazed out over the wind-tossed trees of the park, to distinguish, if possible, in the waning moonlight and through the falling rain, a glimpse of the white weathercock on the roof of the house by the stream; but the low dwelling had vanished, as it were, and all was quiet there, although Kitty hourly expected that some messenger sent thence would rouse the inmates of the villa with evil tidings.

From the other window she had seen the councillor arrive. In a twinkling, as if sprung from the ground, the villa servants had ranged themselves about the carriage with their lanterns; the yellow light illumined the white pillars of the porch, and sparkled and shone on the silver-mounted harness and the sleek coats of the horses,—nay, it was even powerful enough to bring into relief one or two of the marble figures in the shrubbery on the other side of the drive. It all looked most aristocratic. The councillor of commerce had sprung lightly from the carriage, in his rich, fur-lined travelling cloak, every motion of his lithe, youthfully-elastic figure proclaiming the man of wealth just grown wealthier still,—a gleaming comet, to whose sparkling track the glittering stream of gold was magnetically attracted. He had conducted his guests to their apartments, leaving the house himself, accompanied by a couple of lantern-bearing servants, towards two o'clock, to seek his rooms in the tower. Then all had gradually grown quiet in the villa; but the wind, whistling and shrieking about the house, still drove repose from Kitty's eyes. At daybreak, however, she fell asleep, to her great annoyance, for it made her late: instead of being in the house by the river at six o'clock, as she had intended, it was nine before she left the villa.

The morning was clear and beautiful. The tempest of wind had moderated to that soft southern breeze that brings upon its wings the fragrance of the first spring flowers, and caressingly but persistently seeks to draw the brown veil from the soft, shy buds. The birds were twittering upon the roof of the doctor's house, the boughs of the cherry-trees at one of its corners were sprinkled with the tender white of the opening blossoms, and the young grass could no longer hide from the light in the glorious morning sunshine. The former bleaching-ground was covered, as it were, with a misty green veil.

As Kitty crossed the bridge the waters were flowing clear and sunlit, almost peacefully, beneath its decaying wooden arches. Strange! The waves that last evening had received into their depths the rejected ring were far on their way towards the distant ocean; they alone could tell of the treacherous white hands that had burst asunder an oppressive chain.

The house by the river was pervaded by what seemed almost an air of festal solemnity. The red tiled floor of the hall was strewn with fine white sand, and there was perceptible a delicate pastille fragrance; the little table near the hall-door was covered with a fresh napkin, and upon it stood an antique clay vase filled with evergreens, snowdrops, and anemones. The faithful old cook-maid was once more installed in her kitchen, with sleeves rolled up and a dazzling white apron tied around her waist, her round red cheeks shining with good humour and content. And why was the dean's widow thus early in the morning dressed in dark-brown silk, with a fine old white lace barbe upon her gray hair, and the same delicate material around her neck and wrists? Kitty's heart sank within her. Was it all in honour of the false love who was expected to-day to visit her sick sister?

The old lady said not a word with regard to it. She only seemed agitated, and in her eyes and in her voice there were traces of tears. She greeted Kitty with the joyful intelligence that the invalid had passed an excellent night, with no return of the hemorrhage.

In gratitude for this good news Kitty kissed the delicate hand extended to her, when suddenly the widow, usually so reserved, clasped her arms about the girlish figure and pressed her to her heart like a daughter, before leading her into the sick-room.

Henriette was sitting propped up in bed while her maid was arranging her abundant hair, the doctor having retired to take some rest only an hour previously. The sick girl's long, thin face, in which the cheek-bones stood out prominently and the large eyes were encircled by dark rings, looked almost death-like, and Kitty was shocked at the alteration produced in it by the last twenty-four hours, although its expression was much happier. She could not say enough of the doctor's kindness and care, nor of how comfortable and content she felt in the dear old room, which she dreaded to think of ever leaving. She begged Kitty to return to the villa to get a book which she had promised to the widow. Flora had borrowed it of her sister and must be asked where it was. And then she whispered in Kitty's ear that Flora and her grandmother must not weary her by coming to see her too often. She had not the slightest suspicion of the scene that had been enacted at her bedside on the previous evening, and that by her means the long-threatened storm had broken forth.

Kitty could hardly bear to meet her eye, and breathed a sigh of relief when the invalid concluded by begging her to fetch the book as soon as possible, and to bring her several articles from her writing-desk, the key of which she handed to her.

In an hour, therefore, the young girl re-entered the villa. She was thoroughly possessed by the melancholy impression made upon her by Henriette's whole appearance,—the waxen pallor of her face, the sunken features, and the large, brilliant eyes. She recoiled as if from a blow when through the open door of the conservatory she saw the breakfast-table set out with flowers and silver and every costly delicacy that could be procured. A thick Turkish carpet covered the entire marble floor of the Moorish room. The feet of the guests must be made warm enough, and their heads also, to judge by the flasks of choice wine just arrived from the tower cellar.

Kitty ascended to Henriette's room and collected all the articles the sick girl had asked for, and then she dutifully went to bid the Frau President good-morning. As she passed along the corridor her light step was unheard in the hall below by two of the servants, one of whom had just received a parcel from the letter-carrier.

"Good gracious, here is this parcel back again for the third time!" he said, fretfully. "I am tired of the sight of it. I shall have to wrap it up again to-morrow and put a fresh address upon the cover. Our Fräulein must think we have precious little to do." He turned the parcel about irresolutely. "The best thing would be to throw it into the kitchen fire and——"

"What is inside?" asked the other.

"Quantities of paper; and the Fräulein has written upon it herself, in big, sprawling letters, 'Woman.' It may be all very fine——" He paused, in terror, and put on a respectful air: Kitty had descended the stairs and passed by him to the Frau President's apartment.

She was not admitted. The maid came out and informed her that her mistress was occupied in receiving an early visit from one of the ladies of the court. Therefore Kitty went to Flora's room to get the book Henriette wished for. She felt a repugnance to crossing the threshold, her heart beat almost audibly from inward agitation, and she was obliged to admit to herself that with this sister she had not one single spark of sympathy. All the indignation which she had so tried to conquer during the night stirred again within her and threatened to master her.

Perhaps Flora experienced similar sensations. She was standing in the middle of the room, beside a large table covered with books and pamphlets, and looked up with flashing eyes at the intruder. Ah, no; her anger was probably due to the returned parcel. There it lay, torn open, and its beautiful mistress had just scornfully tossed into the waste-paper basket the letter that had accompanied it. It was well that Fräulein von Giese, the malicious maid of honour, was not looking on. Flora's "little finger" had apparently made a small mistake with regard to the destiny of "Woman."

"You have just come from Henriette," Flora said, hastily covering the rejected manuscript with the blue paper in which it had been wrapped. "I hear she is doing very well; I sent over at eight o'clock to inquire. Moritz has no consideration; he sent me a note, written over-night, in consequence of which I was obliged to rise early to be dressed in time, as he wished *à tout prix* to present his guests to grandmamma and me before breakfast. As if the fate of the world hung upon this presentation! Grandmamma will not be greatly edified."

She looked charming. It has been said that we are all apt involuntarily to dress in accordance with the mood of the hour. If this be true, Flora's awakening must have been unusually gay and glad, for her whole figure was draped in the blue of the summer skies. Even in her light curls there was a blue ribbon.

The dress harmonized but ill, to be sure, with the apartment, which looked gloomy and chilly to one entering from the brilliant sunshine outside, and would have been a more fitting background for the figure of some pale, worn scholar than it was for this graceful azure fairy. Neither did the bright and yet delicate hue suit the lady's expression of countenance, which betokened ill humour and a depression not to be concealed. Not a word was said of the occurrences of the previous evening. Apparently they were buried and forgotten; even the finger so lately stripped of its ring had found indemnification for its loss, and sparkled in the splendour of diamonds.

At Kitty's request, Flora went to a book-shelf and took from it the wished-for volume. "Henriette is not going to read herself?" she asked, over her shoulder.

"Doctor Bruck would hardly allow it; his aunt wishes to read the book," Kitty replied, coldly, as she took the volume from her sister.

A sneer hovered upon Flora's lips, and vexation shone in her eyes. She evidently regarded this mention of Bruck's name as great want of tact upon Kitty's part.

Kitty turned to go. But, as she opened the door, the councillor made his appearance, in a state of great hurry and agitation, although he looked quite radiant.

"Stay, Kitty!" he exclaimed, gaily, and stretched out his arms to bar her way. "I must convince myself that you are well and uninjured." He led her back into the room, closed the door, and threw his hat upon the table. "Now tell me, for heaven's sake, the truth of this harrowing story which Anton has been narrating to me as I have been dressing!" he went on. "My people, foolishly enough, said not one word of it all to me last night, for fear of spoiling my night's rest. I have strictly forbidden any such ill-judged forbearance for the future." He ran his hands through his hair. "I am outraged! What will the world think of my want of feeling? Henriette sick in bed, and a formal breakfast arranged for this morning! Tell me the truth of it. They say you were attacked by a mob of furies."

"*I* alone was the object of the attack, Moritz," said Flora. "Henriette and Kitty suffered only because they were with me. I cannot help saying that, to my mind, the principal blame in allowing matters to come to such a point is your own: you ought to have taken decided measures at the first hint of discontent among these wretches. A man of sufficient force of character is always master of such a situation. But your perpetual dread of offending and shocking makes you so weak——"

"Yes, weak enough with you, and with grandmamma," the councillor, pale with vexation, interrupted her. "You, especially, never rested until I recalled the promise I had given my workmen, and so irritated them intensely. Bruck is right——"

"I beg you spare me there!" Flora angrily exclaimed. "If you have no other authority upon whom to rely——"

The councillor approached her and looked into her eyes

with amazement in his own. "What, Flora, still so hostile?"

"Do you imagine me so deplorably weak that I can assume and lay aside my views as one puts on and takes off a garment?" she asked, in reply.

"No, not that; but are you not rash thus to defy our whole cultivated society?"

"What is society to me?" She laughed aloud. "'Our whole cultivated society!'" she repeated. "Will you tell me how you can possibly find any connection between it and your poor failure of a protégé?"

The councillor shook his head, and took her hand in his he was almost speechless with surprise. "Why, is it—can it be possible? Do you not know——"

"Good heavens! what is there to know?" she interrupted him, with an impatient frown, and a slight stamp of her small foot.

At this moment the door opened, and the Frau President entered. She was simply dressed in violet silk. It might have been that the colour made her face look shrunken and sallow, or perhaps she had had a restless night as the result of her yesterday's agitation,—she certainly looked haggard and old.

The councillor hurried towards her and kissed her hand respectfully, reminding her that he had been desirous of paying his respects to her half an hour before, but had been informed that she had not yet left her sleeping-apartment, where she was receiving a visit from Fräulein von Berneck, one of the court ladies.

"Yes, the good creature came to express her sympathy for Henriette's illness and the shameful attack made upon Flora," she said. "We shall have a most trying day to-day: the whole town is ringing with what has occurred, and our friends are indignant; they will all be here to inquire for us."

She sank wearily into an arm-chair; her voice trembled,

and all the elasticity which usually triumphed so victoriously over her years seemed gone. "Fräulein von Berneck had another reason, and a principal one, be sure, for coming," she began again. "I know her well: she is one of those who long to be the first to tell a piece of good news, and is quite careless as to whether it may still be a court-secret or not. She came to tell me privately of the good fortune that has befallen our family." She rose and clasped her hands. "And yet what a terrible dilemma for me! I cannot tell absolutely whether to mourn or to rejoice. It certainly is most distressing that at court, where the best example ought to be set, the old proverbial ingratitude should be shown. What sacrifices Bär has made for the royal family! And suddenly he is set aside as if the faithful old man were not in existence. And so full of vigour as he is, in body and mind,—they are going to pension him!"

"And this is old Von Berneck's good news?" Flora asked, indignantly.

"Of course not!" the Frau President replied, emphasizing her words strongly. "Flora, the strangest things are happening every day. Could you have thought it possible an hour ago that Bruck should be Hofrath and physician to the royal household?"

"Nonsensical court-gossip! What will not idle brains contrive!" laughed Flora. "Hofrath and court-physician! And you listened to such ridiculous stuff, grandmamma, and were congratulated upon it?" And she broke again into a ringing laugh.

"Do you really live so far here from the civilized world that you read no newspapers?" exclaimed the councillor. "Do you actually know nothing—positively nothing—of all that has occurred, and that concerns us so nearly? Why, I have returned a day earlier on this very account. I could not rest for joy. All the papers are full of the wonderful skill Bruck has shown in L——g: it is the topic of the day in Berlin society. The Crown-Prince of R——, who is studying in L——g, had a fall from his horse, and his head was so seriously and dangerously injured that no surgeon could be found willing to undertake the only operation that could save his life: even the famous Professor H—— refused to operate. But he remembered that Bruck had treated successfully a similar case in his last campaign, to every one's astonishment. So he instantly summoned him by telegraph——"

"And you imagine this to have been *your* Bruck, your protégé?" Flora interrupted him. She tried to smile, but her ashy lips, as well as her whole pale, mocking face, seemed paralyzed to marble.

"It certainly was *my* Bruck, as I am proud to call him," the councillor replied, with evident satisfaction. He was rejoiced indeed at this fortunate turn of affairs. True, he had long ceased to have any scruples with regard to his silence in a certain matter; the manner of the miller's death no longer troubled his repose,—for he was a genuine child of the times, an egotist, who, when the choice was to be made between "another" and "self," was never for a moment in doubt that "self" was to be preferred. "And, besides this, a pamphlet he has just published has made an immense sensation in medical circles," he continued. "They say he has made a surgical discovery of great importance to the profession. Oh, there is no denying it,—a brilliant career awaits Bruck."

"Impossible!" Flora said, in a strangely altered tone. She looked like a player who stakes his last guinea upon one card. "I am not to be imposed upon! Either there is some mistake here as to the name, or—the whole story is a fabrication."

At this obstinate and unjustifiable incredulity the councillor fairly forgot the courteous forbearance and self-control he was wont to exercise in his intercourse with the ladies of his household. He stamped his foot angrily and turned away.

H*

The Frau President stood by the table, her white, wrinkled fingers playing nervously upon its surface, her eyes fixed anxiously upon her grandchild. She entirely understood what she must feel upon hearing thus extolled the man whom she had so shamefully depreciated and slandered. It was a lamentable defeat; but these were moments in which a true woman of the world was bound to assert her supremacy.

"You cannot help yourself, Flora," she said, calmly; "you will have to believe it at last. For my part, strange as it is, I doubt no longer. The Duke of D—— is uncle on the mother's side to the crown-prince; of course he is rejoiced at his nephew's recovery, for yesterday evening I saw the order of the D—— royal household lying upon Bruck's writing-table."

"And you tell me this *now* for the first time, grand-mamma?" Flora almost screamed. "Why was I not told yesterday? Why have you kept it from me?"

"Kept it from you?" the Frau President repeated, so indignantly that her head shook with the tremulousness that frequently attacks the old when angry. "What impertinence! What, I should like to know, could induce me to keep such a matter to myself, except the fact that during the last few months you have resented the mention of Bruck's name in your presence? I have certainly avoided it——"

"Because my views on the subject were quite in accordance with your own, chère grand'mère."

"Not at all; but because my whole soul revolts at outbursts of passion. You have been his bitterest opponent; you have judged him more harshly than the severest of his colleagues: the slightest attempt to excuse him always provoked a scene. Poor Henriette and Moritz can tell a tale upon that subject. And have you not this very moment shown how any favourable intelligence with regard to him is received by you?" She must have been agitated indeed so far to forget her almost invariable rule of silence upon disagreeable topics as thus to pass in review before others Flora's misconduct.

Flora was silent. She stood at the window, her back turned to the rest, but her gasping breath showed the struggle through which she was passing.

"And, besides, tell me when I could have told you," the Frau President continued. "Hardly yesterday, when you scarcely showed yourself in the drawing-room, after you came home, to say 'good-evening' either to me or to my guests. Neither was there any time to tell you while we were never alone at the doctor's, when the meagre comforts of his home had put you into such an ill humour."

"They were a source of annoyance to you, my dear grandmother, you will please to remember. You are mistaken as regards myself."

Kitty opened wide her honest brown eyes at this audacious denial; the anathema hurled yesterday against the "dreary old barn" still rang in her ears.

"There is no reasoning with you. I know you well. With all your boasted love of honesty and straightforwardness, you are ready to hide behind a falsehood as soon as it suits you to do so!" the Frau President, by this time thoroughly angry, declared, and, as she moved her hand upon the table, she pushed aside the bundle of manuscript lying there. The cover again fell off, revealing the "big, sprawling letters" of the title.

"Ah, is this here again upon its zigzag journey through the world?" she asked, pointing to the papers. Her tone showed how malicious she, the advocate of moderation in all things, could be. "I should think you might at last allow it its natural rest in the waste-paper basket. This perpetual offering of it for publication, with the consequent repeated rejection of it by the publishers, is, since you are so nearly connected with me, becoming unendurable. I should like to know how you would bear it if one of us should even hint a doubt of your 'great intellectual capacity;' and yet it comes to you from others every four or five weeks, put down in black and white——"

"Do not chafe yourself needlessly, grandmamma. You, as well as certain other people, may easily be mistaken," Flora interrupted her, glancing the while angrily towards her young sister. Had not the chit heard a like unfavourable judgment passed upon her mental powers on the previous day? "You are out of sorts, because you have lost in Von Bär a good friend at court,—and indeed I cannot but sympathize with you, for Bruck will hardly understand how to further your small interests there, even for my sake. It is hard for you, very hard, and yet I cannot see why I should be your victim. I will ask permission to withdraw until the household skies are again clear." She gathered together her papers, and vanished, like a blue cloud, behind the door leading to her dressing-room.

"She is so very eccentric," the Frau President said, with a sigh. "There is nothing in her of her mother, who was all gentleness and docility. Mangold did very wrong in placing her at the head of his household while she was so young. I did all I could to prevent it, but I might as well have talked to the wind. You know well enough, Moritz, how obstinate Mangold could be."

Kitty went towards the door to leave the room. It was undeniable that Flora's early release from all authority had been an injury to her, but the young girl could not stay and hear her dead father so blamed for—refusing, for excellent reasons, to allow his mother-in-law to take the lead in his household.

The councillor followed her and took her hand. "You are so pale, Kitty, so grave and quiet," he said. "I am afraid you are still suffering from the effects of the events of yesterday, my poor child." It was not said at all in the tone of an elderly guardian.

"Kitty has been pale and silent for some days now," the Frau President hastily remarked. "I know what is the matter with her: she is homesick. You need not wonder at it, my dear Moritz. Kitty is used to the quiet life of the middle classes; they make an idol of her in Dresden; everything in the modest household revolves about the wealthy foster-child. With the best will on our part, that cannot be so here. We live too much in the world; all our social customs, the elements of our society, are so different, that she must necessarily feel oppressed and uncomfortable with us." She approached the young girl and gently stroked her cheek. "Am I not right, my child?"

"I am sorry to be forced to say 'no,' Frau President," Kitty replied, firmly, and, as she spoke, she drew back her head, evidently in protest against further caresses. "I am not made an idol of; everything in the household does not revolve about the heiress." She laughed archly. "The poor heiress has more than ever expected of her, and her errors find less indulgence than they did before she was rich. And the distinguished elements of your social circle are by no means so foreign to me as you suppose. The Prime-Minister Von B—— is a near friend of my foster-parents. Our drawing-room is, it is true, too small to accommodate card-tables, but it is a rendezvous for eminent literary men, and is often sought by musical celebrities, when, I assure you, my poor little cottage piano does good service." And again a charming and merry smile hovered upon her lips,—not, however, devoid of sarcasm: there was, indeed, an antagonistic vein in her composition.

"Thank God, my temperament is such as not to allow of my being homesick wherever I know that I am of use," she said, turning to the councillor. "So do not be afraid, Moritz, but rather give me leave to remain here for an indefinite length of time—for Henriette's sake."

"Good heaven, I have no more earnest desire than to keep you here!" he exclaimed, with an eagerness that struck even Kitty as strange.

The Frau President was again standing by the table, turning over the leaves of a book, at which she was looking so earnestly that she seemed to have neither eyes nor ears for aught else. "Of course, my dear Kitty," she said, indifferently, "you will remain here as long as you are content to do so; only your stay must not partake in the smallest degree of the character of self-sacrifice,—that we must most decidedly prohibit. Nanni is an excellent nurse, and my maid is ready to assist her if necessary. You can leave your dear invalid without anxiety."

"Let the motive be what it may, dearest grandmamma, it suffices that Kitty wishes to stay with us," the councillor eagerly interposed. He could not turn his eyes away from the young girl, who stood entirely unmoved by the words either of the Frau President or of her guardian. "Why, in the joyful hope that you would stay with us, I ordered the new grand piano——" He broke off to breathe an ecstatic kiss upon the closed thumb and forefinger of his right hand. "Kitty, you have an instrument now in comparison with which the one in the music-room is a mere spinnet. I ordered it, I say, sent directly here."

"Oh, Moritz, that is not what I meant!" cried the young girl, thoughtlessly, with a look of actual terror in her eyes. "God forbid! Dresden is and always must be my home, and Villa Baumgarten only a temporary abode." She laughed merrily. "A grand piano would be a clumsy piece of luggage to carry about with me."

"I venture to predict that you will entertain another opinion with regard to Dresden one of these days," he rejoined, with a meaning smile. "The grand piano will be here to-morrow, and will be placed for the present in your room."

The Frau President closed her book and rested her small white hand upon the cover. "You have made other arrangements than those we agreed upon," she said, with apparent composure. "They embarrass me somewhat, but I willingly comply with them. I will write to Baroness Steiner to-day and postpone the visit she was to pay us during the month of May."

"But I cannot see why——"

"Because we cannot accommodate her, my dear Moritz. Her companion, who comes with her, was to have Kitty's room."

The councillor shrugged his shoulders. "I am very sorry, then. Of course my ward must stay where she is."

He opposed her! He dared to look calmly into the irritated old lady's angry eyes and think it quite natural that the Frau Baroness von Steiner should give place to Kitty,—he who once would have moved heaven and earth, who thought no sacrifice too great, if thereby he might tempt any person of distinction to be his guest! The thin coating of social varnish which his intercourse with refined society had given him had suddenly been rubbed off, exposing the coarse, common nature of the parvenu. True, he now possessed rank, and was wealthier than most others of his present station,—he had just reaped another golden harvest,—he could plant himself defiantly upon his money-bags, and—this he was doing.

The old lady bit her lip. "I will write immediately," she said, and gathered up her train to go. "The situation in which I find myself placed, from no fault of my own, is scarcely an enviable one, I must say," she said, in a tone of some bitterness, elevating her eyebrows and speaking over her shoulder.

"And all on my account!" Kitty exclaimed, approaching,

and extending her hand to detain the Frau President. "Moritz, you cannot mean that I, young girl as I am, should exclude any friend of the Frau President's. It cannot be. Have I not my own home in the mill? I shall take up my abode there when Frau von Steiner arrives."

"That you certainly will not, my dear Kitty; I decidedly protest against that," the Frau President rejoined, coldly but firmly, and all the haughty arrogance of her nature shone in her eyes. "Your mother never had any unkindness upon my part to complain of; but this intimate association of the villa and the mill is repugnant to my very soul, and least of all would I expose such a connection to the severely critical eye of my refined and aristocratic friend." She stiffly inclined her head. "I shall be in the blue drawing-room, Moritz, in case you wish to present your guests." And she left the room.

The councillor waited with a scornful air until the rustle of her silken robes had died away and the door of the music-room had closed audibly, and then he indulged in a low chuckling laugh.

"You have had your lesson, Kitty," he said. "There is no doubt that the velvet paws conceal sharp claws. Yes, yes, the old cat knows how to scratch. I myself could show scars enough. But, thank Heaven, her turn has come! She must endure what she most abhors; she is no longer dangerous. With Von Bär pensioned, her influence at court and in society is destroyed." He rubbed his hands in smiling satisfaction. "Not a hair's-breadth shall you stir, my dear child; you have a better right in my house than all the rest of them, —remember that!"

He was interrupted. A servant entering announced that the guests awaited their host. Moritz hastily seized his hat, and would have given Kitty his arm, but she slipped past him into the corridor. This transformed guardian, with his bewildering tenderness of voice and manner, pleased her not at all; his cold, business-like letters had been much more to her taste. What a strange change there was in him! Involuntarily she thought of her recent reception in this house; she seemed still to hear the anxious whisper in which the councillor had reminded her of the respect she owed to the Frau President; and here he was, sneering at her behind her back, and beginning to set bounds to her power, hitherto so unquestioned beneath his roof. All this terrified the young girl; it was inexplicable, and as uncomfortable as the close crimson room, with its musty odour of books and papers, upon which she now turned her back to return to the house by the river.

CHAPTER XV.

By the afternoon of this day the sick-room in the doctor's house looked precisely as it had done when the invalid had first been carried into it forty-eight hours before. At her earnest entreaty, the doctor had banished thence the elegant intruders from the villa. Outside, in the wide hall, upon the rough tiled floor, stood ranged against the wall the apple-green arm-chairs and the elegant screen, while about the simple earthen vase containing the spring bouquet stood the gilt porcelain toilet service. The stoneware was again advanced to honour, and the old-fashioned cushioned chairs, with their black serge covers, were in their former places. The little fountain shot up its tiny spray from a circle of plants growing in earthen pots, and upon a table stood the large cage in which were Henriette's canary-birds, brought hither by the wish of the sick girl. The pretty little golden creatures fluttered in and out, perfectly at home, flying around the bed, eating sugar from their mistress's waxen hand, and swinging in the hanging-baskets of vines suspended in the windows.

Nanni, the maid, had been sent to the villa to rest about noon, and the dean's widow had taken upon her the charge of the invalid for the day. The old lady was still in the brown silk dress, over which she had tied a large white linen apron to deaden the rustle of the silk.

Henriette already knew of the change that had taken place. Her maid had told her how a gentleman from court had been received in the hall by the doctor's aunt and conducted by her into the doctor's study,—a gentleman from the court with Bruck, who had so lately been only dispensary physician! This, in addition to the festal attire of the dean's widow and her joyful face, had excited Henriette's curiosity; she grew restless, and never ceased asking and conjecturing until the doctor sat down by her bedside and in his simple, quiet way informed her of what had occurred. This he had done while Kitty, in Flora's room, was a witness of the scene occasioned by the nearly simultaneous announcement by Fräulein von Berneck and the councillor of their startling news.

In the afternoon Kitty sat at Henriette's bedside. The doctor had been summoned to an audience with the prince, and his aunt was absent to arrange some household matters; the two sisters were alone for the first time. Henriette's face fairly shone with the happiness she dared not speak in words: rest and silence had been prescribed for her. The doctor had strictly forbidden her to indulge again in the fervent expressions of delight which she had terrified him by uttering when he first told her all she asked to know. She obeyed him like a child, and had asked of him or of his aunt no further question; but now when his eye was no longer upon her, when the door had closed behind the careful old lady, she suddenly raised herself up among the pillows, and asked, in a hurried, eager whisper, "Where is Flora?"

"You know your grandmamma sends over every hour to tell you how she longs to be here, but that the visits of sympathy she is obliged to receive to-day have given her no chance to leave the villa."

"Oh, grandmamma!" the invalid repeated, peevishly, with an impatient movement of her head. "I am not asking for *her;* I am speaking of Flora." She clasped her hands and lifted them above her head. "Oh, Kitty, what a brilliant justification of Bruck this is! Thank God, I have lived to see it! If only he is not tempted to stop at the villa on his way home from the palace! Flora must meet him again for the first time here,—here by my bedside. I long to see her in the dust before him!"

"Do not excite yourself, Henriette," Kitty entreated, in a trembling voice.

"Oh, let me speak!" she rejoined, hurriedly. "If Bruck only knew how he tortures me with his injunction of silence! My stifled emotion almost chokes me. I feel as I did yesterday before I lost consciousness." She propped herself on her elbow and buried her hand in the masses of fair hair from which she had tossed away the muslin cap. "Do you remember how contemptuously Flora alluded to this journey from which he has returned so famous, calling it a 'pleasure-trip'?" she asked, looking up at her sister, with eyes gleaming with scorn and anger, while her voice fell into the same tone in which she had uttered the delirious fancies of the previous day, which had been the cause of such a terrible struggle. Kitty shuddered. "Do you remember how she sneered and laughed when Moritz came so near the truth in surmising that the doctor had been called to some patient in L——g? No: although she should entreat his pardon on her knees, she can hardly atone for such wicked folly, such unexampled arrogance. I should like to have one look now into the depths of her soul. Such a crushing mortification! She will scarcely be able to lift her eyes to him or to us when she first sees him."

Kitty had folded her hands in her lap, and her eyelashes drooped above her cheeks as if she were the guilty one. Her poor, passionately-moved sister had no idea that this first meeting never would take place, that Flora's foot would never more enter the "dreary barn." Neither she nor the rest knew that the false love had freed herself by a violent effort, that the symbol of the tie that had bound her—the "simple" golden circlet—lay in the depths of the river beneath the bridge, if the waves had not borne it far away.

"Do say something, Kitty," Henriette complained. "You must be cold-blooded indeed to be so calm in the midst of all this. It is true, you have had no chance to become intimately acquainted with the circumstances, and consequently you may not be able to view matters from a correct point of view. Bruck, for example, can scarcely interest you,—you see him too seldom, and have certainly not spoken ten words to him; but you have been a witness of Flora's detestable manœuvres; you have heard the most heartless expressions from her lips. I should suppose that the sense of justice inherent in every healthy nature might inspire you with a desire, a thirst, to see the offender punished."

Kitty looked up with a strange gleam in her eyes. Certainly the blood was not cold that suddenly dyed crimson her forehead and cheeks, and even the round, snowy throat: it was so stirred that for one moment she forgot that she was sitting by an invalid's bedside, and that it was her duty as a conscientious nurse not to allow even the mention of any exciting subject. "And what then?" she asked, eagerly. "What if Flora should acknowledge with shame how wrong she has been? Could it really matter much to a man so insulted, so outraged? As you yourself say, Flora has openly testified her dislike of him. If he were made a prince, it could not transform this dislike to affection."

"Yes, it would do so instantly in a nature as vain and ambitious as Flora's," Henriette replied, in a tone of bitter scorn. "And Bruck? You will see how at her first advance he will ignore the past as if it had never been." She leaned back and closed her eyes for a moment. "Yes, yes; love is such a profound mystery!" she continued, in a half-whisper, to herself. "And he loves her still; how else explain his patient submission and long-suffering?" She opened her eyes, and there shone in their unearthly brilliancy a mixture of pain and irony. "Even although a demon looked at him from her eyes, and she should strike him with her hands, he would love her still, and kiss the hand raised against him." There was a heart-breaking smile upon the emaciated face, which she turned and buried in the pillow. After a short pause, she said, with firmness, "The change in her will make him happy, and therefore we, on our part, must do all we can to obliterate the memory of these last few miserable months."

Kitty said not a word. The sick girl was awaiting with intense impatience the moment that should see the man whom she idolized as her physician happy once more. How if Flora did not come,—if Henriette should learn at last that the false love had put an end, with her own hand, to what she said had been a long torture to her? "Then you will never mention our names again," Henriette had wailed to Bruck in her delirium of the previous day. The chaos of yesterday still reigned in Kitty's mind. Her conception of moral law was distinct and clear; she was still inexperienced enough to believe that rewards and punishments are just consequences of individual action; and here, in this strangely perverted world, she found it was eagerly desired that falsehood, treachery, and a systematic denial of duty should not only go unpunished, but should even be rewarded by rare good fortune. All pains were taken to breathe no syllable of the wrong done; the criminal must be petted, and thanked most humbly for a conversion which, if it really should occur, would not be the result of repentance, but the effect of a change of outward circumstances. And he whom she had so trampled beneath her feet,—would he take her instantly to his heart again if she condescended to return? Of course; he had never released her, even when she told him that she hated him. And Kitty glowed with indignation at the thought of the pitiable weakness which could induce a man to play so unmanly a part. She would have liked to drown in a passion of tears this knowledge which for a moment darkened all life, even the glorious sunny world of nature; but she suppressed all expression of the strange, sharp pain, and sat still, apparently more "cold-blooded" than ever. Weep? What was the whole miserable story to her? She had nothing to do with it, and nothing further to think about it, except with regard to some wedding-present for her sister, some costly piece of embroidery, which she must begin immediately if the marriage were to take place at Whitsuntide.

The dean's widow came in to lay a branch of budding syringa upon the invalid's coverlet as a greeting from the golden spring that was flinging abroad all sweet odours and the songs of birds upon its health-giving breezes. She insisted upon resuming her place by the bed, declaring that Kitty was not needed there at present, but must go out into the garden and breathe the fresh, sunny air; she surely needed it, for her face still showed traces of yesterday's agitation.

The young girl left the room. Yes, air and sunshine had always proved her good friends, bringing the delicious consciousness of youthful vigour, clearing her moral perceptions, and dispelling all morbid sensations. And the dean's widow was right: the world was all May, the promise of the year was everywhere, and the mild air saturated with sunshine breathed health into mind and body. Kitty went out of the house-door and stood upon the steps, inhaling the fresh breeze as she involuntarily extended her round, firmly-moulded arms. Then, descending into the garden, she looked beyond the low picket-fence into the blue distance, beyond the meadows, beyond the river rolling through them, beyond the cottage-roofs and the church-spire. Oh, mysterious human heart, that in presence of all this glory was still so sad and cast down!

From the low wood-shed at the bottom of the garden came a constant, melodious twitter, and from beneath the eaves darted small, feathered creatures, their backs shining with a steely lustre, their throats rusty brown. The first swallows had come. Those eaves had been their nest for years. How often, as a child, had Kitty, lying in the grass, watched their outcomings and ingoings! but then their chatter had sounded lonely and sad in her ears, accompanied by the monotonous murmur of the water, the only other sound that broke the desolate silence reigning about the deserted house, unless upon autumn days, when the ripe fruit would now and then fall with a soft thud upon the sod. Now spoiled petted birds were trilling their songs from the open windows; the smoke from the chimney soared aloft, and spread a thin, sun-gilded veil above the meadow; beside the shed stood the kennel, and the cross, bristly house-dog tore at his chain and snapped at a pretty little light-brown hen that boldly ventured near him to get a few scattered grains of wheat. The housemaid had brought from her village house a cock and some hens, at the widow's requesi. Yes, everything must revive the memory of the country parsonage of long ago.

Kitty chased the cackling hen away from the cross, growling dog, and wandered slowly about beneath the fruit-trees The dry, dead grass of the old year was here and there dashed with that blue which calls up a gleam of pleasure into the saddest eyes: the first violets were blossoming, and the tall, shapely girl bent as eagerly to pluck them as had the little "miller's mouse" years ago. How strange it seemed to her that only a few weeks before, as her grandfather's heiress, she had been mistress here! The sum which the doctor had paid for this little homestead belonged to her,—the honest, careful savings thrown in with the hoarded wealth of the grasping corn-dealer. She started, and involuntarily dropped the violets she had plucked. The same keen sensation of disgrace and humiliation which she had experienced yesterday in the midst of those furious women again assailed her. At the first shock she had protested against the terrible accusation; but now, whenever she called up in her memory her grandfather's coarse, hard face, she could not but admit to herself that he might have said the cruel words about the "starving mice," and in positive pain she clenched her hands. She knew well that on her mother's side she was sprung from the lowest class of society; she had never dreamed of wishing it otherwise,—she had rather gratefully acknowledged the splendid gift of perfect health and vigour bequeathed to her by her grandmother, whose stalwart arm had wielded the axe in the bracing woodland air; but the coarseness and brutality with which the former mill-servant had treated the poor in his pursuit of wealth disgusted and sickened her, and she could not bear to think of the iron safe with its hoarded treasures.

Without knowing it, her walk towards the river quickened almost to a run. Just where the hawthorn hedge bounding the little garden ran for a short distance along the river-bank, glittered some scattered splinters of white glass, the fragments of the little vessel from which she had on the previous evening drunk the soothing mixture. The maid had carelessly thrown them where the water might perhaps carry them away. A sharp pang shot through Kitty's heart, and tears rushed to her eyes, as she thought of that scene in the doctor's house. How far she had been carried by her impulsiveness! Although the refined, reserved man had instantly spoken soothing words of excuse for her rashness, he must inwardly have smiled in scorn of the strong, healthy girl whose brain could be so filled with sickly sentimental fancies. Never again would she be so misled by her weakly sympathetic nature! No; she would rather pass for cruel, hard,—yes, even shrewish. And the doctor should never have cause to laugh at her again,—ah, he would soon have no opportunity to do so. In a little while Henriette would be removed to the villa; all connection between it and the house by the river would be at an end; the doctor would not even mention the names of the inmates of Villa Baumgarten. After what had occurred yesterday e ening,—that scene of which she had been the sole witness, —Flora's return was impossible, however firmly Doctor Bruck might insist upon his rights; this very day must convince him. All must be at an end between himself and Flora, if she kep away. (r would he fulfil Henriette's fears?—would he be unable to repress the desire, upon his return from the interview with the prince, to tell Flora himself of the change in his affairs? If he did stop at the villa, the diamonds upon the finger where he had placed he betrothal ring would tell him instantly, and far more plainly than in words, what he had to expect.

Suddenly Kitty ran back from the river-bank to the garden; a terrible noise, that might possibly disturb Henriette, was heard from the direction of the wood-shed: the chickens were flying screaming and cackling in all directions, and the dog, with loosened chain dragging after him, was making straight for the unfortunate yellow hen that had previously aroused his ire. Kitty ran to the rescue; she seized him by the collar just as he had torn a mouthful of feathers out of the tail of his unhappy victim.

She laughed like a child at the rumpled hen running with a querulous cackle into the wood-shed, and dragged the dog back to his kennel. The unruly beast tugged and resisted, snapping at the strong, girlish hand that was firmly leading him back to captivity.

This struggle for mastery might well have looked dangerous to a spectator, for the dog was vicious, savage, and large, of a strong, muscular build, and the tawny stripes on his back and sides gave him a tiger-like appearance; but he struggled and writhed in vain. With her left hand Kitty fastened the chain again into the iron ring in the side of the kennel, and then, suddenly releasing the animal, gave a backward spring; the brute rushed after her, but only succeeded in tearing off a piece of the hem of her dress.

"You villain!" she said, shaking her finger at him, and then picking up her skirt to examine the injury it had sustained. She heard hasty steps approaching from the bridge, and knew that it was the doctor returning from town, but she did not look up. She hoped he would go into the house without observing her. Perhaps he was coming from the villa in most melancholy mood. He had been so quiet and silent to-day, it almost seemed to her that with the gentle, lingering "Good-night! good-night!" of the previous evening he had meant to mark a boundary between his former and his present life.

He did not go into the house, however, but came directly towards Kitty, raising his cane at the growling, barking dog, who, thus threatened, became silent, and lay down at the door of his kennel. The doctor took a stone and hammered the link of the chain farther upon the hook. "I shall have to get rid of this brute: he is too savage and unmanageable," he said, as he threw away the stone. "His capacity as a watch-dog is not worth the terror he occasions. You, it is true, seemed to have small fear of him; I am afraid that in your consciousness of strength you might be easily led into rashness." This he said in a grave, almost reproachful tone; he had probably been a witness of the scene that had just occurred as he approached on the opposite side of the river.

She laughed. "Indeed you are wrong! I have as much capacity of terror as other girls," she replied, bravely. "Strange dogs, in particular, are my aversion, and I get out of their way whenever I can. But in critical situations there is no help for it; one must not give way to weakness; so I shut my teeth tight and take hold, and I suppose it looks very brave."

The doctor was following with his eyes a swallow flying away from the wood-shed, and he too now smiled, but without looking at Kitty. To her this smile seemed one of incredulity; he probably thought her boasting of her heroism, and unfemininely proud of her strength,—when nothing could be more foreign to her taste or to the truth.

"You doubt it?" she asked, with a glance that was only half merry. "Let me tell you that not until very lately did the heroine before you learn to rise superior to the dread of ghosts in the dark." An arch smile played about her lips and deepened the dimples in her cheeks. "You must know that the castle mill swarms with gnomes and fairies; its princely founder sometimes sees fit to descend from his worm-eaten frame to inspect the bags of grain himself; and there are not wanting the ghosts of dishonest millers who gave short measure during their lives. You may be sure that Susie never kept one such incontestable fact from my youthful ears; and I believed them all as firmly as if I had been brought up in a Thuringian spinning-room. Not a word of this 'fearful joy' could I utter to my father or my dear Lukas,—Susie would have been scolded, and I should have been ashamed; so I resigned myself to go when it was required of me from garret to cellar in black darkness, and to conquer my fears, although my teeth chattered as if from an ague-fit."

"Then you were early accustomed to make heavy drafts upon your power of self-control. How, then, did it happen that you were so ready to ascribe to a man an act of cowardice and weakness?"

She crimsoned. "You forgave me that yesterday," she said, evidently hurt, and yet not without self-assertion, as she stroked a stray lock of hair from her brow in hopes of thus concealing her blushes.

He shook his head. "You should not use that expression, after my assurance that you had done nothing to displease me," he rejoined, involuntarily lowering his voice, as if touching upon some matter known only to her and himself, the knowledge of which the rest of the world was not to share. "I only meant to say that I cannot imagine from what source your yesterday's conjecture sprang."

Kitty glanced towards the house; once more she looked rosy, lovely, and fresh as an apple-blossom; her head, with its crown of braids, seemed almost too young for her Juno-like figure. She pointed to the window of the corner room. "In old times a noble lady lived there——"

"Ah, the romantic story told, too, in many a peasant's spinning-room!" he interrupted her. "Then it was the tragical end of that forsaken dame——"

"Not that only. Henriette made me very anxious and unhappy——"

"Henriette is ill. The morbid state of her nerves makes thought and sensation unnatural in her case. But you are healthy in body and mind."

"Yes, that is true; but there are certain things for which youth and ignorance have no scale of measurement, upon which their judgment cannot be brought to bear——"

"Love, for example," he hastily interposed, with a rapid glance towards the girl.

"Yes," she assented, simply.

He bowed his head, and, lost in thought, tapped mechanically with his cane a large block of sandstone lying in the middle of a grass-plot opposite the house. In former years it had served as a curious but most delightful table for little Kitty, who had thought it placed there chiefly that there might be a spot where childish hands could deposit fallen fruit, flowers, and collections of pebbles. Now she knew that it had once been the base of a statue; the remains of a delicate little naked foot were still to be seen upon its mossy surface.

Kitty passed her slender hand caressingly over the relic. "Some nymph or muse once stood here," she said. "The airy form stood lightly poised upon one foot, with extended arms. I can imagine the whole figure from this fragment. Perhaps her lovely face was turned towards the bridge, and she saw the horseman cross it with his haughty bride in her gleaming brocade——" Involuntarily she paused; his thoughts were evidently far away,—he did not hear what she was saying. What occupied him must have been sad indeed, for for the first time, she saw a look of unmistakable distress on his fine face, usually so composed and calm. Flora! She was this man's curse; his passion for her would be his ruin.

The young girl's sudden silence made him look around. "Ah, yes," he said, evidently recalling his thoughts; "the worthy people who lived here for so long took the liberty of destroying the statues. The garden must once have been adorned with these figures: there are several pedestals still standing in the shrubbery. I shall try to restore the place to what it was formerly. In spite of the neglect of years, the original plan of the garden can still be traced."

"Then it will be all very fine and grand here; but the view of all this lovely wild greenery will be lost; your study——"

"My study will be occupied after next October by a dear

friend of my aunt's," he calmly interrupted her. "In the autumn I shall remove to L——."

She gazed at him in amazement, and involuntarily clasped her hands. "To L——?" she repeated. "Good heavens! are you going to leave her? What does she say to it?"

"Flora? Of course she will go with me," he said, coldly, but his eyes gleamed as with an angry pain. "Do you suppose I shall leave your sister here? Be easy on that score."

Kitty had alluded to his aunt, but she could not correct the mistake: his reply had so startled her, he spoke with such certainty. "You come from the villa?" she asked, timidly, but eagerly.

"No, I have *not* been to the villa," he said, with emphasis. It sounded almost as if he who never condescended to a sneer were indulging in sarcasm. "I have, indeed, not been so fortunate to-day as to see any one from there. I should have liked to see Moritz; but his guests, who were just leaving him as I passed there, were so noisily gay that I preferred to go by without speaking to him."

He had not, then, spoken with Flora since the evening before, and yet was so decided. What could it mean? Kitty wished she were away from it all; she seemed to herself like no one but Priam's ill-omened daughter, the only one who saw where all were blind. It was fortunate that at this moment the poor hen once more ventured too near her grim enemy: it gave Kitty a pretext for breaking off the conversation; she chased the fowl into the shed, closed the door and bolted it.

CHAPTER XVI.

WHEN she turned round, the doctor was still standing where she had left him, but his gaze was directed towards the bridge, and he had grown slightly pale. His profile, with the tightly-compressed lips, reminded her of the moment in the castle mill when she had asked him about her grandfather's death; he was struggling with intense emotion of some kind. Involuntarily her eyes followed the direction of his own, and she could not have been more startled and shocked by the apparition of the drowned woman of former times than she was by the sight of her beautiful sister advancing across the ancient structure with as easy a grace as if she had gone hence on the previous evening with a gay "au revoir." Could it be? She glided lightly over the place where she had declared herself separated forever from the man whom she despised; only a few hours had passed since she had heaped every epithet of scorn and contempt upon his home, which she had vowed never again to enter; and here she was, with her lovely, smiling face, confronting the "dreary barn," her little feet confidently pressing the grassy paths. No wave rolled higher, no breeze stirred, to whisper to her of wrong, wilful treachery, and miserable inconstancy, while the sunshine played about her graceful form, illumining it as if she were of all earth's children the most dear.

She had on a dark dress. Rich black lace covered her fair curls, and, lying upon the snowy neck, fell in long ends over her shoulders and down her back, like the drooping wings of an angel of night. Behind her walked the councillor; he looked very animated, and was conducting the Frau President with an air of such respect that Kitty in all seriousness began to wonder whether she had only dreamed his contemptuous looks of the morning and his expressions with regard to the "old cat" and her "velvet paw."

The doctor slowly advanced to meet the approaching group, while Kitty stood by the shed as if rooted to the spot, still unconsciously holding fast the bolt which she had just pushed home. She saw the usual greetings exchanged. Nothing extraordinary happened; no angry word was uttered. The councillor warmly congratulated the doctor; the Frau President graciously smiled, showing the white tips of her teeth;—and Flora? For one moment her cheeks were dyed with a rosy flush, and her glance, usually so self-assured, wandered from the doctor's countenance to the ground at his feet, but she extended her hand with her accustomed air of good-fellowship, and the tips of her fingers were taken, if not retained, very much as they had been upon Kitty's arrival, and when Doctor Bruck turned round, his features were once more composed to marble.

As she entered the garden, Flora had hastily scanned her young sister from head to foot, smiling scornfully the while, and then turning to make some apparently malicious remark to the councillor; but now, upon her nearer approach, Kitty saw gleaming in her eyes suppressed anger, amounting to a kind of hostility.

"Well, Kitty? You seem to be perfectly at ease here," she exclaimed; "you really look quite at home, as if the keys to every drawer and closet were hanging at your girdle."

The young girl made no reply as she slowly turned from the door she had just bolted and gazed at her sister. Was there no shame in this wayward creature? no shrinking from the sound of her own voice here upon this spot? But yesterday she had declared, "This house shall never again see me within its walls," and now here she stood, about to enter it and to return to the "sordid surroundings."

"Does Flora's jest annoy you, my dear child?" the councillor asked, hastily approaching her. He drew her hand through his arm. "Console yourself with the knowledge of the charming picture you presented among the hens and chickens. Only wait, and you shall possess the finest collection of them that can be got together."

The Frau President, who was ascending the steps, paused a moment, as if her breath had suddenly failed her; her head, trembling nervously, was turned for an instant with an of contempt towards the tender guardian, and then she hastened her entrance into the house. "Brainless fop, he will never cease to be the vulgar bagman!" she muttered, angrily, to Flora, who put her handkerchief to her lips to hide a laugh.

Kitty, as if unconsciously, let her hand remain within her brother-in-law's arm. She scarcely heard what he was saying; she did not observe Doctor Bruck's mute surprise as he stood motionless and allowed the pair to pass him: she only saw Flora's hand, the one in which she held the handkerchief to hide her laughter, and which was covered with a delicate lace mitten that harmonized well with the lace of her dress and by contrast made her hand more snowy white than ever. The diamonds had disappeared from the third finger, where the "simple circlet of gold that weighed upon her like iron" again gleamed dully through the meshes of the lace. Impossible! It lay beneath the waters of the rolling stream. Kitty suddenly felt as if all about her were unreal; her eyes and ears were no longer to be trusted.

"What does this mean?" the Frau President asked, with a frown, pointing to the assemblage in the hall of the furniture from the villa.

"I thought it best to humour Henriette in her desire that these articles should be removed from her room," said Dr. Bruck.

"She was perfectly right. Begging your pardon, grandmamma, it was a ridiculous idea to crowd the sick-room with all those things," Flora remarked, with a shrug. "The poor child is often oppressed for breath; this well-stuffed furniture must have been stifling."

Her grandmother evidently meditated a severe retort, but the doctor was present, and the maid was standing at the door of the kitchen; so she refrained, and went on to the sick-room. As she entered it, she started. Henriette was leaning out of bed, so wasted and pale, and yet with such an eager expectancy in her large wide-opened eyes, that the Frau President feared she was again delirious. The invalid's cool greeting relieved her, however, and she saw that the look which had startled her was directed towards Flora, who had entered the room directly behind her.

The beautiful woman instantly went up to the dean's widow, who had arisen at the entrance of the visitors, and grasped her hand, as if she would thus atone for the neglected farewell of the previous evening, and then she turned to the bed. "Well, dear," she said to the sick girl, "you are wonderfully better to-day, we hear——"

"And you, Flora?" Henriette interrupted her, with irrepressible impatience, as she accorded an absent greeting to the councillor, who stood by her bedside.

Flora suppressed a mocking smile. "I? Oh, tolerably well only! Yesterday's fright is still telling upon my nerves, but my self-control and firm will stand me in stead. Yesterday I was indeed in a wretched state; I was really ill, almost insane, I verily believe, with nervous agitation; at all events, I have but an indistinct remembrance of what happened after that terrible walk,—and no wonder! Daniel in the lions' den was scarcely worse off than I surrounded by those furies——"

"But Kitty defended you nobly," Henriette said. "She

stood like a shield between you and them,—my poor, brave Kitty! Moritz, they tore the clothes from her back and pulled down her hair——"

"This beautiful hair!" the dean's widow said, tenderly, as she stroked the shining waves that rippled back from the girl's brow.

"Well, yes; the furies did not deal very gently with her," Flora admitted, with a frown; "but I must decline taking all the blame for it upon my shoulders. It was mostly due to her mania for wearing stiff silk dresses. Those people envy us our wealth and elegance; her silk dress irritated the women, and they dinned into her ears, and unfortunately into ours also, how her grandmother went barefoot, how the castle miller was once only a mill servant, and amassed the money, now hers, by usury; and various other edifying facts. Kitty's appearance upon the scene greatly increased our danger; their indignation against the wealthy heiress was unbounded. Am I not right, Kitty?"

"Yes, Flora," the young girl replied, in a trembling voice, with a bitter smile. "I must work hard indeed to atone for the wrong done by my grandfather."

While Flora was speaking, the Frau President seemed to dilate with satisfaction. This laying bare of a scandalous pedigree was like music to her ears. She looked fixedly at the councillor. It was impossible that the new-made nobleman should not shrink at the thought that people would point at his wife and whisper everywhere the tale of her descent and of how her fortune was acquired. "Nonsense, Kitty! that sounds too ridiculously sensitive and silly," she said, shaking her head. "What do you propose to do?"

Flora laughed. "Open her safe, of course, and scatter her stocks abroad among the people."

"As Flora did yesterday the contents of her purse in defence of her charming complexion," Henriette remarked, with an air of easy banter. Her rising indignation conquered for awhile her burning desire to see Flora in the dust at the doctor's feet.

"I should never be guilty of such folly," Kitty said, calmly, but seriously, to Flora, who bit her lip at Henriette's remark. "If a curse rests upon the money——"

The councillor's laugh interrupted her. "Never vex yourself about that, child. A curse! I tell you there is a charm about your money; the dividends from some new investments I have just made for you are enormous."

The Frau President's eyelids, usually drooping over her eyes in aristocratic lassitude, opened wide at this expression. The word "dividend" had power to kindle those eyes with an eager glitter which the desire for conquest in her time of youth and beauty could scarcely have called forth.

"Enormous?" she repeated. "Mine are by no means so large. I will sell out, and invest in this new stock."

"That can easily be arranged, dearest grandmamma; I will take the necessary steps immediately. Yes, yes, the saying is quite true, 'Where doves alight there doves will flock,' and never truer than in the present wondrous age. The capitalist is a rock upon which the waves toss up treasure of their own accord——"

"That is not the opinion of the prudent men of the day, Moritz," said Doctor Bruck. When Henriette made her eager retort he had advanced to the bedside and had taken her hand soothingly in both his own, and he was still standing thus. He was in full dress beneath his light overcoat, and looked a most distinguished figure, but in the face which he now turned full upon those present there was perceptible a certain strange look of suffering which Kitty had noticed to-day for the first time. "There has been a good deal of mistrust lately about these sudden gains, and people begin to call them by a very ugly name——"

"Swindling, I suppose you mean," the councillor gaily interrupted him. "My dearest doctor, I have the highest respect for your scientific attainments, but you must permit me to excel you in a knowledge of business affairs. You are a most distinguished surgeon, and have just achieved fame——"

Henriette here sat upright, and asked, eagerly, panting as if almost overcome by her feeling of triumph, "Do you know that, Flora?"

"Of course I know it, you silly child, although the Herr Doctor has hitherto not thought it worth while to give me any personal information of his fortunate cure at L——," Flora lightly made answer, while her eyes boldly and as if in challenge encountered Henriette's gaze. "I also know that the sun of princely favour has suddenly shone full upon him in a most unexampled fashion. Of course this is still a court secret, to be kept even from his betrothed." Her lips parted in an enchanting smile, and the rosy flush that tinted her cheek at her last words became her charmingly.

Henriette fell back disappointed among her pillows,—even she had been mistaken in this chameleon nature.

The Frau President, standing beside the doctor, tapped him almost affectionately upon the shoulder. Never before had she treated him with such condescending familiarity. "May we not know something further? Are the preliminaries not yet arranged?" she asked, in a gentle, flattering tone.

"He has just returned from an interview with the prince," his aunt said, never turning her gaze from her darling, her eyes beaming with proud affection.

"Ah, then the report that Herr von Bär has been pensioned off is true?" the old lady asked, with well-feigned indifference, masking her eagerness.

"I do not know; that is no affair of mine," the doctor quietly replied. "The prince desires that as long as I remain here I shall take charge of his chronic inflammation of the foot——"

"As long as you remain here, Bruck?" Flora interrupted him, quickly. "Are you going away?"

"I shall establish myself in L—— in the beginning of October," he coldly answered, without looking at her. His eyes were fixed upon the budding apple-tree outside of the window.

"What! you have declined a position and a title at our court?" the Frau President exclaimed, clasping her hands in amazement.

"I am not permitted to decline the title." An ironical smile flitted across his features. "Evidently his Serene Highness thinks it contrary to all the laws of etiquette to be attended by an untitled physician. He insists upon making me Hofrath."

As he spoke, his aunt, struggling against her evident emotion, held out her hand to him, and he—usually reserve itself—put his arm around her slender form and clasped her close to his breast. The suffering, the calumniation, which they two had steadfastly endured together isolated them, in the moment of recompense, from the rest of the circle.

Flora turned away and walked to the window, biting her lip until it nearly bled; one could see how she longed to thrust away the faithful friend from the place which the false love had forfeited.

"But he is going away, aunt," Henriette said, in a low, hoarse tone.

"Yes, to where fortune and fame await him," the old lady answered, lifting her tearful face from his shoulder. "I can gladly stay behind in the home which his filial love has provided for me, if I know him appreciated, honoured, and esteemed where he is. And, besides, my mission is almost at an end,—another is to take my place." The tenderness of her tone gave way to profound seriousness, as her eyes, usually so gentle in their expression, looked almost sternly towards the beautiful woman at the window. "She, with her rich endowments of intellect, will appreciate more fully than I can the sanctity and, at the same time, the frequent trials of his profession, and will surely create for him a home whither he may flee from the cares that beset his public career, and where affection and serenity will abide *uniformly.*" The emphasis she placed upon the last word told Kitty that the widow had observed, and ascribed to caprice, Flora's behaviour on the preceding day.

"That is all very charming and delightful, my dear Frau Dean, and I have no doubt that Flora will make an admi rable professor's wife," the Frau President remarked, evidently piqued by the tone which the simple widow of a dean had adopted towards her grandchild; "but nowadays there can be no home without comfortable apartments, and I am having an immense amount of trouble in arranging them. I have just had a most fatiguing discussion with the cabinet-maker; he insists—Heaven knows why!—that it will be impossible to have Flora's buhl furniture, ordered months ago, finished by Whitsuntide. And Flora, too, has had trouble with her trousseau,—the workwomen have been so dilatory that it cannot be ready before the beginning of July. What is to be done?"

"We will wait," Doctor Bruck said, briefly, and took up his hat and cane to put them in the hall.

The Frau President started, and a perplexed expression crossed her countenance; but she instantly recovered herself, and, laying her hand on his arm, said, "How kind and good you are, my dear doctor, to help us thus out of our dilemma! I was afraid of encountering your opposition. Whitsuntide has been quite a nightmare to me, you so insisted upon that time."

"Yes; but my removal to L—— makes some change necessary," he said, quietly, and left the room.

"And what does Flora think?" the dean's widow asked, in an uncertain tone; she was apparently rather shocked at the doctor's cool behaviour, and the sudden, embarrassed silence on the part of the others.

Flora turned towards her a beaming countenance. "I am very glad of the postponement, since my future position is to be so different from what I had expected. There is need of much preparation and reflection. Good heavens, think of the change! A very different mode of life is looked for by the world from the wife of a famous professor from that expected of the wife of a simple doctor, Hofrath and physician to the royal household though he be." There was undeniable arrogance in her whole bearing; every word she said showed the exultation she could not suppress: she had reached the pinnacle of her most ardent aspirations.

The councillor rubbed his hands in a state of great satisfaction; he would have liked to laugh in her face. But the Frau President had some trouble to conceal her rising indignation; her grandchild evidently contemplated achieving at her husband's side a higher social position than she herself, the wife of an exalted government official, had ever attained.

"What are you talking of, Flora?" she said, with a disapproving shake of her head.

"Of my brilliant future, grandmamma," she replied, with a supercilious little smile, as she turned away with the air of one who would not by any word or look be reminded of a disagreeable past.

"And now I resign myself entirely to you, dear aunt," she said to the dean's widow, who was closely observing her every look and word. "Do with me what you will. I will obey you in everything; only show me how I can make Leo happy; I will sew, cook——" And, as she spoke, she drew off her lace mittens as if impatient to begin; but, as she did so, she made a grasp at the empty air, with a sudden exclamation of dismay,—the "simple golden circlet" had slipped from her finger. No one had heard it fall on the floor; every one looked for it, but in vain: it seemed to have vanished into air.

"It must be among your pillows, Henriette," Flora declared. She had grown quite pale. "Let me raise you up for a moment and see——"

"That I cannot allow," the dean's widow firmly interposed. "Henriette must not be disturbed, nor her position unnecessarily altered——"

"Unnecessarily," Flora repeated, reproachfully, pouting like a child. "Why, aunt, it is my betrothal-ring."

Kitty fairly trembled at these words. Was Flora really such a child of good fortune that some miracle had restored to her the ring she had flung away? or was this all a brazen falsehood? In vain did she look for an answer to this in the anxious eyes of the beautiful sphinx.

"It is an unlucky accident," the dean's widow said, "but the ring cannot be lost; we shall find it when Henriette's bed is made, and my servant shall take it over to the villa to you."

"She shall be rewarded with a handful of gold if she brings it to me this evening," declared Flora, who was evidently much disturbed.

The Frau President and the councillor seated themselves by the bedside of the sick girl, who had taken no further part in the conversation. Only once had she raised her head, with her lips opened as if to speak. When her grandmamma had said she could not understand the delay upon the part of the cabinet-maker, she had been upon the point of saying, "Because your orders have been all but countermanded." But she remembered before it was too late that the past must never again be alluded to.

CHAPTER XVII.

The dean's widow left the room, to provide some refreshment, and Kitty followed her. Disgust and aversion drove her from the room in which such a farce had just been played. She begged the old lady to resign to her for an hour her household cares, and the widow willingly handed her her keys. "Here, my dear, dear child, my faithful, true-hearted Kitty," she said, gently, in a voice which trembled as if she were suppressing a sigh, and then she put her arm around the girl's waist and drew her towards her. "It rests me only to look into your frank, sweet face. I am always reminded of Luther's beloved Catharina, the true wife standing so firmly and boldly by her husband's side." And then she sighed deeply as she released the blushing girl and returned to the sick-room.

Kitty brought from the store-room the coffee, and a cake baked in honour of the day, and, while the stout, good-humoured maid made the fire in the stove, she filled the pretty old-fashioned bowl with sugar, and was just cutting the cake in slices, when she heard some one leave the sick-room. The kitchen-door was ajar, and through the wide opening she saw Flora come into the hall.

The beautiful woman looked around her with a troubled, uncertain air,—the geography of the "dreary barn" was unknown to her,—but it seemed as if those searching eyes had magnetically attracted the doctor. At that moment he came out of his aunt's sitting-room.

Flora flew towards him with open arms. Her long black robe swept the floor, and the ends of her black lace scarf streamed behind her like loosened tresses of dark hair. With her white hands, which the black lace ruffles made to seem childishly small, and her pale face, she looked like one of those fair, ghostly dames who, according to popular superstition, arise from the grave to murder those whom they attract.

"Leo!" It was gently breathed, and yet it vibrated through the hall.

Kitty listened with bated breath,—it pierced her very soul.

Was that Flora's voice? Did that delicious sound of soft entreaty, of trembling longing, really issue from the lips that could utter such stinging words, that could smile in such cutting scorn? The young girl turned away, and cast down her eyes; the knife trembled in her hand. She longed to shut the door, that she might neither see nor be seen, but strangely enough she lacked the force and courage to stir. There was no answer without, and no further step was heard.

"Leo, look at me!" Flora spoke louder, half in entreaty, half in command. "Why torture yourself by thus doing violence to your own heart? I know how manfully you are struggling to suppress your most sacred impulses, that you may seem hard and cold, to punish me. And why? Because yesterday I was half wild with what I had suffered, and did not know what I did or said. Leo, my life which belongs to you had been in danger, my blood was in a ferment, and—then you irritated me further."

Kitty involuntarily looked up. Beside her stood the maid, with a broad grin on her good, fat face: it certainly was delightful to hear the pretty lady begging something of her young master. Kitty instantly recovered her self-control; she took the plate of cake in her hand and went out into the hall. She saw the doctor standing with folded arms and averted face gazing through the open house-door; his brown cheek looked pale, his teeth were firmly and angrily set, while

Flora's trailing black figure hung upon his neck, clinging to him like the fabled vampire.

At the noise made by the opening door, the doctor started, and his glance encountered Kitty's. He recoiled as if detected in some crime. Flora's eyes followed the direction of his own, but the lovely arms were not unclasped from about his neck. "It is only Kitty," she murmured, and leaned her head upon his breast.

Kitty glided past them into the sick-room. Her heart beat almost audibly with terror and shame: she had interrupted a love-scene à la Romeo and Juliet. With trembling hands she placed the plate upon a table, and by Henriette's desire, who feared that her pets might make an inroad upon the cake and sugar, she lured the fluttering canaries into their small aviary and closed its door behind them.

As she did so, she saw the ring that had eluded their search lying upon the clean white sand on the floor of the cage. Oddly enough, it had dropped through the wires and upon the soft sand without noise. Kitty took it up and slipped it into her pocket, and then she should have gone into the kitchen to superintend the making of the coffee, but she almost shivered with terror and dislike. She seemed to herself about to be thrust forth to death, to destruction. She still stood by the table, busying herself with the birds, while the Frau President, in a pleasant, subdued voice, talked on about Flora's trousseau, and the dean's widow reckoned up upon her fingers the various additional articles that the change of residence would make necessary; the old lady seemed quite convinced that her distinguished nephew was about to marry a kind of princess.

Kitty was released from torment sooner than she had anticipated. The doctor entered the room after a few minutes, and she slipped past him without looking up. The hall was empty. Flora must have gone into the garden. The grinding of the coffee-mill was heard in the kitchen ; perhaps that harsh noise, and not, as she had suspected, her appearance, had terminated the reconciliation scene thus quickly.

Her duties were soon concluded, and, while the maid was putting on a clean apron preparatory to carrying the coffee to the guests, Kitty went to the window and examined the ring, which with a throbbing heart she took from her pocket. E. M., 1843, was engraved on the inside,—Ernst Mangold. Then she held in her hand the betrothal-ring of Flora's mother.

She stood paralyzed by the utter frivolity with which Flora had thus discovered a means of relieving herself from all embarrassment. Hers was one of those feminine natures which master a situation by a bold stroke as soon as it is comprehended, and by a reckless ignoring of all that is unpleasant in the past come down upon their feet in any change of circumstances and instantly take up afresh the threads of their intrigues and continue to weave them successfully. And this was the sister before whose intellectual and moral superiority her childish soul had prostrated itself in timid awe!

The unpretending symbol of conjugal fidelity worn by Flora's gentle mother to the hour of her death had been desecrated by the daughter's wanton hands. It seemed almost to burn Kitty's fingers. She would have liked to throw it far away, never to be found again by human hand; but it was her sister's by inheritance, and must be returned to her.

She left the kitchen and went into the garden, at the bottom of which Flora stood gazing abroad over the picket-fence. Her back was turned to the house, and her arms folded across her breast, while the sunlight tinged her fair hair through the meshes of the lace with pale gold. The watch-dog was barking incessantly and angrily at the mute, strange figure, with the long, rustling train lying dark upon the grass.

The dog's barking drowned the noise of Kitty's approaching footsteps; Flora did not observe her until she stood close beside her. Then she started and turned round, her face still flushed with agitation; she was evidently in a very irritable frame of mind, for she frowned still more darkly, and her eyes flashed with anger.

"Are you here again, like an inevitable Deus ex machina? Awkward creature, to come blundering in!" she exclaimed, as if there stood beside her not this stately, dignified young girl, but an ill-bred, naughty child, whom the discipline of the rod awaited.

Righteous indignation almost overpowered Kitty; hers was no submissive nature; her youthful blood did not flow so gently in her veins as to prompt her to turn the other cheek to so insulting a reception: but she controlled herself. "I bring you your ring," she said, briefly and coldly.

"Give it to me!" Flora's features assumed a more tranquil expression, as she hastily took the little circlet from Kitty's open palm and put it on her finger. "I am very glad to have the truant once more. It is such bad luck——"

"You are not alluding to any evil omen in this case?" The young girl's voice almost failed her at the display of such incredible audacity.

"And why not? Do you suppose people of our position in life are necessarily free from superstition? Napoleon the First was as superstitious as any village crone, let me tell you; and I, child, also confess to a faith in omens." She looked fixedly at Kitty, as if to defy criticism and to bar all allusion to the past, nay, even all memory of the display on the part of her youthful sister.

But there confronted her now a being undeviatingly true, whose indignant blood was boiling. "You forget," Kitty said, "that you were not standing alone there last evening." And she pointed to the bridge.

Flora laughed angrily. "This comes of having one's footsteps dogged by a younger sister. In the true school-girl fashion, she puts on an air of confidential familiarity, and delights in hinting at what were best gone and forgotten. Did you not hear me say just now that the adventure of yesterday in the forest so shattered my nerves that I could not be responsible for anything that occurred afterwards? I suppose, my esteemed Kitty, that, in your profound sagacity, you would remind me that I cannot connect any omen with my betrothal-ring because—well, because it lies at the bottom of the river. Eh, my dear?" Again she laughed. "What if, in spite of my agitation and confusion of mind, my indignation at an unjust and prejudiced criticism that had just been launched at me, I had yielded to a feeling of compunction, and had *not* thrown away my precious jewel? Did you hear the ring drop, child? Certainly not! for here it is," and she turned the ring about on her finger, "after having really been upon the point of leaving me of its own accord——"

"Because it is too large for you. Your fingers are more slender than your mother's were," Kitty sternly interrupted her.

Flora raised her hand in menace. "Viper!" she muttered, between her teeth. "In the first moment that I saw you I felt, I knew, that your clumsy person would cast an ugly shadow upon my life! How dare you undertake to play the spy upon me? Upon *me?* These honourable principles are the fine effects of the teachings of your excellent Lukas!"

"No need to mention my Lukas!" said Kitty, who opposed a perfectly calm demeanour to this passionate outburst. "My education has had nothing to do with my mode of thought and action in this instance. These 'honourable principles' I inherit from a good father. I detest deceit, and would rather die than call falsehood truth. You may be able to silence those about you by your treacherous audacity, and thus make them accomplices in your deceit, but this you cannot do with me, young and inexperienced though I be. I am not to be blinded: I have excellent eyes and a good memory——"

"Very sound natural endowments; hardly to be equalled by any one gifted with delicate sensibilities and refined feeling!" Flora exclaimed. While Kitty was speaking, she had several times turned as if to leave "the chit." She had clenched her hands, bitten her lip, and mercilessly stripped of its first green leaves one of the boughs of a bush that stood near, but she had not gone, and now she spoke as composedly as though she had not for a moment lost her self-possession.

"Will you ever understand me, child?" She shrugged her shoulders. "I think not; you cling with childlike credulity to your tiresome code of what you call morality, and can never appreciate the soul of things, estimating everything by your rule, as the tradesman does his stuffs by the yard, be they coarse or fine, green or red; but I will try to make myself clear."

She approached her sister, so closely that Kitty felt her breath upon her cheek. "Yes, you are right," she said, in a low tone, and with a hasty side-glance towards the window of the house, "my betrothal-ring is lying in the depths of the river. I flung it away in a paroxysm of despair, in utter disgust,—disgust at the prospect of a life of poverty at Bruck's side. Girls of your stamp cannot, of course, understand this. You choose a husband for certain qualities, a good figure, perhaps, or a fine beard, and when once you have said 'yes' you follow him through thick and thin; and rightly,—such girls make excellent mothers of well-taught sons. They cower in the domestic nest and timidly and humbly close their eyes when an eagle soars to dizzy heights above them. But such an eagle must be my mate. Upon those heights I breathe my native air; close by his side, I cheer him onward and encourage his lofty flight——"

"And if some malignant arrow lame his wing, you proclaim him a crow and leave him like a coward," Kitty interrupted her, thus trenchantly stigmatizing her ambitious sister's shameless treachery; and, as she spoke, she stood with folded arms, the personification of indignant womanhood. "You did not even have the grace to go quietly to work about your faithless schemes, as is the wont of traitors, but you openly declared your bitter hatred, and proclaimed yourself deceived, betrayed, on this very spot, where now you stand again——"

"Bruck's idolized love, who needed to pass through all her errors to appreciate the magnitude of her good fortune," Flora completed the sentence, in a tone of triumph. Then, with a malicious gleam in her eyes, she added, "But you can be excessively impertinent, child. I am really struck by the fine turn you gave to my simile. I admit that a fair share of quite respectable intelligence has fallen to you,—just enough, indeed, to mislead you entirely in your estimate of genius, of a soul of fire. What can you know of a psychological problem? If I had uttered yesterday one word of friendship forfeited, you would be right in your indignation at my sudden change, for nothing of passion can come of friendship; while *hate* and love are close akin in the human soul,—they enkindle each other; excess of love often lies at the foundation of what seems bitter hatred. You, with your blunt sensibilities, can never understand this. You would propitiate your husband by some triumph of cookery, while a nature like mine, in the intensity of its desire to atone, might commit a crime for him, nay, even suffer death."

She pressed her clenched fist to her breast, as if she were even then thrusting a dagger into her heart. "And now let me tell you, never have I loved Bruck so passionately, so intensely, as since I have known how he has endured like a martyr, like a hero, in silence,—since I confessed to myself how bitterly I have wronged him; and never,"—she suddenly seized Kitty's hand in a clasp that was as cold as the wind which came blowing from the water,—" and never," she whispered, "have I been so fiercely jealous. Heed what I say, child! This is *my* domain. And although you are the last to be held dangerous by me,—he has no liking for you, as I have long observed, and, besides, will never have eye or ear for any other save myself,—still, I am not disposed to endure the presence near me of any one who so evidently seeks to please. Your 'homely' ways and conduct here, your intimate going and coming, do not suit me. For the future all this must cease. Do you understand, child?"

Having thus spoken, she picked up her train and turned hastily towards the house, as if to bar all reply,—a needless precaution, for Kitty's pale lips were firmly closed. Youth and innocence had no reply for such a heaped-up measure of arrogance, waywardness, and deceit.

CHAPTER XVIII.

It was May. The trees had shaken off their snowy blossoms, and the huge beds of hyacinths and crocuses, which had been so admired on the lawn before the villa, had quite done blooming. The lilacs and syringas were in flower, the tender green buds were just peeping forth upon the rose-bushes, and the shade in the shrubbery and in the linden avenue was growing deeper and darker. The river ran once more clear through the garland of green that bordered it on either side, and over the dear old house upon its bank there clambered a web of greenery that, day by day, concealed more and more of the white walls. The healthy grape-vines drooped their tendrils even above the overhanging eaves.

The guest-chamber stood untenanted once more. Henriette had been removed some time since to the villa, apparently quite recovered; indeed, her disease seemed to be checked: its progress was not perceptible; and this beneficial change the dean's widow ascribed to Kitty's nursing. The two sisters in their third story led a pleasant, isolated existence that was full of fresh charm since the new piano had been placed in Kitty's room. Not to Kitty's care alone was Henriette's improvement due: her intimate intercourse with the doctor's aunt had proved of great advantage to her. Her views of life and of its duties and pleasures had undergone a change in the quiet of the house by the river. She no longer recoiled from the thought of a retired life,—the whirl of fashion and society aroused in her now no eager longings.

And, in truth, the councillor's home had never been so gay in a worldly sense as at present, since the elevation of its master to the aristocracy. There were many occasions, and very welcome ones, for festivities of various kinds, and the Frau President's invention and the councillor's purse seemed alike inexhaustible. The man's good fortune was wondrous indeed. Disturbed by no loss, no failure, whatever was touched by the enchanted wand of his business genius seemed to turn to gold,—his wealth was estimated by millions. And he thoroughly understood how to wear the glory of his new distinction, how to make it interesting, an inexhaustible theme of wonder and admiration for rich and poor. The road past Villa Baumgarten became a fashionable promenade; strangers were shown the magnificent estate which was always being added to and improved. They told of costly pictures and statuary, of rare collections gathered together within those marble walls of a plate-room not to be equalled in the royal palace. The crowd halted and gaped when one of his equipages waited before the gates, and wondered whether the light cloud of sand, stirred by the wind upon the gravel-walks, were not gold-dust.

Large additions were building, making long stretches of road through the park almost impassable, heaped up as they were with blocks of granite and marble to be used in these additions and in the new stables, the old ones, although spacious and convenient, having long been too small for the councillor's passion for fine horses. The ground selected for the artificial lake proved rather unsuitable for such an adornment, and this, with the new tropical conservatory, absorbed enormous sums of money. And one day a multitude of workmen arrived to undertake the repair of an extensive and very elegant pavilion, which had been hitherto locked up and in disuse. It was situated in the forest, at a considerable distance from the villa, but from its upper windows there was a good view of the road and the town. A graceful wing was added to the original building, the windows were all provided with plate-glass, and from time to time the councillor would produce from his pocket patterns of stuffs for covering furniture, or drawings for parquet floorings, and beg the aid of the Frau President's taste in their selection. On such occasions she was wont to be very curt and ungracious, while Flora smiled behind her pocket-handkerchief; but the old lady was forced to choose, in spite of her declaration that she was not at all interested in the renovation of the old "barracks," and had quite enough of work to last her lifetime in the arrangement and ordering of the villa, without troubling herself about a lodging-house for business friends of the councillor's, a place where she certainly never should set her foot. Therefore she steadily ignored the new building, in spite of the incessant noise and hammering that resounded thence, much as the ambitious spouse of a reigning sovereign ignores her future dower-house.

In all this bustle, this hurry of beginnings and endings, the councillor came and went like a bird of passage. He made many business excursions, but these were shortly all to have an end, he said, and then he should purchase a large estate in the country and become really one of the landed aristocracy. Whenever he had two or three holidays, he spent much time in the third story; he drank coffee there regularly in the afternoon, to the great vexation of the Frau President, who thereby lost her favourite hour in her conservatory; for she was naturally far too attentive to leave "dear Moritz" to the society of a peevish invalid and an unformed school-girl, and almost always made her appearance with him.

This was a great relief to Kitty, who had conceived an unconquerable, shy dislike of her guardian since he had grown so strangely affable and even tender in his demeanour towards herself, and so false, so deceitful in his external politeness towards the Frau President. Involuntarily she adopted, in her intercourse with him, the dignified reserve of a woman, where she had formerly shown the confidence of a child. And this very change seemed to please and encourage him in his new, strange rôle. He divined her wishes and fulfilled them; he had long since consented that the unused portion of the mill-garden should be sold to the workmen. He placed no obstacles in the way of any of her benevolent schemes, and, when her purse was empty, filled it without a word of remonstrance. "Deny yourself the fulfilment of no whim, Kitty; I shall soon have to buy you another iron safe," he said, in allusion to the astounding increase of her capital. She listened in gloomy silence. With all his finesse and diplomatic replies to her grave inquiries, he had never yet disproved the complaint made by the people, that her wealth had been gained by pitiless usury,—a complaint to which the Frau President never lost an opportunity of alluding. The naïve childish delight Kitty had formerly taken in being so rich had been converted into a kind of dread of the money which was so swiftly, so strangely accumulating, only, it might be, to fall upon and crush her at some future day in just retribution.

She had grown notably graver. The sunny smile that her lively temperament had so often called up upon her face was now rare. She was never unreservedly gay, except in the house by the river, and there only at certain times. The dean's widow had been for some time charitably teaching a number of poor children to knit and to sew, every Wednesday and Saturday afternoon. In this little scheme Kitty, with the joyful consent of the old lady, had taken part. Intercourse with children was something entirely novel in her experience, stirring chords in her nature the existence of which she had never suspected. She took heartfelt delight in the little creatures, and admitted to herself that the care and instruction of them was an occupation beyond all others to her in interest.

She clothed them when they needed it,—there was always an apron or little dress in her work-basket,—and she provided (which the dean's widow could not have offorded) fruit and biscuit for their refreshment when the hour of industry was over. In the summer the lessons were given in the garden, and when they were over the children, for the most part living in the closest and darkest alleys of the town could enjoy a romp on the grass in the shade of the fruit-trees. Kitty had provided portable benches for seats, and balls and hoops for the hour of recreation that followed work.

Flora was greatly vexed at all this, which she chose to regard as an infringement of her rights with regard to the doctor's aunt, but she was wise enough to suppress all evidence of her annoyance in the house by the river, since "the old woman took it so very ill if the tall girl with vulgar red cheeks and genuine Sommer features was not regarded as a perfect pattern-card of every imaginable virtue." The beautiful betrothed visited the house daily; she had had a dozen embroidered white aprons made, trimmed with lace, and never appeared without this domestic adornment, which became her admirably. No one could accuse her of not making every exertion to gain the approval of the doctor's aunt. She exposed her delicate face to the heat of the kitchen fire that she might learn how to bake cake; she took lessons in pickling and preserving, and once even took the flat-iron from the maid-servant's hand and herself ironed a table-napkin; but, in spite of these tremendous exertions, she never succeeded in inducing the dean's widow to depart in the smallest degree from the courteous but excessively reserved demeanour that she had adopted towards her nephew's betrothed ever since that most unlucky evening. She seemed to know perfectly well how, after these efforts, Flora would withdraw to her dressing-room as if fatigued to death, there to pull off her apron and toss it into a corner, and then usually to refresh herself by a round of visits in the carriage to her friends, whose ill-concealed envy was an inexhaustible source of satisfaction for her. These friends maintained unanimously that the university professor's future wife gave herself the airs of a full-plumaged peacock as she rolled along in her coupé, and that her arrogance was almost unbearable.

The sudden change in Doctor Bruck's career was still a nine-days' wonder. Many could hardly yet believe that the calumniated and depreciated young physician of a few weeks since now walked the streets of the capital an actual Hofrath. The man grew daily in the estimation of court and public; and, since his removal to L—— would in future make him unattainable, every sufferer was desirous of benefiting by his skill. Thus it happened that Doctor Bruck was actually overwhelmed with patients. His manuscript lay untouched upon his writing-table; he slept in his lodgings in town, taking his meals there usually, and thus declining to avail himself of the councillor's daily invitations to dine; any time spent at the villa or with his aunt had to be stolen, as he expressed it, from his patients.

Kitty saw him but seldom, and was all the more struck with the great change in him, probably in consequence of hard work, she thought. He looked pale and wearied; his former quiet but gentle reserve had become gloomy taciturnity. With Kitty he had scarcely interchanged two words since she had surprised his tête-à-tête with Flora in the hall, and his curt manner towards her had been such as to convince her that her inopportune appearance on that occasion had greatly angered him. It wounded her that it should be so, and she avoided him whenever she could.

In his conduct towards Flora, on the other hand, there was not the slightest change; he was the same grave, dignified person whom Kitty had seen the first time she had seen the betrothed pair together. Sometimes she half believed that the terrible scene by Henriette's bedside was either a freak of her own imagination, or else that Doctor Bruck possessed a power, common to no other mortal, of forgetting, of absolutely obliterating from his memory, disagreeable occurrences. Flora had evidently expected that her entreaty for forgiveness, her manifest repentance, would restore the intimate intercourse of the first weeks of their betrothal. Loving her so passionately as he did, must he not be intensely happy in knowing her now irrevocably his own again? Perhaps the happiness was there, only concealed for the present, and his beautiful betrothed might console herself by reflecting that a man of Bruck's stamp was not too easily appeased, that all would be as she would have it by September, the month now fixed for the marriage.

In the mean while, the twentieth of May, Flora's birthday, had come. Every table in her room was covered with flowers, the usual gifts of her friends. Even the princess had sent a magnificent bouquet to the betrothed of the Hofrath, whom she delighted to honour, and the most flattering congratulations poured in from various grandees of the court. Yes, it was a day of triumph for Flora; a day to strengthen her in the conviction that she was a favourite of the gods, one destined to an exceptionally brilliant career.

And yet there was a cloud upon her brow, and now and then she frowned darkly upon the table in the centre of the room. Among the gifts from her grandmother and her sisters stood a handsome mantel-clock of black marble. Doctor Bruck had sent it to her early in the morning, with an accompanying congratulatory note, excusing his non-appearance before the afternoon, on the ground of anxiety concerning a patient who was very ill.

"I cannot understand why Leo could find nothing prettier for me than that clumsy thing," she said, as she pointed to the clock, to the Frau President, who had taken the princess's bouquet from a vase and was smelling it eagerly, as if it must exhale a peculiar perfume. "No one likes to give a *black* birthday present; for my part, I consider it at least very bad taste."

"The clock is very suitable, chosen quite in accordance with your taste, Flora; it is intended to complete the decoration of this room," said Henriette. She was lying on the crimson couch, and, as she spoke, she glanced contemptuously at the black marble pedestals in the corners of the room.

"Nonsense! you know as well as I that I cannot take this furniture away with me. Moritz furnished this room entirely according to my desire, it is true, but so far as I know he has given me neither the furniture nor the hangings. And I would not take them away with me if he offered them to me,—one grows just as tired of a stereotyped style of furnishing as of a dress that has been often worn. What in the world shall I do with that black thing in L——, in my new boudoir that is furnished in lilac with bronze ornaments?"

"I, too, should have preferred a fresh bouquet; but you are not sentimental, Flora," Henriette remarked, not without a shade of malice. Kitty, dressed in white to-day for the first time, was standing beside a beautiful myrtle-bush which the dean's widow had reared herself and sent as her gift. The girl, with a sorrowful smile, passed her hand as if in a caress over its shining tender leaves. No one appreciated this beautiful present, which it must have cost the giver a pang to resign.

In the afternoon, also, the reception-rooms were open, for visitors were still coming with congratulations. The entire suite of these lower rooms, when opened, presented a charming coup-d'œil. The warm air blew in through the gilt bronze tracery of the balcony, bearing on its wings the odour of the lindens in the avenue and of the opening flowers on the lawn; the golden May sunshine streamed through the high windows. In the crimson room alone it was powerless to awaken a single bright reflection. There all looked dark and cold as ever,—it seemed cruel to imprison all the lovely flowers upon the tables within those four dark walls.

Henriette reclined in a rocking-chair opposite the open door of the balcony. She would have liked to look as like the May as Kitty, and her emaciated figure was enveloped in clouds of white muslin; but she was cold, and had wrapped about her shoulders a soft white shawl of embroidered crape, over which her abundant hair fell in rich waves; it had never been coiled up since her last attack.

Thus lying motionless in the flickering sunlight, with her large dark-blue eyes wide open, shaded by their long dark lashes, and her snowy skin only near the temples tinged with faint carmine, she looked like a waxen doll. She had sent Kitty to the piano in the music-room, and was awaiting, with hands folded in her lap, the beginning of Schubert's "Lob der Thränen." Suddenly the faint flush near her temples deepened to rose, and her clasped hands involuntarily sought her heart—Doctor Bruck entered the drawing-room.

Flora flew towards him and hung upon his arm. She scarce gave him time to speak to the others, but drew him into her room to look at her birthday gifts. The beautiful woman who had endeavoured for so long to impress all with her learning and studious habits of research, to-day, on her twenty-ninth birthday, manifested the naïve grace of a girl of sixteen, and was indeed, with her lovely animated face and supple lithe movements, charmingly youthful.

Kitty stood by the music-stand, looking for the notes of the song, as the pair passed her on the way to Flora's room. She looked around for an instant, to receive Bruck's half-embarrassed bow, and then went on diligently with her search.

"Look, Leo, to-day I close with the past, wherein I erred so sadly and almost destroyed the happiness of my life," Flora said, in her irresistibly sweet voice, as Kitty took from the shelf a thick portfolio of music. "I would not recall the memory of that wretched evening, when I lost all self-control and, in my excitement and agitation, uttered words in which my heart and soul had no share; but, for the truth's sake, and because I owe it to myself, I must tell you that you too were wrong then in your adverse criticism of me. It was no desire for notoriety that drove me to authorship, but true talent, —to speak plainly, genius. Ask me no further! I can assure you I could have made my way by my work, 'Woman,' which you have never seen. According to the verdict of competent judges, it is indeed calculated to win me name and fame in the world; but how could I desire, by your side, to follow any path of my own, or to exercise any of my special gifts? No, Leo, I will bask solely in the light of your fame, as is fitting for a woman, and, in order that temptation may never in the future again assail me, these pages, the result of diligent study and of the fount of poesy in my soul, must vanish from the world."

Kitty, who had just found the notes she had been seeking, turned at this moment to take her place at the piano. She saw Flora hold a lighted match to her manuscript, and throw it, blazing, into the fire-place. The beautiful woman turned her head towards the window where the doctor was standing; perhaps she wished that he should make an attempt to hinder her from what she was doing; but no step was audible, no hand was extended to snatch the precious fuel from the flames. The smoke of the burning paper, borne on the wind of spring, floated into the music-room; and as Flora, biting her under lip, and with a strange gleam in her eyes, stepped back from the fire-place, Kitty took her seat at the piano and began Liszt's arrangement of the "Lob der Thränen."

Kitty would not listen to Bruck's reply; it was terrible to her to be perpetually an involuntary witness of these scenes between the betrothed pair; it would end in Bruck's hating her. But she was indignant at the farce she had again seen played. The battered manuscript, repeatedly pronounced to be worthless by competent critics, had been dragged out once more, to play the part of a tragic sacrifice made by a high-minded woman, who thus in submission to a stern lord and master renounced the genius which she was aware she possessed.

Through the melody that Kitty's fingers evoked from the piano the girl could hear a continuous murmur of sound, in which she distinguished the grave tone of the doctor's voice, although, to her great satisfaction, no distinct word was audible. As she concluded, Flora entered the room to pass through to the balconied apartment. She no longer hung upon Bruck's arm, but walked beside him with the princess's bouquet in her hand, looking like a child who has been reproved and dares not reply. Flora had found her master. She darted an angry glance towards her sister, whose hands were just lifted from the keys of the piano at the close of the piece. "Thank heaven, you have done, Kitty!" she said, standing still. "You bang away so that I can scarcely hear my own voice. You see, you play your own little things very fairly,—they are nursery airs, without any depth; but really you ought not to attempt Schubert or Liszt; you have neither sufficient taste nor execution."

"Henriette asked for that piece," Kitty calmly replied, as she closed the instrument. "I do not pretend to be a skilled musician——"

"No, my darling, indeed you do not; you do not care to make people stare at your wonderful dexterity," suddenly interrupted Henriette, appearing upon the threshold of the door as she spoke; "but never was there girl who could interpret Schubert as you can. Or does Flora think that the tears you bring to our eyes start entirely out of conventional politeness?"

"They come from morbid nerves, nothing more!" replied Flora, laughing, as she followed the doctor into the drawing-room, whither the Frau President had called him.

The old lady was looking somewhat perplexed, as she sat with her eye-glass in one hand, and in the other a letter, which the servant had just brought her. "Ah, my dearest Hofrath,"—she used this title as often as she possibly could, for the sound of it flattered her ear,—"my friend Baroness Steiner writes me that she is coming here in a few days to consult you. She is very anxious about her little grandson, the hope of the ancient family Von Brandau. The boy has limped a little for some time, and our most skilful physicians have searched in vain for the cause of the trouble. Will you examine the child, and take him in charge?"

"Certainly; provided the lady does not make too great a demand upon my time." He well knew how fond the high-born dame in question was of being waited for, and that she chose to have a cold in any one of her family respected as if it were a mortal illness.

The Frau President was evidently offended at the indifference with which her request was treated; she made no reply.

"The Baroness seems piqued by my recent postponement of her visit," she said, addressing Flora; "this letter," tapping it with her eye-glass, "is full of satire; if she had not been worried and anxious, she never would have written to me. I can hardly tell you how it pains me. Now she wishes to take rooms in the best hotel that can be found, where our Hofrath can visit her, and begs me *at least* to do her the favour to secure a suite of five apartments for her." And as she spoke she cast an annihilating glance from beneath her drooping eyelids towards the lovely girl in the white dress, who, standing opposite her, behind a large arm-chair, rested her arms upon the back of it, and grew alternately red and pale as she listened to what was, every word of it, intended as a reproach for her.

"She might be very comfortable on the third floor, if she did not really need five rooms," the Frau President continued. "But she must have a drawing-room for herself and her daughter Marie, a school-room for little Job von Brandau and his governess, and three sleeping-rooms at the very least. Of course she brings her maid." Much out of humour, she leaned her head on her hand, in anxious reverie.

"All of which means that, during the visit of this preten

tious Baroness, Kitty will be in the way," Henriette angrily exclaimed.

"I have offered to go to the mill," Kitty said, without a trace of irritation, as she passed her hand soothingly over Henriette's hair.

"Oh, no; I have thought of a far better plan, Kitty, if you must go," the invalid cried, with sparkling eyes. "We will beg the dean's widow to give you her lovely spare room; I know she will be delighted, for she fairly dotes upon you. Your piano can be taken over there, and I can go to you whenever I choose——" She stopped as her eyes met those of the doctor. He had turned away at first towards the window, but he looked around now with undeniable disapproval on his face,—he scarcely seemed like himself.

"I propose what seems to me far more fitting and practicable, that the boy and his governess shall be lodged in my house," he said, coldly.

The Frau President loosened the cloud of lace beneath her chin, and could not suppress a fleeting, ironical smile. "That can scarcely be arranged, my dear Hofrath," she replied. "Nothing could induce my old friend to be separated from Job, and then—you have no idea what a spoiled child he is. Our own little prince is not so delicately brought up as this last and only scion of the Brandaus; the poor, puny little creature is bedded in satin and down. Yes, those people think such luxuries only en règle. But we are put to it to make them comfortable."

"And why, Leo, should you prefer to give your aunt the trouble of having that little monster—the petted scion of the Von Brandaus is positively the naughtiest and most good-for-nothing little wretch in the world—in her house?" Henriette indignantly asked; her nerves were in just the irritated state that prompted her to say what she might hereafter regret. "What has Kitty done to you? It has pained me for some time to see how unjust you are to her. Do you despise her because her grandfather was the castle miller? You hardly ever speak to her; and it is ridiculous, for at all events she is Flora's sister. She is the only one of us who never addresses you by your Christian name."

"My dear," Flora interrupted her, "I have long objected to that familiar address, and if my wishes were consulted, no one would use it. To tell the truth, I grudge an iota of my right to any one else. With regard to yourself, Henriette, I let it pass; but I really entreat that Kitty may not allow herself such a liberty." And she put her hand within the doctor's arm and looked tenderly up in his face.

Embarrassed, perhaps, by this public display of affection, or irritated by Henriette's reproof, the doctor started as if the white hand had been an odious reptile, and his colour changed.

Kitty turned to leave the room. She could have burst into tears of wounded feeling, but she bravely endured her pain and maintained a calm demeanour. Just as she reached the door, it opened, and the councillor entered. She forgot for the moment the dislike she had felt for him of late, remembering only that he was her guardian and stood in a father's place with regard to her, and as a result of this she lightly laid her hand on his arm in greeting.

He looked surprised, but with a satisfied smile and an arch twinkle in his eyes he pressed the little hand to his heart. His own hands were not free: they held a small chest, which he placed upon the table by which the Frau President was sitting. His entrance interrupted a most painful scene, and Henriette, who had been the cause of it, could have fallen upon his neck in gratitude to him for the easy, happy tone which he adopted in his unconsciousness.

"Now I am content; my birthday gift for you, Flora, has come at last," he said. "My Berlin agent accuses the manufacturers of the delay in its arrival." He lifted the cover.

"Apropos, I have another birthday pleasure for you," he added, with a gay, jesting air. "I have just heard that you are avenged,—the leader of the attack upon you in the forest, she of the menacing nails, has been sentenced to-day to a considerable term of imprisonment; the others, who were either very young or misled by her, have escaped with a reprimand."

"I cannot think that your news will really give Flora any pleasure," cried Henriette; "of course such offences must not go unpunished, and it can do that fierce Megæra no harm to be shut up alone for a while; but there was something so terrible for us all in that whole adventure, it is so dreadful to be so hated, that I wish you had said nothing about it, Moritz."

"Do you think so?" Flora asked, with a laugh. "Moritz knows me better; he knows I am quite above being moved by it, and would not stir a finger for the sake of popularity. And you were the same a while ago, Henriette. I should like to know what you would have said eight months ago if any one in our circle had advocated the rights of the people; all that was entirely beneath your notice. But since Kitty has been here, such questions and discussions are the order of the day on the third floor, to such a degree that one stands abashed in presence of such Spartan virtue and feminine heroism. I should not wonder if Kitty had already been searching her cook-book for recipes for nourishing soups to keep the culprit strong in her confinement."

"No, not that," Kitty bravely replied, looking full into the beautiful and impertinent face turned towards her; "but I have made inquiries about her family. She has four little children, and her unmarried brother, who was one of Moritz's workmen and helped to provide for the fatherless little ones, has been lying ill for a long time. Of course these five helpless creatures must not suffer; and I have undertaken to provide for them as long as they are thus destitute."

The councillor turned round, and a remonstrance seemed

hovering upon his lips. "Yes, Moritz," the young girl said, hastily, "at such moments I have less horror of my grandfather's hoards."

The Frau President pushed back her chair impatiently. This "maudlin sentimentality" was beyond a jest. "These are most extraordinary statements and strangely perverted views of life and the world! Wealth could not possibly fall into more dangerous hands," she cried. "Yes, my dear Hofrath, I see you look in wonder at the hand now laid so beseechingly on Moritz's arm because he would fain restrain it from such wilful expenditure."

Kitty instantly withdrew her hand. She saw the doctor gloomily avert his gaze, but he made no reply to the Frau President's remark.

"Ah, grandmamma, that was surely no glance of disapproval," Flora cried, as she watched suspiciously the changing colour on the doctor's cheek. "Bruck always was a kind of enthusiast for the lower classes——"

"He surely is so no longer, my child,—now that he frequents the court and enjoys the prince's most distinguished regard."

"And why should such intercourse undermine my principles?" the doctor asked, with apparent composure, although his voice sounded uncertain, as if he were undergoing a mental struggle.

"Good heavens! you would not ally yourself with the revolutionary party—with those social democrats?" the Frau President cried, in dismay.

"I think I have already explained several times that, for very humanity's sake, I belong to none of these extreme parties. I endeavour to preserve that clear judgment which party hate is sure to cloud, and which is most desirable if one wishes to labour for the true weal of his fellow-mortals."

Meanwhile, the councillor had been busy unpacking the

chest. He especially disliked to have any topic touched upon the discussion of which might endanger the peace of his household. He now unfolded a piece of rich maize-coloured satin and another of violet velvet. "A couple of toilettes for your first débût as the wife of a distinguished professor," he said to Flora.

His end was gained. The splendour of the stuffs was too attractive for female eyes; even Henriette forgot her irritation at sight of a couple of exquisite fans, and some boxes of artificial flowers from Paris. But the contents of the chest were not yet exhausted. "The other ladies of my household must not go empty-handed, especially since I am to be at home now for some time and shall have no other opportunity of bringing them gifts," the councillor continued.

The Frau President, with a gracious smile, accepted a costly lace shawl, and Henriette a white silk dress, while into Kitty's reluctant hand the councillor, with a peculiarly significant glance, put a tolerably large morocco case.

This glance aroused in an instant in the girl's soul a perfect tempest of emotion, calling into life all the aversion that had of late stirred within her towards her guardian and brother-in-law. No, no, a thousand times no,—he should not gaze at her thus, as if together they shared a secret which none else might know; once for all, she would put a stop to this. Shame, annoyance, and an almost irresistible desire openly to proclaim her aversion now before every one, filled her soul and were mirrored on her face, although its changing expression was misunderstood.

"Well, Kitty, is it such a novelty for you to receive a present?" asked Flora. "What has Moritz given you? We must be told the sweet secret some time. Let me see it, child." She took the case as it was nearly dropping upon the floor, and pressed the spring that opened the lid. A crimson light flashed from the stones forming the necklace that lay inside upon black velvet.

The Frau President put up her eye-glass. "Superbly set; almost too artistically antique for imitation, although modern fashion certainly sanctions its being worn. This paste is uncommonly clear and sparkling." She negligently extended her hand for the case, that she might more conveniently examine its contents.

"Paste?" the councillor repeated, much piqued. "How, grandmamma, can you accuse me of such want of taste? Is there a thread here that is not genuine?" He passed his hand over the pile of glistening silks. "You ought to know that I never purchase imitations."

The Frau President bit her lip. "I do know it, Moritz; but really in this case I am astounded,—these are such rubies as even our beloved princess does not possess."

"Then I am sorry that the prince cannot afford to give them to her," the councillor rejoined, with a conceited smile. "I certainly should be ashamed to present Kitty with a valueless gift,—Kitty, who in a couple of years will be her own mistress and will be able to buy as many jewels as she pleases. Any imitation would then be tossed contemptuously aside."

"I agree with you there," the Frau President remarked, ironically. "Kitty has a decided preference for the solid and expensive,—witness the heavy silks which she always wears. But, my child," and she turned to the young girl, who had folded her trembling hands again on the back of the chair by which she stood, and made no motion to possess herself of the jewels, "a knowledge of how to dress one's self must be the result of taste, acquired by intercourse with people of refinement. Such gorgeous stones are not befitting your eighteen years; a plain cross or locket is more becoming so youthful a neck. The most you should wear would be a simple coral or pearl necklace."

"But Kitty will not always be eighteen, or always a girl,

grandmamma," Flora exclaimed. "We know that well enough, —eh, Kitty?"

The young girl's eyes flashed indignantly at the air and tone of the speaker. She turned proudly away to depart without a word.

"Only see how dignified the child can look!" Flora said, with a forced laugh. She could not succeed in quite concealing her vexation. "She behaves as if my harmless trifling had betrayed a state secret. Is it a crime, then, to want to be married? Nonsense, you little prude! Never deny in public what may be confessed in confidential moments." She ran her fingers over the sparkling rubies with a mischievous and significant glance at the councillor. "Yes, Moritz, this certainly is a necklace fit only for—the wife of a millionaire."

The Frau President now arose, hastily gathered up her letters and her eye-glass, and drew her scarf over her shoulders to leave the room. "I hope you will never falter in your love of the genuine, my dear Moritz," she said, coldly. "The champagne in which we drank Flora's health to-day was wanting in that quality: it has given me a headache. I must lie down for a while."

At the door she turned once more. "When I have refreshed myself a little, I must beg you to come to some conclusion," she said, holding out a letter to the councillor. "Read that, and you will see that the Baroness must not be put off and offended a second time. I yielded the other day for the sake of peace, but indeed I cannot submit so entirely again. People of position really cannot be pulled about like puppets and shaken off at pleasure. Remember that, I beg you, Moritz."

She left the room with a stately inclination and an air of severe dignity.

CHAPTER XIX.

"You will have hard work, Moritz," said Flora, pointing towards the door through which the Frau President had vanished. "Grandmamma is evidently on her mettle and armed to the teeth."

The councillor laughed gaily.

"Well, well," Flora continued, "you will see whether she will yield one inch of the authority you have allowed her to exert so absolutely. I have warned you repeatedly; now see——" She suddenly interrupted herself, and anxiously seized Bruck's hand. "For heaven's sake, tell me, Leo, what is the matter with you?" she cried, passionately. "You are struggling with some grief which you would conceal from me. Ah, you cannot deceive me! Here, and here"—she passed her white fingers across his forehead, that flushed to the roots of his hair—"I see lines that distress me. You are working too hard. After to-day, I shall take the liberty of sending one of the servants every day to your house in town to deny you positively to that tiresome crowd, who, after defaming you in every possible way, are killing you with their importunity."

Henriette stared at the speaker like one dismayed, and the councillor cleared his throat and stroked his delicate moustache to conceal a slight sneer, while the doctor, whose face had hitherto maintained a rigid composure, smiled a faint smile of bitter contempt. "That you will certainly not do, Flora," he said, in a peremptory tone. "I must decidedly forbid any interference with my practice, either at present or in future. Just now," and he turned to the councillor, "I have a word to say to you on behalf of a very sick man, quite broken down physically and mentally by violent business excitement; will you let me speak with you alone?"

"A very sick man?" the councillor repeated, dubiously. He knitted his brows, and the lines about his mouth grew hard and pitiless. "Oh, yes; I know whom you mean,—that hair-brained fellow Lenz. The man has been speculating in the wildest way, and wants me to save him from ruin. No, I thank you."

"Will you not wait until we are alone to discuss it?" the doctor asked, with emphasis. "At present you and I are the poor man's only confidants with regard to his terrible situation; even his wife does not know of it——"

"Well, well, I will hear how far you are able to plead for him, but I hardly think I can hold out even a finger to save him. It is a hopeless affair, I tell you." He shrugged his shoulders. The sudden accumulation of wealth was fast making the really kind-hearted man hard and cruel; he found it quite impossible to sympathize with a fellow-mortal beset by torturing cares. "You, of all men, should be the last to say a word for him,—he was one of the most violent of your accusers."

"Ought that really to influence me?" Bruck asked, gravely, as he prepared to accompany the councillor into an adjoining room. The man of science looked at this moment immeasurably the superior of the mere moneyed man beside him.

The three sisters were left alone. Flora rang for her maid to take away the councillor's gifts, and Kitty took up her parasol.

"Are you going out, Kitty?" asked Henriette, who was again seated in her rocking-chair.

"To-day is a class-day at the Frau Dean's; I am late, and must hurry——" The young girl paused involuntarily,—Flora's face had grown so dark and angry.

"I cannot express how your conduct disgusts me," Flora

said, peevishly. "The dean's widow, personification that she is of duty, stern duty, declined my invitation to coffee to-day because those wretched little things from the lowest quarter of the town could not on any account be sent away without their instruction; and Kitty sets off to second her efforts, with an air of the most righteous devotion to the welfare of humanity."

She bit her lips, and waited until the maid had left the room, when she turned and laid a detaining hand on Kitty's arm. "Patience for a moment! Let me tell you that your conduct forces me to play a part insufferably wearisome to me. September is still far off. Of course the dean's widow expects her nephew's betrothed to exercise the same heroic self-sacrifice practised by her model sister. I am to take those children's dirty fingers in mine and patiently initiate them stitch by stitch into the mysteries of knitting and netting. I am to wash their faces, comb their hair, and play games with the little wretches by the hour. I have tried it; ugh! And if I fail to do it, his aunt's complaints stamp me in Bruck's eyes as a kind of monster, an unwomanly, heartless creature, who does not love children. For this reason, in view of my rights in the matter, I forbid now and in future this kind of intercourse on your part in the house of my future husband. Do you hear?"

"I hear, but I shall nevertheless continue to follow the dictates of my own conscience," Kitty replied, calmly, freeing her arm from her sister's grasp. "Your rights which you once scorned, and in my presence declared yourself weary of——"

"Yes, yes!" Henriette interrupted, suddenly standing by Kitty's side in defiance of her arrogant sister.

"These rights I in no wise interfere with, as I am fully conscious," Kitty continued. "Matters must stand ill with you, Flora, when you see in the kindly actions of others a hostile element, that can imperil your position——"

"Imperil?" Flora repeated, clapping her hands, with a laugh. "Dearest and wisest of young moralists, you are under a slight mistake. Love that could pass unharmed through the fiery trial which I intentionally prepared for it can be imperilled by nothing in this world."

"Too true," Henriette murmured, in a sad, subdued tone. "It needs all my remembrance of Bruck's former firmness of purpose and true manliness to prevent his appearing to me now utterly weak."

"Of course," Flora continued, noticing Henriette's remark only by a slight shrug, "I am speaking merely with regard to the time between now and September, during which courtesy prompts me to make every concession to the dean's widow. In L—— everything will be different: matters will arrange themselves, and Bruck will find in the first weeks of our marriage that such a wife as his aunt would choose for him would be not only an insupportable burden, but an actual impossibility. When he sees me presiding in society he will acknowledge my superiority,—he will enjoy the lustre that my ease and grace as mistress of his household shed upon his distinguished position, when he finds that my holding aloof from housekeeping cares entails no pecuniary sacrifice on his part. I have calculated everything, and find that besides my pin-money I shall have quite sufficient income to pay out of my own pocket the wages of a housekeeper and capital cook."

As she spoke, she looked at her nails with a smile, and then turned aside with a haughty bend of her head. The tall mirror reflected a face and figure of dazzling beauty, but it was impossible to imagine that woman bending in love and anxiety over the couch of a sick child, or engaged in the thousand offices of affection and care to which the true wife and mother is prompted by the loftiest impulses of her nature.

Her gaze wandered from the contemplation of her own loveliness to the girl clad in white standing before the blue velvet portière, that brought into relief the youthful beauty of her figure, the incomparable freshness and delicacy of her colour beneath the heavy plaits of hair that crowned a face in which the dark eyes shone like stars. If in Flora was seen the woman of intellect who had already attempted to pierce the mystery of existence, her youngest sister was the type of maidenly innocence and spotless purity. Perhaps this displeased her, for she smiled and nodded scornfully at the young girl's reflection in the mirror.

"Yes, yes, little one, you will not long preserve that modest-violet air, and the domestic duties which Lukas has in her exaggerated ideas of this world so foolishly insisted upon your performing, will be as much out of place in your sphere of life as in mine. Moritz will never endure the jangle of a bunch of keys at your girdle,—rely upon that, even although he should gallantly promise you ten poultry-yards. He, with his brand-new stamp of rank, will insist more upon the aristocratic whiteness and softness of his wife's hands than does our most gracious prince himself."

Long before she had finished Kitty had moved, with a blush, to where the mirror no longer reflected her image. "What do Moritz's views upon the subject matter to me?" she asked, half turning round, while she looked in inquiring surprise at her sister.

"Oh, Flora, Flora, how can you be so thoughtless?" Henriette exclaimed, with a timid glance towards Kitty's expressive face.

"Nonsense! Moritz will be very grateful to me for breaking ground for him. And do you suppose Kitty has not known all about it this long time? Never was there a girl over fifteen whose nerves of sensibility were not electrically aware of a man's preference for her. Whoever denies it is either stupid or a refined coquette." Again she contemplated herself in the mirror, and pulled the curls lower over her brow.

"Any one who has observed our youngest's confiding, clinging manner in a certain direction cannot well be mistaken; eh, Kitty,—you understand me?" And from beneath her raised arm she smiled archly at her sister.

"No, I do not understand you," the girl replied, hastily; an undefined mixture of indignation and intuitive dislike stirring within her.

"Come, Kitty, let us go," said Henriette, passing her arm around her sister's waist, to draw her towards the door. "I cannot bear this!" she added, angrily.

"Nonsense! do not be vexed, Henriette," laughed Flora, holding out the jewel-case to Kitty. "Here, my child; do not leave this here, where the servants are coming and going continually."

Like a child, Kitty involuntarily put her hands behind her. "Moritz must take them back," she said, decidedly. "Your grandmother is quite right;—it is an unsuitable gift; such a necklace would not become my neck."

"And you expect me to believe in such naïve unconsciousness?" Flora asked, as if quite out of patience. "Such affectation is absurd in a girl of your age. There is the lace shawl that Moritz gave grandmamma;—she scorns it; she is more sensitive than your sisters, who think it very natural that your gift should outvalue theirs fourfold,—and you pretend not to understand why? Do not be ridiculous! You hear the hammering yonder in the pavilion every day from morning until night. The entire household, down to the very workmen, know that a home is being arranged there for grandmamma, so that the councillor's young wife may preside here alone. Well, little innocence, shall I speak still more plainly?"

Hitherto the young girl had stood motionless, following her sister's words with a dawning comprehension of their meaning, as if some dangerous serpent were slowly uncoiling its slimy folds in her presence. But now her lip curled in a proud smile. "Do not trouble yourself,—at last I understand you," she said, slowly, her astonishment revealing itself in the clear ring of her voice. "You have gone about it far more wisely than did your grandmother to make my further stay in this house impossible."

"Kitty!" Henriette exclaimed. "No, there you are wrong. Flora has been heedless and thoughtless, but she never meant that." She went close to her sister's side and looked tenderly in her face. "And why should such words drive you away from the house, Kitty?" she asked, in a caressing but anxious whisper. "Are you really unconscious of the love so unequivocally displayed for you? See, I have often wished for death,—but if it were possible that you should ever be mistress here in our father's house, I could——"

Kitty extricated herself impatiently from the encircling arm. "Never!" she cried, shaking her head indignantly, her whole maidenly soul in revolt against the consciousness to which she had been so suddenly and rudely awakened.

"Indeed,—never?" Flora repeated. "Perhaps the *parti* is not sufficiently distinguished, eh? You are waiting for some needy count or prince, who, after the fashion of the day, will come to release, not Dornröschen herself, but her money-bags from the spell. Well, the present time is by no means poor in such marriages! And we know, too, how that unfortunate incumbrance, the wife, usually fares. If you would hear perpetually how your grandfather drove the mill-wagon and your grandmother went barefoot, then marry into some noble family. I really should like to know what you find to object to in Moritz, or rather what can justify you in rejecting his hand. You are very wealthy, to be sure, but we know where your money came from. You are young, but no beauty, child; and as for your talent, which you well know how to bring forward, it is but a spark assiduously fanned into a little flame by ambitious teachers, and will soon be extinguished when they can no longer look to you for the rich reward of their services."

"Flora!" Henriette interrupted her.

"Be quiet! I speak in your interest now," Flora continued, dismissing her remonstrance with a decided wave of her hand. "Perhaps, Kitty, you think Moritz ought to display a more passionate affection for you. My dear child, he is a middle-aged man, who has long outlived a school-girl's romantic idea of love. It is, besides, a question whether you will ever be loved for yourself alone,—that must always be a question in the case of such an heiress. I cannot understand you. Hitherto you have devoted yourself to the care of an invalid, as any confirmed old maid might have done, because—well, apparently because no one desired you to do so; and now, when Henriette makes her future existence dependent upon your remaining here, you wish to go. For my part, I should be far more content in L—— if I knew that you had our sister in charge; and as for Bruck, you have just had a proof, poor child, of how little there is of sympathy between you,—he prefers to have that spoiled boy Job Brandau beneath his roof, to your constant presence there; but, nevertheless, I am sure that, since he is obliged to leave his patient here, he would like to know that she has some one with her whom she really loves."

Henriette, pale as ashes, leaned against the wall, incapable of speech, so great was her distress at Flora's ruthless and heartless enumeration of everything that could humiliate and wound her sister's heart. Kitty, however, had entirely recovered her self-possession.

"We two will discuss this alone, Henriette," she said, calmly; but the lips with which she touched the invalid's brow quivered, and the fingers that clasped Henriette's thin hand were cold as ice. "Go to your room now, I pray you;" she looked at her watch; "it is time for you to take your drops. I will come back shortly."

She left the room without looking again at Flora.

"Conceited as ever! I verily believe she is offended at being thought no beauty, and thinks that such men as Bruck should follow in her train," the beautiful woman said, ironically. Then, while Henriette silently gathered up and carried away her gift and the jewel-casket, she passed on, humming a gay air, to the room whither the two gentlemen had withdrawn, and, tapping lightly at the door, called to them that it was very impolite to leave the heroine of the day alone for so long a time.

CHAPTER XX.

For a long while Kitty wandered aimlessly in the park, through its quiet leafy alleys to its most secret recesses. She did not wish, in her present agitated state, to meet the observant eyes of the dean's widow; she knew the old lady would question her, and if she confessed the cause of her distress she would probably learn that her old friend also desired her marriage with the councillor. Upon this point every one was against her, Flora, Henriette, the doctor. Egotism ruled each and all of them, she now comprehended. But she would not be imprisoned in the gilded cage; she would escape them all. Her thoughts were full of bitterness as she paused, wearily, before the ruin, which she had reached in her walk. The sun was low in the heavens; its declining rays bathed in purple and gold the clouds, the dark forest of firs in the distance, and the encircling water on either side of the hill. The mound, crowned with the tower, stood out from the glittering background like a monument of black marble, and the group of chestnuts in full leaf showed like a many-pointed silhouette, through which gleamed here and there the glow of colour in the western sky.

The young girl gazed moodily at the picture across the water. There, where the heavy silken curtains fell like a dark crimson blood-stain behind the huge panes of glass, stood the detested safe. Hitherto she had feared it, but to-day she hated those four iron walls that had thrust her own individuality aside to stand in the stead of a girl filled with youthful hopes and desires and a profound longing for the true happiness of life. When lovers sued for her hand, their tender glances were for the monster that dogged her steps; they wooed the heiress in her. This was the attraction for Councillor von Römer; the wealthy man wished to be still wealthier. Certainly no worm gnawing at the core of a delicious fruit could be more pernicious than this ever-recurring torturing thought which Flora had wantonly cast into the virgin soil of her sister's mind.

And below, at the foot of the tower, yawned the dark cave where the rich man's costly wines seethed and sparkled in flasks and casks. Only lately the councillor had taken the Frau President and his three sisters-in-law through the cellar. He had just increased the precious stock, and it was all ranged carefully in the huge vaults that burrowed deep into the hill on all sides of the tower.

The air was cool and dry below there; the tiled floor shone as if polished; not a grain of dust, not a cobweb, could be seen upon the stone ribs of the mighty arches, and the glasses on the shelves, the green for hock, the clear for champagne, were bright as crystal; it was easy to see that no more care was expended on the drawing-rooms than upon these subterranean halls. And where the finest wine was stored, where only a faint glimmer of daylight pierced the vaulted gloom, in the very darkest corner, stood the two barrels of historic gunpowder, in such complete preservation that Kitty had lately declared with a laugh that she was sure they must be renewed from time to time, like the famous ink-spot at the Wartburg. She never liked this corner; she could not understand how the rich man could endure it night and day beneath his feet; and when her fancy conjured up the ghostly ancestress of the Von Baumgartens gliding hither and thither with her gleaming torch, she shuddered with horror.

Her gaze wandered over the blackened pile; one single spark alighting there below, and the old tower, built for eternity though it seemed, would burst asunder, and everything of price or value that human hands had there treasured up would be dispersed abroad in atoms; those iron walls would be broken down, and the papers, to which clung the curses of the poor, be scattered to the winds.

She shrank from the thought, and yet thus her own personality might be delivered from the golden mask that excited the greed of the avaricious. Horrified at the picture of destruction which her imagination had conjured up, she had covered her eyes with her hands, and now, letting them drop, she looked up with a deep-drawn sigh into the golden air above the tower, where Henriette's doves were wheeling, while before the window in the steep wall, that bore upon its top the last remnants of the stately colonnade, hung the thrush's cage belonging to the councillor's servant. Rosemary and marigolds were blooming upon the window-sill, from which drooped a green curtain of wild hop-vines. The little bird was singing at the top of his voice, incited thereto by the flapping of the doves' wings, while the deer had come noiselessly down the grassy incline and were gazing across the water at the tall, slender mortal whose fancies had been so terrible, so full of despair.

The deer and the doves knew her well,—the young girl used often to feed them with crumbs and biscuit; but to-day she only took a silent leave of them, although the doves were alighting on the grass on the other side of the bridge, and the boldest of them were venturing across it, looking for the accustomed food. Kitty walked along the bank of the stream, and soon heard the merry voices of children mingling with the murmur of its waters. The Frau Dean's little pupils were still at play in the garden, and in spite of the girl's depression of spirits, in spite of her mental suffering, the source of which she hardly understood herself, the sound brought a sensation of pleasure to her soul. Those little creatures, with their innocent eyes and happy hearts, did not love her as the heiress; they did not even know of the existence of the iron safe; they took gratefully their simple evening meal, and hardly asked whence it came. To them she was the dear "Fräulein Kitty," whose words of praise they strove to win, to whose ear they confided the troubled confession of childish wrong committed or childish injustice endured. Here at least she was loved,—honestly loved for herself alone.

She hastened her steps; the nearer she drew to the house the more it seemed to her that she was returning to her true home. The maid appeared between the two poplars that stood on either side of the bridge, and walked, basket on arm, towards the town to make her evening purchases. She, too, was a faithful creature, whose services were not all rendered merely for the sake of money; her good-natured, honest face seemed to belong of right to the household in the modest house by the river.

As Kitty crossed the bridge the children were not in sight: they were playing behind the house; the watch-dog greeted her with a lazy flap of his tail as he lay at the door of his kennel. He had long been her good friend, and his character had undergone such a change for the better that the yellow hen was allowed to parade the green within an inch of his nose without molestation.

The house-door stood wide open, and, as the maid was absent, the dean's widow was probably within. Kitty was just ascending the steps, when she heard the doctor speaking in the hall. She stood as if rooted to the spot.

"No, aunt; the noise wearies me. I have this constant trouble in my head," he said. "If I have a moment to spend in this green retreat, I wish to rest. I need rest,—rest!" Was that voice, trembling with nervous impatience and suppressed pain, really his? "I know, aunt, that what I ask of you is a sacrifice, but nevertheless I implore you to suspend your classes during the few months of my remaining here. I will gladly hire a room in town and engage a teacher for the time, so that your pupils may not lose anything——"

"Oh, my dear Leo, you know you have only to speak the word," his aunt interrupted him. "How could I suspect that my classes had suddenly grown so wearisome to you? You shall never hear another sound from them,—I will take care of that. I am sorry only on one account,—Kitty——"

"Always that girl!" the doctor exclaimed, as if his aunt's gentle mention of that name had destroyed the last remnant of his patience and self-control. "You never think of *me*."

"Dear Leo, what do you mean? I verily believe you are jealous of your old aunt's affection," the old lady said, in surprise.

He did not reply; the girl outside heard him advance towards the hall-door.

"My poor Kitty! It is impossible that her noiseless beneficence, her kindly presence, should be disagreeable to any man on earth," his aunt said, following him. "I have never seen a girl who combined such childlike innocence with so much womanly dignity, such keenness of intellect with such kindness of heart. I am irresistibly attracted by her; and I cannot believe that my Leo can be so unjust as to deny merit to any woman save to the one whom he adores as his future wife."

Kitty started; the doctor burst into a laugh, so bitter, so loud, that she recoiled in terror. Involuntarily she turned to flee; no, she would remain,—she was the cause of that scornful laugh,—she would hear how the doctor would refute his aunt's good opinion of her, undeserved though it were.

"You are wont to be keen-sighted, aunt, but here you fail lamentably," he said, pausing suddenly in his inharmonious laughter. "Let it go! I shall not dispute what you say; why should I? I have but one request to make of you: that until my departure we may be together as we have been hitherto,—*alone.* You used to be content without other society than mine; try to be so again during the few months of my stay here. I do not wish to have any one coming and going."

"Not even Kitty?"

A sound as of an impatient stamp of the foot upon the sanded tiles of the hall-floor reached the young girl's ears. "Good heavens, aunt, will you force me to——" he exclaimed, angrily: the voice was hardly to be recognized as his.

"God forbid, Leo! everything shall be as you wish," the old lady interrupted him, terrified, and yet attempting no concealment of her regret. "I will do all that I can to banish her as kindly as possible, that she may not suffer more than is necessary. But how agitated you are, Leo, and how your hand burns! You are ill. You are wearing yourself out for your patients. At least you shall have repose here in your own home, rely upon it! Let me mix you a glass of lemonade."

He thanked her, but refused the proffered kindness. Kitty heard the aunt go towards the kitchen, probably to arrange the evening meal, and immediately afterwards the doctor appeared at the hall-door.

CHAPTER XXI.

JUST outside stood the young girl, leaning against the door-frame; pale, and with a hard, determined gaze, she looked abroad beyond the man at her side into the empty air,—she *would* not see him.

He recoiled at sight of her, then stood for one moment speechless before her motionless figure. "Kitty!" he called, softly, in the anxious, hesitating tone of one who seeks to arouse another from some heavy, troubled dream.

She drew herself up to her full height, and slowly descended the steps. "What do you wish, Doctor Bruck?" she asked, over her shoulder, when she stood upon the grass below. She might have been some automaton, but for the indignant light that flamed in her eyes.

He blushed like a girl, and approached her. "You heard—" he asked, with hesitation, but with intense eagerness.

"Yes," she interrupted him, with a bitter smile, "every word. Another reason why you should rid your house of intrusive strangers,—the walls have ears." She moved away from the steps, as if to be quite clear of the threshold she was no more to cross.

Meanwhile he had recovered himself; he threw his hat upon a garden-table near, and stood erect before her, no longer blushing, but with an air of relief, as if matters had taken a wished-for turn, and chance had come to aid him. "Fear of being overheard has no part in what I have been telling my aunt. This quiet home has no secrets, and those which one must imprison in his own breast will not escape, even where the walls have no ears," he said, with calm gravity. "You heard every word,—you know, then, that only the desire for present rest induces me to ask for undisturbed quiet. Unfortunately, I must resign any attempt to justify my rude egotism. You certainly cannot conceive that there are those who are perpetually fleeing from thoughts and—images; but perhaps you may more easily imagine the angry pain, the torture of a man so fleeing, who, hurrying exhausted to his home, finds there just what he seeks to escape."

As he spoke, he had approached her more nearly, and she now looked him keenly and inquiringly in the face. Yes, he was in earnest; he not only described this torture, he felt it at this very moment; his strangely disordered glance, the pallor that overspread his countenance, left her no room to doubt it; but—he did not flee from his future wife, or from the innocent children; and none others frequented his room, except herself. It was really true, then, as she had frequently told herself, that she had become utterly distasteful to him since she had several times been the witness of scenes between himself and Flora; he did not wish to see her in his house, and he had begged his aunt to put a stop to her afternoon classes, that her further intercourse there might cease. As this conviction crept over her, her lovely features lost their usual mobility, and their expression grew stern and hard.

"There is no reason why you should justify your proceeding; you are master here,—that suffices," she replied, icily. "But what an unbounded esteem you must entertain for the Baroness Steiner, since you sacrifice your coveted repose to her, and wish to receive her spoiled grandchild and his governess beneath your roof!" It was a harsh reproof to come from girlish lips which were wont to be frank and outspoken, but which had never hitherto uttered words to show how sharp and cutting the clear, bell-like voice could be. "No, no; do not speak!" she cried, with sudden passion, as he opened his lips to reply. "I would not have you stoop to frame a false excuse for courtesy's sake, and say what you do not think. I know too well what motives influence you!" She evidently struggled to keep down angry tears. "I have most inopportunely crossed your path on several occasions, and entirely understand the irritation with which you exclaimed, a moment ago, 'Always that girl!' I cannot forgive myself for my awkwardness, although upon one occasion only did I wilfully interfere. But you judge me still more harshly,—you persecute me in consequence."

Doctor Bruck did not contradict her, but it seemed as though he had a struggle to resist the temptation to speak. He looked down upon her with eyes full of an inexplicable expression, and his right hand leaning upon the garden-table was tightly clenched. As he stood thus, every lineament of his handsome face showed the strength and resolution that would to the last resist being forced to an explanation.

"It cost me much to return hither," she began again. "The Frau President"—she pointed towards the Villa Baumgarten—"poisoned my childhood with her pride of rank whenever it was in her power to do so, and I can never forget the bitter tears which her perpetual insolence wrung from my poor Lukas. You know how, upon my arrival, I shrank from meeting my clever sister Flora, and how, in sight of the villa, I longed to turn back and flee to my Dresden home. Would that I had done so! In addition to pride of rank and of office, the arrogance of wealth is now rampant in the villa. In that air, filled with pretence and gold-dust, no healthy thought or feeling can survive. By my very nature I am incapable of striking root in such a soil; but here,"—she extended her arms towards the house and garden,—"here I was at home; here I could even have forgotten my dear Dresden; why,—I do not know myself!"

How lovely she was, standing there in spotless white, thoughtfully inclining her head with its crown of heavy braids! "I think your dear old aunt has cast a spell upon me," she added, with a bright look; "the simple, noble beauty of her character helps me to a true balance of mind; she goes her way calmly, noiselessly, and never yields one iota of what she holds to be just and right, although no word of contradiction or self-assertion ever passes her lips. It is refreshing indeed, in contrast with such unjustifiable pretensions, such deceitful appearances, and—yes, such pitiable weakness assailing even the strong masculine intellect." She tossed contemptuously aside a spray of blossoms with which she had been toying as she spoke.

The gesture evidently irritated the man who stood before her. A gloomy fire shone in his eyes; he understood her. "You have forgotten to enumerate one virtue possessed by my 'dear old aunt,'—caution and gentleness in judgment," he said, reprovingly. "She never would have uttered such condemning words as those you have just spoken, for she knows how easily we may be mistaken, and that often—as, indeed, in the case to which you so evidently allude—what looks like weakness demands every possible exertion of strength." He spoke with exceeding earnestness; the calm demeanour, which had never forsaken him even when there had been such wonderful and sudden changes in his career, had vanished entirely.

In her first surprise, Kitty's eyelashes drooped upon her hot cheeks, but she felt that she was right: he was utterly weak towards himself in his love, as in his dislike. Had she not had proof of the latter?

At this moment the children in their play came running round the corner of the house. As soon as they saw Kitty they rushed to greet her, shouting with joy. They paid no heed to the doctor's stern face, and in a second the young girl was surrounded and almost overborne by the merry throng, in their eagerness for some kind word or caress from their "dear Fräulein."

In spite of her agitation, Kitty almost laughed outright, for the wild onslaught of the children in their affection fairly made her stagger; but the doctor became more angry than she had ever before seen him. He harshly reprimanded the little ones, and ordered them to return behind the house and stay there until they were dismissed.

Confused and frightened, the children retired.

Kitty looked after them compassionately until they had all disappeared. "I should like to go with them to comfort them, but I cannot again seek the spot which I have left forever," she said, half in pain, half in anger.

"'Comfort!'" the doctor rejoined, almost derisively. "Confess that you would now like to stamp me monster as well as weakling. Be consoled: children carry their comfort with them, their smiles and tears are closely akin. Do you not hear them laughing already?" And he pointed over his shoulder with a fleeting smile. "I'll wager their merriment is at my expense. I sent them off on your account; I could not endure——How could you bear such an attack? They are uncouth, rude——"

"Because they are fond of me? Thank God that it is so! There at least I may still have faith!" she cried, pressing her clasped hands to her bosom. "Or would you perhaps persuade me that this exhibition of affection is also due solely to my money? Oh, no, here I stand firm; I will not be defrauded of this satisfaction, rely upon it!"

He recoiled in amazement. "What strange idea has——"

"Ah! is it really so surprising that at last I have been aroused from the state of childish confidence in which I have lived, imagining that true honest feeling was worth something in this world? It has taken a long time, has it not, to induce my clumsy German comprehension to open its eyes and see how unspeakably ludicrous were all its old-fashioned ideas of right and wrong, truth and falsehood?" She grew pale and shuddered. "There is something horrible in the sudden conviction that one has no existence as a genuine human creature, with a right to be happy after one's own fashion."

He turned away his eyes, and she continued: "At our first meeting you asked me how I liked my sudden accession to wealth; now for the first time I am able to answer your question. I seem drowning in this ocean of money; many hold out a hand to me, to be sure, to rescue me, not for my own sake, but for the golden waves that surround me."

The doctor interrupted her. "In heaven's name, what induces you to take such a view of your life?"

"Can you ask? Am I not forced to accept this view with every draught of air that I inhale, every drop of water that I drink? In my dear Dresden home I am cajoled as the 'heiress,' my teachers exalt the faint spark of musical talent which I possess for the sake of the high price I pay for my lessons, and the guardian wooes his ward because he knows better than any one else—how rich she is."

As she spoke, her gaze had wandered aimlessly over the distant hills; now she looked at the doctor; he started as if from an electric shock. "Has it gone so far?" he stammered, passing his hand over his eyes as if overcome by dizziness. "And you of course are pained to think that such thoughts should influence Moritz," he added, after a moment's pause.

She listened in wonder, his voice sounded so faint and broken. "It wounds me still more deeply that every one seems to feel justified in having a voice in the matter," she replied, as, standing erect, she looked the personification of a protest against unwarranted assumption of authority. Then, shaking her head gravely, she continued: "Such an unfortunate heiress as I must be on her guard lest she become a pitiable plaything in the hands of egotism; and this I will not be, absolutely will not. And you, Herr Doctor,—you too are one of those who think that an orphan girl should submit herself, her will, her goings and her comings, to the convenience of others. Here you would exile me, there you would fetter me to the spot. I should like to know what justifies you in this despotism, or—no"—her lips quivered in the struggle to keep back the tears,—"I would ask, with Henriette, 'What have I done to you?'"

The last passionate words died upon her lips: the doctor grasped her wrist with fingers that were like cold iron.

"Not a word more, Kitty," he said, in a whisper that terrified her. "Did I not know that there is not in your nature a trace of falsehood, I could not but believe that you had devised this torture to wring from me a secret which has been strictly guarded,"—he dropped her hand,—"but I too say, this shall not be, absolutely shall not!"

He folded his arms, and walked away for a few paces as if to go towards the house, but suddenly, turning, he said, "I should like to know how I would fetter you to the villa." His tone was calmer, and he came again and stood before her.

Kitty blushed crimson; for one instant maidenly timidity delayed her reply, then she answered, firmly, "You wish me to be—mistress of Villa Baumgarten——"

"I?—I?" He laughed again the hard, scornful laugh that had startled Kitty awhile before in his conversation with his aunt. "And upon what do you base this accusation? Why should I wish to see you mistress of Villa Baumgarten?" he asked, controlling himself with difficulty.

"Because, as Flora says, you would not have Henriette left alone," she replied, with frank decision, born of a determination to leave no point unexplained. "You see how fond I am of my poor invalid sister, how gladly I undertake the care of her, and you would like to have her future home and comfort secured by my becoming—the wife of the councillor."

"And you believe me to be at the head of this family scheme? You seriously believe this? Have you forgotten how I protested long ago against your sacrificing yourself and remaining longer in Römer's house?"

"Since then much has been changed," she replied, bitterly. "In September you will leave M—— forever; it will then be a matter of indifference to you who rules in the villa; your comfort will no longer be disturbed by an unsympathetic presence there——"

"Kitty!" he gasped.

"Herr Doctor?" She calmly met, with head proudly erect, his glance of fire. "The excellence of such an arrangement is plain, and no one who was not as dull of comprehension as myself could have been blind to it for so long," she added, with apparent composure, and with a gravity of tone and manner that seemed to come of suddenly-added years of knowledge and experience. "Then no strange element would intrude upon the family circle; every domestic arrangement could remain as it is; the habits of all in the villa, as well as in the tower, need not be disturbed; nothing, not even my iron safe in Moritz's 'treasure-chamber,' would have to be moved from its place. Oh, it is all so sensibly contrived——"

"And is so natural, that you have not hesitated for a moment to remain," he completed her sentence, breathing quickly, and with a look which in its impatience seemed to chide the lips that delayed confirmation of his words.

"No, Herr Doctor, you exult too soon," she cried, with a kind of triumph in her tone. "The obstinate heiress refuses to be led in chains. I am going, going this very day. I came here only to take my leave of your aunt, and should have laughed at your decree of exile awhile ago, if it had not pained me. My sisters have at length opened my blinded eyes, and revealed to me in a dazzling vista the 'happiness' to which I have been destined. At the moment of revelation I felt as if there were but one path open to me from the Frau President's drawing-room,—the road leading directly to the railroad depot,—and I should have pursued it immediately, had I not remembered the duties here which I had undertaken to fulfil. I am not going to stay away longer than will suffice to convince Moritz that he can never be more to me than my legal guardian, and that he arouses my dislike as soon as he attempts to assume any tone towards me except that of a fatherly friend and adviser."

She drew a long sigh of relief, and, although she had crimsoned to the roots of her hair with maidenly shame at speaking such words, it was easy to see that she was now fully determined that all should be plain and clear between herself and the man who, as she spoke, seemed to become more erect and elastic in form, as if some oppressive weight were suddenly removed from his shoulders.

"Since the day when Henriette was carried fainting into your house, a strong tie has been formed between the Frau Dean and my poor sister," Kitty continued, more quickly, "and I can go away with an easy mind, leaving Henriette to your aunt's care. I wished to bespeak her kind services in this matter, and came hither for that purpose. I shall now write to her from Dresden, for you must be aware that she whom you have banished from your house will never again intrude upon your domain."

With these words she turned to go. "Good-bye, Doctor Bruck!" she said, with a slight inclination, and walked towards the bridge. As she reached the poplars that grew on the other side of the river, she turned once more to take a last look at the dear old house. Around the corner the children were peeping curiously, but the doctor still stood by the garden-table, both hands resting upon the top, and leaning heavily forward, while his face, which was ashy pale, was turned to her with a wild expression of despair.

Oh, mystery of a girl's heart! Without thinking what she did, she flew back across the bridge, over the path she had thought never to tread again,—she would have traversed the world to come to his aid.

"Ah, you are ill!" she stammered, laying her warm supple hands anxiously upon his own.

"No, not ill, Kitty, only what you declared me to be a while ago, although in a different sense,—a pitiable weakling!" he replied, impatiently, shaking back a lock of hair that had fallen over his brow. "Go, go! can you not see that in my present condition every word of sympathy, every kind look, is like a dagger-thrust?" he cried, harshly, while quick as thought he stooped and pressed his lips for one instant passionately upon the white hand that lay upon his own.

Startled though she was, for a moment Kitty's heart throbbed fast and loud with an indescribable sensation of happy tenderness, and the words hovered upon her lips, "No, I will not go,—you need me." But at the same moment he stood erect before her, mute and pale, and pointed commandingly towards the bridge. She turned once more, and fled as though the angel with the flaming sword stood by his side.

A few hours later she noiselessly descended a back staircase in the villa, her travelling-bag in her hand. She went as she had come, suddenly, unexpectedly. Henriette, although shocked and distressed at her departure, had acquiesced in her remaining away for a time, since Flora's thoughtlessness had made such mischief. She consented that Kitty should leave thus privately, and write what she thought best to say from Dresden, she herself engaging to inform the household of her departure. One condition she strictly exacted, however, and that was, that Kitty should instantly return whenever her invalid sister needed her support and care.

Henriette stood at the top of the staircase with arms extended in farewell, while Kitty drew her veil down over her swollen eyelids. Every hall and passage of the house was bathed in light, and carriage after carriage rolled up to the door. For a moment Kitty was obliged to take refuge in a side-corridor, whence she saw ladies in full dress rustle by to the drawing-room. Footmen threw open the folding-doors, and, within, Flora appeared in light-blue silk and white lace, beautiful and gracious as a princess, to receive the guests assembled in her honour. The councillor was celebrating her birthday by a large ball.

As she looked, Kitty's heart ached to breaking. There stood her haughty sister, the favorite of fortune that dogged her footsteps although she had thrust it from her, and here cowered hopelessness like crime. Why should every gift of heaven, all the wealth of love, be heaped upon this one head, —that did not prize them,—while a weary life of self-sacrifice lay before the other sister in the midst of her hoarded gold?

The doors were closed, and Kitty hurried out into the park, filled with such despair as alone can assail a young and ardent nature; and while the maid awaited her in her room to dress her for the soirée, she was knocking at the door of the mill to request Franz to accompany her to the railroad depot.

CHAPTER XXII.

More than three months had passed, during which Kitty had studied as never before, giving hours to her music daily, and trying to find forgetfulness in devotion to duty. Henriette kept a kind of diary, which she sent every week to her sister. It told her how the life in the villa had gone on since her departure. She could "read between the lines" that the Frau President had been evidently much relieved thereby, and had established a rule in the villa more despotic than ever. Henriette told how her grandmother had praised Kitty's "thorough good taste" in what she had done, while Flora shrugged her shoulders and spoke of "school-girl's nonsense." She herself had informed the councillor of his ward's absence on the evening of the ball; he had turned quite pale with anger, and had been out of humour with her for days in consequence of her share in the affair. Flora, too, had been cross and out of sorts all that evening, for her lover had excused himself from appearing, on the plea of professional duties.

The councillor had written to Kitty announcing a visit to Dresden in June, when he had "an explanation to make;" but Henriette, as the time approached, told of his being overwhelmed with business, of the myriads of telegrams that were sent from Berlin to him as soon as he left that capital, where, indeed, he passed more time than in his home. The visit remained unpaid; a short business letter now and then was all she received from him, and her last remittance was sent through his bookkeeper,—an unprecedented occurrence.

Kitty breathed more freely,—the dreaded conflict was not

to take place. Her guardian had seen from her reply to his letter that his hopes were futile, and had quietly acquiesced. The young girl might then have returned to her post as Henriette's nurse, but the doctor's wife decidedly opposed this scheme, because Kitty, as she often anxiously remarked, had returned home from her former visit much changed, having lost all her youthful spirits and the fresh colour in her cheeks. Besides, the Baroness Steiner, with her suite, had now been quartered in the villa for two months, and had left no vacant corner on the third floor.

Kitty herself shuddered at the thought of a return so long as there had been no removal to L——. She knew too well that it would be impossible for her in that circle to maintain her outward self-possession. In Dresden she was obliged to exert all her strength of character not to show that her peace of mind was fled, that she was always struggling fiercely against the sweet bewildering force that had taken up its abode in her heart, and which seemed like a crime. Henriette had never recalled her, in spite of the passionate declaration repeatedly made that she longed for her "true, strong sister;" on the contrary, she spoke with enthusiastic gratitude of the tenderness and care lavished upon her by the dean's widow. Her diary was a continued narrative, in which two people played the principal part,—the doctor and his aunt. Every occurrence in the house by the river was duly detailed, even to the untimely death of the yellow hen, a victim to a recurrence of savage hatred on the part of her enemy the house-dog; and the unusual plenty of the grapes in the garden. It was even thought worth while to tell of a "snow-white kitten, whose favorite place was the Frau Dean's own chair." These were innocent items; but the diary was usually gloomy and melancholy in tone; in some parts it read as if the pages had been wetted with tears, in others as if the pen had been guided by a hand of fire. Of the relation between Flora and the doctor not a word was said, but great distress was expressed that the latter had been so changed by the wearing anxieties of his profession: only towards his patients was he uniformly gentle and kind; in general society he had become taciturn and irritable, while in appearance every one noticed how greatly he was altered.

Thus gradually the time appointed for the marriage drew near. Flora had neglected to invite her distant half-sister; Henriette wrote that her head was full of a series of fêtes that were being given in her honour, and that with regard to her trousseau and her marriage festivities her whims had almost driven the trades-people to despair. The invalid seemed in great distress of mind; she repeatedly dwelt upon her inability to sustain alone all the bustle and excitement of the approaching marriage. The dean's widow could be of no assistance to her at that time, since she herself was suffering greatly at the thought of a separation from her nephew, and was often absent-minded and sad. These complaints grew more and more frequent, until one evening a few days before the marriage a telegram arrived which ran, "Come instantly; I am miserable and ill."

No delay was to be thought of; even the doctor's wife consented that Kitty should go immediately; and the girl herself —she shivered in nervous dread of what was to come, and yet she exulted in the blissful thought that she should see once more the man who was—her future brother-in-law.

Again on a morning in September she found herself in the large room in the castle mill. She had come by the night train, having telegraphed to Franz to meet her. And certainly a mother's h nds could not have prepared everything for her arrival more lovingly than had old Susy. The room, illumined by the green light pene rat ng the chestnut-boughs before the windows, was redolent with the fragrance of the heliotrope, roses, and mignonette upon the window-sills, fresh white covers had been put upon all the tables, a tempting snowy bed stood in the recess, and upon the large oaken table stood the familiar copper "machine" full of hot coffee. Even the home-made cake was ready strewn with sugar, beside the gilt china cup that had been the pride of the corner cupboard during the lifetime of the old miller's wife.

Again the girlish tread was heard upon the white scoured floor, and through the open window came the cooing of the doves and the murmur of the distant weir,—she was at home. She would visit her invalid sister from here, and upon no account accept the councillor's hospitality, in spite of the Frau President's scorn of "familiar intercourse between the villa and the mill."

Kitty was in a strange mood. Dread of her first visit to the villa; painful longing for the house by the river, the weather-cock upon the roof of which she discerned with a beating heart from her southern window, and which she might not approach; passionate impatience to see, if only once more, the tall figure which she had first seen here in the mill, and which it was torture to confess to herself, as she did daily, she had loved from that moment; all this stirred within her, in addition to the strange, inexplicable foreboding and anxiety that possessed her soul. For months the columns of the newspapers had been filled with sensational intelligence in regard to the bursting of the great swindling bubble of the day in Vienna, and shortly afterwards of a similar catastrophe in Berlin. The destruction of this modern Tower of Babel was the topic of the day in every public place, in every drawing-room; it had been discussed even in the small æsthetic circle in Kitty's Dresden home. In the railway-carriage on the road from Dresden to M—— it had been the inexhaustible theme for conversation among her fellow-travellers, and now with her own eyes Kitty could behold one of the results of this calamity. Through the cooing of the doves and the distant murmur of the weir came the sound of excited human voices, and just behind the last chestnut the young girl had a view of the gravelled space in front of the factory. It was swarming, as she had seen it once before, with workmen, some silent and gloomy, others gesticulating wildly and talking loudly. The stock company that had purchased the factory of the councillor had failed; the officers of the law had already appeared in the building, and the employés had not yet recovered from the shock of the sad news.

"Yes, yes, so it goes," said Franz, as he brought in Kitty's trunk. "Those people were too well off, and they thought they deserved more,—now they will live for a while from hand to mouth, and then from bad to worse. All of them would like to pick up money off the streets; and who can blame them, when their betters do the same? He's a fortunate fellow who gets safely through the stream," he went on, slapping his pockets; "'an honest store by work made more' is my motto; no need to lie awake o' nights then. Those who don't know how to speculate had better let it alone. There's the Herr Councillor, to be sure, firm as a rock; he's too long-headed to be touched." Then, with an air of great wisdom, raising his forefinger, "Yesterday he got back from Berlin, finer than ever. I had just taken a load of corn to the station,—hey, how his black horses flew past! He understands it all. They said he had just made another lucky hit, and he looked like a man with millions at his command. He has been away for a long time, and I dare say would not have returned now but for the fine doings they are to have over there to-night."

To-night! The wedding was to take place on the next day but one, and immediately afterwards the newly-married pair were to set off upon a bridal tour. Kitty knew it, she had read it often enough in Henriette's diary, and yet the thought came to her now with a shock of terror.

"They are to have a fine time at the villa to-night," Susy

said, as she handed her young mistress a cup of coffee. "I was talking yesterday with the councillor's Anton, and he says they haven't room enough for all the guests who are coming. They have built a theatre, and ever so many young ladies from town are to dress up, and the evergreens have been coming by wagon-loads to ornament the house."

The factory clock was striking eleven as Kitty walked over to the villa. The murmur of voices was still audible as she went through the mill-yard, but scarcely had the small door in the wall separating the park from the mill-garden closed behind her before an aristocratic silence reigned around.

Franz was right; one felt here that the noise and confusion of the money-market could not touch the rich man and his belongings; that the devouring waves of misfortune and ruin could not even wet the soles of his feet. Ah! there stretched the beautiful lake. It had absorbed the azure of the sky, and lay a giant sapphire of spotless purity. It had been finished thus quickly at an enormous expense of money and labour. Swans were gliding to and fro upon its placid waters, and near the shore rocked a gaily-painted boat, fastened at the end by a chain. Kitty had left the park a mass of tender spring green; now the shadows had deepened. The sun's fiery rays, pouring down in all their summer splendour, had burned away the delicate colours of the flowers of spring, and had kindled in their stead the torches of the cannas and the straight stems of the gladiolus upon every bit of lawn that peeped forth among the shrubbery.

How many hands must be employed to maintain such exquisite neatness everywhere! Not a fallen leaf lay upon the paths, not a blade of grass broke the even line of the gravelled roads, no fading blossom was left upon the bushes. And in the distance, among the groups of majestic trees, appeared the imposing façade of the new stables; their erection also had been so swift as to seem almost the work of magic. For all there had been expended immense sums; whatever was flung abroad in the stock market, the golden stream here seemed inexhaustible. None of the electric shocks that had wrought such destruction in the business world had been felt here.

Passing on beneath the shady arches of the linden avenue, Kitty approached the villa. Never had the fairy structure seemed to her so aristocratically unapproachable as to-day in the golden light of morning, the gay flag waving from the roof,—a fluttering sign of welcome floating on the air. Involuntarily the young girl laid her hand upon her throbbing heart; she had not been invited, and yet she had come. It was a sacrifice indeed to sisterly affection, this crushing down of her own proud nature. Behind the bronze tracery of the balcony, the Frau President's lap-dog was running to and fro, barking at the visitor with all his old hostility, and the parrot, in his gilded cage in the blue drawing-room, screamed in chorus.

As Kitty entered the door, a lady glided past her, holding her handkerchief to her face, and above its lace border she glanced shyly at the young girl from eyes swollen and red with weeping. Kitty recognized her; it was the gay young wife of a major, accustomed to every luxury. The elegance and variety of her toilettes had been the talk of the capital. She hurried around the corner of the house towards the shrubbery, probably to remove there the traces of tears before she was seen upon the public highway.

"There is nothing left for her husband but to shoot himself; they say he has lost every stiver," Kitty heard one of the servants say, as she passed through the hall. "Serves him right! What has an army officer to do with speculating in stocks that he knows nothing of? Then his wife comes to our master, and cries her eyes out to beg him to help them out of the mire. A pretty piece of business! If he were to help all those who have been to him lately, he might take up his staff and beg on the road; he would have nothing left for himself."

Another victim, then, of the terrible crisis! Kitty shuddered, and ascended the stairs unperceived. A solemn silence reigned in the third story. Mechanically she opened the door of the room that had formerly been assigned to her. It was plain that the Frau Baroness Steiner reigned here no longer; but the room had evidently not been arranged to receive another guest. Much of the furniture had been removed, and in its stead the walls were lined with draped tables covered with a profusion of articles, displayed with great taste and care,—the gorgeous trousseau of the professor's wife in spe; in the centre of the room, upon a tall dress-stand, hung a robe of snowy satin, covered with lace and orange-blossoms, the heavy train lying long upon the floor,—Flora's wedding-gown. Kitty turned away her eyes, and closed the door; and in a few moments she clasped in her arms Henriette, who, at sight of her sister, broke into such a transport of joy that it seemed the result of relief from terrible pain.

The sick girl was alone. No one had any time to give her to-day, she said. The councillor had taken upon himself all the arrangements for the festival given in honour of Flora's marriage, and everything was to be conducted upon a scale of great magnificence. He was determined to show the capital what money could do. To be sure, this was the weak point in his character. With her usual inconsequence, she had neglected to tell any one of the telegram she had dispatched to Kitty. Such an announcement would have been entirely superfluous, she declared, in reply to Kitty's look of surprise and dismay; every one knew that she had promised to return and nurse her poor Henriette whenever she was sent for, and as for an unexpected encounter with the councillor, Kitty might rest perfectly easy; Moritz had "a new flame" in Berlin, whence he had returned of late, and especially yesterday, remarkably absent-minded; only smiling archly, and making no denial, when Flora had rallied him.

To these communications Kitty made no reply; she was possessed by the conviction that it had been high time for her to return. She found the sick girl much changed, and in a state of feverish agitation. The hard hollow cough shook her emaciated frame much more frequently than formerly, her hands were burning hot, and her breath came with great difficulty. She had hitherto always denied herself the relief of tears; her will was of iron. But to-day her beautiful eyes were swollen and disfigured with weeping. She was consumed by fear, she wailed, hiding her head on Kitty's breast, lest Bruck, with all his love for Flora, should be wretchedly unhappy; and although nothing had been said by the dean's widow about it, she was sure the old lady felt as she did, and was miserable. Kitty admonished her, rather curtly, that this was solely Bruck's affair; no one had had more opportunity than he of being thoroughly aware of Flora's egotistical nature. If he persisted in making her his wife, he was surely prepared to meet the consequences. Henriette started up in alarm; the words sounded so harsh. Indeed, there seemed a strange alteration in Kitty; a kind of stern reserve was in her whole manner, as though she had accepted her fate after a hard struggle.

CHAPTER XXIII.

Not long afterwards, Kitty, carefully supporting her invalid sister, descended the stairs to announce her arrival to the family. They passed through the narrow corridor where Kitty had taken refuge for a moment on the evening of her departure. It ran near the ball-room, which occupied almost the entire floor of a wing of the villa.

"They are rehearsing for this evening, and the men are decorating the room at the same time," Henrietta said, listening, with a quiet, scornful laugh, as dramatic declamation, mingled with knocking and hammering, was heard through the open doors. "Those girls are utterly disgusting! They would one and all be glad to scratch the bride's eyes out as they stand upon the stage, and yet they spout away about the 'loveliest flower' lost from their circle, the genius of poesy having kissed her brow, and the like wretched stuff. And Moritz, with his boundless extravagance, is behaving like a fool. Yesterday evening, after his return from Berlin, he scolded the workmen as if they had been school-boys. They had to tear down the 'worthless trash' they had put up, because in two dark corners they had substituted woollen for silken damask. Always the same parade of his millions! Just look here!"

She noiselessly opened a little wider one of the doors, through which was visible a magnificent canopy of crimson velvet fringed with gold, beneath which the bridal pair were to stand in the evening.

"Think how *he*, with his pale, gloomy face, will look beneath all that finery!" Henriette whispered, leaning her blonde head upon her sister's shoulder. "And she will stand beside him, victorious, triumphant as ever, in her studied toilette of innocent white muslin and marguerites. Oh, Kitty! there is something strange and inconceivable in the whole affair. I often feel as if a miserable secret were lurking behind it all, like a glimmering spark beneath gray ashes."

In the dining-room the Frau President was sitting at breakfast with Flora and the councillor. Flora's beautiful morning dress was of white, trimmed with pink, and a charming breakfast-cap covered her hair, which was *en papillotes.* Kitty was startled,—her beautiful sister's strongly-marked profile looked so sharp and thin without the golden glory of the curls above her brow; for the first time she saw that Flora was no longer young, that at last her restless ambition had begun to grave deep lines in the lovely oval of her face.

"Heavens, Kitty! what put it into your head to drop down upon us to-day?" she cried, with an irritation which she did not care to conceal. "I cannot tell you how it embarrasses me. I must assign you some place now whether I will or not, and I have twelve bridesmaids already,—you see yourself I cannot want a thirteenth——" She paused with a faint exclamation.

The councillor had been sitting with his back to the door, and had just poured out a glass of Burgundy which he was raising to his lips, when Flora's words apprised him of the entrance of the sisters. Either the glass slipped from his hand in his surprise, or he did not look to see how he placed it upon the table,—its dark crimson contents were spilled upon the white damask cloth and stained Flora's dress.

For a moment he stood confused, dismayed, his face colourless, his eyes staring at the door as if some bodiless phantom were entering there instead of the stately girl with serious eyes and an assured bearing. But he recovered himself quickly. Apologizing to Flora for his awkwardness, he rang the bell for servants to repair the disaster, and then, hastening to Kitty, drew her into the room. There was in his air and manner not a trace of the rejected lover; in every word, as he took her hands kindly, there spoke only the former fatherly guardian who rejoiced to see his ward again. He patted her on the shoulder and bade her welcome.

"I did not venture to invite you," he said, "and indeed I have been too busy with business matters of late to be able to think much of Dresden. You must forgive——"

"I am here solely upon Henriette's account, and as her nurse," Kitty hastily interrupted him, without the least air of offence at Flora's unsisterly reception.

"You are kind and good, my child," the Frau President said, with a smile of relief; every fear was banished from her mind by the entire ease of this meeting. "But where shall we put you? Your former room is occupied by Flora's trousseau, and——"

"Therefore you must permit me to remain in my own home, where I have just established myself," Kitty courteously and modestly finished the sentence.

"I am afraid there is no help for it," the old lady replied, in the best of humours. "This afternoon our house will be full to overflowing, and everything is in the greatest bustle and confusion,—our breakfast-table is in the only peaceful spot. From early dawn they have been hammering and rehearsing——"

"Yes; they fairly shake the walls with their declamation in the ball-room," said Henriette, wearily leaning back in the arm-chair the councillor had placed for her. "As we passed, we heard 'Pallas Athene,' 'the roses of Cashmere,' and 'learned professor,' in admirable confusion——"

"Ugh!" Flora exclaimed, putting her fingers in her ears, "it is really too bad to force such an amateur production upon me, when I have performed myself in so many of our court fêtes. And there one must sit and not move a muscle of one's face, when the ridiculousness of the thing is half killing one with inward laughter——"

The Frau President imposed silence upon her by an emphatic gesture, for the amateur performers, who had taken a cup of chocolate in the dining-room before the rehearsal, made their appearance now in search of the hats and parasols they had left behind them.

Flora slipped into the adjoining boudoir.

With an affectation of great delight, the maid of honour, Fräulein von Giese, hastened up to Kitty and welcomed her among them once more. Then, holding out her hand to the councillor, she exclaimed, "So glad to see you, my dear Herr von Römer. Now we can thank you in person for the delightful way in which you have seconded our efforts to make our fête this evening charming. Everything is superb, like the work of enchantment." She rapturously kissed her finger-tips. "Only in Villa Baumgarten can one enjoy such 'Arabian Nights' Entertainments:' every one agrees to that. Apropos, have you heard the terrible news about Major Bredow? He is totally ruined, and many others are trembling in terror. Good heavens! what times these are in which we live! Shock follows shock with such rapidity——"

"But Major Bredow has been speculating so insanely," the Frau President said, indifferently, adjusting herself comfortably among the cushions of her arm-chair. "How could any one act so entirely without sense or reason?"

"It is his wife's fault. She spent too much: three thousand a year on her dresses alone."

"Oh, my dear, she might easily have done that if her husband had shown more sense in his investments; but he mixed himself up with projects that carried swindling on the face of them." She shrugged her shoulders. "In such matters one should always take the best advice, as I have done; eh, Moritz? we need have no fears."

"I should think not," he replied, smiling with easy assurance, and, filling his glass with Burgundy, he emptied it at a draught. "Of course, in such a general crash no one is entirely untouched; here and there small sums vanish that have been risked just for the sake of trying,—pin-pricks, that draw no blood——"

"Ah, that reminds me that I have not had my newspaper to-day," the Frau President interrupted him, with animation. "It usually comes punctually at nine o'clock."

He shrugged his shoulders. "Some negligence of the post-office, or it may have slipped in among my papers and been sent to the tower. I will see about it." And he filled his glass again.

"I beg pardon, ladies," he said, alluding to these repeated draughts. "I am threatened with an attack of headache, to which I am subject, and my best mode of prevention is a brimming glass of wine." His face did indeed seem to have borrowed the dark hue of the wine he was drinking.

He hastily opened a bottle of champagne and filled several glasses. "I pray you drink with me to the success of our evening's entertainment," he said to the ladies, who each followed his example in taking up a glass. "To the flower-fairy and her train! To youth and beauty, and the delights of life, so dear to us all,—ay, to existence itself!"

The glasses clinked, and the Frau President shook her head, with a laugh.

Involuntarily Kitty had withdrawn to a window recess, in which stood Henriette's arm-chair. She saw a tear tremble beneath the invalid's eyelid at the thoughtless toast as she bit her lip in indignant pain; for her, existence was a rack of torture,—for her, the delights of life were purchased by suffering with every breath she drew. The young ward had taken no glass, and the guardian had offered her none. The girl's glance rested gravely and searchingly upon his mobile features.

She had never suspected that a tempest of feeling could arise behind the man's smooth, passionless face; and yet there it was, plainly indicated in the uncertain wandering eyes, in the quiver of the lips, in the forced merriment of the voice.

Her guardian seemed conscious of her look; involuntarily he glanced towards the window, and then hastily placing his glass upon the table he passed his hand across his brow and ran his fingers through his hair,—an attack of dizziness seemed to threaten him for an instant, in addition to the headache which evidently defied his remedy.

CHAPTER XXIV.

By the afternoon, preparations for the evening greatly increased the noise and confusion. The families of rank from the neighbouring estates arrived, and apartments had to be assigned them. Trunks filled with costumes were brought from town: the performers were to dress in the villa. Barbers and milliners came and went, and through it all the gardeners were bringing palms, orange-trees, and tropical plants from the conservatories.

In spite of all the noise and bustle that could be heard in her room, Henriette had fallen into what seemed a refreshing slumber. In the adjoining dressing-room sat Nanni, sewing spangles upon a cloud of gauze that was wanted by the decorators of the stage below-stairs. Kitty softly opened the door, and, bidding the girl pay special heed to her sleeping mistress until her return, she left the room and went down-stairs to go to the mill, where she still had some arrangements to make.

She avoided the large hall,—it was swarming with people, coming and going,—and turned into the passage beside the ball-room. It was quieter, but at the low door at the end of it leading into the open air stood the councillor, a straw hat on his head, apparently about to go to the tower. He was instructing Anton, his servant, who lodged in the tower, with regard to commissions which he was going to town to fulfil. "Take time enough," he called after him; "I shall not dress before six o'clock."

Kitty walked slowly on along the corridor in hopes he would now leave the door and go into the park, but he thrust his hands mechanically into the pockets of his light coat and stood still. He was standing on the topmost of three or four steps, and the view obtained thence of a considerable portion of his beautiful domain apparently delayed his descent. Perhaps he had never before so enjoyed this view in all its wondrous beauty, when the rosy light of the charming afternoon invested it with a tender splendour. The movement of his head showed that his gaze was wandering hither and thither, but the young girl also saw that he was trembling with profound, suppressed emotion, as with his right hand he suddenly covered his eyes. He must have been struggling with the illness of which he had spoken, and which he was determined should not disturb the evening's festivities.

She walked more quickly and with less caution, and he turned hastily at the sound of her approach.

"Is your headache worse?" she asked, kindly.

"Yes; and I have just had a slight attack of giddiness," he answered, in an uncertain voice, as he pulled his hat down over his eyes. "No wonder! If I had had the least idea of the thousand annoyances inseparable from this ball I never would have given it," he added, more calmly, although his manner was not natural. "Those stupid workmen have made all kinds of mistakes in my absence; they did not understand my ideas, and what they had been hammering away at for a week had to be pulled down and put up again in twelve hours. That is why this bustle and noise must go on until the very moment when the curtain rises."

He descended the steps slowly and cautiously, as if everything were again swimming before him.

"Shall I go back and get you a glass of Seltzer-water?" she asked, as she stood in the door-way; "or would it not be better to send for the doctor?"

"No, thank you, Kitty," he replied, in a strangely gentle tone, and his moistened glance rested lingeringly upon the girl who had expressed such kind anxiety, "And indeed you are mistaken if you think Bruck is to be had so easily. He is overwhelmed with practice; I believe he will have to be sent for to leave some sick-bed to come to his very marriage, the day after to-morrow." A sarcastic smile flitted across his face. "My best remedy is, I know," he instantly added, "my vaults in the tower. I am just going there to select the wine for this evening; the air in those cellars will act like a cooling bandage."

Kitty arranged her hat upon her head and came out upon the door-steps.

"And you are going to the mill? No farther, I hope?" he said, looking at his watch. It was a simple question, and negligently uttered, and yet it seemed to Kitty that he caught his breath as he asked it.

Descending the steps, she told him her errand to the mill, and then, nodding a farewell, she crossed the road while the councillor turned towards the tower. Behind the first group of shrubs, she turned and looked after him; he was surely suffering more than he would admit. His knees seemed to tremble beneath him; he had thrust back the hat from his forehead as if his brow were burning, and his eyes were wandering aimlessly over the park.

Suddenly her temples throbbed; a vague terror assailed her. That sick man tottering so uncertainly alone in the tower-cellar! Like some fever-bred phantom, the horrible thought that had shocked her once before in sight of the tower again occurred to her. "I pray you, Moritz, be careful with the light," she cried anxiously after him.

He might have been deep in thought, or perhaps his nerves were in that unusually irritable state when a loud voice suffices to terrify; he started as if struck by a shot.

"What do you mean by that?" he called back, hoarsely. "Are you seeing ghosts by daylight, Kitty?" he instantly added, with a burst of laughter that mortified his ward, as he vanished among the trees, waving his hand and holding himself erect.

Scarcely half an hour later, Kitty was walking along the river-bank. Her errand to the mill accomplished, she found she had time to snatch one sweet, stolen glance at the house by the river. How her heart beat as she saw the weather-cock on the roof gleaming in the sunlight through the quivering birch-leaves! How she started at the crunching of the gravel on the path beneath her tread! She came like an exile to have one last look of a beloved country. She leaned against the trunk of the poplar that stood by the bridge, whence she had stamped that last scene so ineffaceably on her memory,—the peeping children, their heads showing against the brilliant landscape beyond as upon a golden background, the strong stern man by the garden-table seeming crushed by some inexplicable emotion.

All was quiet now in the shaded garden. The trees, then in all the pride of spring, were now bending with the load of bright-coloured fruit that filled the air with its fragrance, and the trellis was hardly seen beneath its purple load. Only one shy glimpse towards the corner window, where stood the doctor's writing-table. He was not at home; he was hastening from one bedside to another, driven by professional cares. And he no longer occupied that room. White muslin curtains adorned the window; upon the sill, among the pots of Alpine violets in full bloom, lay a snow-white kitten, and two knitting hands and a woman's head crowned with snowy hair beneath a muslin fichu could be distinguished there; the Frau Dean's old friend was already established. He too had burned his ships behind him; he was ready to go, and the day after the morrow, the "last moment" would come, when her proud, heartless sister would stand beside him in glistening white satin, to become mistress of the mansion to a man of note. Had she once struggled as bitterly—that fair young dame of by-gone days—as did the girl who now, in a burst of tears, clasped her arms about the poplar's slender stem and pressed her brow painfully against the rough, hard bark? She of the legend had once been loved, if deserted at last; no blame could be attached to her; but here an evil jealousy was gnawing at the heart of one unloved, and she whom she envied was—her own sister.

A loud footfall behind her made her look around. Franz the miller, with an iron crowbar over his shoulder, was passing by, to look after the upper weir, he said. His presence sent the blood to her cheeks and scared her from her post of observation. While Franz hurried on she walked slowly along the bank of the stream. She could not yet make up her mind to return to the villa; her toilette for the evening would be completed long before Henriette, who was determined to be present at the fête, had half finished the adornments which were to make the ravages of disease less conspicuous.

The solitude here was so delicious; there was no one to see how red her eyes were, or how angrily her wayward heart was battling with the sinful desires that had urged her hither,—yes, they had been the cause of her coming. She would not spare herself or lie to her own soul! She had not come to

24*

see the quiet house, and the dear old friend whose home it was, and she had not been sure that he was not there. She had hoped—what? And when another face than his had appeared at the window the whole place had been to her lonely and deserted.

Franz had vanished in the distance. She was approaching the ruin. The circle of water about it glistened, and through the shrubbery she could see the graceful bridge spanning the ditch. At the moment a man was crossing it from the tower. A thick reddish beard covered the lower part of his face; he wore a labourer's blouse, and was driving two roes before him with his stick. They leaped across the bridge and fled into the recesses of the park.

Kitty would have paid the man no especial attention—workmen were continually employed in and about the tower—if his conduct had not seemed strange to her. The councillor was very fond of these roes; he was provoked when they strayed into the park, and here this stranger was intentionally chasing them across the ditch! Was he one of the discontented crowd of factory-hands who envied the rich man and wrought mischief to his possessions whenever they could? He turned into a path leading through the park-gates out upon the high-road; she followed him with her eyes until he was lost in the thicket. The resemblance was wonderful! In his carriage and height, in his whole make, indeed, the man in the blouse might have been the councillor's twin brother.

She stood involuntarily rooted to the spot, looking towards the tower whence he had come. How charmingly the landscape here harmonized with the structure! How well the modern architect had known how to spare and now to efface so as to weave about the old ruin a romantic charm!

Silence reigned again; no sound was heard but the faint flapping of the doves' wings; those graceful sailors of the air were floating in the crimson evening light, slipping through the interstices of the mural crown of the tower as it showed clear against the western sky—No, it was no mural crown! in a flash it was a burning crater, vomiting forth with a noise like thunder a cloud of pitchy vapour into the serene skies. The ground seemed to be torn from beneath the girl's feet. She was dashed to the earth and in an instant immersed in the cool waters of the fosse.

What was it? Every one came running from the villa to take refuge in the garden. The house tottered from foundation to roof-tree. An earthquake? As if bereft of all sense, the members of the household stood still in the open air as though expecting to see the earth yawn at their feet. Little rills of water were trickling through the grass of the lawn. The air began to be filled with smoke, and to scatter everywhere on the gravel walks particles of burned material. The panes of plate-glass in the windows were broken; and in the ball-room the huge mirror stretching from floor to ceiling lay shattered into a thousand pieces, the silk and velvet draperies had dropped from their fastenings around the stage, and the workmen had with difficulty escaped injury from the falling framework.

Passers-by rushed in from the road, among them Anton, who was just returning from town. "There! there!" they cried to the Frau President, who was leaning half fainting upon Flora's arm, and as they spoke they pointed to the distant portion of the park. There was a fire in that direction, and huge volumes of smoke were pouring upwards so thickly that the sparks showed in its pitchy blackness like rockets in a dark night.

"The powder in the tower has exploded!" a voice cried from the midst of the throng.

"Nonsense!" Anton replied, with an attempt at a laugh, although his teeth were chattering in his head with terror.

"That old stuff has long been past exploding, and the few pinches of fresh which the Herr Councillor had stored there in jest could not have stirred a tile from its place."

Nevertheless he ran wildly in the direction of the tower across the flooded lawn,—he knew his master had gone thither. The crowd followed him, whilst the fire-alarm from the neighbouring town began to toll.

What had become, in a moment almost too brief to suffice for one human breath, of the Eden which wealth and luxury had evoked from the ruins of knightly splendour? When the black vapour darkened the heavens there had burst into air the infernal force as if from some subterranean fountain; huge masses of granite had been tossed forth to lie here and there half buried in the soft sod of the lawn, having broken strong trees like reeds in their descent, while towards the south the new conservatory stood like a sieve of glass, each splinter sparkling and gleaming in the evening light. There must have been a perfect hailstorm of stones poured upon it, thus to shatter the exquisite toy, so lately the admiration of the capital.

It was indeed a sight to horrify the breathless crowd as they emerged from the shrubbery that had partially concealed the extent of the disaster. Had the ghostly ancestress of the Baumgartens indeed lighted the train to put an end to the farce which the modern parvenu was playing above the hoary ruins of the home of her race? Those builders of old must have cemented their walls with iron. The upper portion of the tower, with its machicolated summit, was indeed scattered to all the four winds of heaven, but of the lower and more ancient building only the smaller part had been destroyed; it lay in huge masses near the fosse, whilst the rest still stood threateningly erect in air, and from its depths the yellow flames ascended, greedily devouring every particle of wood or inflammable material within.

"My poor master!" Anton groaned, stretching his arms in despair across the ditch, the waters of which had been raised from their bed by the force of the explosion to flow here and there over the park. They were now pouring back again, and dashing once more upon their accustomed way, carrying with them gravel, grass, and the bleeding bodies of slain doves and rooks. The pretty arches of the bridge had vanished, the green artificial hill was seamed by huge rifts, and the old chestnuts which it had nourished were thrust forth from its bosom to lie stretched on the ground, their boughs interlaced like the horns of deer dead in mortal conflict.

Of what use were the crowds of men hurrying hither with their fire-engines? There was nothing to save. Where in that glowing crater could be found the costly furniture, the famous collection of ancient tankards, the pictures, statuary, ivory carvings, and rich carpets? As if in ghastly mockery, a crimson silk curtain that had floated uninjured from one of the windows was still hanging from a fragment of stone sill down over the remains of the outer wall, like a stream of blood flowing from some terrible wound.

And among the crowd there ran whispers of the piles of gold and silver—or no, papers, bundles of papers, representing incalculable sums, factories, mines, landed property,—all of which the old tower, with its mighty walls, its impregnable locks, and its fosse, had guarded like a dragon. Where were they now? Where were the sheets of iron that had imprisoned them? Had the safes fallen undestroyed into the vaults of the cellar, to await there a future resurrection in defiance of the flames?

And what had become of him,—of the man who, as Anton declared, had gone to the tower an hour before to select the wine for the evening's entertainment? All gazed helplessly at the flaming mass, while the faithful servant ran to and fro on the bank of the ditch, wringing his hands, and shouting his master's name across the water. It had been inconceivable folly to keep the powder there where an unguarded lamp was so frequently used.

"The old historic powder has had nothing to do with this. Some very different explosive material has been at work here," a loud voice said from the crowd. The speaker was an engineer, and had been passing by the villa at the moment of the catastrophe.

"But how came anything else in the cellar?" Anton stammered, standing still, and looking at the speaker with wonder and inquiry.

The man shrugged his shoulders with a meaning look, and, turning, was lost in the crowd, whilst the engines did their work.

As long as the fire raged, the jets of water hissed upon the flames, the alarm-bell tolled unceasingly, firemen brought planks and poles from the villa to construct some kind of a bridge over the fosse, and the noise and confusion increased from moment to moment. In the midst of it all, a piercing shriek was heard at some distance; on the path leading to the upper weir Franz the miller had been found; a heavy stone had prostrated him and crushed in his chest; the man was dead.

This shriek, uttered by his wife as she threw herself upon the body, seemed re-echoed from all parts of the park, it was so resounded with cries from hundreds of throats.

"Moritz,—they have found him!" the Frau President murmured, with a start. She had sunk down upon a garden-seat not far from the house,—her feet refused to carry her farther. She now made an effort to rise; in vain! The infirmity of age, hitherto so resolutely ignored, asserted itself at this moment of nervous agitation. "Have they found him? Is he dead? Dead?" she stammered, incoherently, her eyes, usually so coldly calm, staring wildly in the direction of the ruin, whilst she clutched the arm of Flora, who was standing beside her.

The beautiful woman alone preserved her composure. There above the trees the thick vapour rolled lazily and heavily upwards, painting the heavens far and near in dull ashen gray, and here before the house, with its shattered window-panes, the orange-trees were overturned upon the lawn, where the water trickled and flowed in little rills, to gather in pools in the deep furrows cut by the fire-engines. The air was filled with wild outcries, crowds of people were rushing past each moment from the town, and in the midst of this desolation stood a lovely woman, clad in white, with marguerites on her breast and in her fair curls, pale to the lips, but collected and self-assured in her demeanor,—a being set apart from all personal misfortune.

"If you would only loosen your hold of my arm, grandmamma," she said, impatiently, "I might possibly convince you that you are needlessly alarmed. Why must Moritz have perished? Pshaw! Moritz, with his constant good fortune! I am perfectly sure that he is there in the midst of the crowd, safe and sound, and those stupid servants, who, by the way, pay us no attention, except to shout out some unintelligible nonsense in passing, are so frightened that they do not know their own master when they see him." She looked down at the wet sod, and then at her white boot that peeped forth from beneath the flounces of her muslin dress. "One would say I too had lost my senses," she continued, with a shrug, "but I must go and see——"

"No, no, you must stay here!" cried the Frau President, grasping the skirt of white muslin. "You will not leave me alone with Henriette, who is still more helpless than I, and is of no use to me? Oh, God, I shall die! If he should be dead, if—what then?" Her head sank upon her breast, that gleamed with diamonds; she looked old and infirm, and her form seemed bent and shrunken in the stiff folds of her yellow moiré dress.

Henriette crouched upon the seat beside her, ashy pale, with wide, terrified eyes. "Kitty! Where can Kitty be?" she repeated to herself with trembling lips, as if it were a sentence she were learning by rote.

"God in heaven grant me patience!" Flora muttered between her teeth. "Such weakness is terrible. Why in the world, Henriette, are you continually asking for Kitty? No one means to take her from you!"

She looked impatiently towards the house, but no one was to be seen who could relieve her of her charge; every one had gone to the ruins,—the newly-arrived guests, the footmen, the servants from the kitchen; even the neatly-shod ladies' maids had run through the wet towards the scene of the disaster. But aid approached from town in the persons of the amateur performers, who came breathlessly round the corner of the house.

"For heaven's sake, tell us what is the matter!" cried Fräulein von Giese, rushing up to the lonely group of women.

Flora shrugged her shoulders. "We know nothing more than that there has been an explosion in the tower. Every one runs past us; no one answers our questions; and I cannot stir from the spot, because grandmamma has lost her head, and in her agitation is positively tearing the clothes off my back. She imagines that Moritz is killed."

The young girls stood as if turned to stone at this horrible idea,—the strong, handsome man who only a few hours before had emptied his glass to the "delights of life" already perished in the flames or crushed to atoms! It could not be. "Impossible!" exclaimed Fräulein von Giese.

"Impossible?" the Frau President repeated, with a mingling of sobs and wild laughter; she had struggled to her feet, but she tottered like a drunken man as she pointed a trembling finger towards the nearest grove. "There—they are bringing him! My God! Moritz, Moritz!"

In solemn silence an object was being borne along, and within the circle of those who were accompanying it walked Doctor Bruck, without his hat, his tall figure towering above the rest.

Flora flew towards him, whilst the Frau President burst into a fit of convulsive weeping. At sight of the lovely commanding figure the group involuntarily parted. Flora gave one hasty glance at the form extended upon a litter, and instantly turned back to say soothingly, "Be calm, grandmamma! It is not Moritz——"

"It is Kitty,—I knew it," Henriette murmured hoarsely, in a voice that was half sob, half whisper, as she staggered across to where the bearers had put down their burden for a minute to take breath.

The poor girl lay upon the old-fashioned couch from the doctor's study. Her dress hanging over its side was dripping with moisture. Soft pillows were beneath her back and head; with her eyelids so gently closed and her hands resting so calmly upon her breast, one might have imagined her sleeping, but for the bandage above her brow and the blood trickling down her cheek.

"What has happened to Kitty, Leo? What was she doing near the ruin?" Flora asked, approaching the couch, both in tone and in manner displaying more irritation at her sister's supposed forwardness than terror at what had happened.

At her previous remark, intended to soothe her grandmother, the doctor had turned in sudden anger; now he seemed not to hear her speaking, so firmly closed were his lips, so stolid was the look which passed her by to rest with interest upon Henriette.

The poor invalid stood before him gasping for breath, looking up to him with eyes dimmed with tears. "Only one word,

Leo; is she alive?" she stammered, raising her hands clasped in entreaty.

"Yes; the concussion and loss of blood have stunned her; the only danger at present to be apprehended is from her wet clothes. The wound on her temple is trifling, thank God!" he answered in vibrating tones, which seemed to come from the depths of his heart, while with all a brother's tenderness he put his left arm around the frail form that could hardly stand upright. "Go on," he said to the bearers, with evident anxiety and impatience.

The accompanying crowd dispersed; there was no danger here, and most of them returned to the ruin. The couch was carried on towards the house, past the Frau President, who gazed at the unconscious form as if bereft of all capacity to understand and appreciate. The group of horrified girls stood huddled together, looking helplessly towards the young physician who walked beside the couch without noticing them. He kept his left arm around Henriette's waist; his right hand he had laid lightly upon Kitty's brow, as if to shield her from any shock if consciousness should return. He who was usually so reserved, who so carefully concealed all emotion, the man whom of late all had seen so gloomy and constrained, was now looking down with unconcealed tenderness upon the pale face lying upon the pillows, as if nothing existed for him in the world except this most sacred and dear treasure which he had just snatched from the grave.

Flora followed the silent group apart, as if bound by no tie to the three people whom misfortune had suddenly shown to be so closely allied. On the spot where the bearers had rested the water was standing in little pools; she walked through them not heeding the wet, and her long muslin train dragged damp and dirty over the gravelled path. Suddenly she tore the wreath of marguerites from her hair; it was a bitter mockery in the midst of all this horror; she plucked and pulled it to pieces mechanically as she walked along, and the little white stars lay scattered upon the ground over which she had passed.

She too passed her grandmother and her friends without heeding them. Her flashing glance rested immovably upon her lover's tall, commanding figure; evidently she momentarily expected that he would turn to her, and thus she followed him step by step to the house and across its threshold. The Frau President called after her; the earth was shaken by another loud crash from the ruins, followed by shouts and cries. She did not look round; the world might be dissolved behind her; she was inexorably resolved to assert her "rights."

CHAPTER XXV.

A SILENT night of anxious, breathless suspense ensued upon this horrible day. No one went to bed; the gas was lighted all over the house, the servants glided noiselessly about on tiptoe, or huddled whispering in corners, and when some fireman passed near the house, or a door was softly opened, all started as from an electric shock and hurried into the corridors, sure that some intelligence would be brought of the master of the house. But the night waned, and the dawn peeped in at the windows,—he never, never came.

The rosy light of a glorious morning shone upon Villa Baumgarten, making the broken window-panes glitter and shine. It entered the ball-room and kindled the crimson of the fallen canopy, it kissed the fading leaves of the festoons of green and the broken boughs of the plants brought from the conservatory;—what chaos reigned there! One single minute had converted the costly but frail "Arabian Nights' Entertainment" into a heap of ruins and fragments. The charming verses in praise of the bride were unspoken, and upon the spot where the bespangled genius should have hovered in a rosy cloud, the keen morning breeze toyed mockingly with shreds of pink and white tulle.

It was the first time, perhaps, that the light of dawn had seen these splendid interiors; no shutter had been closed, no shade drawn down,—it even stared in upon the gorgeous bedroom in the northeastern angle of the building, upon the violet silk draperies, the richly-carved bedstead covered with lace, and it might mirror itself in the diamonds strewn among the puffs of the Frau President's hair. The maid had not dared to offer her services to the old lady, who now and then would totter through the long suite of apartments, dragging after her her heavy yellow train among overturned furniture and statues toppled from their pedestals.

The cloud of tulle which she always wore about her neck and chin had become loosened, and the sharp, withered outline of the lower portion of her face and of the throat was painfully evident. Yes, she was very old, and the sun of her life was low on the horizon; nevertheless, her aged brain was busy with but one absorbing thought, "Who is Moritz's heir?" She herself had not the slightest claim upon the wealth of the man so suddenly snatched away, not even upon the bed in which she slept or the plate from which she ate. The councillor had been early left an orphan; so far as she knew, he had no existing relatives of his name; but had he not continually sent a subsistence to a sister of his mother's living on the Rhine? Would she inherit his wealth? The idea was maddening. The wife of an obscure clerk, a needy seamstress, would then take possession of this colossal fortune, and the Frau President Urach, who for years had not been able to conceive how any one could move without silken-cushioned equipages, how any one could dine without lackeys in waiting, or sleep unless in a bed canopied with silk, would have to rout out her old furniture from the garrets whither it had been banished, and hire narrow lodgings where there were no stables filled with horses, no liveried servants and princely *ménage*, for neither she nor her granddaughters were connected by any tie of blood with the millionaire who had gone out of the world intestate.

The guests invited from the neighbourhood had remained with the old lady until midnight, and, although no distinct mention had been made of this subject, there had not been lacking allusions to the business complications that must ensue upon the catastrophe, since the councillor had kept all his ledgers and business papers of every description in the tower, and not a scrap of them was to be found.

But, although enormous sums had thus been destroyed, did not she, the Frau President, at present make her home upon an estate valued at many thousands? Were not the vaults of the plate-chamber beneath her feet? Were not the stables full of thorough-bred horses? And was not the collection of paintings of incalculable value? All this would more than suffice to ensure a luxurious existence to the old lady to the end of her days, if only she could prove that one drop of blood in her aristocratic veins came from the same source that had given life to the rope-maker's son.

And they spoke also of her who lay at present above-stairs, in Henriette's sitting-room, the castle miller's granddaughter; they knew that her entire fortune had been kept in the tower. Upon this theme the Frau President in her nervous agitation did not care to speculate; what was the old miller's hoarded wealth to her? Flora, on the contrary, maintaining an entire self-possession in spite of the horrors of the day, pondered long upon the possible consequences to her half-sister of the destruction of the safe in the tower.

There was an angry frown upon her brow as she came down from the third story about ten o'clock in the evening. She, the admired centre of a large and aristocratic circle, the beautiful woman whose intellectual force and ripe judgment had been the wonder of her acquaintances, had been obliged, to her intense disgust, to play the pitiable part of a supernumerary in the sick-room. In addition to Henriette, who had taken up her position on a couch and would not consent to leave the room, the dean's widow had made her appearance as Kitty's nurse. She had sought refuge in the villa, for the house by the river being the nearest to the tower had suffered much from the explosion; the chimneys had been thrown down, the southern wall was much damaged, the windows were shivered to pieces, and none of the doors would latch or bolt. The friend and companion had gone with the maid to Susy, at the mill, and the doctor had left two watchmen to guard the house during the night.

There had been no place for Flora at the wounded girl's bedside. At the head sat the dean's widow, her eyes red with weeping, and opposite her the doctor. "The old woman" had behaved as if the trifling injury that Kitty had sustained were the gravest consequence of the disaster, and the doctor had never stirred from his post, only relinquishing his clasp of Kitty's hand when the bandage upon her brow needed renewing. It required more patience and self-control than Flora had at command to look quietly on at such anxious care bestowed upon "a tall, robust girl, with nerves and muscles inherited from the former woodcutter's daughter."

Weary of the perpetual whispering, and perceiving that there was no sensible word to be extorted from all these frightened people, the beautiful woman had at last left the room alone and greatly irritated; the doctor had not even accompanied her to the door. Of course she did not go to bed; she took off her evening dress, and, putting on a white cashmere dressing-gown, reclined towards morning upon her crimson lounge.

The former study looked desolate and dreary enough. The black writing-table had been emptied of all its papers, and stood dusty in the recess by the window; most of the books had been taken from the shelves and were packed in boxes in the middle of the floor; the pedestals were overturned, while, over all, the hanging lamp but carelessly lighted by the servants threw a pale uncertain gleam, which, now that the morning air and dawning light came freshly in through the broken panes of glass, swung to and fro in its white globe like the last faint spark of fire from the ruins.

When the day had fairly broken, Flora sent up-stairs to request the doctor to come to her, and as his firm, military step was heard in the corridor she hastily arranged her curls beneath her lace morning cap, leaned back among the crimson cushions, and looked from under her half-closed eyelids towards the door by which he was to enter.

He came in. Never had she seen him thus, and involuntarily, mechanically, she arose as if to greet a stranger.

"I am not well, Leo," she said with hesitation, not turning her glance of surprise from his face, which although pale and weary was as if inspired by some light from within that had totally changed its character. "My head burns; fright and wet feet must have brought on an attack of fever." She added this uncertainly, whilst his eyes dwelt upon her with the cool searching gaze of the physician. The look irritated her.

"Have a care, Bruck!" she said, in a perfectly calm tone, but her breath came quick, and her finely pencilled eyebrows contracted so that two deep lines showed between them. "For months I have borne to see that your practice is your best beloved, to which I am subordinate." She shrugged her shoulders. "I can foresee that such must be my fate, and possess magnanimity enough to acquiesce in it, since such devotion to his profession will bring fame to the man whose name I shall bear." She turned her head as she spoke with a haughty air, as if looking through a world filled with his renown. "But I protest against being set aside when I have need of your medical skill," she continued. "We have all suffered from the terrible catastrophe. It was my task, and one of indescribable difficulty, to protect and soothe grandmamma, who was half insane with terror, and Henriette; and yet it has never occurred to you to ask, 'How have you borne all this?' "

"I have not asked because I know you pride yourself upon subordinating all emotion to the intellect, and because I can see at a glance how little your physical condition has been affected."

She listened amazed to his tone, which, with all its wonted calmness, trembled audibly as if in consequence of throbbing pulses.

"With regard to your second assertion you are wrong," she said, after a moment's silence. "My temples throb with nervous excitement. Your first may be correct; I do strive to compose myself in view of every event whatsoever, that I may bring my calm judgment to bear upon it. From your tone you would seem to disapprove of this method of mine, although just at present it certainly deserves your praise. I have never been induced to speculate with my paternal inheritance; I have never been tempted by fortunate chances; were it otherwise I should stand here this moment with empty hands, my dowry would have been dispersed upon the air like the papers that were destroyed yesterday. Yes, look dismayed if you will, Bruck,"—she lowered her voice,—"I am not deceived, and I choose to call things by their right names. Grandmamma is pacing her room and wringing her hands in fear lest the 'colossal fortune' should fall into stranger hands.

Our precious guests spent half the night bewailing the fate of the wealthy man, fortune's darling, torn by cruel destiny so tragically from his earthly paradise. But *I* say, this theatric exit was tolerably well put upon the stage, nevertheless there is a rent in the curtain which lets in the light of reality upon the corpse. In a short time, perhaps in a day or two, the fact will be spread abroad that Römer was at first only a bold speculator, it may be, but in the end—a scoundrel."

There could not have been a more striking illustration of the wayward turns of fortune than was presented at this moment. There stood the beautiful woman in her white Iphigenia robes, the crimson carpet beneath her feet, the swinging lamp above her brow, upon the very spot where in the preceding December she had stigmatized as pretended her lover's medical skill, and had declared, "I cannot endure concealment of my opinion."

Flora was right; she certainly called things by their right names; she gave utterance to what the man standing before her could not in his inmost soul deny, and which since yesterday had caused him great pain; but to hear the naked fact thus boldly stated by those finely chiselled lips, in order that their owner might vaunt her keen insight, naturally offended deeply his sense of delicacy and refinement.

"Ah, I see I am so unfortunate to-day as to displease you," she began again, half sarcastically half poutingly, as she followed him to the window recess whither he had gone in evident irritation. "It may be that my speech was too downright; perhaps in view of many little kindnesses shown me now and again by Römer it would have been well to be less frank and true,"—she elevated her eyebrows and shrugged her shoulders,—"but I am the sworn foe of all hypocrisy and have reason enough for indignation. My sister Henriette, with whose inheritance Römer has been speculating, will be a beggar; and Kitty?—rest assured that not a stiver of all her immense fortune is left."

"So much the better!" came as if only breathed from the lips that seemed at this moment to be curved beneath the thick moustache in a tender smile.

Faint as was the sound, Flora's ear caught it. "So much the better?" she asked, in surprise, half laughing as she clasped her hands. "Our youngest is certainly not much to my taste, but what crime has she committed, that her ill luck should so content you?"

He bit his lip, and, pressing his forehead against the window-frame, looked abroad into the garden, where the golden morning light was just touching the head of the marble nymph at the fountain.

"Of course Kitty will not be so badly off as Henriette; she will have the castle mill, and that is worth a good round sum," she added, after a pause. "She can live there when matters are arranged; and indeed I know of no better refuge for our poor invalid. The sisters are very fond of each other, and would like to be together. In fact, no other arrangement is possible, for grandmamma's limited income will make it impossible for her to take charge of Henriette, and of course I should not think of burdening you with my sick sister." She suddenly put her hand within his arm and looked up at him tenderly. "Ah, Leo, how thankful I shall be when we are seated together in the carriage to-morrow, leaving behind us all this disaster and misery!"

With a passionate gesture and a face in which shone an indignation she had never seen there before, he snatched his arm from her clasp. "Would you really forsake them all, leave them helpless and alone to meet the terrible shocks of the near future?" he cried, as if beside himself. "Go then whenever you choose,—I remain here!"

"Leo!" she almost screamed, and then stood for a moment

speechless, overpowered by anger. She laid her clenched hand upon her heart, as if she had received a stab. "Surely you do not estimate the full meaning of your hasty words," she said, slowly and emphatically. "I will regard them only as they call for this reply from me. If we do not set out upon our tour to-morrow, before further revelations are made as to Römer's affairs,—and surely no one can take it amiss of us that we quietly carry out plans so long decided upon,—our union must be indefinitely postponed."

He made no reply, but stood motionless in his former position, looking from the window. His silence evidently irritated her further: passion gleamed in her large gray eyes.

"I said before that I am willing to yield the first place in your heart to your practice, to your devotion to your profession," she went on, with increasing emphasis, "but I will not yield one jot of my rights to other women,—remember that, Leo! I cannot see why I should be forced to struggle through the fearful crash that must come here, with grandmamma and my sisters, when I have the right to flee to the calm protection of the home you have promised me. Can I do anything to alter the state of affairs? Nothing whatever. Why, then, do you wish to consign me to needless suffering? Must I too be an object for universal compassion? I would sooner depart on the instant. I *will not* be pointed at and pitied."

She paced the room in agitation. "You have not the faintest excuse to make me for remaining here," she said, standing at a distance from him, frowning darkly, when she had waited in vain for a reply. "You cannot even plead the necessity here for your professional aid. You would have had to leave Henriette to her fate; and as for Kitty, you will not assert that the scratch on her forehead which you yourself declared to be trifling demands all your medical skill. To tell the truth, I could scarcely suppress a laugh last night at your aunt's conduct and your own. It is allowable for Henriette to shed childish tears over a few drops of blood,—she is weak and nervous,—but for you to behave as if our youngest, the robust child of a race of peasants, were framed of snow and air——" She paused at the menacing look that Leo turned upon her as he raised his finger, unable longer to control the expression of his indignation.

She laughed angrily. "Do you think I am afraid? I return menace for menace. Take care, the 'yes' has not yet been uttered before the altar; it still lies with me to give a turn to affairs that you would hardly like. I repeat that your whole conduct yesterday with regard to Kitty was distasteful to me. Am I not to sneer at your treating her like a princess——"

"No, not like a princess,—like the best beloved of my heart, like my first and only love," he interrupted her, in a deep, melodious voice.

She started as if the earth had suddenly yawned at her feet; involuntarily she raised her arms towards heaven, and then she approached him.

He extended his hands as if to ward off her touch, and stood erect and decided. "Yes, I confess to you what I have hitherto struggled fiercely to lock within my own breast, from a shame that was the result of a perverted idea of right and wrong. I do it without a word of excuse or self-justification——" His voice sank. "I have been faithless to you from the moment of my first meeting with Kitty."

Flora slowly dropped her arms. Plain and distinct as the words were, they were the most incredible she had ever heard. Pshaw! why had she betrayed such foolish terror? It was true that the petted Flora Mangold had ensnared many a man's heart to reject it pitilessly in wanton love of power: not a season had passed without bringing her such triumphs; but that a man should prove faithless to her—ridiculous! The idea was too absurd; no one in the capital would credit it, herself least of all. It was far easier to believe that Doctor Bruck had at length summoned courage to attempt to revenge himself. She had pushed her fiery trial to extremes; in her justifiable irritation she had threatened to withhold her "yes" on the very altar-steps, and his long-suffering was exhausted; he was trying to punish her by arousing her jealousy. Her boundless vanity and frivolity postponed for a few minutes the bitterest experience of her life.

She curled her lip ironically and folded her arms. "Ah, at first sight, then!" she said. "Was that outside in the corridor, where she made her appearance like a genuine child of the people, the dust of travel on her boots and the poetic kerchief bundle in her hand?"

It was plain that her trifling irritated the man almost to madness. At this terrible moment, when his "first and only love" had asserted itself after suffering and struggles unspeakable, he was laughingly taken to task like a school-boy. He controlled himself, however. This question must be decided now; to see that it was decided with dignity was his task.

"I had then been Kitty's guide and companion from the mill, where I first saw her," he replied, with tolerable composure.

A dark blush of surprise crimsoned Flora's cheek. Her eyes sparkled: she bit her lip. "Ah! this is the first I have heard of that. She too,—the hypocrite of the 'pure' heart had her reasons for suppressing all mention of this interesting meeting." She laughed a short, hard laugh. "And what more, Bruck?" she demanded, her arms still folded, one foot advanced upon the carpet.

"If you persist in this tone, no explanation is possible for me except in writing." And he indignantly attempted to pass her.

She stepped before him. "Good heavens! how tragically you take it! I am only doing my best to play my part in your little farce. What! you would strive with me in a warfare of the pen? Dear Leo, believe me, you would come off the loser there, in spite of the telling medical brochures you have given to the world."

The arrogant smile that accompanied her words faded upon her lips in the presence of the stern cold glance that met her own. Gradually the suspicion dawned within her that he was indeed in earnest, bitter earnest; not as to his pretended affection for Kitty,—that passed all belief,—but as to his resolution, in spite of his passionate love for herself, to break with his capricious betrothed at the last moment rather than submit to a life-long "fiery trial." She regretted the words she had spoken, but arrogance and vanity retained their mastery of her.

"Then go!" she said, stepping aside. "I will not bear such looks as the one you have just given me. Go! I will not stir a finger to keep you." She burst into a scornful laugh. "Oh, rare masculine nature, so vaunted and so sung! There was a time when I begged almost upon my knees for my freedom; the chains were only the more closely riveted upon me. Look then, and learn from me what in such moments is the sole and only stay even for a 'vain, weak, feminine nature:' pride——"

"It was pride that then made me inexorable,—invincible pride, although a very different quality from the mixture of anger and defiance which you designate as such," he interrupted her. "I confess I was wrong,—very wrong. I will trouble you, as I have said, with no self-justification that might seem to throw blame upon others however remotely. The motive for my conduct then sprang from a fancied need to assert my own force, my masculine will, which as I thought should rise superior to all vagaries of feeling. I would not give you back your troth because I had been accustomed to regard my own when once plighted as pledged for all eternity. From that point of view our betrothal was as indissoluble as a Catholic marriage. I do not deny that the relics of my student days had weight with me in a false conception of honour. I spoke of one spring of action to you on that evening, and I refer to it again. I did not choose to join the throng of those who had been bound to your chariot-wheels only to be publicly rejected. I repeat that this was a boyish, unformed view to take, since in such cases it is not the man's honour, but the woman's, that is compromised."

She turned from him and drummed angrily with her fingers upon the table. "I never concealed from you the fact that I had been wooed repeatedly before our betrothal," she said, with proud indifference.

"You never did, nor did any of my acquaintances," he interposed. "But you must not forget that you were the lofty ideal of my boyhood. At the university, in my last campaign, I was spurred on by the thought that the proud heart so often wooed had never inclined to any, that it would bless him who should win it——" He broke off; he would not refer to the coquetry she had displayed; he scorned to bring the slightest recrimination to his aid.

"And do you assert that I ever loved a single one of this throng of inevitable adorers?" she asked, indignantly.

"*Loved?* No, Flora, not one; not even myself," he exclaimed, carried away for the moment. "You *loved* only the incomparable beauty, the elegant carriage, the vaunted wit, the future fame, of the petted Flora Mangold."

"Aha! I have looked in vain for loving flattery from your lips. Even in the first days of our betrothal you had no caressing words for me, and now in your anger you paint a picture of me with which I may well be content."

He blushed like a girl. It was long since he had kissed

that beautiful mouth, and yet that he had ever done so now seemed to him an offence against that other, whose purity made her the first and only true embodiment of his ideal woman. Involuntarily he withdrew his glance from the eyes that gazed at him with laughter in their depths.

Ah, she had done well to remind him of those happy first days,—the game was her own. "Did you really come to me, Leo, only to find fault and quarrel with me?" she asked, approaching him again and hastily laying her hand on his arm.

"You forget that you sent for me, Flora," he replied, gravely. "I should not have come of my own accord. I have two patients above-stairs; Henriette's condition became critical towards morning. If you had not expressly desired my presence I should not have left her, nor should I, at this miserable and unhappy time, have brought affairs to the crisis you have just provoked."

"Crisis? Because in a fit of childish vexation I told you to go! How can you take girlish pique in such bitter earnest?" What words from one who usually repudiated all maidenly emotion as unworthy her masculine intellect! This slippery eel-like nature was hard to grapple with.

The doctor looked dismayed. Her capricious words had caused him merely to describe a circle; he was no farther with her than he had been at the beginning of the interview. "There I do not blame you," he answered, with a passionate impatience that would not be suppressed. "I allowed myself to confess to you——"

"Ah, yes, you told me of your masculine will, which must rise superior to all vagaries of feeling. Has it played you false at last?"

"No, not played me false, but submitted to better and purer convictions. Flora, I told you awhile ago that my refusal to dissolve the engagement between us was the result of a false principle. I had long known that in your heart there was not a trace of true self-sacrificing love for me; and I too had entirely outlived my feeling for you, which had never been a warm genuine emotion of the heart, but merely enthusiastic admiration. We had both been mistaken. True, I suffered severely in the thought of the loveless future that awaited me,—me to whom nature had given a heart craving affection; but I resigned myself to it, and you had less difficulty in reconciling yourself to your pretended rival, my profession, because our estrangement required of you no real sacrifice."

She was silent, and her eyes sought the ground; she could not look into the grave intense face of the speaker and contradict the truth he uttered.

"And I clung to keeping my troth to the letter, all the more that my spirit was faithless to you——"

"Ah!—indeed?"

"Yes, Flora, I have struggled with my inclination as with a deadly foe." He sighed heavily. "From the first moment I have dealt cruelly with myself, and with the girl who inspired me with this invincible passion. I would not permit the slightest, the most innocent approach upon her part. I would not even endure in my room the flowers she had held in her hand and thoughtlessly forgotten. She liked to be in my house. I forbade her coming as if she had desired to fire my roof. I was coldly uncivil to her even while I looked into her face that was heaven to me——"

"Ah, yes, one can well conceive it. Divine to the eye of a physician,—round and healthy, pure white and red painted in strong colours by Nature herself." With these words the breathless listening figure awoke to life. "And you dare to tell me th's? What! this naïve, innocent creature throws flowers into the rooms of the men whom she would ensnare——"

"Hush!" He raised his hand with an air of such command as silenced even those wayward lips. "Overwhelm me with reproaches, I shall not justify myself; but in defence of Kitty I am armed to the teeth. She never wittingly attracted me; she returned to Dresden with no knowledge of my heart or—of her own. Why she went you well know. Whilst from one quarter she was met by persuasions to contract a loveless marriage, from another she was informed that the rooms which she occupied were needed for the comfort of a high-born guest. I was witness to this uncivil treatment, and almost forgot myself so far as to remonstrate indignantly with the Frau President; yet when an indirect request was made to me to receive the unwelcome inmate in my house I had no room there for her; nay, more, an hour afterwards she was an involuntary auditor of my request to my aunt to break off all intercourse with her until I should have removed to L——. And she went, wounded to the core of her proud firm and yet gentle nature, and I was brutal nay wicked enough, for the sake of a false principle, for the sake of the idol of clay which represents certain ideas of honour, to persist in the monstrous lie which I tried to make credible to her, to myself, and to the world about me."

As if overpowered by his own description, he paused for some seconds. Flora threw herself upon the couch and clasped her head between her hands, as if she chose to hear no more; but he continued: "I pitilessly allowed her to go, and breathed again; now I should be better of this mental torture. Folly, folly! I did not see that at the moment she vanished from my sight a demon glided to my side and clutched my very heart-strings. It was not the cares of my profession that hollowed my cheeks and made me gloomy and taciturn in society,—incessant labor is my delight and steels my nerves and muscles,—it was longing, a longing that increased as the days went by."

He had left the window, and was pacing the room in evident agitation of mind, while Flora sat upright and tossed back the curls from her forehead.

"Upon Kitty's account?" she cried, with a bitter laugh. "Oh, if papa could only see now how just was the instinct that guided his first-born when she refused to call the miller's daughter mamma, and when she turned away in anger from his youngest born because she already had two *real* sisters and did not want a half-sister! And it is no false principle which you have hitherto adopted as your spring of action,—no! How many thousand 'monstrous lies' are maintained and rule men's actions for the sake of this principle!—and those who maintain them victoriously will be respected as honourable men forever——"

"I vowed to myself that during this decisive interview I would not allude to the past," he interrupted her, standing still, his voice trembling, but evidently determined to make an end of the matter, "yet you force me to refer to the scene between us which took place after the attack upon you in the forest. I then allowed my betrothed to tell me to my face that she hated me, or rather despised me, because untoward chance seemed to prevent my proving to be the celebrity to whom she had first plighted her troth. The following day I endured the unexampled transformation of this hatred into fond affection, in consequence of my title of Hofrath conferred upon me by the prince, and I silently suppressed my contempt and dragged on my chain, because I wished to be 'respected as an honourable man.' And I should have carried out the detestable falsehood if we two had been the only ones concerned in the matter, if the burden of a ruined existence had been mine alone to bear. I should like to summon these three human hearts for judgment before the bar of true morality; one pronounces the solemn 'yes' before the altar because she thereby ensures to herself a desirable worldly position, and the two others who have suddenly become conscious of the true sacred love that unites them,—who belong to each other although they may be as far asunder as the poles——"

A half-stifled cry interrupted him. "Did she really dare then, hypocrite that she is, to raise her eyes to her sister's betrothed? Has she avowed her sinful love to you?"

He looked at her for an instant with speechless indignation. "However base the accusations you may utter, you cannot sully the stainless purity of that character," he said, firmly. "Since that departure I have never heard one word from her lips, not even during the past night when with returning consciousness she opened her eyes. She returned yesterday, but I did not know of it. I had retired to my garden to avoid the noise and bustle of the evening's entertainment, reports of which had pursued me from patient to patient during the day, when I suddenly saw her upon the bridge, an exile who dared not cross it, banished thence by my cruel words." He paused, and his face flushed; never could he confide to these ears how then and there the entrancing conviction had possessed his soul that the girl weeping by the poplars loved him.

"After the fearful catastrophe I sought her in the park," he continued, forcing himself to proceed calmly, "and as I raised her from the ground I told myself that death had passed her by that I might yet be happy. I tore myself loose from the fetters of conventionality and a false sense of honour, I rose superior to the malice of a calumniating world, and resigned all claim to the title of a 'respected' hypocrite."

During his last words Flora's air and manner underwent a transformation; she had lost her game, all was at an end, and the cold designing woman used her quick wit to become mistress of this situation also. All that was defiant in her bearing vanished, and was replaced by a soft cat-like suppleness. She hurriedly drew her morning cap over her curls, and looking up from beneath them with a Satanic smile that showed her sharp white teeth, she said, as if in reply to his last declaration, "What! without asking *me*, Herr Doctor? Well, let it go! In view of all these naïve confessions, I cannot but ask, with a sigh of relief, 'What would have become of me at the side of such a sentimental enthusiast?' And therefore it happens well, well for each of us. I give you back your troth, but only as one might let loose a bird tied fast by a string that has one end wound around one's finger." She smiled again, and touched the betrothal-ring upon her hand with her delicate finger-tip. "Woo the most charming girl in the capital, one who hates and envies me,—and there are enough who do so,—and I will resign the ring to her, but never to Kitty, never! Do you hear? Although you should flee across the ocean together, or stand before the altar in the most obscure village church, I shall be there at the right moment and forbid the union."

"Thank God you have no power to do so!" he said, drawing a deep breath, and very pale.

"Do you think so? Trust me to bar the fulfilment of your hopes in the future, pitiable traitor that you are, who could trample down a superb flower-bed to pluck a daisy! You shall hear from me again!"

With a low, sneering laugh, she hastily retired to the next room, locking the door behind her, and almost at the same moment a footman knocked, to request the doctor to come instantly to Fräulein Henriette, who had suddenly become much worse.

CHAPTER XXVI.

For years nothing had excited such universal interest and sympathy in the capital as the explosion in the tower, to which not only the Councillor, but also Franz the miller, had fallen a victim.

Two days had passed since the catastrophe, and in these forty-eight hours the horror and grief occasioned by the death of the millionaire had gradually been replaced by dark reports, alarming the business world, and carrying dismay among the labouring classes. The rich man's name, it was said, represented upon various books many thousands of indebtedness. The councillor had undertaken all the improvements upon his Baumgarten estate at the same time, and consequently only a small portion of their cost had been defrayed. The statement made upon the spot immediately after the explosion by the engineer, and afterwards confirmed by others, began to be widely circulated, and Von Römer's debtors asked one another anxiously how the explosive material came to be in the vault just below the chamber containing all his bonds and securities. They did not wait long for a reply. Confidential letters from Berlin, where news of the councillor's terrible death had not yet been received, spoke of immense losses which he must have sustained from the failures in quick succession of various houses there. He had indeed understood as few speculators ever had done how to keep his confidential business friends in ignorance of his money transactions; even the former book-keeper of the factory, whom after its sale he had retained as his private secretary, had no knowledge of his affairs. He had also been able so to dazzle the eyes of those with whom he had dealings by the splendour of the golden cloud in which he enveloped himself, that the dark side of his schemes and speculations never was evident to them. And thus, in spite of these revelations as to his losses, his fate might always have been bewailed as a result of his antiquarian love for the historic powder in the ruins, had he not made the mistake of selecting for his instrument of destruction a modern explosive material. This was the rent in the curtain which let in the light of reality upon the corpse, as Flora had said.

While the town was thus being prepared for the avalanche of ruin which must ensue, certain changes were taking place in the house of mourning. On the first day crowds of friends had hastened to offer their sympathy, and, although every one stepped softly and spoke in whispers, there had ensued in consequence a certain noise and bustle. The second day on the contrary was marked by a profound and gloomy silence, which reigned below- and above-stairs,—all the more oppressive since in most of the rooms the shutters were closed behind the broken panes of glass, causing a vague, uncertain twilight. The Frau President did not yet dream that a second shock was to follow the terrible event in the ruin; all her thoughts were occupied with speculations as to the amount of the immense fortune left by the unfortunate man, and the heir to whom it would fall. With all the egotism of old age her mind had already ceased to dwell upon the dead man himself. The selfishness that animated alike the grandmother and her eldest granddaughter had never been so evident as in this time of trial.

Immediately after her interview with the doctor, Flora had briefly informed the Frau President that her engagement was broken off, without assigning any reason for the fact, and the old lady had shown no curiosity upon the subject, merely rousing herself from her self-absorption for a moment to listen, and then shrugging her shoulders by way of reply. This change in her granddaughter's prospects appeared to her of but small consequence compared with the tragedy which threatened to plunge an aristocratic, high-born woman from a position of princely luxury into all the horrors of straitened circumstances. Flora then withdrew to her own room, and under the pretence of a violent headache denied herself to visitors, spending her time in packing and arranging her effects.

In the servants' hall the day which had been so long looked forward to as the wedding-day was marked by a confusion and subversion of all custom and order, such as only sudden preparations for departure can produce. The reports current in the town had fallen among the crowd of domestics and hangers-on like a bomb-shell, all the more terrifying since some among them on the morning after the disaster had hazarded a suspicion that "matters might not be quite straight." They hourly expected the officers of the law to make their appearance; each one looked out for himself or herself; the long tables set for the ball were stripped of everything eatable, and the bowls of punch were drained to the dregs.

From these regions the first intimation came to the Frau President Urach that her rule in Villa Baumgarten was considered by others as at an end; whereas formerly her first touch upon her bell had been answered instantly, she was now obliged to ring repeatedly—yes, even to call—before her orders were sullenly obeyed. She could hear too how her lap-dog, once caressed by the servants as their mistress's pet, yelped under many a kick slyly administered, while eyes that had been wont to be cast down respectfully in her presence now stared her boldly in the face.

The inmates on the third floor of the villa knew nothing of this changed demeanour on the part of the servants. Henriette had always been kind and considerate; the men and maids had regarded the poor invalid as doomed to death; they had been used to walk on tiptoe in her presence, and to speak in whispers;

and in this respect they now redoubled their efforts, since "the Herr Hofrath" had told them that her state at present was critical.

Yes, she lay in her bedroom, scarcely to be recognized except for her marvellously beautiful blue eyes, resigning at last willingly and without a pang her frail weary frame to the dark power that had dogged her footsteps for so many years. She was perfectly conscious that she was dying, and had put away from her with loathing all the gaudy colours with which she had always seemed to hope to borrow a show of youth and health. As if in a snow-drift, she reclined among spotless linen, shaded by soft muslin curtains. She was to be spared the pain of being turned away from her home to seek, according to Flora's arrangement, a refuge in the castle mill. She would be gone before the law in the name of hundreds of anxious creditors laid its hand upon the remains of the fabulous wealth which had been dispersed upon the winds; she was to depart before hearing her brother-in-law's memory branded with disgrace and crime,—his terrible end had loosened her last weak hold upon earth. And her ardent desire was fulfilled: her beloved physician watched over her to her latest breath; he promised that he would remain with her and not go to L—— until she was "much better." Once more she was as happy as she had been in the house by the river; Doctor Bruck watched over her, and Kitty was his aid,—the two people whom she loved most in the world.

Kitty recovered very quickly, leaving her bed on the afternoon of the second day. She wore a narrow bandage about her brow, and the heavy braids of hair, too massive to be worn around her head for the present, hung down her back; but this was all the change that could remind one that the terrible explosion had hurled her to the ground and overwhelmed her with the waters of the fosse, where she must have perished if loving eyes had not sought and loving hands rescued her.

Her bearing was as energetic and assured as ever, whatever tempests might assail her soul. In addition to her profound sorrow for her dying sister and Römer's tragic fate, the certainty forced itself upon her mind that her guardian was not without blame in what had occurred; Doctor Bruck, to whom she had hinted her fears, had said not one word to contradict them. He was as quiet and taciturn as ever. This might well be the result of Henriette's condition, but there was a peculiar solemnity in his reserve, which seemed also to have infected the dean's widow.

The old lady on the afternoon of the first day had issued from the room adjoining Henriette's, where she had had an interview with the doctor, her eyes full of tears, but evidently agitated by pleased surprise. She had then taken her leave to superintend the removal of various articles of furniture from her home to the doctor's town-house, where she was to take up her abode with her friend until the repairs in the house by the river should be concluded. She came to the villa from time to time to see Henriette for a few moments, always avoiding any meeting with Flora.

The beautiful woman had only come up-stairs once to see Henriette, just at the time when Doctor Bruck had obeyed an urgent request for his presence from the prince. It was strange that she should pass through the room where Kitty lay without even a glance towards the wounded girl, who lifted her head to address her. She left Henriette's bedside and went down to her own apartments without again entering the adjoining room, and Nanni reported that Fräulein Flora was preparing shortly to leave the house.

Once or twice during the day the Frau President ascended the stairs, a cloud of black crape around her gray head, her countenance troubled, and utterly bereft of that proud composure the maintenance of which in times of trial she had always asserted to be the distinguishing characteristic of a well-balanced mind. She could do nothing but weep and wring her hands convulsively at the terrible change that one moment had made in the villa and its inmates. The exhausted invalid always breathed more freely when the door closed upon the melancholy figure shrouded in black.

On the morning of the third day after the explosion, the old lady suddenly opened the door of Flora's study and tottered across the threshold, holding in her hand a newspaper. Flora was busy writing tickets for her various trunks and packages; she arose, with a foreboding of what was to come, and approached her grandmother, who had sunk into an armchair.

"My four thousand thalers!" she moaned. "Child, child, I have been robbed by scoundrels of my little all, the miserable pittance left me by my grandfather! My four thousand thalers which I guarded like the apple of my eye——"

"No, grandmamma, tell the truth,—your four thousand thalers which you foolishly risked!" Flora interrupted her, harshly. "I warned you, but I was laughed at and scorned because I would not invest my bonds and securities in the same way. The company in which you took stock has failed, I suppose."

"Disgracefully! wickedly! Read that! I shall have hardly fifty thalers to call my own," the Frau President cried, with a failing voice, covering her face with her hands. "But there is one thing I cannot understand," she said, starting up again as Flora was hastily perusing the article in question: "the paper refers to earlier statements; the crash must have come four or five days ago; and Moritz knew nothing of it,—impossible!"

"Might it not have something to do with your not receiving your newspaper a few days since?"

"Ah! you think, then, that our poor Moritz wished to spare me the shock during the marriage festivities, and suppressed the paper? Oh, yes,—of course! And he would have made good the loss to me, I am sure; he himself persuaded me to do as I did. There is consolation in that thought at least, for if necessary I can swear that Moritz assumed the responsibility of my investment; and surely I may hope to be repaid my four thousand thalers from his estate."

Flora tossed the paper upon the table. Regardless as she was wont to be of the feelings of others, in this case she scarcely knew in what words to dispel the illusion under which her grandmother laboured. She had been silent upon this point until now, in hopes that some one of their dear friends from town would undertake the task of enlightening the Frau President; but the dear friends had absented themselves; on the previous day not one had been near the villa, and now she must speak herself. She could not permit her grandmother to expose herself to ridicule by this inconceivable want of all suspicion of the truth.

"Grandmamma," she said, in an under-tone, laying her hand upon the old lady's arm, "the first thing to be considered is the possible value of the estate to which you allude."

"Oh, my child, only look out of the window and you will acknowledge that the payment of my poor four thousand would scarcely be felt by the heir, whoever it may be. Even if the enormous capital employed by Moritz in his business operations be lost in consequence of the destruction of his books and papers, the real estate and personal property which he owned will amount to a handsome fortune." She sighed sadly,—"I should be thankful indeed if I were his acknowledged heir."

Flora shrugged her shoulders. "You might never come into possession——"

The Frau President started up. "Are you mad, Flora? Weak as I am, I would run for hours, and fast for weeks, if I might thereby win the right to claim this inheritance. It is incredible that fate should be so cruel! I, I, in my position, to be thrust forth from the house that owes its splendour, its aristocratic prestige, to me alone, and an obscure old woman, who has spent her life in darning linen, to be installed here in my place!"

"That need not vex you, grandmamma; his old aunt upon the Rhine will no more inherit than you will."

"Ah! Other heirs have appeared, then?"

"Yes,—his creditors."

The Frau President staggered back to her arm-chair, with a low cry.

"Hush! Pray do not make a scene," Flora said, almost in a whisper. "The people below-stairs know it much better than I; they are all ready to flee from the house like rats from a sinking ship. I cannot and must not leave you any longer in ignorance of the state of affairs. We must be *au fait* if we would not be laughed at as dupes." She drew the cloud of black tulle closer about her grandmother's chin and neck and rearranged her disordered hair. "No one must see you thus, grandmamma," she said, sternly. "We must retire as gracefully as possible: the affair is too dishonourable and disgraceful; there is no longer any doubt that the explosion was the work of despair—to give it its right name, a piece of villainy—on Römer's part."

"The wretch! The infamous scoundrel!" shrieked the Frau President, rising, and fairly running to and fro in the apartment, rage lending strength to her feeble limbs.

Flora pointed to a window before which there hung no protecting shade. "Remember, every one outside can hear you!" she said. "Since early dawn tradesmen have been hovering near the house; the excitement in the capital is tremendous; some people have almost lost their senses with anxiety. Everything consumed by this large household for the last six months is unpaid for. The butcher has even dared to invade the house and demand that you should be called to speak with him. He wishes, of course, before the officers of the law appear, to extort from you, as the head of the household, the six hundred thalers owing him. He was insolent enough to tell my maid that the ladies of the house, as well as the councillor, had eaten his meat."

"Ugh! what a slough that miserable fellow has thrust us into, while he has made his own cowardly escape!" the Frau President exclaimed, half choked with rage, and yet instinctively withdrawing from the open window. She wrung her hands. "Gracious heaven! what a fearful situation! What is to be done?"

"First of all, we must pack up everything that is our own and leave the house, if we would not have the officers seal up our effects also; we might wait long before they would be returned to us. I am just going up-stairs to put away my"—she interrupted herself with a laugh—"my trousseau in chests and trunks. Then I am going to make an inventory of the household articles, and if you yourself will not take charge of handing them over——"

"Never——"

"Then the housekeeper can do it. We have reason enough to plead illness." She took from her writing-table the key of the room where her trousseau was, whilst the Frau President retired to place her possessions if possible beyond the risk of being officially sealed up.

CHAPTER XXVII.

THE morning air came, blowing over the tops of the trees in the park, through the open window, bringing into the church-like stillness of the bedroom a dreamy murmur of waters from the distant river, and breathing the fragrance of mignonette and heliotrope above the white face of the sleeping invalid. The crimson leaves of the wild vine that wreathed the window-frame quivered in the soft, gentle breeze that seemed to have plucked the reddened leaves as it passed to strew them upon the white coverlet, the fair hair, and the pale hands. Henriette had asked to have them brought to her, "as a farewell from the summer that was *also* passing away."

Kitty sat by the bedside watching her sister's slumber. She had, by a gentle gesture, scared away the robin that, accustomed to find crumbs scattered for him upon the window-sill, had boldly ventured into the room, his gentle twitter sounding alarmingly loud in the profound silence, in which each gasping breath issuing from the narrow chest was painfully audible. Doctor Bruck had been obliged to leave his patient for half an hour; the prince made a point of seeing at least once a day the physician who had cured him in a few weeks of a trouble of long standing. And so Bruck had chosen for this visit a time when Henriette was sleeping and would not miss him.

The maid had taken her place with her sewing behind the bed-curtains to be within call if needed. Every now and then she glanced towards the motionless figure in the arm-chair. They had declared below-stairs that the "Fräulein from the mill" would be the worst sufferer from the master's failure, but it seemed to Nanni that a girl who had just lost half a million must show it in some despairing way, and not look at all like the fair young creature who, with a bandage about her brow, and dressed in soft creamy white, sat watching by the bedside, grave but composed, and motionless as a statue. "So young, but so steady, so fresh and blooming, but with so little care for the good things of life," the maid thought after true lady's-maid fashion: the beautiful Fräulein packing up her trousseau in a neighbouring apartment was far wiser. She was taking care of everything belonging to her; sending her maid up- and down-stairs for every pocket-handkerchief that might have been mislaid; she was determined to lose nothing—nothing. Ah, she had always known how to take care of herself, and was just as rich as ever: she had not lost a penny. Now she was going to set off for L—— before her lover, with all her trunks and boxes, and so get rid of the trouble that might come upon the villa at any moment. It was vexing enough, but everything prospered with her; she might do as she pleased, and every one thought it all perfectly right. Suddenly there was such a noise in the trousseau-room that the sick girl started and moaned in her sleep.

"Fräulein Flora is packing up her things there," Nanni said, with affected unconcern, as Kitty started up and laid her hand soothingly upon that of her half-awakened sister.

Henriette's boudoir separated the two rooms, and Flora had of course supposed that no noise she made could be heard in the bedroom, or she would have been more careful in having her trunks moved. Kitty arose, and, closing behind her the door of the bedroom, crossed the sitting-room and entered the apartment whence the noise proceeded.

Flora uttered a low cry—whether from fright or vexation was doubtful—as the tall white figure appeared upon the threshold and in a low voice begged for quiet for her sleeping sister.

"I am sorry. I did not think the noise made in moving the trunks could be heard in Henriette's bedroom," she said, curtly. "You glide about so white and noiseless that one might suppose the ghostly Baumgarten ancestress, now that her wanderings in the tower are no longer possible, had taken up her abode in the villa. Mischief enough attends you. A good Christian ought to cross herself three times at sight of you."

She motioned to her maid to leave the room. "Stay!" she cried, tossing aside her bridal veil, as Kitty was about to follow the girl. "If there is a spark of honour alive in you, answer me now."

Kitty quietly released her dress from the detaining hand that grasped it, and turned back into the room. "I am at your service," she said, her clear, earnest eyes fixed calmly upon her sister's agitated face. "Only I must beg you not to speak so loud, lest Kenriette should be disturbed."

Flora made no reply; she seized Kitty's hand and drew her towards a window. "Come here! Let me look at you! I must see how wooing suits you."

The young girl recoiled from the bold, flashing eyes, which, together with the insulting words, sent the blood to her face. "As the elder sister, you should be ashamed to adopt such a tone——"

"Oh, divine innocence! I tell you that, as the youngest sister, you should be ashamed to raise your eyes to your elder sister's betrothed."

Kitty stood paralyzed. Who had searched the depths of her heart, and plucked thence the secret which she had guarded with all the force of her nature? She was conscious that she lost colour; she felt that she was standing like a culprit detected in some crime; and yet no word came from her pale lips.

"See what a guilty conscience! It could not be more perfectly personified," Flora said, with a laugh, touching the girl's breast with her finger-tips. "Yes, yes, you will admit, my dear, that for all your fine plots there is no duping your elder sister. She sees through such 'purity of soul'; her keen eye detects each tender approach, from the first spring flowers left in the man's room, in the innocent hope that they may attract his notice."

Life now returned to the motionless figure. Involuntarily she clasped her hands. It seemed to her that ever since she had set foot upon the soil of her native place her unconscious, secret soul had been tracked like some wild animal by the huntsman. Was it possible that such hateful designs could be attributed to her because of the trifling negligence which had already caused her tears of vexation? Righteous indignation stirred within her.

"I have already regretted my negligence on the occasion to which you seem to allude," she said, proudly. "But whoever spoke of it to you——"

"Whoever? He himself, child!"

"Then it is you who represent the trifling circumstance in an entirely false light."

"Ah, take care, take care, child! The passion so long suppressed gleams in your eyes," Flora exclaimed, and, although she smiled coldly, her foot tapped the floor impatiently. "*I* am false, then? Not *he*, when he boasts of his conquest?"

Again the colour left Kitty's cheek as she firmly shook her head. "No! Although you should repeat that to me a thousand times, I would not believe it! I would sooner doubt all that I have been taught to believe in as good and true! He—even think a falsehood? He, like some brainless fop, boast of a conquest? He, who——" She paused, as if terrified at the passionate tone of her own voice. "You calumniated him vilely when I first came home," she added, controlling herself. "Then I could not answer you, although instinctively I espoused his cause; but now that I know him I will not have a word breathed against him. It is monstrous that I must say this to you. How can you find it in your heart,—how dare you persist in attainting the honour of the man whose name you will shortly bear?"

As she uttered these last words Flora turned and gazed at her incredulously, as if doubting the evidence of her senses. "Either you are a most finished actress or—a declaration of love must be handed to you in black and white before you can understand it. You really know nothing of it?" With an impertinent smile, she laid her hands upon Kitty's shoulders and gazed keenly into the clear brown eyes. Then thrusting her from her, she exclaimed, "Pshaw! What more do I need? Have you not just fought for him as if you were willing to spend your last breath in his defence?"

Kitty turned towards the door. "I cannot see why you detained me here," she said.

"Ah! was I too figurative, then? Must it be said plainly in good German? Well, then, my dear, I wish nothing more or less than to know what has passed between Bruck and yourself yesterday and to-day."

"What passed between us," Kitty replied, "you may readily learn word for word. He took great pains, and I made his task very hard, to destroy my blind reliance upon some future improvement in Henriette's condition; he took pains to prepare me"—her voice trembled and tears glistened in her eyes—"for her departure."

Flora, in evident confusion, walked away to the window. With all her idolatry of self, the suspicion faintly dawned upon her that she played but a poor part in contrast to these two people. "Child, you must have long known of that," she said, in a subdued tone. "And have you not felt that we all ought to pray that the poor sufferer might be released from the burden of pain she has borne so long?" She approached the girl once more. "And was that really all that was said, word for word?"

A feeling of unutterable scorn awoke in Kitty's mind. This, she thought, was the jealousy, not of a loving woman, but of a vain one, who would watch her lover stealthily, and control, if she might, every word that he spoke. "Do you suppose that in an hour when he lends support and consolation to the dying, Doctor Bruck has either mind or heart for aught else," she asked, with grave reproof in her tone, "and when, besides, in the sufferer to whom he ministers he loses the dearest friend he has upon earth?"

"Yes, she loved him," Flora said, coldly.

Kitty's cheeks burned. Flora fairly exulted in the girlish embarrassment which was so evident. "Yes, yes, the man may congratulate himself upon the charm which he unconsciously possesses, and which attracts female hearts as the light of a candle allures moths. The world will laugh to learn that all the daughters Mangold the banker left behind him succumbed to the spell. Stay!" She had spoken in what was almost a playful tone, until Kitty once more hastened towards the door, and then the authoritative word came like a command from her lips. The young girl paused as if rooted to the spot, for fear lest a louder repetition of the word might arouse her sleeping sister. "Even our youngest, the fair miller's maid, hardy of limb and strong in soul, has proved weak," Flora continued. "Oh, you may protest as you please, with that defiant air and that pitiable pretence of offended pride. Well, I will believe you; you can clear your fame, if you will retract the eulogium you pronounced upon Bruck just now with such incomparable emphasis——"

"I do not retract one iota!"

"Do you not see, wicked girl, that you are bound hand and foot in the fetters of your sinful love? Look in my eyes! Can you look your betrayed sister in the face and say 'No'?"

Kitty raised her bowed head and looked back over her shoulder; she put her hand up to the wound in her forehead, which was beginning to throb, but it was done mechanically; even if her life-blood had been streaming from it, she would hardly have heeded it at this moment, when thought and feeling were concentrated upon one point. "You have no right to require from me an answer to such a question," she said, firmly, although her heart throbbed loud and fast; "and I am not bound to reply to you. But you have called me wicked, and have spoken of treachery; these are the very words with which I reproached myself until I understood the true nature of the affection which you call sinful——"

"Ah, a confession after the most approved style!"

A soft smile played about the pale lips; the face, white it seemed as the bandage about the brow, was transfigured for the moment. "Yes, Flora, I confess, because I have no cause for shame. I confess too for our dead father's sake. I will not, in view of that dear memory, bear upon my soul even the appearance of treachery towards one of my sisters. We are not responsible for our feelings, but for the power that we allow them; this I know after a fruitless struggle with a mysterious affection, which seems to have been born with me, to have been present with me always, though slumbering. Is it a crime to approach reverently another's domestic altar? Is it a crime to look up gladly at a tree growing in another's garden? Is it a crime to love and not covet? I desire nothing of you; I shall never cross your path or your lover's. You shall never hear of me again; you need never even remember me. How can it harm either of you that I shall love him while I have breath, and be faithful to him as to one taken from me by death?"

A low laugh interrupted her. "Take care, child! In a moment your rhapsody will clothe itself in rhyme."

"No, Flora, that I leave to you, although I know that my whole conception of life has been more exalted since this affection has had lodgment in my heart." She stepped back into the room, past the stand upon which hung the wedding-gown. Without knowing it, she brushed by the hanging train, and, with a low rustle, the whole silken fabric fell upon the floor.

Kitty stooped to raise it, but Flora pushed the satin scornfully aside with her foot. "Let it lie!" she said, bitterly. "Even the lifeless stuff rebels against a sister's treachery."

"And are you free from blame, Flora?" Kitty asked. Her blood was easily roused; her sense of justice was strong, and not even for the sake of peace would she submit to the persistent injustice of wayward egotism. "What was it that first filled my heart? Sympathy, unutterable sympathy for the noble man whom you misunderstood, whom you reviled to the world, and from whom you struggled to be free. If all this were not wrong, why did you ask forgiveness? I have seen you penitent——When you threw the ring into the river——"

"Good God, Kitty! do not retail again that old vision of yours," Flora cried, putting her fingers to her ears for a moment, and then turning to her sister and holding up her hand before her eyes. "There, there it is. And I can assure you it is genuine; the letters engraved inside leave nothing to be desired. And besides let me tell you, to put an end to the matter. that the thing will play no further part in my life, except that of a wire with which to guide a puppet. My engagement with Bruck is broken——"

Kitty started in amazement. "You tried in vain to break it a while ago," she stammered.

"Yes; then the fellow had some remnant of strength in him; now he has become weak as a child."

"Flora, he has released you?"

"Good heavens, yes! if you must hear the joyful news a second time."

"Then he never loved you. Then he insisted upon his

rights, prompted by some other motive. Thank God, he may yet be happy!"

"Do you think so? I still have a voice in the matter," said Flora. She laid her hand with a firm pressure upon her sister's arm, and looked with a diabolic expression into the honest brown eyes. "I will never forgive him for letting me beg in vain for my freedom. He shall know now what it is to have the cup dashed from thirsting lips. I will never resign his ring——"

"The counterfeit——"

"How can you prove that, child? Where are your witnesses? Your accusation of me has not a foot to stand upon. I have been rightly credited with legal acumen. But do not be alarmed. I would not be so cruel as to forbid marriage altogether to my former betrothed; he may marry—to-morrow, if he pleases; but only one whom he does not love,—I have not the least objection to a marriage of convenience. I shall haunt his path, detect every emotion of his soul which he may happen to betray. Woe be to him should he attempt to defy me!"

She had picked up one of the sprays of orange-blossoms scattered about the room, and as she waved it to and fro she looked like some beautiful tigress circling with subtle, supple windings her destined prey.

"Well, Kitty, since you love him, do you not wish to beg for him?" she began again, slowly emphasizing her words. "Look, I have his happiness in my hands. I can crush it, or bid it live and flourish, according to my pleasure. This absolute power is priceless to me, of course, and yet I can hardly resist the temptation to resign it, chiefly to test the strength of what is so vaunted as true love. Suppose I were to place this ring in your hands, with the right to dispose of it as you please,—understand me, I myself should from that moment resign all claim, all right of protest,—would you, in order that Bruck might from this time be free to choose, submit to any conditions that I should impose?"

Kitty had involuntarily pressed her clasped hands tightly to her throbbing breast,—there was a terrible conflict going on within her. "I will comply with any even the hardest conditions immediately, if only I may free him from your toils," came hoarsely but resolutely from her lips.

"Not too fast, my child. You might possibly destroy the happiness of your own life by too ready a self-sacrifice."

The young girl paused for a moment, and put one hand up to her aching head. Evidently, strong though she was, one support after another was failing her, her youthful ardour, the elastic force that breeds self-reliance, faith in her own power of self-conquest: her will alone remained firm. "I know what I mean; there is no need for reflection," she said.

Flora held the orange-spray before her face as if she were inhaling the fragrance of the artificial blossoms. "What if his choice—perhaps only to humiliate me—fell upon yourself?" she asked, looking askance at her young sister.

Kitty's breath failed her. "It never will,—he never liked me!"

"True. But suppose he should tell you that he loves you, the pledge of his freedom would scarcely be safe in your hands, I am afraid. Some day he would woo his beloved, and I might fare ill with my conditions. No! I will keep my ring!"

"Just heaven! can it really be that one sister can so torture another?" Kitty cried, in indignant pain. "And yet at this very moment, seeing as I do your incorrigible egotism, your pitiless nature, your invincible passion for intrigue more clearly than ever before, I am all the more impelled to deliver your former lover at any price from the vampire that thirsts for his life-blood. You *must* not retain any hold upon him. He shall begin his life anew, in a home where he will find happiness and peace, now that he is no longer condemned to lead a mere life of society by the side of a heartless coquette——"

"Many thanks for your flattering description! You show far too much enthusiasm for his happiness to allow of my entrusting my treasure to your keeping."

"Give it to me; you may do so without fear."

"Even if he should indeed and in truth love you?"

The girl's lips quivered in absolute agony, she wrung her hands as in despair, but she was firm. "What if it were so? I should be no irreparable loss. He can easily find a better than I. His past bitter experience is warrant that he will not again deceive himself. Give me the ring, the counterfeit. Although I know that not the least particle of value attaches to it in reality, I promise you to respect it as the one now lying in the river, since it is a sign and pledge of Bruck's enfranchisement." She held out her hand.

"I know you to be honourable enough never to use it for your own advantage," Flora said, slowly and with emphasis, drawing off the ring. A tremor shook Kitty's limbs as the gold touched her palm, and her fingers closed tight upon the circlet, while a contemptuous smile hovered upon her lips; she was too proud to assert by a single syllable her purity of purpose.

"Well?" Flora cried.

"I have given you my word; now I am the puppet whom you rule by this wire,"—she raised her closed hand,—"are you satisfied?" And she left the room.

As she crossed the threshold, Doctor Bruck was ascending the opposite staircase. He glanced towards the two figures, the one erect and triumphant in the middle of the room, coldly smiling, while the girl, issuing from it flushed and agitated, almost broke down at sight of him.

He hurried to her side, and, regardless of all else, put his arm around her to support her. The door closed behind them to the accompaniment of a low, mocking laugh.

CHAPTER XXVIII.

In the afternoon the tempest which flying reports had presaged, as sea-mews announce the coming storm, broke over the house. The legal authorities had been expected since the early morning, and yet when they made their appearance it was like an electric shock. They came too soon for every one. The servants were engaged in moving the Frau President's old-fashioned mahogany furniture, with its dusty and torn coverings, from the garrets down into the hall; Flora's trunks were still awaiting the tardy express-wagon; the cellars were still filled with the wine that there had been no time to remove.

The Frau President proudly retired to her bedroom, refusing to see the gentlemen; but, although they were perfectly respectful in demeanour, they could not regard her nerves, but were obliged to ask if the furniture of the room belonged to her, and, when answered in the negative, to request her to remove to an adjoining empty cabinet, since the room must be officially sealed up. In this small apartment the old furniture was placed, the bed aired, and covered with the faded brown silk coverlet which the Frau President had not seen for years, and which caused her a shudder of disgust. Her maid arranged everything as comfortably as possible, putting flowers upon the little mahogany table, and bringing from the bedroom many a trifle that her spoiled mistress had been accustomed to use; but the old lady never noticed the pains she was taking: she sat by the window gazing towards the pavilion, the new roof of which was just visible among the trees.

This dreaded and detested "dower-house" had grown into a fairy habitation. Rich curtains hung at the windows; everything shone in newness and beauty,—the smooth floors, the elegant furniture, the frescoes, the chandeliers; even the kitchen was thoroughly fitted up, down to the commonest iron spoon. This "bijou" was to have been hers as long as she lived, and she had scorned it for fear lest it might exile her from the society wont to gather at the councillor's. And now —and now!

Meanwhile, Flora was contending for her possessions; but all her arguments, even her appeal to the testimony of the servants, were in vain. "Fräulein Mangold," the officials courteously persisted, "might reclaim her own afterwards, but at present everything must be placed under seal." And for hours there was a passing to and fro, up and down stairs. All the plants adorning the house were placed in the conservatories, one key after another was turned in the lock, and every open window was closed. It was dreary to mark the silence and darkness that settled down wherever the officials had finished their work. Amidst it all the servants grumbled openly about the wages due them; but each one made ready to leave the house, where every comfort lay behind lock and key, and where the flesh-pots no longer simmered on the fire. The gardener alone remained, and was lodged in the servants' hall.

While this confusion reigned, the soul of the sick girl above-stairs unfolded its wings to leave, calmly and peacefully, after the conflict of years, the worn and weary body.

Henriette's room was unvisited by the officials; everything about the dying girl was her own. Great pains were taken to avoid even a loud footfall on the third floor, and nothing approached the parting soul that could startle or annoy it. She looked through her window into the rosy heavens; she watched the swallows, their white breasts and wings looking like silver crosses floating among the pink evening clouds. On the previous day, thin wreaths of vapour had still floated above the ruin, and distant noises had troubled the sick girl's mind, causing it to dwell painfully upon the terrible spot where the crashing walls had buried beneath their fragments the "rash man" to whom, with all his weaknesses, she had clung in sisterly affection. But at this solemn evening hour, at the close of the day and of a brief mortal existence, there was nothing to remind one of previous horrors.

The doctor sat by Henriette's bedside. He saw how the rapid finger of death emphasized and sharpened each outline of the face, still informed for a brief space of time with consciousness. The ebbing stream of life moved her pulses in faint isolated throbs, like retreating waves returning now and then to plash once more upon a deserted shore.

"Flora!" the dying girl whispered, with a speaking glance.

"Do you wish to see her?" he asked, making ready to go for her.

Henriette faintly shook her head. "You will not be vexed that I wish to be alone with you and Kitty until——" She did not finish the sentence, but plucked at the fading crimson vine-leaves upon the coverlet. "I will spare her, and she will be grateful,"—there was a faint shade of irony in her smile,—"she detests touching scenes. You will take her my farewell, Leo."

The doctor silently inclined his head. By his side stood Kitty. Her heart beat fast; her dying sister had no suspicion that the relations upon which her mind was dwelling no longer existed. Should she learn the truth? She glanced anxiously at the doctor's face: it was grave and composed; no sudden and unexpected announcement should disturb the peace of the departing soul, and for preparation there was no time.

Henriette's eyes wandered to the evening sky. "How exquisitely clear and rosy! It must be a heavenly delight for the freed soul to bathe in such splendour!" she whispered, fervently. "Will it ever be allowed to look back here? I only want to look once, to see"—she turned her head on the pillow with difficulty, and gazed, with eyes glowing for the first time with unutterable love, full at Bruck—"if you are happy, Leo. Then I care not how distant are the starry worlds to which I may be borne." Even in this her last hour the poor girl could not bring herself to say, "I must know you happy, or I shall not be content, for I have loved you intensely with every fibre of my heart."

A transfiguring glow seemed to illumine the doctor's bowed head. "All is well with me, Henriette," he said, with emotion. "I dare to hope that I shall not pass a lonely and embittered life; nay, better still, I *know* that even at the eleventh hour my dream of the true happiness of existence will be fulfilled. Does that content you, my sister?" He pressed his lips upon the small hand that was growing cold in his own. "I thank you from my soul," he added.

A blush, faint and rosy as the evening sky, came and went upon the cheek of the dying girl; her timid glance involuntarily sought her sister, who, her hand leaning upon Bruck's chair, was evidently struggling to control her grief. At sight of her Henriette's heart melted in pity and sympathy.

"Look at my Kitty, Leo!" she said, imploringly, in a failing voice. "Let me tell you of what has so often distressed and pained me. You have always been so cold to her,—once harsh even to cruelty,—and yet there is none to be compared to her. Leo, I have never understood your prejudice against her. Be kind to her—befriend her——"

"To my latest breath! while life lasts!" he interrupted her, scarce able to master his emotion.

"Then all is well! I know you will take care of her,—and my strong, brave darling will stand between you and all annoyance——"

"Like a faithful sister, which from this moment I am," Kitty completed the sentence, in a choking voice.

An ecstatic smile hovered about Henriette's mouth. She closed her eyes, and did not see the shudder that shook her strong sister's frame as the doctor held out his hand to her and she rejected it as if she had no right to its mute pressure. The smile faded, and the dying girl struggled for breath. "Say farewell to grandmamma. Now I would rest,—ah, give me rest, Leo, I entreat!" she gasped.

"In ten minutes you will fall asleep, Henriette," he said, in a low, soothing tone. He laid her hand upon the coverlet, and softly put his arm beneath the pillow supporting her head; she lay like a child upon his breast,—a happy death!

And before the ten minutes were passed she slept. The fluttering vine-leaves at the window stirred, as if lightly touched, and the rosy light in the sky, in which the parting soul had longed to bathe, suddenly glowed to deepest crimson. The little tame bird perched upon the window-sill as usual at sunset,—his soft twitter towards the waxen face upon the pillow was heard for the last time,—and then these windows also were closed, not to be opened until the councillor's house had passed into stranger hands.

The Frau President came up to the room, bowed as with a sudden added weight of the age she had so steadily tried to ignore. The white cloud of tulle once more enveloped cheek and chin: no mourning should be worn for a scoundrel, she said. She went to the bedside, and a spasm passed over her features as she gazed upon the calm countenance of the dead. "She is happy," she said, in a broken voice. "She has chosen the better part,—she need not go into exile,—she is spared the bitter, bitter struggle with poverty."

But Flora came and went without a word. She took no note of the two faithful guardians at the bedside. She kissed her dead sister upon the brow, and then walked with head erect to the door by which she had entered. She paused, it is true, upon the threshold, but she never turned either her eyes or her head towards where the doctor stood and gravely delivered to her her sister's last message. She bent her head almost imperceptibly in token that she heard what was said, and then rustled down the stairs, to put on her bonnet and go to the nearest hotel, where she had engaged lodgings for herself and her grandmother. No one, not even the dead, was permitted to pass another night beneath the criminal's roof.

And when, after nightfall, Henriette's form had been borne away to the hall, where all, clad for the grave and heaped with flowers, await the opening of their latest earthly portal, the last room on the third floor was closed and locked, and the doctor and Kitty descended the stairs together. Their steps echoed drearily through the silent, deserted house. The lantern carried before them by the gardener shed abroad a ghostly light over the lonely walls and passages, where so lately the stream of life had flowed in luxurious evidence of what was after all but a false, fleeting show of wealth.

The soft night air, as they walked along, was as balm to Kitty's burning eyes. A clear, starry sky canopied the silent park, the single groups of trees could be distinguished, and the mirror of the pond gleamed like dull silver through a misty veil. The gravel crunched beneath their tread, and from afar was heard the water of the weir, but not a leaf or a twig stirred,—it was as quiet as it had been for hours in Henriette's room. And therefore Kitty started in terror when the doctor's full deep voice broke the silence. They had reached the leafy entrance of the avenue, and he paused.

"I leave the capital in a few days, and I fear that, until then, you will neither visit my aunt nor allow me to come to the mill," he said, with both sorrow and eagerness in his tone. "I tell myself also that we are walking together for the last time,—that is, for the present——"

"Forever!" she interrupted him, sadly but firmly.

"No, Kitty!" he said, as firmly. "It would be a separation forever if your words spoken a few hours since could not be gainsaid. I do not want a *sister.* Do you think a man can content himself with sisterly letters when he is thirsting for loving words from beloved lips? But no,—I did not mean to speak thus to-day. Only selfishness could betray me into such entreaties while you are suffering as at present. One thing I must say to you, however. This afternoon you had an interview which, when I met you, had agitated you profoundly. You had been told what has happened, and of course the whole odium that always attaches to the sudden rupture of an engagement had been thrown upon me,—I saw that in your face; and afterwards, when for love of Henriette you promised to be a *sister* to me, I *heard* the power that evil whispers had gained over you,—thank God, not for always! I know—I know that your clear, just insight may be dimmed for a while; but this cannot last. Kitty, on that terrible afternoon I was in my garden, and saw how, on the opposite river-bank, a girl leaned her brow against a tree and wept bitterly."

Kitty turned as if to flee down the avenue, but Bruck had taken her hand and held it in a firm grasp. "I saw before me the girl whom I was longing to clasp in my arms. I had just been victorious in the last of those self-conflicts from which I had suffered for months; victorious, because I had liberated myself from false views of life and had admitted that I should be a perjured traitor if I contracted a hated marriage while my whole being was filled with an invincible passion. There stood the one who was dearer to me than all else beside, and my heart leaped, for her streaming eyes did not look towards my aunt's windows, but——" He paused, and pressed the hand which he held to his lips, while she leaned against the trunk of a linden, incapable of uttering a word.

"I cannot blame her who was to have been my wife; that

matters have been allowed to go so far is my fault,—mine only. I was weak enough, for dread of what the world might say, to continue our engagement after I had discovered, with shame and anguish, that I had been attracted by a beautiful exterior animated by no qualities of mind or heart that did not crumble to insignificance if subjected to the slightest test. This discovery I made in the first weeks of our betrothal."

He was wrong; the qualities enshrined within that lovely form were not insignificant. Flora's was a nature incredibly malicious. She had known then of Bruck's love for her sister, of course from his own confession. What a contemptible plot! Her victim had the ring in her possession; she had bought it with a price; her word was pledged even though Bruck should woo herself. The young girl's eyes wandered in despair to the starry heavens. She knew that Flora would never release her from her promise although she should implore her on her knees. There would be no need even of Flora's eloquence to convince the world that she was betrayed and deceived, the dupe of her younger sister, who had lured her lover from her. That this was the colour she would give to what had taken place was clear as the stars above. How they sparkled, those shining worlds! To which of those golden orbs had the spirit of her sister been borne upon the rosy evening air? Could she look back to see how the happiness of the man whom she had loved would be wrecked?

"You do not speak, Kitty. Your silence rebukes me; I ought not to have spoken to-day," he began again. "I will not press you further. I do not ignore the fact that my desires will arouse a conflict within you: you were not else the strictly just and honourable girl that you are; but I know also that I shall attain the goal I so long for without stormy arguments and entreaties. I will leave you time for consideration and recovery from the grief that now fills your soul and colours every thought and feeling. I go without the assurance that alone can give me peace, but—I shall come again. And now we will go on to the mill. Take my arm in full confidence that no brother could care for you with less thought of self than fills my soul at this moment. You might with equal tranquillity put yourself in charge of my aunt and myself when we set out on our way to L——."

"I shall not return to Saxony," she said. She had placed her hand within his arm, and they walked slowly along the avenue. The girl's limbs seemed possessed with a mortal torpor that clutched at her throbbing heart and deadened the voice that came so hard and cold from her lips. "I found when I was last in Dresden that in my present state of mind there is no help for me in incessant study or the performance of my trifling household duties. I must have some occupation requiring sustained absorbing labour day after day. Until a few days ago I hesitated to express this need; I knew my first hint at such a thing would arouse a storm of expostulation from my guardian. The heiress's duty was all marked out for her, and consisted in spending her income as brilliantly as possible. All that is past. The dreaded safe is no longer in existence, or rather its paper contents were worthless before it was destroyed. This I have been quite sure of, since Nanni whispered to me this afternoon that everything was being sealed up. I am right, my hundreds of thousands have vanished, have they not?"

"I hardly think anything can be saved——"

"But I still have my mill, and there I will stay. I shall, perhaps, lay myself open to your serious disapproval when I tell you that from this time I wish to attend to my affairs myself. It savours, perhaps, of 'women's rights' for a young girl to undertake the management of business affairs and represent a firm in her own person."

"I am not so prejudiced; I advocate warmly such independence upon a woman's part, and I know that you, with your force and energy, would do well; but it is not your vocation, Kitty. Your place is at the head of a happy home, not standing day after day reckoning up columns of figures at a desk in a counting-room. Do not begin it! For at some future day you will be carried off without a question as to the debit and credit in your books, and terrible confusion might be the consequence."

If the light of the stars could only have illuminated the dark avenue, the speaker would never have allowed the girl at his side to leave him, so hopeless a despair was painted on her face; he would have taken her in charge then and there, and wrung from her the thoughts that were torturing her. But the darkness covered the terrible struggle that was going on beside him, betrayed by no word or sign, not even a sigh, and he ascribed the depression and discouragement which had made her voice so dull and monotonous to the misery of the parting scene she had gone through with her dead sister.

Now and then a pebble rattled from beneath their feet on the gravelled road, and the rushing of the waters of the stream sounded loud and near in the silence that followed the doctor's last words. The lindens of the avenue retreated; the heavens stretched broadly above, and standing clear against their sparkling depths were the two slim poplars that flanked the wooden bridge.

At sight of them the doctor involuntarily pressed the girl's arm closer to his side. "There, Kitty," he whispered; "there you used to look for the first violets. I promised you you should do so in future, and I can keep my word: I shall always spend my Easter holidays here."

Kitty pressed her clenched hand to her breast; she thought the violent throbbing of her heart would suffocate her; and yet she asked, quietly, "Will your aunt accompany you to L——?"

"Yes; she will undertake the care of my household so long

as I am alone. She sacrifices much to do so, and will be thankful to shake the dust of the large city from her feet and return hither to her green country home. I know that the brave, true heart for which I sue will not delay her release too long," he added, in a tone of tender entreaty.

A light appeared twinkling from the mill window. Franz the miller had been buried this afternoon, leaving behind him a widow and three children. The roof that still sheltered them did not belong to them, and the miller's small savings were not sufficient for their support. Susy had been to the villa for a few moments to look after her mistress, and had described to Kitty the despair of the poor wretches, and mourned over "the topsy-turvy state of the business without any master."

The bow-window of the room in the lower story looking towards the park was dark. The outline of the mill buildings rose black and shapeless against the sky,—it all seemed lonely and deserted; the bark of the watch-dog, who resented the approaching footsteps, sounded lost as in some endless desert. The wheels were silent, and the huge room was so empty and echoing that one might have fancied that, since the strong human hand so lately working here had stiffened in death, each friendly busy elf had pulled his cap over his peevish face and slipped away.

The doctor drew the young girl towards him before he opened the gate. "I seem to be leading you into exile," he said, anxiously. "You ought not to give me the pain of knowing you alone after this sad and weary day. Come with me; my aunt will be only too happy to receive and take care of you."

"No, no!" she said, hurriedly. "Do not think that I shall resign myself to a passion of useless grief when I am alone. I have no time for it, and I shall not do so. I must," and she pointed to the bow-window, where the dim light of a lamp began to shine behind the chintz curtain, "play the part of comforter there. Those four poor people are dependent upon my energy and assistance."

"Dear, dear Kitty!" he said, clasping her right hand in both his own and pressing it to his breast. "Go then in God's name! I should hold it a crime to place one stone in the hard but sure path you have chosen through your present suffering. Only remember that you are not yet quite recovered. Do not make too great a demand upon your strength; and wear the bandage upon your forehead for a few days longer. And now farewell: at Easter, when the last wintry mist has flown, when the ice and snow are thawed, when human hearts throb joyously,—at Easter I shall return. Until then, think of one whose every thought is yours, and do not let slander or mistrust come between us!"

"Never!" This one word came almost like a groan from her lips. She withdrew the hand he pressed to his lips, and the gate in the wall clanged to behind her. She took no step forward; leaning against the cold damp wall, her face buried in her hands, she listened breathlessly to his departing footsteps. What was death in comparison with the tortures of this wildly-beating heart condemned to live? She listened until the soft night air, brushing her cheek, brought no sound upon its wings, and then, with tearless, weary eyes, she passed on into the house, to enter upon her mission of comforter and protector.

Three days later, immediately after Henriette's burial, Doctor Bruck and his aunt left the capital. Kitty had not seen the doctor again, but his aunt had repeatedly passed an hour with her. The same day Flora left also, accompanied by the Frau President. The old lady was to visit the baths; and Flora went to Zürich, where, report said, she was to devote herself for a time to the study of medicine.

CHAPTER XXIX.

More than a year had passed since the day in March when Kitty Mangold, grandchild and sole heir of the wealthy castle miller, had been walking upon the high-road from the town on her way to present herself at her guardian the councillor's in her new character of heiress.

Those who now turned aside into the by-road leading to the mill found upon their right a row of pretty little cottages, that belonged to the workmen in the factory, and had been erected upon the waste portion of the mill-garden,—the strip of land that Kitty had begged of her guardian for the convenience of these men. And the townspeople liked much to walk in this direction. Formerly the high massive wall enclosing the mill-grounds had cast its shade so far that the footpath beneath it was almost always damp and had long been avoided. Now the wall had gone, and the pretty path was planted with acacias. The cottages looked neat and trim, with their air of Dutch cleanliness, the pretty porch in front of each, and the small gardens which had been planted the previous autumn with all kinds of flowering shrubs.

Behind them loomed the castle mill, hoary with age, its windows looking in the opposite direction, as if angry that its ancient mantle of green had been thus bordered with gay embroidery. It had undergone no alteration, save that the shabby old dial had been brightened, and the little gate leading through the wall into the adjacent park had been walled up. There was no longer any connection between the mill and the former estate of the vanished Von Baumgartens from whom the old structure had derived its high-sounding title. But the deafening noise, the throbbing heart of the old pile went on with rejuvenated vigour, and the road to the mill-yard was more frequented than ever,—the masterless business was directed by a firm cool hand and a prudent head. Kitty's undertaking had been attended with success. She had found an experienced foreman, and poor Lenz, the merchant who had lost his all, was her assistant book-keeper.

She set herself to work in the office she had fitted up in the mill, to learn the mysteries of business, and her thorough education and excellent capacity soon enabled her to acquire all that Lenz could teach. She did actually work like a man, "day by day;" the business increased, and produced such results as would have astonished the old castle miller himself. And the sight of the contented faces about her smoothed the rough path she had chosen to tread. She had taken charge of poor Franz's widow and orphans, giving them rooms for life in a small out-building of the mill, which she had fitted up for their occupation. The woman continued, as heretofore, to assist Susy in her housekeeping, while the children received such an education as their father, whose mind had been occupied entirely with material considerations, had never dreamed of giving them.

It was true that of all the vast wealth left behind him by the castle miller nothing remained for Kitty but the mill and a few thousand thalers which she had induced her guardian to allow her to lend to the workmen to enable them to build their cottages upon the mill-land. Her hundreds of thousands had vanished in the flames, and the small amount of gold and silver recovered in a melted condition from beneath the ruins was far more likely to be the remains of tankards and platters than of coin. In the disastrous confusion that followed the explosion there were many creditors whose claims even the real estate and valuable collections were not sufficient to satisfy; the failure proved to be one of the worst and most hopeless that occurred in that time of ruin and uncertainty. Villa and park passed again into the hands of an old and noble family, and the new owner had the ruins of the ancient tower cleared away, the ditch filled up, and even the artificial mound levelled, that there might be nothing upon the aristocratic soil to bring to mind the miserable parvenu who had there met his wretched and disgraceful death. And the ancient wooden arched bridge leading across the stream to the house by the river was also destroyed. The doctor's house was now reached by a stone bridge, crossing the river near the factory, and a pretty footpath along the opposite shore.

The house, which had been completely restored late in the autumn, was still unoccupied; the Frau Dean's old friend had passed the winter in the doctor's former town-house, and was to move out only with the return of fine spring weather. Kitty used to stroll hither almost every day. Although the autumn mists hung dank and chill, although snow-flakes filled the air, and the wind blew keen from the north, at the approach of twilight she would lay aside her pen, put on her wraps, and sally forth into the open air.

Then for half an hour she would throw away all thought of the columns of figures, the dry business details in which she sought all day to bury her warm, longing heart. She was no longer the strict mistress, whose watchful eye never overlooked the smallest irregularity, who exacted a rigid performance of duty from herself as well as from her people, inducing it in the latter case by such a judicious mixture of praise and blame that no harsh word was ever needed from her lips. At this twilight hour she was only the young ardent girl, who, hard and stern as she might be to the passion that possessed her soul, still permitted herself some moments of dreaming melancholy, of unrestrained suffering.

Then she would pass through the narrow, creaking wicket-gate leading out into the fields; the gate to which, after the attack in the forest, she, with Henriette in her arms, had bent her weary steps. As she reached the moss-grown fragment of a pedestal in the centre of the grassy lawn, beside which she had stood with Bruck, she would pass her hand lightly over it, as if in a caress, and then seek the spot where the garden-table had stood, where the doctor, as she now knew, had so suffered for her sake. She walked around the lonely house, with its closed shutters, its new unblackened chimneys, and its creaking weather-cock, to mount the damp, slippery steps and listen at the house-door. Through the key-hole came the soft, low sigh caused by the draught of air sweeping through the wide hall, the withered vines about the doorway rustled, and now and then a belated sparrow would dart in beneath the eaves. This was the only sign of life stirring in the loneliness, but the girl looked for it eagerly; at least the silence was not that of the grave. The right to open this door belonged to beloved hands, and some day footsteps would resound within and dear faces look from the windows; this was sure, although Kitty, at the thought of it, told herself that then she should leave her home and wander afar, until—Bruck should conduct hither some bride to whose hand she might confide the ring.

His career in L—— was a brilliant one. His reputation spread from day to day. Large and distinguished audiences attended his lectures, and several fortunate cures, of which the objects were individuals of high rank, were everywhere talked of. His aunt's letters to Kitty—she wrote frequently—breathed peace and content; they were a source of immense enjoyment to the young girl, but also of terrible mental conflict, for which reason she replied but seldom and briefly. The doctor himself never wrote,—he adhered strictly to his promise not to assail her with entreaties, and contented himself by sending some message of remembrance, which she kindly and punctually reciprocated.

In this solitude her young life passed, day after day. She

never dreamed that she was a subject of great interest in the town, that her bold assertion of her independence, her resolute and energetic assumption of authority at the head of her affairs, excited far more attention and respect than had ever been awarded to the heiress. The distinction thus falling to her lot was the cause of a series of visits to the castle mill, of which the first when paid was received with no little astonishment. The Frau President Urach when walking with her faithful maid no longer disdained to make the mill a resting-place, in order, "as her duty to her poor dear lost Mangold required, to look after his youngest child."

The old lady had returned to the capital a few weeks after her departure from the villa. She occupied a couple of rooms very high up in a narrow little street, living in a pinched way, in accordance with her very small means, and half forgotten by the world. The councillor of medicine, Von Bär, had purchased a country-seat, and grumbling turned his back upon the capital; for her he had vanished entirely, and of all her former acquaintance her only visitors were some few of the friends of her youth and the pensioned Colonel von Giese, who sometimes came to play cards with her.

She suddenly found it very comfortable "in this fine old room in the castle mill, where there is really space to breathe in," and, weary with her walk, she would seat herself contentedly in the old-fashioned chintz-covered sofa, that had once sustained the castle miller's burly form, and enjoy the delicious coffee which Kitty always prepared for her, making no sort of remonstrance when Susy, at a nod from her young mistress, hung upon the maid's arm a basket filled with fresh butter and eggs.

It was best not to speak to her of Flora, who of course had not lost one penny of her fortune, and who now indeed paid the rent of her grandmother's rooms and the wages of her maid, but could do nothing more, since, as she wrote, she needed all the rest of her income for herself, and could hardly manage to live upon it. She had soon quitted Zürich, where the study of "that disgusting medicine irritated the nerves almost to madness." She was one of those intellectual coquettes who pose for a certain part, greedy for notoriety and a reputation for profound and thorough attainment, while in reality they recoil from the slightest amount of genuine serious study.

Easter was at hand. For several weeks improvements had been going on in the garden of the house by the river. The doctor had sent a gardener from L——, who laid out new paths, or rather tried to restore the pretty old garden to its original plan. Many men were busy digging and planting, and places were arranged for some statues which had arrived from L—— and were still unpacked in the hall. The shutters of the house had been thrown open for two weeks; the rooms had been freshly painted and papered, and a flag-pole had been erected upon the roof. Then the Frau Dean's friend moved out from town, bringing with her a host of charwomen, who made the house a shining mirror of neatness and cleanliness from garret to cellar.

Kitty had not discontinued her walks. On the very day before Easter she came hither once more, at noon. The men were still at work in the garden, but the evergreens that had overgrown the land belonging to the house, forming here and there an impenetrable thicket, had been thinned and left only within the boundaries first assigned them, while from among their dark foliage gleamed the new statues. The winding paths were freshly gravelled, the old creaking wooden gate had been replaced by one of wrought iron; the Frau Dean's arbour had been freshly painted, and behind the house a high picket-fence enclosed a new poultry-yard.

Upon the familiar stone pedestal before the door stood a

Terpsichore with arms gracefully extended, just as Kitty had imagined her from the remains of the little marble foot.

"The statue is very pretty," the strange gardener said to her with a shrug, "but it ought to be more elegantly placed. This lawn," and he looked around upon the old bleaching-ground, "is quite wild, by no means in proper order, but the Herr Professor strictly forbade my touching it." Kitty stooped with crimson cheeks and plucked the first violet, which had opened fully in all its fragrance at the base of the pedestal. "Yes, the grass is full of weeds," the man said over his shoulder, as he walked on.

And the house, now really a little castle, actually shone with freshness and beauty—"fitted up as if for a bride," the Frau Dean's old friend remarked to Kitty with an unsuspecting smile. The snow-white kitten came softly to the door over the new tiles of the hall. In the Frau Dean's sitting-room, behind the cròcheted curtains, in the midst of the laurels and large-leaved plants that had been moved out from town, the canary-bird piped his clear shrill song. The former life was beginning here anew, and the Frau Dean herself was to arrive by the afternoon train. She was to bring a guest with her, her old friend had remarked with a mysterious twinkle of the eye; who it was she did not know, but she had been commissioned to provide the guest-chamber with new furniture. And as she spoke she threw open the folding-doors leading into it from the hall, and tears filled Kitty's eyes as she thought of Henriette, who had lain here in such pain, and yet peaceful and happy as never before in her sad life. But even while her thoughts were thus occupied she was conscious of a sharp, unfamiliar pang of jealousy. Who was this guest who had become so dear to the Frau Dean's heart that she had been invited to stay with her?

The gay rose-covered curtains and the hanging-baskets filled their old places, but the rickety furniture had made way for what was new and pretty, although very simple, and instead of the faded illustrations of Vosz's "Luise" some fine landscapes hung upon the freshly-papered walls. The well-remembered room had been converted into a pretty sitting-room, and an adjoining cabinet that had formerly stood empty had been arranged for a sleeping-apartment.

All this Kitty looked at once more, with tear-dimmed eyes, and then walked home to place herself at her desk and answer several business letters. Lenz was to return in the evening from a business trip he had undertaken, and his young mistress was anxious to have all in readiness to be entrusted to his hands while she spent the next fortnight with her foster-parents in Dresden.

Ah, how difficult it was to fix her attention! Her pulses throbbed, and the handwriting, usually so clear and firm, looked scrawled and careless. She was interrupted too by the Frau President's maid, who came with a large empty market-basket on her arm, on her way to make her Easter purchases of provisions, and the Frau President had told her, since it was only a little out of her road, to stop at the mill and give Fräulein Kitty Fräulein Flora's letter to read. It had just come.

Susy was immediately instructed to fill the basket with all sorts of delicacies from her pantry, but the letter lay untouched upon Fräulein Kitty's writing-table long after the maid had returned to her mistress.

The Frau President had several times previously sent the young girl her step-sister's letters. The sheets had seemed to burn beneath her touch, but she had dutifully read them through that she might not seem ill-natured. And now a flickering flame seemed creeping towards her from the perfumed envelope lying near her elbow. Impatiently she moved her arm and pushed it beneath a pile of bill-headings. She could not see why, to-day, she should give herself the pain that the reading of these letters always caused her, made up as they were of frivolity, arrogance, and conceit.

She took up her pen again, but only for a few moments. In her agitation she bent her head, as towards a protecting talisman, over the violet she had just placed in a tiny vase of water, and inhaled its sweet cooling fragrance; she went to her piano and played a soothing, peaceful air; she opened one of the windows and stroked the tame doves perched upon the sill, trying to persuade herself meanwhile that the sending of the letter was in fact only a masked advance upon her pantry; —but there must have been an evil spell in the mischievous envelope. She could no longer resist the impulse to open it, but pushed aside the pile of papers, and removed the cover.

As she did so a sealed enclosure fell from it. She did not notice it: her eyes wandering over the first page opened wide in amazement, and involuntarily, strong girl as she was, she grasped at some support. Flora wrote thus from Berlin:

——"You will laugh and exult, dear grandmamma, but I now see that it is best,—an hour ago I was betrothed to your former favourite, Karl von Stetten. He is uglier and more awkward than ever, and his bull-dog physiognomy is not improved by the blue spectacles he has lately begun to wear. *Fi donc*—I shall never be very proud to walk by his side, but his dog-like constancy to his really insane passion for me has moved me at last, and since through the unexpected death of his young cousin he has suddenly fallen heir to Lingen and Stromberg, and stands very well at court here and in society, I really had no further objection to make——"

The letter was tossed upon the table. Bruck was free,—no longer fettered so that he could not come to the castle mill. Ah, what a change after all these seven terrible months of torture, of effort to train and bend her stubborn heart,—to scourge each wandering thought so that she might attain at last to the strong stoicism that would enable her calmly to transfer the hated ring to the hand of his betrothed, and then to pursue her own course, lonely but blameless!

She covered her eyes with her hand, as if some phantom had appeared in the midst of her bewildering delight. Perhaps she had not read the words aright! Could it be so? Flora was betrothed? At the eleventh hour, after so many unsuccessful attempts to achieve fame, was she taking refuge in matrimony? Kitty again took up the thick perfumed sheet,—yes, yes, there it really was in the "sprawling hand." And then followed long and exact instructions as to how the betrothal was to be announced in the capital; and there was much talk of the marriage, which was to take place upon Easter Monday. Then came the invitation to her grandmamma to be present. This was all as clear as daylight; but the girl grew deadly pale and felt faint and sick as she read on. Flora wrote further:

"On my way to Berlin I stopped for a day or two at L——. It will interest you to hear that a certain Hofrath and Professor has achieved not only name and fame, but also won the heart of a fair countess. I was everywhere told that he has been privately betrothed to this charming patient of his, whose cure he effected after her case had been given over as hopeless by all other physicians. The noble parents are abundantly content with their daughter's choice, and the dear and pious old aunt has not refused to bestow her blessing upon the pair. I saw her seated beside them in a box at the theatre, as eminently peaceful and virtuous as ever, wearing, if I am not mistaken, cotton gloves upon her hands. The girl is very pretty,—a doll's face with no expression. And he?—I can speak out to you, grandmamma, and confess that I bit my lip until it bled, with vexation that stupid chance should have made this man the object of universal homage and consideration, and that he could stand there behind the chair of his betrothed so calm and self-assured, as if all this distinction were his by right, and as if he knew nothing of weakness or dishonour——! Let Kitty have the enclosed note——"

Yes, there it lay, closely sealed, upon the writing-table, bearing the address, "Kitty Mangold." The room grew dim about her, and the slip of paper trembled in the hands that shook as if with a fever-fit. It contained only these words:

"Have the kindness to deliver to the Countess Witte the ring entrusted to you, or, if you choose, throw it into the river after the other! FLORA."

Kitty suddenly grew calm; mechanically she folded up the note and laid it with the letter. Was the beautiful countess the guest for whom the guest-chamber had been prepared? She shook her head decidedly, and her brown eyes began to beam brightly as she clasped her hands upon her throbbing breast. Was she worthy ever to look him in the face again if she could doubt him for an instant? He had said, "I shall come at Easter;" and he would come, although the most brilliant eloquence should persuade her to the contrary. She would believe nothing save that he loved her and that he would come. No, no, a haughty lord might have the heart to present to his former love a proud new mistress of his home; but not he,—he in his singleness of soul. He would not break his promise to the miller's granddaughter for the sake of another, even were that other a countess.

An ecstasy possessed her soul in which all thought seemed lost. She flew to the southern window to get one glimpse of the dear old house. A gay flag was floating above its roof. Had the guests arrived, then? Should she hasten to embrace the dean's widow? No, agitated as she was, she could not go. She must banish the traitorous colour from her cheeks and quiet the throbbing of her heart before she could meet the gentle lady's clear kindly eye. Rest, rest! She went to her writing-table.

The huge ledger lay open upon it; in that drawer were six business letters which ought to be answered to-day; and she could hear the rumbling in the court-yard below of one of the clumsy mill-wagons laden with grain. The dogs were barking furiously at a beggar to whom Susy was throwing a piece of bread from her window. Here was enough of prosaic reality. And the rude pictures, which, as they had formerly been the objects of her grandfather's admiration, still adorned the walls, were as little calculated to excite emotion as the stout stuffed cushion of the sofa above which they hung, or the tall Schwarzwald clock standing stiff and straight against the wall, swinging its weary pendulum behind the ground glass.

The young girl's glance lingered among all these glories, till finally she took a sheet of paper and dipped her pen in the ink. "Messrs. Schilling & Co., Hamburg,"—oh, no one would be able to read that! In despair she passed her hand over her forehead, parting the brown curls so that a faint crimson scar was disclosed. Thus she sat for a moment, motionless, her left hand covering her eyes, her right still holding the rebellious pen. Suddenly she felt a cool air upon her cheek; the draught came from an open door or window; she looked up, and there he stood upon the topmost step of the small flight leading into the room, smiling and radiant with the joy of return.

"Leo! I knew it!" she exclaimed; and, throwing down her pen, she ran towards him and was clasped in his arms.

Susy came running from the hall. What was the matter? The door was wide open, and she had heard the cry. She stood open-mouthed; the corner of her blue apron, with which she had been about to wipe her heated forehead, dropped from her hand in dismay, for there upon the well-scoured boards of her sacred castle-mill room stood Doctor Bruck, clasping her Fräulein in his arms as if he never in his life meant to release her. Lord save us! if they were betrothed no one knew it.

She cautiously crept nearer to close the door, but Kitty saw her, and with a burning blush tried to extricate herself from her lover's embrace.

The doctor laughed, the gay musical laugh of former times, and held her fast. "No, Kitty, you came, to be sure, of your own accord, but I cannot trust you yet," he said. "I should be a fool to give you a chance of transforming yourself into a *sister* again. Come in, Susy," he cried over his shoulder to the old housekeeper; "you must witness the fact that we are betrothed, before I can let her go."

Susy wiped her eyes, and was profuse in her congratulations, after which she hurried across the court-yard to tell the news to her gossip and crony, poor Franz's widow, lamenting at the same time that the good times at the mill were nearly over, since the Fräulein was to be married.

The doctor went to the writing-table and solemnly closed the huge ledger. "The career of the lovely miller's maiden is at an end, for—Easter has come," he said. "How I have counted the days of this time of probation, which I myself ordained that I might not lose you altogether! You cannot tell how hard it is to live on from hour to hour in uncertainty, when the whole happiness of life is at stake. My only consolation I found in your letters to my aunt, in which, in spite of the character and force of will that they showed, I fancied I could detect your love. But how few and short they were!" He took her hand and drew her towards him again. "I knew that a time of renunciation must intervene between the unhappy past and my complete happiness; I bore in mind all your sorrow for your sister; but to this hour I have never been able to understand why you would have renounced me forever and lived a lonely unblessed existence." He paused suddenly, and his face flushed,—there beside the closed ledger lay a folded note; he knew the large uncertain characters only too well: such missives had frequently been sent him in the early days of his former engagement.

Firmly Kitty laid her hand upon the paper. Why expose this detestable intrigue? Let it lie buried forever; there was no longer any obstacle in the way of her happiness. But the doctor gravely drew the note from beneath her detaining fingers. "There must be no secret between us, Kitty," he said, "and this seems to be one."

He read, and then insisted upon a full confession. Kitty told him of what she had endured, and through it all he could not but gratefully perceive the depth of the unselfish affection that would have foregone the happiness of an entire future to secure his freedom.

"And what about the lovely Countess Witte? I thought she was coming with your aunt to take possession of the guest-chamber," Kitty said at last, smiling through her tears, wishing to change the current of thought which deprived her lover of all his wonted composure. She succeeded: he laughed.

"*I* shall take possession of the guest-chamber," he replied. "I had reasons for not advising you beforehand of the time of my arrival, and I see they were good. As regards the young countess, she was an inmate of our household for three months while under my professional care, and is perhaps slightly demonstrative in the expression of her gratitude for the cure I was happily able to effect,—that is all. You will see her in a fortnight, when, my darling, I propose to bear away my bride to L——. Ours has been a long betrothal, —seven months! Will you not consent to kneel before the altar there?"—he pointed through the window to the spire of the neighbouring village church,—"I always had such an affection for that place."

"You shall take me whither you will," she said, softly, "but I have duties here——"

"Nonsense! the ledger is closed, and your faithful Lenz can say what is right to 'Schilling & Co.,' Hamburg."

She laughed. "Well, then, command, and I obey!" she

rejoined. "I will retire;—good news for Lenz, who will rent the mill and soon make good his losses."

They left the house, and Kitty, leaning on the doctor's arm, walked along the path she had traversed so often in the wintry weather. To-day it was delicious to wander there beneath the arching, budding boughs. The soft willow buds brushed the girl's glowing cheeks; a gentle evening breeze was blowing, and the stream flowed rippling between banks clothed in the tender green of early spring. The park lay beyond, quiet and grand as ever; they saw the swans slowly gliding upon the lake, and high above the tops of the trees a blue-and-yellow flag fluttered from the roof of the villa. The lord of the mansion was at home.

What a tide of recollections flooded the two hearts that had just plighted their troth for time and for eternity!

"Do you know," whispered the doctor, "that they say Moritz has been seen in America?"

She nodded. "A few days ago Franz's widow received five hundred thalers from an anonymous friend in California. She cannot imagine who her benefactor is; but I know him." And she told Leo of the light-bearded workman who had driven away the roes to save them from a cruel death because they had been his pets in former happy days.

There stood the dear old house in the fading evening light. The labourers had left the garden. A solemn silence brooded over it all, the statues gleamed white among the evergreens, and the dean's widow came down the steps from the hall-door, her arms extended to clasp to her motherly heart her "own dearest Kitty," whose love she had so long prayed might bless her darling.

Deep and full came the sound of the chimes in the distant town; they were ringing in—Easter!

THE END.

www.ingramcontent.com/pod-product-compliance
Lightning Source LLC
LaVergne TN
LVHW010152110826
845151LV00002B/500

* 9 7 8 1 4 2 5 5 3 7 1 0 4 *